Genghis Khan

Genghis Khan

Introduction by
David Curtis Wright

General Editor: Jake Jackson

**FLAME TREE
PUBLISHING**

This is a FLAME TREE Book

FLAME TREE PUBLISHING
6 Melbray Mews
Fulham, London SW6 3NS
United Kingdom
www.flametreepublishing.com

First published 2022
Copyright © 2022 Flame Tree Publishing Ltd

22 24 26 25 23
1 3 5 7 9 8 6 4 2

ISBN: 978-1-80417-233-9

The cover image is © copyright 2022 Flame Tree Publishing Ltd, including elements
courtesy of Shutterstock.com/Tooykrub/Andrey Burmakin

All inside images courtesy of Shutterstock.com and the following:
Kristina Birukova, Steinar, Maryna Yakovchuk and Zvereva Yana.

The classic texts in this book derive from *Makers of History: Genghis Khan* by Jacob
Abbott, published by Harper & Brothers Publishers, New York and London, 1901;
in addition to chapter extracts from *The Mongols: A History* by Jeremiah Curtin,
published by Little, Brown, and Company, Boston, 1908. The texts have been edited
slightly for this volume.

Printed and bound in the UK by Clays Ltd, Elcograf S.p.A

Contents

Series Foreword

STRETCHING BACK to the oral traditions of thousands of years ago, tales of heroes and disaster, creation and conquest have been told by many different civilizations in many different ways. Their impact sits deep within our culture even though the detail in the tales themselves are a loose mix of historical record, transformed narrative and the distortions of hundreds of storytellers.

Today the language of mythology lives with us: our mood is jovial, our countenance is saturnine, we are narcissistic and our modern life is hermetically sealed from others. The nuances of myths and legends form part of our daily routines and help us navigate the world around us, with its half truths and biased reported facts.

The nature of a myth is that its story is already known by most of those who hear it, or read it. Every generation brings a new emphasis, but the fundamentals remain the same: a desire to understand and describe the events and relationships of the world. Many of the great stories are archetypes that help us find our own place, equipping us with tools for self-understanding, both individually and as part of a broader culture.

For Western societies it is Greek mythology that speaks to us most clearly. It greatly influenced the mythological heritage of the ancient Roman civilization and is the lens through which we still see the Celts, the Norse and many of the other great peoples and religions. The Greeks themselves learned much from their neighbours, the Egyptians, an older culture that became weak with age and incestuous leadership.

It is important to understand that what we perceive now as mythology had its own origins in perceptions of the divine and the rituals of the sacred. The earliest civilizations, in the crucible of the Middle East, in the Sumer of the third millennium BC, are the source to which many of the mythic archetypes can be traced. As humankind collected together in cities for the first time, developed writing and industrial scale agriculture, started to irrigate the rivers and attempted to control rather than be at the mercy of its environment, humanity began to write down its tentative explanations of natural events, of floods and plagues, of disease.

Early stories tell of Gods (or god-like animals in the case of tribal societies such as African, Native American or Aboriginal cultures) who are crafty and use their wits to survive, and it is reasonable to suggest that these were the first rulers of the gathering peoples of the earth, later elevated to god-like status with the distance of time. Such tales became more political as cities vied with each other for supremacy, creating new Gods, new hierarchies for their pantheons. The older Gods took on primordial roles and became the preserve of creation and destruction, leaving the new gods to deal with more current, everyday affairs. Empires rose and fell, with Babylon assuming the mantle from Sumeria in the 1800s BC, then in turn to be swept away by the Assyrians of the 1200s BC; then the Assyrians and the Egyptians were subjugated by the Greeks, the Greeks by the Romans and so on, leading to the spread and assimilation of common themes, ideas and stories throughout the world.

The survival of history is dependent on the telling of good tales, but each one must have the 'feeling' of truth, otherwise it will be ignored. Around the firesides, or embedded in a book or a computer, the myths and legends of the past are still the living materials of retold myth, not restricted to an exploration of origins. Now we have devices and global communications that give us unparalleled access to a diversity of traditions. We can find out about Indigenous American, Indian, Chinese and tribal African mythology in a way that was denied to our ancestors, we can find connections, match the archaeology, religion and the mythologies of the world to build a comprehensive image of the human adventure.

The great leaders of history and heroes of literature have also adopted the mantle of mythic experience, because the stories of historical figures – Cyrus the Great, Alexander, Genghis Khan – and mytho-poetic warriors such as Beowulf achieve a cultural significance that transcends their moment in the chronicles of humankind. Myth, history and literature have become powerful, intwined instruments of perception, with echoes of reported fact and symbolic truths that convey the sweep of human experience. In this series of books we are glad to share with you the wonderful traditions of the past.

Jake Jackson
General Editor

Introduction to Genghis Khan

THE RISE OF CHINGGIS KHAN (Genghis Khan, Jenghiz Khan) and the subsequent spread of the Mongol empire were, in the words of the peerless French Orientalist Paul Pelliot (1878–1945), parts of 'the most extraordinary adventure that the world has ever known'. This was not hyperbole on Pelliot's part. Chinggis Khan and his successors founded the largest land empire the world has ever known, not excepting the former Soviet Union. The Mongols are *it* as far as world empires are concerned.

Temujin

The story of the Mongols and their empire began with the Great Khan himself, who, during his youth and rise to power, was known as Temujin. There is no universal consensus about the year of Chinggis Khan's birth. 1155, 1162 and 1167 are all possibilities, with a majority of scholarship on his life placing his birth sometime during the 1160s.

He was born on the Onon River as Temujin to his father Yisugei (Yezonkai in Abbott's spelling and Yessugai in Curtin's spelling), a leader of the Mongol tribe, and his mother Hö'elun (Olan in Abbott's spelling and Hoelun in Curtin's spelling), whom his father had stolen from the Merkits, a rival tribe. At his birth, Temujin clutched in his hand a blood clot the size of a knucklebone, which was taken as a propitious omen and later interpreted by shamans as portending him holding the great seal of state.

Temujin spent his early childhood with his siblings on the banks of the Onon River, the site of Yisugei's main encampment. Like all Mongol children, he learned to shoot arrows and ride during his early years. His closest childhood friend was Jamuka (Chamuka), with whom he had concluded a covenant of blood brotherhood by drinking drops of each other's blood in cups of milk. From this time forth they were *anda*, or sworn brothers, and sworn brotherhoods were generally viewed on the steppe as more binding than ties of direct, literal blood relationship.

Temujin Falls in Love and Is Orphaned

When Temujin was eight or nine years old, he was smitten with a girl named Börte (Purta in Abbott's spelling), one year his senior, in the Boskur band of the same tribe. The girl, according to the *Secret History of the Mongols*, an account written down from oral tradition sometime in the early to mid-thirteenth century, had a striking visage and flashing eyes. Later during his teens, Temujin remembered the fetching lass Börte and returned to take her as his bride. Börte's father originally wanted Temujin to stay with him and his daughter for a few months, and Yisugei assented.

Temujin ended up going home with his father and not staying with his bride-to-be and his future father-in-law. On their way home from the betrothal, Yisugei and Temujin encountered a group of Tartars, an enemy tribe. Yisugei, being hungry, dismounted and asked for a meal, which the Tartars were obliged to provide due to time-honoured steppe traditions holding that people were required to feed hungry strangers on the steppe, even if they were enemies. But the Tartars, recognizing Yisugei as an enemy leader, poisoned his food, and he died from it soon after returning home.

Survival, Grit and Gumption

Yisugei's Mongol tribe abandoned him, his mother and his siblings after Yisugei's death, leaving them to fend for themselves on the steppe, likely in the hope that they would perish, be eaten by wild beasts or absorbed into another tribe. But the sturdy and strong-willed mother Hö'elun was determined, along with her sons and especially Temujin, that they would survive, thrive and eventually recover their lost leadership status among the tribe. For several years they subsisted on wild vegetation and small game, which Temujin and his brothers hunted. Temujin did fight with his brothers and ended up killing one of them, much to the towering rage of his mother.

Soon after this fratricide, during his 15th or early 16th year, Temujin was captured by the Tayichi'ut (Taychot in Abbott's spelling) tribe, placed in a cangue (wooden yoke), and held under close guard. He managed to escape, however, with the help of a sympathetic Tayichi'ut guard who was later to become one of Chinggis Khan's trusted generals.

Temujin's captivity among the Tayichi'ut was a traumatic and defining period in his life. He may have been subjected to sexual abuse during his captivity, which the *Secret History* hints at by indicating that he was passed around from tent to tent, spending one night in each tent. He learned during this time not to trust family members merely because of bloodline ties, but to trust non-kin who demonstrated loyalty through actions. Later, as Chinggis Khan, Temujin did not run his empire as a mafia of blood relatives, sworn or otherwise, but as an imperium of trusted commanders and comrades.

Soon after his return home, young Temujin and his family were the victims of rustlers who stole all but one of their horses, leaving them in potentially desperate straits. Temujin wanted his horses back, but he was smart enough to know that he should not attempt to recover them alone. He met up with a 13-year-old son of a tribal leader with whom Yisugei had had friendly relations, and together they found the stolen horses, recaptured them and took them home. This was Temujin's first experience with the importance of securing alliances or allegiances, a crucial lesson he remembered for the rest of his life.

Alliances and Expansion

When Temujin was 15, he decided to go find Börte, the love of his childhood, and bring her home to live with him and Hö'elun. He found her soon enough, and her father permitted her to go with Temujin. Fifteen was the age at which steppe nomads were thought to have reached their majority, and Temujin, toughened as he was by his childhood and early youth experiences, began seeking ways not simply to survive, but to achieve greatness. He sought out Bo'orchu, the young man who had helped him recover his stolen horses, who instantly dropped everything he was doing and followed Temujin. He was Temujin's first follower and ally. Temujin, his brothers and Bo'orchu then sought an alliance with a large tribe, a crucial matter if they were to expand their power and influence. Temujin took the precious sable coat that came with Börte as her dowry and sought out Toghrul, the leader of the Kerait tribe.

This alliance with the Keraits made young Temujin a man of some note on the steppe, and he began to attract the attention of other important tribes, most notably the savage Merkits. Memories and grudges lasted long on the steppe, and the Merkits had never quite forgotten that Yisugei had stolen his wife Hö'elun from them years earlier. Now, with the young upstart Temujin seemingly on the rise, the Merkits decided it was time to cut him down to size and, in the process, exact revenge for the kidnapping of Hö'elun. Three hundred Merkit horsemen attacked Temujin and his family, and everyone, including Hö'elun herself, fled on horseback. Börte, however, was left with no horse and thus fell into Merkit captivity. But having captured her, the Merkits decided to leave off any further attacks against Temujin; capturing his wife was vengeance enough for them for the theft of Hö'elun years earlier.

Temujin was thus safe for the moment, but never considered letting the matter over the Merkit kidnapping of Börte drop. He approached his Kerait overlord Toghrul about joint operations against the Merkit. Toghrul readily assented to this, saying that in gratitude for the sable coat he would rescue Börte even if it meant slaughtering every last Merkit.

Toghrul was ready to commit 20,000 mounted archers against the Merkits, and, as it turned out, Temujin's sworn brother or *anda* from his childhood on the Onon River, Jamuka, was also ready to field an equal number of horsemen. Jamuka, like Temujin, had been through a difficult and traumatic childhood but had risen to leadership over the Jadarat tribe, and he remembered well his sworn brotherhood with Temujin and was now eager to help him. Jamuka had also come to Temujin's attention because he, like Temujin, had Toghrul as his overlord.

Their allied attack against the Merkits took place during the 1180s, perhaps when Temujin was in his late teens, and it was a smashing success. He caught up with his beloved Börte, recaptured her alive and then called off the campaign against the Merkits. But she returned to him pregnant with a Merkit child who would be born as Jochi, the father of Batu, the future first khan of the Golden Horde in Russia. Temujin never begrudged her the pregnancy; as the *Secret History* and centuries of Mongol folklore delight in retelling, he was only too happy to have his Börte back.

Falling Out with Jamuka

During and after their campaign against the Merkits, Temujin and Jamuka revived their childhood *anda* and spent 18 months together, displaying great affection for each other, sleeping apart from others and under the same blanket. But the two sworn brothers eventually had a falling out and came to a clash of arms, and the reasons for it are not altogether clear. It does, however, seem fairly obvious that both had enormous ambitions of unifying all of the pastoral nomads of the steppe lands north of China under their individual rule.

Temujin's break with Jamuka was another defining moment and turning point in his life. His successes against his enemies led many people and tribes on the steppe to believe that he was favoured of heaven and destined to unify under his rule all people in what we now call Mongolia. But the followers of Jamuka thought much the same of their leader, so conflict between the two was, in historical hindsight, inevitable.

Toghrul, the leader, or khan, of the Kerait, saw that the two captains nominally under his authority would eventually clash and he would have to choose which one to support. Jamuka, for his part, was busy forming an alliance of tribes against his former *anda* and commenced hostilities with Temujin and his forces in 1184, at first securing significant victories against him. At the same time, Toghrul lost sway over the Keraits for a time and fled west to the lands of the Kara Khitai, the descendants of the Khitans, who had ruled over most of the steppe and part of northern China during the Liao dynasty (907–1125).

Temujin's fortunes improved to some extent after Toghrul's flight, and he soon joined in alliance with the Jurchens of the Jin dynasty (1115–1234), then in power over portions of the steppe and northern China. In securing this alliance, he convinced Toghrul to return and assist him, although Toghrul had also recovered his power and was now known as Ong Khan (perhaps the Prestor John of European legend and rumour). But Temujin no longer thought of himself as Ong Khan's vassal, so the stage was set for eventual conflict between these two leaders as well. There were now three contenders for ultimate hegemony over the steppe lands: Temujin, Toghrul and Ong Khan.

When the entente between Temujin and the Jurchens against the Tartars fell apart, Temujin attacked the Jurchens and secured their submission to him, at least for the moment. Temujin and Ong Khan had patched up their differences and jointly waged the campaign against the Jurchens, many leaders of whom were executed in the winter of 1196–97. But Ong Khan's power was still growing independently, as was Jamuka's, who was elected *Gurkhan,* or chief khan, the political and military implications and ramifications of which were only too obvious. The three-way struggle between Temujin, Ong Khan and Jamuka the *Gurkhan* was now well underway.

Meanwhile, however, Temujin and Ong Khan for a time pursued joint action against the Naimans, the elite and single most powerful tribe in the steppes, only to be talked out of it by Jamuka, who was likely jockeying for his own ambition. Temujin resented Jamuka's intervention, and with good reason: Jamuka was actively working to curtail or circumscribe Temujin's growing influence.

Temujin's campaign against the Tartars was eventually back on track, and he went to war with these ancient archenemies of his Mongol people – the enemies who had poisoned his father Yisugei years earlier. Temujin destroyed the Tartars and wiped them out as a people, sparing only those who were shorter than the linchpin of a wheel of a cart – in other words, only the little children, whom he distributed among other tribes.

Temujin's genocide against the Tartars greatly increased his renown, power and ambition, and he turned against Ong Khan, whom he defeated and set to flight in 1203. (Later that year, Ong Khan was killed by a Naiman guardsman who did not recognize him.) With this, the mighty Kerait people came completely under Temujin's control. Now he and Jamuka were alone in their struggle for supremacy over Mongolia.

Final Triumph as Chinggis Khan

The Naimans were Temujin's next and final nemesis. Power among the Naimans was not really held by their khan Tayang (Tayian in Abbott's spelling), but by the dominant harridan who was his mother. Sensing that a clash with the Mongols was imminent, she sought to provoke them into a war by saying that the Mongols smelled bad and were good for nothing, except that the best of the Mongol women might be abducted, taught to wash their hands and then employed as the Naimans' milkmaids.

The Merkits and the Jadirat under Jamuka allied with the Naimans for the great showdown with Temujin. Together their numbers were superior, but Temujin prevailed over them all, taking care to capture the Naiman khan's mother alive and mock her in person for saying that the Mongols smelled bad and were good only as milkmaids.

But the Merkits fled their defeat in 1204 rather than submit to Temujin, so he took to the field once again and decimated their numbers. Jamuka, who had also fled defeat, hid for a time but was soon captured by his own followers and presented to Temujin. But Temujin, who since childhood had loathed betrayal and disloyalty, had the people who brought him Jamuka executed for daring to lay hands on their legitimate leader. But Temujin hesitated to kill Jamuka, since killing an *anda* was, in Mongolian culture, a more hideous and perfidious act than killing one's literal bloodline brother. Jamuka, however, refused not to be executed, requesting only that he be dispatched bloodlessly to avoid having the great blue heavens above see a leader's shed blood on the ground, an ancient steppe taboo. Temujin ultimately, and reluctantly, assented to Jamuka's execution, as recounted in melodramatic detail in the *Secret History*'s chronicle of the final meeting between the two former *andas*.

Having defeated the Naimans and executed Jamuka in 1206, Temujin was now the undisputed master of the steppe lands north of China. That same year, at a *khuriltai,* or grand assembly, of steppe leaders, Temujin was proclaimed Chinggis Khan (Jenghiz Khan in Persian; Anglicized as Genghis Khan), which title probably means Oceanic Khan, or Khan from Ocean to Ocean, connoting the vastness of territory that heaven had given to him. Temujin accepted the title modestly and gave credit to his earlier followers and supporters, particularly his boyhood friend Bo'orchu. The *Secret History* devotes many paragraphs to Chinggis Khan's recognition and rewarding of those who had assisted him.

Continuing Campaigns North of China

For the next three years, Chinggis Khan organized his empire, introducing universal conscription and decimally designating military units of 10, 100, 1,000 and 10,000. He demanded absolute, blind loyalty and obedience from the new military nobility he created.

In 1209 the Uighurs, a Turkic-speaking people living mostly in modern Xinjiang, submitted to Chinggis. They were the first non-Mongolic people to yield to him, but certainly not the last. Chinggis Khan then turned his attention to the Tangut people and their state of Xi, or Western Xia (Xi Xia), a large state that extended over Ningxia, the Ordos and parts of Gansu. In 1209, Chinggis Khan's forces penetrated into Xia territory, and by early 1210 Xia had nominally submitted to Chinggis Khan but ultimately refused to provide the Mongols with auxiliary troops, a slight the vindictive Chinggis Khan never forgot and eventually avenged.

The Jurchen Jin dynasty in northern and central China was probably Chinggis Khan's main objective after his conquest of the pastoral nomadic peoples of Mongolia. (China, the wealthiest state in the world by far at the time, was divided, with Jin on the north and the moribund, decadent and effete Song dynasty in southern China.) Jin China was a source of the wealth and booty Chinggis had promised to his followers and lieutenants, so securing reliable access to Chinese material wealth was politically essential to him.

Chinggis Khan launched an attack on Jin China in 1210, and from then on refused to pay tribute or respect to the Jurchen rulers – defiances that the Jurchens recognized correctly as acts of war. By the summer of 1211, Chinggis had violated Jin's borders, and by 1214 he was besieging the Jin capital at Zhongdu (modern Beijing) and was in control of almost all cities and towns north of the Yellow River. The siege developed into a stalemate, with both the Jin defenders and Mongol besiegers so short on food that they resorted to cannibalism, the Mongols sacrificing every 10th man among them for the cooking pot. But Chinggis held firm, and by late summer of that year the Jin emperor simply abandoned his capital at Zhongdu and retreated southward to Nanjing. This crushed Jin morale and boosted the morale of the Mongols and their ethnic Chinese siege technicians, and by late 1214 and early 1215 the Mongols had captured Zhongdu, plundered it for a month and then set it alight. Chinggis Khan had begun the war with Jin as a gigantic raid for plunder, but now, under the influence of his ethnic Chinese advisors and technicians, he demanded that large tracts of Jin territory be ceded to him.

Westward Campaigns

In 1216, Chinggis left the campaign against Jin China and returned to Mongolia, where he dealt with one last challenge to his power from the Merkits. Chinggis then tracked down a fugitive Naiman leader out on the Irtysh River in modern Siberia and Kazakhstan. This campaign brought Chinggis into contact with the sultanate of Khwarazm, an Islamic and Persian-Turkic polity located in the Transoxiana region, or mostly what is today Uzbekistan. At first Chinggis only wanted trade and peace with Khwarazm and its sultan, but Sultan Muhammad brusquely rebuffed Chinggis's feelers for peace and contemptuously dismissed the Mongols as idolaters. But Chinggis responded in 1218 by sending three envoys as his representatives, again proposing peaceful relations, and not conveying any demand for surrender or submission. At the same time, a Mongol trading caravan arrived in Ortrar, where the Khwarazm governor suspected them of espionage and had them killed. Chinggis, infuriated at this provocation, sent more envoys to Khwarazm, this time with the demand that the offending governor be turned over to the Mongols. Sultan Muhammad responded to this by killing Chinggis's envoys! Implacably enraged, Chinggis resolved to destroy Khwarazm, including the shah whom he now called a mere bandit and not a king. Chinggis made careful and deliberate plans for war, and by the autumn of 1219 he approached Ortrar with a massive army of Mongol cavalry and Chinese siege technicians, who were non-gunpowder artillerists. The city fell to the Mongols in February 1220. The next to fall was the Khwarazm city of Bokhara, which had the good sense to surrender peacefully and was thus spared general massacre, although it was thoroughly plundered, and Chinggis did require all able-bodied men of Bokhara to serve as cannon fodder for his subsequent sieges.

The treatment of Bokhara was a model for subsequent Mongol campaigns against cities: Those that surrendered peacefully were spared, while those that resisted were massacred of their entire male populations, with the exceptions of scholars and craftsmen, for whom Chinggis had some use. From Bokhara, Chinggis moved to Samarkand, where in March 1220 he drove out the city's population alive, only to allow them to return a few days later, but not before he had massacred the 30,000 Turks who were the city's garrison. Sultan Mohammad fled, only to die in 1221 on the southern coast of the Caspian Sea.

By the spring of 1222, Chinggis Khan left Samarkand under a lieutenant and encamped in the southern Hindu Kush. Here he was visited by a Taoist Chinese monk who, Chinggis believed, might have the secret of immortality, something Chinggis coveted because he feared death. The monk admitted that he had no elixir of immortality, but the great khan still treated him with respect and listened politely to his advice to cease killing his enemies.

Final Campaign and Passing

In 1224, Chinggis spent the summer on the Irtysh River (in modern Siberia and Kazakhstan), and in the spring of 1225, now an aging man, he set off to return to Mongolia. On his way he had one more old score to settle with the Tangut state of

Xia. In addition to refusing to provide him with auxiliary troops years earlier, Xia had had the audacity to rebel against Chinggis Khan over his long absence in Central Asia. By the summer of 1226, Chinggis, though an old man, accompanied his armies in campaign against the Xia capital of Ningxia. His orders to the Xia to surrender were haughtily rebuffed, and in his fury at this Chinggis captured the city, carried out a massacre of its population, killed the Tangut king and took the king's wife as his own.

It was on this campaign that Chinggis Khan died. There is no single accepted account of the particulars of his death, but one persistent narrative has him dying at the hands of the aggrieved and resentful Tangut queen, who cut him in his genitals. Chinggis Khan died in the summer of 1227, having concluded his long and storied career with one final bloodbath.

A funeral cortège carried Chinggis Khan's body back to Mongolia, and all people the cortège encountered on its way were killed, both to accompany their khan in death and to ensure that the secret of his burial place did not become known. Chinggis's body was ultimately buried in Mongolia, officially at the Burkhan Khaldun Mountain, although other sites claim to contain at least some of his remains. The exact location of his main tomb remains unknown to this day, despite extensive attempts during the 1990s to locate it using modern sounding equipment. (Many Mongols had strong reservations about the search for Chinggis Khan's tomb, much less its potential opening by archaeologists.) Today, as a result, the mystery of the tomb's location is the object of endless fascination for wandering romantics, amateur historians and curious explorers. In 1229, Ögedei Khan, Chinggis Khan's son and successor to the throne, ordered that 40 flawlessly beautiful virgins be dressed in fine clothes, bedecked with fine jewels and sacrificed along with several fine horses to the spirit of Chinggis Khan. In death, as in life, Chinggis still wielded the power of life and death over mortals.

The Mongol Empire After Chinggis Khan

Chinggis Khan's empire by no means died with him. His sons and grandsons who succeeded him as Grand Khan expanded the Mongol conquests of the thirteenth century to include, eventually, the Golden Horde over Russia, the Il Khanate over much of the Middle East, the Chagadai Khanate in Central Asia and the Yuan dynasty in China under his grandson Khubilai Khan. By the fall of the Song dynasty and the Mongol conquest of all of China in 1279, the Mongol World Empire became the largest land empire ever known in world history, not excepting even the former Soviet Union.

Chinggis Khan's place in history will always be controversial and debatable. He is the national hero of Mongols in Mongolia, China's Inner Mongolia Autonomous Region and Russia's Republic of Buryatia. In China he is generally thought of ambivalently, with the same ethnic Han Chinese who admire him and his successors for their conquests of the Middle East and Russia often excoriating his memory for how the Mongols conquered and ruled China, even as they credit the Mongols for reunifying all of historically Chinese territory for the first time in well over three centuries. Russia's view of him and his successors in the Golden Horde is mostly negative, and the Russians will likely never cease remembering their period of the 'Tartar (Mongol) yoke' with bitterness. In the Middle East, Chinggis and his successors are widely viewed with opprobrium. During America's wars with Iraq, dictator Saddam Hussein often sought to equate the Americans with the Mongols and their commander Hulegu, who devastated Baghdad in 1256.

Connecting Asia and Europe

During the thirteenth centuries, several Europeans were able to travel overland all the way to Mongolia, including John of Plano Carpini between 1245–47 and William of Rubruck from 1253–55. (One Asian, Rabban Sauma, travelled from East Asia all the way to Bordeaux in France and back.) The famed Marco Polo began his travels to Mongolia and China between 1271 and 1292 and travelled to southern China in the 1280s, just a few years after the Mongol conquest of China was complete. Marco Polo's descriptions of the fabulous wealth of 'Cathay' (China) and the 'millions and millions' of people in the Chinese city of Kinsai (Lin'an, the former Song capital city) enthralled generations of Europeans over the subsequent centuries. After the transportation and communication links between Europe and China were once again broken, Marco Polo returned to Europe and wrote his famous travel tale. The veracity of Marco Polo's account always has and always will attract vigorous debate, but the fine and accurate detail with which he describes much of what he saw in China strongly suggests to most historians that he did indeed make it to China to have an extensive and extended look around.

The Mongols in World History

Chinggis Khan's empire that he left his sons and grandsons kept expanding until it became the largest land empire the world has ever known, excepting neither the British Empire nor the former Soviet Union. His sons and grandsons succeeded him as Khaghan, or Grand Khan, of the empire. At its height in *c.* 1285, the Mongol World Empire had four major divisions or khanates, each ruled by a khan who, in theory if not always in fact, owed and paid allegiance to the Khaghan in Mongolia or, later under Khubilai Khaghan, in China. These khanates were the Yuan dynasty in China, the Chagadai Khanate in Central Asia, the Golden Horde in Russia and Eastern Europe, and the Il Khanate in Iran and large parts of the Middle East.

It is now quite fashionable and popular in academia to see the Mongol World Empire for what it actually was: a big chunk of world history. The Mongols contacted and ruled many peoples. The Mongols worked all manner of devastation over the areas they conquered, to be sure, but they also unified much of Eurasia under their control and, for a time in the late thirteenth century, opened long-dormant overland transportation and communication links from China through Central Asia and the Middle East to the Mediterranean. 'Pax Mongolia', or the Mongol Peace, has long been and remains today an energetically debated notion and concept. Chinggis Khan and his successors did make several important contributions to many civilizations, but it is certainly a mistake to credit them with creating the modern world, as one unwise, recently published book has claimed. The rise of the modern world was a very complex, multivalent phenomenon and is unamenable to reductionist impulses and monocausal explanations.

David Curtis Wright (PhD, Princeton) (Introduction), Associate Professor of History at the University of Calgary, specializes in the history of imperial China's interactions with its pastoral nomadic neighbours, particularly but not exclusively the Mongols. He is the author of *From War to Diplomatic Parity in Eleventh-Century China: Sung's Foreign Relations with Kitan Liao* and is currently finishing a history of the final few years of the Mongol conquest of China.

Genghis Khan

AN EARLY ENGLISH-LANGUAGE BIOGRAPHY of Chinggis Khan (more popularly known as Genghis Khan), Jacob Abbott's work is included in its entirety in this volume. Abbott (1803–79) was an American educator and prolific author whose many biographies were written for adolescent and young adult readers. Among his output were biographies of Alexander the Great, Cleopatra, Cyrus the Great, Hannibal, Julius Caesar, Mary Queen of Scots, Peter the Great, William the Conqueror and Xerxes.

In his book entitled simply *Genghis Khan*, Abbott relates the basic contours of Khan's story in a compelling and readable narrative form. With his intended reading audience in mind, Abbott gives an abbreviated, streamlined, simplified and even somewhat bowdlerized version of the story of Chinggis Khan and his empire. Abbott does not include a welter of proper names in his narrative because he seems to have feared, probably correctly, that this would be overwhelming and distracting to the large majority of his young readers. He also includes some useful and informative background information that even some scholarly biographies of the Great Khan neglect, for instance, the pastoral nomadic lifestyle of the Mongols (Chapter I), a description of Mongolian shelters, archery and ways in war (Chapter II), and even the royal hunt (Chapter XXIII), a topic that was not written up in full scholarly monograph form until the appearance of Thomas Allsen's magisterial *The Royal Hunt in Eurasian History* in 2006. Abbott devotes several chapters of his work to Chinggis Khan's campaigns in Central Asia, especially against the Khwarazmian Empire. This is important because much of Chinggis Khan's reputation for spectacular brutality comes from his campaigns in Central Asia during the 1210s and 1220s.

Chapter I
Pastoral Life in Asia

✗

Four Different Modes of Life Enumerated

THERE ARE FOUR DIFFERENT METHODS by which the various communities into which the human race is divided obtain their subsistence from the productions of the earth, each of which leads to its own peculiar system of social organization, distinct in its leading characteristics from those of all the rest. Each tends to its own peculiar form of government, gives rise to its own manners and customs, and forms, in a word, a distinctive and characteristic type of life.

These methods are the following:
1. By hunting wild animals in a state of nature.
2. By rearing tame animals in pasturages.
3. By gathering fruits and vegetables which grow spontaneously in a state of nature.
4. By rearing fruits and grains and other vegetables by artificial tillage in cultivated ground.

By the two former methods man subsists on animal food. By the two latter on vegetable food.

Northern and Southern Climes – Animal Food in Arctic Regions

As we go north, from the temperate regions toward the poles, man is found to subsist more and more on animal food. This seems to be the intention of Providence. In the arctic regions, scarcely any vegetables grow that are fit for human food, but animals whose flesh is nutritious and adapted to the use of man are abundant.

As we go south, from temperate regions toward the equator, man is found to subsist more and more on vegetable food. This, too, seems to be the intention of nature. Within the tropics scarcely any animals live that are fit for human food; while fruits, roots and other vegetable productions which are nutritious and adapted to the use of man are abundant.

In accordance with this difference in the productions of the different regions of the earth, there seems to be a difference in the constitutions of the races of men formed to inhabit them. The tribes that inhabit Greenland and Kamtschatka cannot preserve their accustomed health and vigour on any other than animal food. If put upon a diet of vegetables, they soon begin to pine away. The reverse is true of the vegetable eaters of the tropics. They preserve their health and strength well on a diet of rice, breadfruit or bananas, and would undoubtedly be made sick by being fed on the flesh of walruses, seals and white bears.

Tropical Regions – Appetite Changes with Climate

In the temperate regions, the productions of the above-mentioned extremes are mingled. Here many animals whose flesh is fit for human food live and thrive, and here grows, too, a vast variety of nutritious fruits, roots and seeds. The physical constitution of the various races of men that inhabit these regions is modified accordingly. In the temperate climes, men can live on vegetable food, or on animal food, or on both. The constitution differs, too, in different individuals, and it changes at different periods of the year. Some persons require more of animal, and others more of vegetable food, to preserve their bodily and mental powers in the best condition, and each one observes a change in himself in passing from winter to summer. In the summer the desire for a diet of fruits and vegetables seems to come northward with the sun, and in the winter the appetite for flesh comes southward from the arctic regions with the cold.

When we consider the different conditions in which the different regions of the earth are placed in respect to their capacity of production for animal and vegetable food, we shall see that this adjustment of the constitution of man, both to the differences of climate and to the changes of the seasons, is a very wise and beneficent arrangement of Divine Providence. To confine man absolutely either to animal or vegetable food would be to depopulate a large part of the earth.

First Steps Toward Civilization

It results from these general facts in respect to the distribution of the supplies of animal and vegetable food for man in different latitudes that, in all northern climes in our hemisphere, men living in a savage state must be hunters, while those that live near the equator must depend for their subsistence on fruits and roots growing wild. When, moreover, any tribe or race of men in either of these localities take the first steps toward civilization, they begin, in the one case, by taming animals, and rearing them in flocks and herds; and, in the other case, by saving the seeds of food-producing plants, and cultivating them by artificial tillage in enclosed and private fields. This last is the condition of all the half-civilized tribes of the tropical regions of the earth, whereas the former prevails in all the northern temperate and arctic regions, as far to the northward as domesticated animals can live.

Interior of Asia – Pastoral Habits of the People

From time immemorial, the whole interior of the continent of Asia has been inhabited by tribes and nations that have taken this one step in the advance toward civilization, but have gone no farther. They live, not like the Native people in North America, by hunting wild beasts, but by rearing and pasturing flocks and herds of animals that they have tamed. These animals feed, of course, on grass and herbage; and, as grass and herbage can only grow on open ground, the forests have gradually disappeared, and the country has for ages consisted of great grassy plains, or of smooth hillsides covered with verdure. Over these plains, or along the river valleys, wander the different tribes of which these pastoral nations are composed, living in tents, or in frail huts almost equally movable, and driving their flocks and herds before them from one pasture-ground to another, according as the condition of the grass, or that of the springs and streams of water, may require.

Picture of Pastoral Life

We obtain a pretty distinct idea of the nature of this pastoral life, and of the manners and customs, and the domestic constitution to which it gives rise, in the accounts given us in the Old Testament of Abraham and Lot, and of their wanderings with their flocks and herds over the country lying between the Euphrates and the Mediterranean Sea. They lived in tents, in order that they might remove their habitations the more easily from place to place in following their flocks and herds to different pasture-grounds. Their wealth consisted almost wholly in these flocks and herds, the land being almost everywhere common. Sometimes, when two parties traveling together came to a fertile and well-watered district, their herdsmen and followers were disposed to contend for the privilege of feeding their flocks upon it, and the contention would often lead to a quarrel and combat, if it had not been settled by an amicable agreement on the part of the chieftains.

Large Families Accumulated

The father of a family was the legislator and ruler of it, and his sons, with their wives, and his son's sons, remained with him, sometimes for many years, sharing his means of subsistence, submitting to his authority, and going with him from place to place, with all his flocks and herds. They employed, too, so many herdsmen, and other servants and followers, as to form, in many cases, quite an extended community, and sometimes, in case of hostilities with any other wandering tribe, a single patriarch could send forth from his own domestic circle a force of several hundred armed men. Such a company as this, when moving across the country on its way from one region of pasturage to another, appeared like an immense caravan on its march, and when settled at an encampment the tents formed quite a little town.

Rise of Patriarchal Governments

Whenever the head of one of these wandering families died, the tendency was not for the members of the community to separate, but to keep together, and allow the oldest son to take the father's place as chieftain and ruler. This was necessary for defence, as, of course, such communities as these were in perpetual danger of coming into collision with other communities roaming about like themselves over the same regions. It would necessarily result, too, from the circumstances of the case, that a strong and well-managed party, with an able and sagacious chieftain at the head of it, would attract other and weaker parties to join it; or, on the arising of some pretext for a quarrel, would make war upon it and conquer it. Thus, in process of time, small nations, as it were, would be formed, which would continue united and strong as long as the able leadership continued; and then they would separate into their original elements, which elements would be formed again into other combinations.

Origin of the Towns

Such, substantially, was pastoral life in the beginning. In process of time, of course, the tribes banded together became larger and larger. Some few towns and cities were built as places for the manufacture of implements and arms, or as resting places for the caravans of merchants in conveying from place to place such articles as were bought and sold. But these places were comparatively few and unimportant. A pastoral and roaming life continued to be the destiny of the great mass of the people. And this state of things, which was commenced on the banks of the Euphrates before the time of Abraham, spread through the whole breadth of Asia, from the Mediterranean Sea to the Pacific Ocean, and has continued with very little change from those early periods to the present time.

Great Chieftains – Genghis Khan

Of the various chieftains that have from time to time risen to command among these shepherd nations but little is known, for very few and very scanty records have been kept of the history of any of them. Some of them have been famous as conquerors, and have acquired very extended dominions. The most celebrated of all is perhaps Genghis Khan, the hero of this history. He came upon the stage more than 3,000 years after the time of the great prototype of his class, the Patriarch Abraham.

Chapter II
The Mongols

Mongols – Origin of the Name

THREE THOUSAND YEARS is a period of time long enough to produce great changes, and in the course of that time a great many different nations and congeries of nations were formed in the regions of Central Asia. The term Tartars has been employed generically to denote almost the whole race. The Mongols are a portion of this people, who are said to derive their name from Mongol Khan, one of their earliest and most powerful chieftains. The descendants of this khan called themselves by his name, just as the descendants of the 12 sons of Jacob called themselves Israelites, or children of Israel, from the name Israel, which was one of the designations of the great patriarch from whose 12 sons the 12 tribes of the Jews descended. The country inhabited by the Mongols was called Mongolia.

A Mongol Family

To obtain a clear conception of a single Mongol family, you must imagine, first, a rather small, short, thick-set man, with long black hair, a flat face and a dark olive complexion. His wife, if her face were not so flat and her nose so broad, would be quite a brilliant little beauty, her eyes are so black and sparkling. The children have much the appearance of young Native Americans as they run shouting among the cattle on the hillsides, or, if young, playing half-naked about the door of the hut, their long black hair streaming in the wind.

Their Occupations

Like all the rest of the inhabitants of Central Asia, these people depended almost entirely for their subsistence on the products of their flocks and herds. Of course, their great occupation consisted in watching their animals while feeding by day, and in putting them in places of security by night, in taking care of and rearing the young, in making butter and cheese from the milk, and clothing from the skins, in driving the cattle to and fro in search of pasturage, and, finally, in making war on the people of other tribes to settle disputes arising out of conflicting claims to territory, or to replenish their stock of sheep and oxen by seizing and driving off the flocks of their neighbours.

Animals of the Mongols

The animals which the Mongols most prized were camels, oxen and cows, sheep, goats and horses. They were very proud of their horses, and they rode them with great courage and spirit. They always went mounted in going to war. Their arms were bows and arrows, pikes or spears and a sort of sword or sabre, which was manufactured in some of the towns toward the west, and supplied to them in the course of trade by great traveling caravans.

Their Towns and Villages

Although the mass of the people lived in the open country with their flocks and herds, there were, notwithstanding, a great many towns and villages, though such centres of population were much fewer and less important among them than they are in countries the inhabitants of which live by tilling the ground. Some of these towns were the residences of the khans and of the heads of tribes. Others were places of manufacture or centres of commerce, and many of them were fortified with embankments of earth or walls of stone.

Mode of Building Their Tents

The habitations of the common people, even those built in the towns, were rude huts made so as to be easily taken down and removed. The tents were made by means of poles set in a circle in the ground, and brought nearly together at the top, so as to form a frame similar to that of a Native American wigwam. A hoop was placed near the top of these poles, so as to preserve a round opening there for the smoke to go out. The frame was then covered with sheets of a sort of thick grey felt, so placed as to leave the opening within the hoop free. The felt, too, was arranged below in such a manner that the corner of one of the sheets could be raised and let down again to form a sort of door. The edges of the sheets in other places were fastened together very carefully, especially in winter, to keep out the cold air.

Within the tent, on the ground in the centre, the family built their fire, which was made of sticks, leaves, grass and dried droppings of all sorts, gathered from the ground, for the country produced scarcely any wood. Countries roamed over by herds of animals that gain their living by pasturing on the grass and herbage are almost always destitute of trees. Trees in such a case have no opportunity to grow.

Bad Fuel – Comfortless Homes

The tents of the Mongols thus made were, of course, very comfortless homes. They could not be kept warm, there was so much cold air coming continually in through the crevices, notwithstanding all the people's contrivances to make them tight. The smoke, too, did not all escape through the hoop-hole above. Much of it remained in the tent and mingled with the atmosphere. This evil was aggravated by the kind of fuel which they used, which was of such a nature that it made only a sort of smouldering fire instead of burning, like good dry wood, with a bright and clear flame.

The discomforts of these huts and tents were increased by the custom which prevailed among the people of allowing the animals to come into them, especially those that were young and feeble, and to live there with the family.

Movable Houses Built at Last – The Painting

In process of time, as the people increased in riches and in mechanical skill, some of the more wealthy chieftains began to build houses so large and so handsome that they could not be conveniently taken down to be removed, and then they contrived a way of mounting them upon trucks placed at the four corners, and moving them bodily in this way across the plains, as a table is moved across a floor upon its castors. It was necessary, of course, that the houses should be made very light in order to be managed in this way. They were, in fact, still tents rather than houses, being made of the same materials, only they were put together in a more substantial and ornamental manner. The frame was made of very light poles, though these poles were fitted together in permanent joinings. The covering was, like that of the tents, made of felt, but the sheets were joined together by close and strong seams, and the whole was coated with a species of paint, which not only closed all the pores and interstices and made the structure very tight, but also served to ornament it; for they were accustomed, in painting these houses, to adorn the covering with pictures of birds, beasts and trees, represented in such a manner as doubtless, in their eyes, produced a very beautiful effect.

Account of a Large Movable House

These movable houses were sometimes very large. A certain traveller who visited the country not far from the time of Genghis Khan says that he saw one of these structures in motion which was 30 feet in diameter. It was drawn by 22 oxen. It was so large that it extended five feet on each side beyond the wheels. The oxen, in drawing it, were not attached, as with us, to the centre of the forward axletree, but to the ends of the axletrees, which projected beyond the wheels on each side. There were 11 oxen on each side drawing upon the axletrees. There were, of course, many drivers. The one who was chief in command stood in the door of the tent or house which looked forward, and there, with many loud shouts and flourishing gesticulations, issued his orders to the oxen and to the other men.

The Traveling Chests

The household goods of this traveling chieftain were packed in chests made for the purpose, the house itself, of course, in order to be made as light as possible, having been emptied of all its contents. These chests were large, and were made of wicker or basketwork, covered, like the house, with felt. The covers were made of a rounded form, so as to throw off the rain, and the felt was painted over with a certain composition which made it impervious to the water. These chests were not intended to be unpacked at the end of the journey, but to remain as they were, as permanent storehouses of utensils, clothing and provisions. They were placed in rows, each on its own cart, near the tent, where they could be resorted to conveniently from time to time by the servants and attendants, as occasion might require. The tent placed in the centre, with these great chests on their carts near it, formed, as it were, a house with one great room standing by itself, and all the little rooms and closets arranged in rows by the side of it.

Necessity of Such an Arrangement

Some such arrangement as this is obviously necessary in case of a great deal of furniture or baggage belonging to a man who lives in a tent, and who desires to be at liberty to remove his whole establishment from place to place at short notice; for a tent, from the very principle of its construction, is incapable of being divided into rooms, or of accommodating extensive stores of furniture or goods. Of course, a special contrivance is required for the accommodation of this species of property. This was especially the case with the Mongols, among whom there were many rich and great men who often accumulated a large amount of movable property. There was one rich Mongol, it was said, who had 200 such chest-carts, which were arranged in two rows around and behind his tent, so that his establishment, when he was encamped, looked like quite a little village.

Houses in the Towns

The style of building adopted among the Mongols for tents and movable houses seemed to set the fashion for all their houses, even for those that were built in the towns, and were meant to stand permanently where they were first set up. These permanent houses were little better than tents. They consisted each of one single room without any subdivisions whatever. They were made round, too, like the tents, only the top, instead of running up to a point, was rounded like a dome. There were no floors above that formed on the ground, and no windows.

Roads Over the Plains

Such was the general character of the dwellings of the Mongols in the days of Genghis Khan. They took their character evidently from the wandering and pastoral life that the people led. One would have thought that very excellent roads would have been necessary to have enabled them to draw the ponderous carts containing their dwellings and household goods. But this was less necessary than might have been supposed on account of the nature of the country, which consisted chiefly of immense grassy plains and smooth river valleys, over which, in many places, wheels would travel tolerably well in any direction without much making of roadway. Then, again, in all such countries, the people who journey from place to place, and the herds of cattle that move to and fro, naturally fall into the same lines of travel, and thus, in time, wear great trails, as cows make paths in a pasture. These, with a little artificial improvement at certain points, make very good summer roads, and in the winter it is not necessary to use them at all.

Tribes and Families

The Mongols, like the ancient Jews, were divided into tribes, and these were subdivided into families; a family meaning in this connection not one household, but a large congeries of households, including all those that were of known relationship to each other. These groups of relatives had each its head, and the tribe to which they pertained had also its general head. There were, it is said, three sets of these tribes, forming three grand divisions of the Mongol people, each of which was ruled by its own khan; and then, to complete the system, there was the grand khan, who ruled over all.

Influence of Diversity of Pursuits

A constitution of society like this almost always prevails in pastoral countries, and we shall see, on a little reflection, that it is natural that it should do so. In a country like ours, where the pursuits of men are so infinitely diversified, the descendants of different families become mingled together in the most promiscuous manner. The son of a farmer in one state goes off, as soon as he is of age, to some other state, to find a place among merchants or manufacturers, because he wishes to be a merchant or a manufacturer himself, while his father supplies his place on the farm perhaps by hiring a man who likes farming, and has come hundreds of miles in search of work. Thus, the descendants of one American grandfather and grandmother will be found, after a lapse of a few years, scattered in every direction all over the land, and, indeed, sometimes all over the world.

It is the diversity of pursuits which prevails in such a country as ours, taken in connection with the diversity of capacity and of taste in different individuals, that produces this dispersion.

Tribes and Clans

Among a people devoted wholly to pastoral pursuits, all this is different. The young men, as they grow up, can have generally no inducement to leave their homes. They continue to live with their parents and relatives, sharing the care of the flocks and herds, and making common cause with them in everything that is of common interest. It is thus that those great family groups are formed which exist in all pastoral countries under the name of tribes or clans, and form the constituent elements of the whole social and political organi the people.

Mode of Making War – Horsemen – The Bow and Arrow

In case of general war, each tribe of the Mongols furnished, of course, a certain quota of armed men, in proportion to its numbers and strength. These men always went to war, as has already been said, on horseback, and the spectacle which these troops presented in galloping in squadrons over the plains was sometimes very imposing. The shock of the onset when they charged in this way upon the enemy was tremendous. They were armed with bows and arrows, and also with sabres. As they approached the enemy, they discharged first a shower of arrows upon him, while they were in the act of advancing at the top of their speed. Then, dropping their bows by their side, they would draw their sabres, and be ready, as soon as the horses fell upon the enemy, to cut down all opposed to them with the most furious and deadly blows.

If they were repulsed, and compelled by a superior force to retreat, they would gallop at full speed over the plains, turning at the same time in their saddles, and shooting at their pursuers with their arrows as coolly, and with as correct an aim, almost, as if they were still. While thus retreating the trooper would guide and control his horse by his voice, and by the pressure of his heels upon his sides, so as to have both his arms free for fighting his pursuers.

These arrows were very formidable weapons, it is said. One of the travellers who visited the country in those days says that they could be shot with so much force as to pierce the body of a man entirely through.

The Flying Horseman – Nature of the Bow and Arrow

It must be remembered, however, in respect to all such statements relating to the efficiency of the bow and arrow, that the force with which an arrow can be thrown depends not upon any independent action of the bow, but altogether upon the strength of the man who draws it. The bow, in straightening itself for the propulsion of the arrow, expends only the force which the man has imparted to it by bending it; so that the real power by which the arrow is propelled is, after all, the muscular strength of the archer. It is true, a great deal depends on the qualities of the bow, and also on the skill of the man in using it, to make all this muscular strength effective.

With a poor bow, or with unskilful management, a great deal of it would be wasted. But with the best possible bow, and with the most consummate skill of the archer, it is the strength of the archer's arm which throws the arrow, after all.

Superiority of Firearms

It is very different in this respect with a bullet thrown by the force of gunpowder from the barrel of a gun. The force in this case is the explosive force of the powder, and the bullet is thrown to the same distance whether it is a very weak man or a very strong man that pulls the trigger.

Sources of Information – Gog and Magog

But to return to the Mongols. All the information which we can obtain in respect to the condition of the people before the time of Genghis Khan comes to us from the reports of travellers who, either as merchants, or as ambassadors from califs or kings, made long journeys into these distant regions, and have left records, more or less complete, of their adventures, and accounts of what they saw, in writings which have been preserved by the learned men of the east. It is very doubtful how far these accounts are to be believed. One of these travellers, a learned man named Salam, who made a journey far into the interior of Asia by order of the Calif Mohammed Amin Billah, sometime before the reign of Genghis Khan, says that, among other objects of research and investigation which occupied his mind, he was directed to ascertain the truth in respect to the two famous nations Gog and Magog, or, as they are designated in his account, Yagog and Magog. The story that had been told of these two nations by the Arabian writers, and which was extensively believed, was, that the people of Yagog were of the ordinary size of men, but those of Magog were only about two feet high. These people had made war upon the neighbouring nations, and had destroyed many cities and towns, but had at last been overpowered and shut up in prison.

Salam – Adventures of Salam and His Party

Salam, the traveller whom the calif sent to ascertain whether their accounts were true, travelled at the head of a caravan containing 50 men, and with camels bearing stores and provisions for a year. He was gone a long time. When he came back, he gave an account of his travels; and in respect to Gog and Magog, he said that he had found that the accounts which had been heard respecting them were true. He travelled on, he said, from the country of one chieftain to another till he reached the Caspian Sea, and then went on beyond that sea for 30 or 40 days more. In one place the party came to a tract of low black land, which exhaled an odour so offensive that they were obliged to use perfumes all the way to overpower the noxious smells. They were 10 days in crossing this fetid territory. After this they went on a month longer through a desert country, and at length came to a fertile land which was covered with the ruins of cities that the people of Gog and Magog had destroyed.

In six days more they reached the country of the nation by which the people of Gog and Magog had been conquered and shut up in prison. Here they found a great many strong castles. There was a large city here too, containing temples and academies of learning, and also the residence of the king.

The Wonderful Mountain – Great Bolts and Bars

The travellers took up their abode in this city for a time, and while they were there they made an excursion of two days' journey into the country to see the place where the people of Gog and Magog were confined. When they arrived at the place they found a lofty mountain. There was a great opening made in the face of this mountain 200 or 300 feet wide. The opening was protected on each side by enormous buttresses, between which was placed an immense double gate, the buttresses and the gate being all of iron. The buttresses were surmounted with an iron bulwark, and with lofty towers also of iron, which were carried up as high as to the top of the mountain itself. The gates were of the width of the opening cut in the mountain, and were 75 feet high; and the valves, lintels and threshold, and also the bolts, the lock and the key, were all of proportional size.

The Prisoners

Salam, on arriving at the place, saw all these wonderful structures with his own eyes, and he was told by the people there that it was the custom of the governor of the castles already mentioned to take horse every Friday with 10 others, and, coming to the gate, to strike the great bolt three times with a ponderous hammer weighing five pounds, when there would be heard a murmuring noise within, which were the groans of the Yagog and Magog people confined in the mountain. Indeed, Salam was told that the poor captives often appeared on the battlements above. Thus, the real existence of this people was, in his opinion, fully proved; and even the story in respect to the diminutive size of the Magogs was substantiated, for Salam was told that once, in a high wind, three of them were blown off from the battlements to the ground, and that, on being measured, they were found but three spans high.

Travelers' Tales – Progress of Intelligence

This is a specimen of the tales brought home from remote countries by the most learned and accomplished travellers of those times. In comparing these absurd and ridiculous tales with the reports which are brought back from distant regions in our days by such travellers as Humboldt, Livingstone and Kane, we shall perceive what an immense progress in intelligence and information the human mind has made since those days.

Chapter III
Yezonkai Khan
1163–75

X

Yezonkai Behadr

THE NAME OF THE FATHER of Genghis Khan is a word which cannot be pronounced exactly in English. It sounded something like this, Yezonkai Behadr, with the accent on the last syllable, Behadr, and the a sounded like a in hark. This is as near as we can come to it; but the name, as it was really pronounced by the Mongol people, cannot be written in English letters nor spoken with English sounds.

Orthography of Mongol Names

Indeed, in all languages so entirely distinct from each other as the Mongol language was from ours, the sounds are different, and the letters by which the sounds are represented are different too. Some of the sounds are so utterly unlike any sounds that we have in English that it is as impossible to write them in English characters as it is for us to write in English letters the sound that a man makes when he chirps to his horse or his dog, or when he whistles. Sometimes writers attempt to represent the latter sound by the word *whew*; and when, in reading a dialogue, we come to the word whew, inserted to express a part of what one of the speakers uttered, we understand by it that he whistled; but how different, after all, is the sound of the spoken word *whew* from the whistling sound that it is intended to represent!

Great Diversities

Now, in all the languages of Asia, there are many sounds as impossible to be rendered by the European letters as this, and in making the attempt every different writer falls into a different mode. Thus, the first name of Genghis Khan's father is spelled by different travellers and historians, Yezonkai, Yesukay, Yessuki, Yesughi, Bissukay, Bisukay, Pisukay, and in several other ways. The real sound was undoubtedly as different from any of these as they were all different from each other. In this narrative I shall adopt the first of these methods, and call him Yezonkai Behadr.

Yezonkai's Power – A Successful Warrior

Yezonkai was a great khan, and he descended in a direct line through 10 generations, so it was said, from a deity. Great sovereigns in those countries and times were very fond of tracing back their descent to some divine origin, by way of establishing more fully in the minds of the people their divine right to the throne. Yezonkai's residence was at a great palace in the country, called by a name, the sound of which, as nearly as it can be represented in English letters, was *Diloneldak*. From this, his capital, he used to make warlike excursions at the head of hordes of Mongols into the surrounding countries, in the prosecution of quarrels which he made with them under various pretexts; and as he was a skilful commander, and had great influence in inducing all the inferior khans to bring large troops of men from their various tribes to add to his army, he was usually victorious, and in this way he extended his empire very considerably while he lived, and thus made a very good preparation for the subsequent exploits of his son.

Katay

The northern part of China was at that time entirely separated from the southern part, and was under a different government. It constituted an entirely distinct country, and was called Katay. This country was under the dominion of a chieftain called the Khan of Katay. This khan was very jealous of the increasing power of Yezonkai, and took part against him in all his wars with the tribes around him, and assisted them in their attempts to resist him; but he did not succeed. Yezonkai was too powerful for them, and went on extending his conquests far and wide.

At last, under the pretence of some affront which he had received from them, Yezonkai made war upon a powerful tribe of Tartars that lived in his neighbourhood. He invaded their territories at the head of an immense horde of Mongol troops, and began seizing and driving off their cattle.

The Khan of Temujin – Birth of Genghis Khan

The name of the khan who ruled over these people was Temujin. Temujin assembled his forces as soon as he could, and went to meet the invaders. A great battle was fought, and Yezonkai was victorious. Temujin was defeated and put to flight. Yezonkai encamped after the battle on the banks of the River Amoor, near a mountain. He had all his family with him, for it was often the custom, in these enterprises, for the chieftain to take with him not only all his household, but a large portion of his household goods. Yezonkai had several wives, and almost immediately after the battle, one of them, named Olan Ayka, gave birth to a son. Yezonkai, fresh from the battle, determined to commemorate his victory by giving his newborn son the name of his vanquished enemy. So he named him Temujin. His birth took place, as nearly as can now be ascertained, in the year of our Lord 1163.

Such were the circumstances of our hero's birth, for it was this Temujin who afterward became renowned throughout all Asia under the name of Genghis Khan. Through all the early part of his life, however, he was always known by the name which his father gave him in the tent by the river side where he was born.

Predictions of the Astrologer

Among the other grand personages in Yezonkai's train at this time, there was a certain old astrologer named Sugujin. He was a relative of Yezonkai, and also his principal minister of state. This man, by his skill in astrology, which he applied to the peculiar circumstances of the child, foretold for him at once a wonderful career. He would grow up, the astrologer said, to be a great warrior. He would conquer all his enemies, and extend his conquests so far that he would, in the end, become the Khan of all Tartary. Young Temujin's parents were, of course, greatly pleased with these predictions, and when, not long after this time, the astrologer died, they appointed his son, whose name was Karasher, to be the guardian and instructor of the boy. They trusted, it seems, to the son to give the young prince such a training in early life as should prepare him to realize the grand destiny which the father had foretold for him.

Explanation of the Predictions

There would be something remarkable in the fact that these predictions were uttered at the birth of Genghis Khan, since they were afterward so completely fulfilled, were it not that similar prognostications of greatness and glory were almost always offered to the fathers and mothers of young princes in those days by the astrologers and soothsayers of their courts. Such promises were, of course, very flattering to these parents at the time, and brought those who made them into great favour. Then, in the end, if the result verified them, they were remembered and recorded as something wonderful; if not, they were forgotten.

Karasher – Education of Temujin

Karasher, the astrologer's son, who had been appointed young Temujin's tutor, took his pupil under his charge, and began to form plans for educating him. Karasher was a man of great talents and of considerable attainments in learning, so far as there could be anything like learning in such a country and among such a people. He taught him the names of the various tribes that lived in the countries around, and the names of the principal chieftains that ruled over them. He also gave him such information as he possessed in respect to the countries themselves, describing the situation of the mountains, the lakes, the rivers and the great deserts which here and there intervened between the fertile regions. He taught him, moreover, to ride, and trained him in all such athletic exercises as were practiced by the youth of those times. He instructed him also in the use of arms, teaching him how to shoot with a bow and arrow, and how to hold and handle his sabre, both when on horseback and when on foot. He particularly instructed him in the art of shooting his arrow in any direction when riding at a gallop upon his horse, behind as well as before, and to the right side as well as to the left. To do this coolly, skilfully and with a true aim, required great practice as well as much courage and presence of mind.

His Precocity

Young Temujin entered into all these things with great spirit. Indeed, he very soon ceased to feel any interest in anything else, so that by the time that he was nine years of age it was said that he thought of nothing but exercising himself in the use of arms.

His Early Marriage

Nine years of age, however, with him was more than it would be with a young man among us, for the Asiatics arrive at maturity much earlier than the nations of Western Europe and America. Indeed, by the time that Temujin was 13 years old, his father considered him a man – at least he considered him old enough to be married. He was married, in fact, and had two children before he was 15, if the accounts which the historians have given us respecting him are true.

Just before Temujin was 13, his father, in one of his campaigns in Katay, was defeated in a battle, and, although a great many of his followers escaped, he himself was surrounded and overpowered by the horsemen of the enemy, and was made prisoner. He was put under the care of a guard; for, of course, among people living almost altogether on horseback and in tents, there could be very few prisons. Yezonkai followed the camp of his conqueror for some time under the custody of his guard; but at length he succeeded in bribing his keeper to let him escape, and so contrived, after encountering many difficulties and suffering many hardships, to make his way back to his own country.

Plans of Temujin's Father – Karizu – Tayian

He was determined now to make a new incursion into Katay, and that with a larger force than he had had before. So he made an alliance with the chieftain of a neighbouring tribe, called the Naymans; and, in order to seal and establish this alliance, he contracted that his son should marry the daughter of his ally. This was the time when Temujin was but 13 years old. The name of this his first wife was Karizu – at least that was one of her names. Her father's name was Tayian.

Death of Yezonkai

Before Yezonkai had time to mature his plans for his new invasion of Katay, he fell sick and died. He left five sons and a daughter, it is said; but Temujin seems to have been the oldest of them all, for by his will his father left his kingdom, if the command of the group of tribes which were under his sway can be called a kingdom, to him, notwithstanding that he was yet only 13 years old.

Chapter IV
The First Battle
1175

IN THE LANGUAGE OF THE MONGOLS and of their neighbours the Tartars, a collection of tribes banded together under one chieftain was designated by a name which sounded like the word orda. This is the origin, it is said, of the English word horde.

Temujin's Accession – Discontent

The orda over which Yezonkai had ruled, and the command of which, at his death, he left to his son, consisted of a great number of separate tribes, each of which had its own particular chieftain. All these subordinate chieftains were content to be under Yezonkai's rule and leadership while he lived. He was competent, they thought, to direct their movements and to lead them into battle against their enemies. But when he died, leaving only a young man 13 years of age to succeed him, several of them were disposed to rebel. There were two of them, in particular, who thought that they were themselves better qualified to reign over the nation than such a boy; so they formed an alliance with each other, and with such other tribes as were disposed to join them, and advanced to make war upon Temujin at the head of a great number of squadrons of troops, amounting in all to 30,000 men.

Taychot and Chamuka

The names of the two leaders of this rebellion were Taychot and Chamuka.

Young Temujin depended chiefly on his mother for guidance and direction in this emergency. He was himself very brave and spirited; but bravery and spirit, though they are of such vital importance in a commander on the field of battle; when the contest actually comes on, are by no means the principal qualities that are required in making the preliminary arrangements.

Arrangements for the Battle

Accordingly, Temujin left the forming of the plans to his mother, while he thought only of his horses, of his arms and equipments, and of the fury with which he would gallop in among the enemy when the time should arrive for the battle to begin. His mother, in connection with the chief officers of the army and counsellors of state who were around her, and on whom her husband Yezonkai, during his lifetime, had been most accustomed to rely, arranged all the plans. They sent off messengers to the heads of all the tribes that they supposed would be friendly to Temujin, and appointed places of rendezvous for the troops that they were to send. They made arrangements for the stores of provisions which would be required, settled questions of precedence among the different clans, regulated the order of march and attended to all other necessary details.

Temujin's Ardour

In the meantime, Temujin thought only of the approaching battle. He was engaged continually in riding up and down upon spirited horses, and shooting in all directions, backward and forward, and both to the right side and to the left, with his bow and arrow. Nor was all this exhibition of ardour on his part a mere useless display. It had great influence in awakening a corresponding ardour among the chieftains of the troops, and among the troops themselves. They felt proud of the spirit and energy which their young prince displayed, and were more and more resolved to exert themselves to the utmost in defending his cause.

Porgie

There was another young prince, of the name of Porgie, of about Temujin's age, who was also full of ardour for the fight. He was the chieftain of one of the tribes that remained faithful to Temujin, and he was equally earnest with Temujin for the battle to begin.

Exaggerated Statements

At length the troops were ready, and, with Temujin and his mother at the head of them, they went forth to attack the rebels. The rebels were ready to receive them. They were 30,000 strong, according to the statements of the historians. This number is probably exaggerated, as all numbers were in those days, when there was no regular enrolment of troops and no strict system of enumeration.

The Battle

At any rate, there was a very great battle. Immense troops of horsemen coming at full speed in opposite directions shot showers of arrows at each other when they arrived at the proper distance for the arrows to take effect, and then, throwing down their bows and drawing their sabres, rushed madly on, until they came together with an awful shock, the dreadful confusion and terror of which no person can describe. The air was filled with the most terrific outcries, in which yells of fury, shrieks of agony and shouts of triumph were equally mingled. Some of the troops maintained their position through the shock, and rode on, bearing down all before them. Others were overthrown and trampled in the dust; while all, both those who were up and those who were down, were cutting in every direction with their sabres, killing men and inciting the horses to redoubled fury by the wounds which they gave them.

Bravery of Temujin and Porgie

In the midst of such scenes as these, Temujin and Porgie fought furiously with the rest. Temujin distinguished himself greatly. It is probable that those who were immediately around him felt that he was under their charge, and that they must do all in their power to protect him from danger. This they could do much more easily and effectually under the mode of fighting which prevailed in those days than would be possible now, when gunpowder is the principal agent of destruction. Temujin's attendants and followers could gather around him and defend him from assailants. They could prevent him from charging any squadron which was likely to be strong enough to overpower him, and they could keep his enemies so much at bay that they could not reach him with their sabres. But upon a modern field of battle there is much less opportunity to protect a young prince or general's son, or other personage whose life may be considered as peculiarly valuable. No precautions of his attendants can prevent a bomb's bursting at his feet, or shield him from the rifle balls that come whistling from such great distances through the air.

Influence of Temujin's Example – The Victory

At any rate, whether protected by his attendants or only by the fortune of war, Temujin passed through the battle without being hurt, and the courage and energy which he displayed were greatly commended by all who witnessed them. His mother was in the battle too, though, perhaps, not personally involved in the actual conflicts of it. She directed the manoeuvres, however, and by her presence and her activity greatly encouraged and animated the men. In consequence of the spirit and energy infused into the troops by her presence, and by the extraordinary ardour and bravery of Temujin, the battle was gained. The army of the enemy was put to flight. One of the leaders, Taychot, was slain. The other made his escape, and Temujin and his mother were left in possession of the field.

Rewards and Honours

Of course, after having fought with so much energy and effect on such a field, Temujin was now no longer considered as a boy, but took his place at once as a man among men, and was immediately recognized by all the army as their prince and sovereign, and as fully entitled, by his capacity if not by his years, to rule in his own name. He assumed and exercised his powers with as much calmness and self-possession as if he had been accustomed to them for many years. He made addresses to his officers and soldiers, and distributed honours and rewards to them with a combined majesty and grace which, in their opinion, denoted much grandeur of soul. The rewards and honours were characteristic of the customs of the country and the times. They consisted of horses, arms, splendid articles of dress and personal ornaments. Of course, among a people who lived, as it were, always on horseback, such objects as these were the ones most highly prized.

Temujin's Rising Fame

The consequence of this victory was that nearly the whole country occupied by the rebels submitted without any farther resistance to Temujin's sway. Other tribes, who lived on the borders of his dominions, sent in to propose treaties of alliance. The khan of one of these tribes demanded of Temujin the hand of his sister in marriage to seal and confirm the alliance which he proposed to make. In a word, the fame of Temujin's prowess spread rapidly after the battle over all the surrounding countries, and high anticipations began to be formed of the greatness and glory of his reign.

His Second Wife

In the course of the next year Temujin was married to his second wife, although he was at this time only 14 years old. The name of his bride was Purta Kugin. By this wife, who was probably of about his own age, he had a daughter, who was born before the close of the year after the marriage.

Purta Carried Away Captive – Customary Present

In his journeys about the country, Temujin sometimes took his wives with him, and sometimes he left them temporarily in some place of supposed security. Toward the end of the second year, Purta was again about to become a mother, and Temujin, who at that time had occasion to go off on some military expedition, fearing that the fatigue and exposure would be more than she could well bear, left her at home. While he was gone a troop of horsemen, from a tribe of his enemies, came suddenly into the district on a marauding expedition. They overpowered the troops Temujin had left to guard the place, and seized and carried off everything that they could find that was valuable. They made prisoner of Purta, too, and carried her away a captive. The plunder they divided among themselves, but Purta they sent as a present to a certain khan who reigned over a neighbouring country, and whose favour they wished to secure. The name of this chieftain was Vang Khan. As this Vang Khan figures somewhat conspicuously in the subsequent history of Temujin, a full account of him will be given in the next chapter. All that is necessary to say here is, that the intention of the captors of Purta, in sending her to him as a present, was that he should make her his wife. It was the custom of these khans to have as many wives as they could obtain, so that when prisoners of high rank were taken in war, if there were any young and beautiful women among them, they were considered as charming presents to send to any great prince or potentate near, whom the captors were desirous of pleasing. It made no difference, in such cases, whether the person who was to receive the present were young or old. Sometimes the older he was the more highly he would prize such a gift.

Vang Khan, it happened, was old. He was old enough to be Temujin's father. Indeed, he had been in the habit of calling Temujin his son. He had been in alliance with Yezonkai, Temujin's father, some years before, when Temujin was quite a boy, and it was at that time that he began to call him his son.

Purta and Vang Khan

Accordingly, when Purta was brought to him by the messengers who had been sent in charge of her, and presented to him in his tent, he said, 'She is very beautiful, but I cannot take her for my wife, for she is the wife of my son. I cannot marry the wife of my son.'

Vang Khan, however, received Purta under his charge, gave her a place in his household, and took good care of her.

Purta's Return – Birth of Her Child

When Temujin returned home from his expedition, and learned what had happened during his absence, he was greatly distressed at the loss of his wife. Not long afterward he ascertained where she was, and he immediately sent a deputation to Vang Khan asking him to send her home. With this request, Vang Khan immediately complied, and Purta set out on her return. She was stopped on the way, however, by the birth of her child. It was a son. As soon as the child was born it was determined to continue the journey, for there was danger, if they delayed, that some new troop of enemies might come up, in which case Purta would perhaps be made captive again. So Purta, it is said, wrapped up the tender limbs of the infant in some sort of paste or dough, to save them from the effects of the jolting produced by the rough sort of cart in which she was compelled to ride, and in that condition she held the babe in her lap all the way home.

Jughi

She arrived at her husband's residence in safety. Temujin was overjoyed at seeing her again; and he was particularly pleased with his little son, who came out of his packing safe and sound. In commemoration of his safe arrival after so strange and dangerous a journey, his father named him Safe-arrived; that is, he gave him for a name the word in their language that means that. The word itself was Jughi.

Temujin's Wonderful Dream

The commencement of Temujin's career was thus, on the whole, quite prosperous, and everything seemed to promise well. He was himself full of ambition and of hope, and began to feel dissatisfied with the empire which his father had left him, and to form plans for extending it. He dreamed one night that his arms grew out to an enormous length, and that he took a sword in each of them, and stretched them out to see how far they would reach, pointing one to the eastward and the other to the westward. In the morning he related his dream to his mother. She interpreted it to him. She told him it meant undoubtedly that he was destined to become a great conqueror, and that the directions in which his kingdom would be extended were toward the eastward and toward the westward.

Disaffection Among His Subjects – A Rebellion

Temujin continued for about two years after this in prosperity, and then his good fortune began to wane. There came a reaction. Some of the tribes under his dominion began to grow discontented. The subordinate khans began to form plots and conspiracies. Even his own tribe turned against him. Rebellions broke out in various parts of his dominions; and he was obliged to make many hurried expeditions here and there, and to fight many desperate battles to suppress them. In one of these contests he was taken prisoner. He, however, contrived to make his escape. He then made proposals to the disaffected khans, which he hoped would satisfy them, and bring them once more to submit to him, since what he thus offered to do in these proposals was pretty much all that they had professed to require. But the proposals did not satisfy them. What they really intended to do was to depose Temujin altogether, and then either divide his dominions among themselves, or select some one of their number to reign in his stead.

Temujin Discouraged

At last, Temujin, finding that he could not pacify his enemies, and that they were, moreover, growing stronger every day, while those that adhered to him were growing fewer in numbers and diminishing in strength, became discouraged. He began to think that perhaps he really was too young to rule over a kingdom composed of wandering hordes of men so warlike and wild, and he concluded for a time to give up the attempt, and wait until times should change, or, at least, until he should be grown somewhat older. Accordingly, in conjunction with his mother, he formed a plan for retiring temporarily from the field; unless, indeed, as we might reasonably suspect, his mother formed the plan herself, and by her influence over him induced him to adopt it.

Temujin Plans a Temporary Abdication

The plan was this: that Temujin should send an ambassador to the court of Vang Khan to ask Vang Khan to receive him, and protect him for a time in his dominions, until the affairs of his own kingdom should become settled. Then, if Vang Khan should accede to this proposal, Temujin was to appoint his uncle to act as regent during his absence. His mother, too, was to be married to a certain emir, or prince, named Menglik, who was to be made prime minister under the regent, and was to take precedence of all the other princes or khans in the kingdom. The government was to be managed by the regent and the minister until such time as it should be deemed expedient for Temujin to return.

Arrangement of a Regency – Temujin's Departure

This plan was carried into effect. Vang Khan readily consented to receive Temujin into his dominions, and to protect him there. He was very ready to do this, he said, on account of the friendship which he had borne for Temujin's father. Temujin's mother was married to the emir, and the emir was made the first prince of the realm. Finally, Temujin's uncle was proclaimed regent, and duly invested with all necessary authority for governing the country until Temujin's return. These things being all satisfactorily arranged, Temujin set out for the country of Vang Khan at the head of an armed escort, to protect him on the way, of 6,000 men. He took with him all his family, and a considerable suite of servants and attendants. Among them was his old tutor and guardian Karasher, the person who had been appointed by his father to take charge of him, and to teach and train him when he was a boy.

Being protected by so powerful an escort, Temujin's party were not molested on their journey, and they all arrived safely at the court of Vang Khan.

Chapter V
Vang Khan
1175

Karakatay – Vang Khan's Dominions

THE COUNTRY OVER WHICH Vang Khan ruled was called Karakatay. It bordered upon the country of Katay, which has already been mentioned as forming the northern part of what is now China.

Indeed, as its name imports, it was considered in some sense as a portion of the same general district of country. It was that part of Katay which was inhabited by Tartars.

Vang Khan's name at first was Togrul. The name Vang Khan, which was, in fact, a title rather than a name, was given him long afterward, when he had attained to the height of his power. To avoid confusion, however, we shall drop the name Togrul, and call him Vang Khan from the beginning.

The Cruel Fate of Mergus

Vang Khan was descended from a powerful line of khans who had reigned over Karakatay for many generations. These khans were a wild and lawless race of men, continually fighting with each other, both for mastery, and also for the plunder of each other's flocks and herds. In this way most furious and cruel wars were often fought between near relatives. Vang Khan's grandfather, whose name was Mergus, was taken prisoner in one of these quarrels by another khan, who, though he was a relative, was so much exasperated by something that Mergus had done that he sent him away to a great distance to the king of a certain country which is called Kurga, to be disposed of there. The King of Kurga put him into a sack, sewed up the mouth of it and then laid him across the wooden image of an ass, and left him there to die of hunger and suffocation.

His Wife's Stratagem

The wife of Mergus was greatly enraged when she heard of the cruel fate of her husband. She determined to be revenged. It seems that the relative of her husband who had taken him prisoner, and had sent him to the King of Kurga, had been her lover in former times before her marriage; so she sent him a message, in which she dissembled her grief for the loss of her husband, and only blamed the King of Kurga for his cruel death, and then said that she had long felt an affection for him, and that, if he continued of the same mind as when he had formally addressed her, she was now willing to become his wife, and offered, if he would come to a certain place, which she specified, to meet her, she would join him there.

Nawr – He Falls into the Snare

Nawr, for that was the chieftain's name, fell at once into the snare which the beautiful widow thus laid for him. He immediately accepted her proposals, and proceeded to the place of rendezvous. He went, of course, attended by a suitable guard, though his guard was small, and consisted chiefly of friends and personal attendants. The princess was attended also by a guard, not large enough, however, to excite any suspicion. She also took with her in her train a large number of carts, which were to be drawn by bullocks, and which were laden with stores of provisions, clothing and other such valuables, intended as a present for her new husband. Among these, however, there were a large number of great barrels, or rounded receptacles of some sort, in which she had concealed a considerable force of armed men. These receptacles were so arranged that the men concealed in them could open them from within in an instant, at a given signal, and issue forth suddenly all armed and ready for action.

Armed Men in Ambuscade – Death of Nawr

Among the other stores which the princess had provided, there was a large supply of a certain intoxicating drink which the Mongols and Tartars were accustomed to make in those days. As soon as the two parties met at the place of rendezvous the princess gave Nawr a very cordial greeting, and invited him and all his party to a feast, to be partaken on the spot. The invitation was accepted, the stores of provisions were opened, and many of the presents were unpacked and displayed. At the feast, Nawr and his party were all supplied abundantly with the intoxicating liquor, which, as is usual in such cases, they were easily led to drink to excess; while, on the other hand, the princess's party, who knew what was coming, took good care to keep themselves sober. At length, when the proper moment arrived, the princess made the signal. In an instant the men who had been placed in ambuscade in the barrels burst forth from their concealment and rushed upon the guests at the feast. The princess herself, who was all ready for action, drew a dagger from her girdle and stabbed Nawr to the heart. Her guards, assisted by the re-enforcement which had so suddenly appeared, slew or secured all his attendants, who were so totally incapacitated, partly by the drink which they had taken, and partly by their astonishment at the sudden appearance of so overwhelming a force, that they were incapable of making any resistance.

The princess, having thus accomplished her revenge, marshalled her men, packed up her pretended presents, and returned in triumph home.

Early Life of Vang Khan – Reception of Temujin

Such stories as these, related by the Asiatic writers, though they were probably often much embellished in the narration, had doubtless all some foundation in fact, and they give us some faint idea of the modes of life and action which prevailed among these half-savage chieftains in those times. Vang Khan himself was the grandson of Mergus, who was sewed up in the sack. His father was the oldest son of the princess who contrived the above-narrated stratagem to revenge her husband's death. It is said that he used to accompany his father to the wars when he was only 10 years old. The way in which he formed his friendship for Yezonkai, and the alliance with him which led him to call Temujin his son and to refuse to take his wife away from him, as already related, was this: When his father died he succeeded to the command, being the oldest son; but the others were jealous of him, and after many and long quarrels with them and with other relatives, especially with his uncle, who seemed to take the lead against him, he was at last overpowered or outmanoeuvred, and was obliged to fly. He took refuge, in his distress, in the country of Yezonkai. Yezonkai received him in a very friendly manner, and gave him effectual protection. After a time, he furnished him with troops, and helped him to recover his kingdom, and to drive his uncle away into banishment in his turn. It was while he was thus in Yezonkai's dominions that he became acquainted with Temujin, who was then very small, and it was there that he learned to call him his son. Of course, now that Temujin was obliged to fly himself from his native country and abandon his hereditary dominions, as he had done before, he was glad of the opportunity of requiting to the son the favour which he had received, in precisely similar circumstances, from the father, and so he gave Temujin a very kind reception.

Prester John – His Letter to the King of France

There is another circumstance which is somewhat curious in respect to Vang Khan, and that is, that he is generally supposed to be the prince whose fame was about this period spread all over Europe, under the name of Prester John, by the Christian missionaries in Asia. These missionaries sent to the Pope, and to various Christian kings in Europe, very exaggerated accounts of the success of their missions among the Persians, Turks and Tartars; and at last, they wrote word that the great Khan of the Tartars had become a convert, and had even become a preacher of the Gospel, and had taken the name of Prester John. The word *prester* was understood to be a corruption of presbyter. A great deal was accordingly written and said all through Christendom about the great Tartar convert, Prester John. There were several letters forwarded by the missionaries, professedly from him, and addressed to the Pope and to the different kings of Europe. Some of these letters, it is said, are still in existence. One of them was to the King of France. In this letter the writer tells the King of France of his great wealth and of the vastness of his dominions. He says he has 70 kings to serve and wait upon him. He invites the King of France to come and see him, promising to bestow a great kingdom upon him if he will, and also to make him his heir and leave all his dominions to him when he dies; with a great deal more of the same general character.

Other Letters

The other letters were much the same, and the interest which they naturally excited was increased by the accounts which the missionaries gave of the greatness and renown of this more than royal convert, and of the progress which Christianity had made and was still making in his dominions through their instrumentality.

The Probable Truth

It is supposed, in modern times, that these stories were pretty much all inventions on the part of the missionaries, or, at least, that the accounts which they sent were greatly exaggerated and embellished; and there is but little doubt that they had much more to do with the authorship of the letters than any khan. Still, however, it is supposed that there was a great prince who at least encouraged the missionaries in their work, and allowed them to preach Christianity in his dominions, and, if so, there is little doubt that Vang Khan was the man.

At all events, he was a very great and powerful prince, and he reigned over a wide extent of country. The name of his capital was Karakorom. The distance which Temujin had to travel to reach this city was about 10 days' journey.

Temujin and Vang Khan

He was received by Vang Khan with great marks of kindness and consideration. Vang Khan promised to protect him, and, in due time, to assist him in recovering his kingdom. In the meantime, Temujin promised to enter at once into Vang Khan's service, and to devote himself faithfully to promoting the interests of his kind protector by every means in his power.

Chapter VI
Temujin in Exile
1182

Temujin's Popularity

VANG KHAN GAVE TEMUJIN a very honourable position in his court. It was natural that he should do so, for Temujin was a prince in the prime of his youth, and of very attractive person and manners; and, though he was for the present an exile, as it were, from his native land, he was not by any means in a destitute or hopeless condition. His family and friends were still in the ascendency at home, and he himself, in coming to the kingdom of Vang Khan, had brought with him quite an important body of troops. Being, at the same time, personally possessed of great courage and of much military skill, he was prepared to render his protector good service in return for his protection. In a word, the arrival of Temujin at the court of Vang Khan was an event calculated to make quite a sensation.

Rivals and Enemies Appear – Plots

At first everybody was very much pleased with him, and he was very popular; but before long the other young princes of the court, and the chieftains of the neighbouring tribes, began to be jealous of him. Vang Khan gave him precedence over them all, partly on account of his personal attachment to him, and partly on account of the rank which he held in his own country, which, being that of a sovereign prince, naturally entitled him to the very highest position among the subordinate chieftains in the retinue of Vang Khan. But these subordinate chieftains were not satisfied. They murmured, at first secretly, and afterward more openly, and soon began to form combinations and plots against the new favourite, as they called him.

Yemuka – Wisulujine

An incident soon occurred which greatly increased this animosity, and gave to Temujin's enemies, all at once, a very powerful leader and head. This leader was a very influential chieftain named Yemuka. This Yemuka, it seems, was in love with the daughter of Vang Khan, the Princess Wisulujine. He asked her in marriage of her father. To precisely what state of forwardness the negotiations had advanced does not appear, but, at any rate, when Temujin arrived, Wisulujine soon began to turn her thoughts toward him. He was undoubtedly younger, handsomer and more accomplished than her old lover, and before long she gave her father to understand that she would much rather have him for her husband than Yemuka. It is true, Temujin had one or two wives already; but this made no difference, for it was the custom then, as, indeed, it is still, for the Asiatic princes and chieftains to take as many wives as their wealth and position would enable them to maintain. Yemuka was accordingly refused, and Wisulujine was given in marriage to Temujin.

Yemuka's Disappointment and Rage – Conspiracy Formed

Yemuka was, of course, dreadfully enraged. He vowed that he would be revenged. He immediately began to intrigue with all the discontented persons and parties in the kingdom, not only with those who were envious and jealous of Temujin, but also with all those who, for any reason, were disposed to put themselves in opposition to Vang Khan's government. Thus, a formidable conspiracy was formed for the purpose of compassing Temujin's ruin.

The conspirators first tried the effect of private remonstrances with Vang Khan, in which they made all sorts of evil representations against Temujin, but to no effect.

Temujin rallied about him so many old friends, and made so many new friends by his courage and energy, that his party at court proved stronger than that of his enemies, and, for a time, they seemed likely to fail entirely of their design.

Progress of the League

At length the conspirators opened communication with the foreign enemies of Vang Khan, and formed a league with them to make war against and destroy both Vang Khan and Temujin together. The accounts of the progress of this league, and of the different nations and tribes which took part in it, is imperfect and confused; but at length, after various preliminary contests and manoeuvres, arrangements were made for assembling a large army with a view of invading Vang Khan's dominions and deciding the question by a battle. The different chieftains and khans whose troops were united to form this army bound themselves together by a solemn oath, according to the customs of those times, not to rest until both Vang Khan and Temujin should be destroyed.

Oath of the Conspirators

The manner in which they took the oath was this: They brought out into an open space on the plain where they had assembled to take the oath, a horse, a wild ox and a dog. At a given signal they fell upon these animals with their swords, and cut them all to pieces in the most furious manner. When they had finished, they stood together and called out aloud in the following words:

'Hear! O God! O heaven! O earth! the oath that we swear against Vang Khan and Temujin. If any one of us spares them when we have them in our power, or if we fail to keep the promise that we have made to destroy them, may we meet with the same fate that has befallen these beasts that we have now cut to pieces.'

They uttered this imprecation in a very solemn manner, standing among the mangled and bloody remains of the beasts which lay strewed all about the ground.

Plan Formed by Temujin – The Campaign

These preparations had been made thus far very secretly; but tidings of what was going on came, before a great while, to Karakorom, Vang Khan's capital. Temujin was greatly excited when he heard the news. He immediately proposed that he should take his own troops, and join with them as many of Vang Khan's soldiers as could be conveniently spared, and go forth to meet the enemy. To this Vang Khan consented. Temujin took one half of Vang Khan's troops to join his own, leaving the other half to protect the capital, and so set forth on his expedition. He went off in the direction toward the frontier where he had understood the principal part of the hostile forces were assembling. After a long march, probably one of many days, he arrived there before the enemy was quite prepared for him. Then followed a series of manoeuvres and counter-manoeuvres, in which Temujin was all the time endeavouring to bring the rebels to battle, while they were doing all in their power to avoid it. Their object in this delay was to gain time for re-enforcements to come in, consisting of bodies of troops belonging to certain members of the league who had not yet arrived.

Unexpected Arrival of Vang Khan – His Story

At length, when these manoeuvres were brought to an end, and the battle was about to be fought, Temujin and his whole army were one day greatly surprised to see his father-in-law, Vang Khan himself, coming into the camp at the head of a small and forlorn-looking band of followers, who had all the appearance of fugitives escaped from a battle. They looked anxious, wayworn and exhausted, and the horses that they rode seemed wholly spent with fatigue and privation. On explanation, Temujin learned that, as soon as it was known that he had left the capital, and taken with him a large part of the army, a certain tribe of Vang Khan's enemies, living in another direction, had determined to seize the opportunity to invade his dominions, and had accordingly come suddenly in, with an immense horde, to attack the capital. Vang Khan had done all that he could to defend the city, but he had been overpowered. The greater part of his soldiers had been killed or wounded. The city had been taken and pillaged. His son, with those of the troops that had been able to save themselves, had escaped to the mountains. As to Vang Khan himself, he had thought it best to make his way, as soon as possible, to the camp of Temujin, where he had now arrived, after enduring great hardships and sufferings on the way.

Temujin's Promises

Temujin was at first much amazed at hearing this story. He, however, bade his father-in-law not to be cast down or discouraged, and promised him full revenge, and a complete triumph over all his enemies at the coming battle. So he proceeded at once to complete his arrangements for the coming fight. He resigned to Vang Khan the command of the main body of the army, while he placed himself at the head of one of the wings, assigning the other to the chieftain next in rank in his army. In this order he went into battle.

Result of the Battle – Temujin Victorious

The battle was a very obstinate and bloody one, but, in the end, Temujin's party was victorious. The troops opposed to him were defeated and driven off the field. The victory appeared to be due altogether to Temujin himself; for, after the struggle had continued a long time, and the result still appeared doubtful, the troops of Temujin's wing finally made a desperate charge, and forced their way with such fury into the midst of the forces of the enemy that nothing could withstand them. This encouraged and animated the other troops to such a degree that very soon the enemy were entirely routed and driven from off the field.

State of Things at Karakorom – Erkekara

The effect of this victory was to raise the reputation of Temujin as a military commander higher than ever, and greatly to increase the confidence which Vang Khan was inclined to repose in him. The victory, too, seemed at first to have well-nigh broken up the party of the rebels. Still, the way was not yet open for Vang Khan to return and take possession of his throne and of his capital, for he learned that one of his brothers had assumed the government, and was reigning in Karakorom in his place. It would seem that this brother, whose name was Erkekara, had been one of the leaders of the party opposed to Temujin. It was natural that he should be so; for, being the brother of the king, he would, of course, occupy a very high position in the court, and would be one of the first to experience the ill effects produced by the coming in of any new favourite. He had accordingly joined in the plots that were formed against Temujin and Vang Khan. Indeed, he was considered, in some respects, as the head of their party, and when Vang Khan was driven away from his capital, this brother assumed the throne in his stead. The question was, how could he now be dispossessed and Vang Khan restored.

Preparations for the Final Conflict – Vang Khan Restored

Temujin began immediately to form his plans for the accomplishment of this purpose. He concentrated his forces after the battle, and soon afterward opened negotiations with other tribes, who had before been uncertain which side to espouse, but were now assisted a great deal in coming to a decision by the victory which Temujin had obtained. In the meantime, the rebels were not idle. They banded themselves together anew, and made great exertions to procure re-enforcements. Erkekara fortified himself as strongly as possible in Karakorom, and collected ample supplies of ammunition and military stores. It was not until the following year that the parties had completed their preparations and were prepared for the final struggle. Then, however, another great battle was fought, and again Temujin was victorious. Erkekara was killed or driven away in his turn. Karakorom was retaken, and Vang Khan entered it in triumph at the head of his troops, and was once more established on his throne.

Temujin's Popularity

Of course, the rank and influence of Temujin at his court was now higher than ever before. He was now about 22 or 23 years of age. He had already three wives, though it is not certain that all of them were with him at Vang Khan's court. He was extremely popular in the army, as young commanders of great courage and spirit almost always are. Vang Khan placed great reliance upon him, and lavished upon him all possible honours.

He does not seem, however, yet to have begun to form any plans for returning to his native land.

Chapter VII
Rupture with Vang Khan
1182-1202

X

TEMUJIN REMAINED AT THE COURT, or in the dominions of Vang Khan, for a great many years. During the greater portion of this time, he continued in the service of Vang Khan, and on good terms with him, though, in the end, as we shall presently see, their friendship was turned into a bitter enmity.

Erkekara – State of the Country – Wandering Habits

Erkekara, Vang Khan's brother, who had usurped his throne during the rebellion, was killed, it was said, at the time when Vang Khan recovered his throne. Several of the other rebel chieftains were also killed, but some of them succeeded in saving themselves from utter ruin, and in gradually recovering their former power over the hordes which they respectively commanded. It must be remembered that the country was not divided at this time into regular territorial states and kingdoms, but was rather one vast undivided region, occupied by immense hordes, each of which was more or less stationary, it is true, in its own district or range, but was nevertheless without any permanent settlement. The various clans drifted slowly this way and that among the plains and mountains, as the prospects of pasturage, the fortune of war or the pressure of conterminous hordes might incline them. In cases, too, where a number of hordes were united under one general chieftain, as was the case with those over whom Vang Khan claimed to have sway, the tie by which they were bound together was very feeble, and the distinction between a state of submission and of rebellion, except in case of actual war, was very slightly defined.

Yemuka – Sankum

Yemuka, the chieftain who had been so exasperated against Temujin on account of his being supplanted by him in the affections of the young princess, Vang Khan's daughter, whom Temujin had married for his third wife, succeeded in making his escape at the time when Vang Khan conquered his enemies and recovered his throne. For a time he concealed himself, or at least kept out of Vang Khan's reach, by dwelling with hordes whose range was at some distance from Karakorom. He soon, however, contrived to open secret negotiations with one of Vang Khan's sons, whose name was something that sounded like Sankum. Some authors, in attempting to represent his name in our letters, spelled it *Sunghim*.

Yemuka easily persuaded this young Sankum to take sides with him in the quarrel. It was natural that he should do so, for, being the son of Vang Khan, he was in some measure displaced from his own legitimate and proper position at his father's court by the great and constantly increasing influence which Temujin exercised.

Deceit

'And besides,' said Yemuka, in the secret representations which he made to Sankum, 'this newcomer is not only interfering with and curtailing your proper influence and consideration now, but his design is by-and-by to circumvent and supplant you altogether. He is forming plans for making himself your father's heir, and so robbing you of your rightful inheritance.'

Sankum listened very eagerly to these suggestions, and finally it was agreed between him and Yemuka that Sankum should exert his influence with his father to obtain permission for Yemuka to come back to court, and to be received again into his father's service, under pretence of having repented of his rebellion, and of being now disposed to return to his allegiance. Sankum did this, and, after a time, Vang Khan was persuaded to allow Yemuka to return.

Temujin's Situation – His Military Expeditions

Thus, a sort of outward peace was made, but it was no real peace. Yemuka was as envious and jealous of Temujin as ever, and now, moreover, in addition to this envy and jealousy, he felt the stimulus of revenge. Things, however, seem to have gone on very quietly for a time, or at least without any open outbreak in the court.

During this time Vang Khan was, as usual with such princes, frequently engaged in wars with the neighbouring hordes. In these wars he relied a great deal on Temujin. Temujin was in command of a large body of troops, which consisted in part of his own guard, the troops that had come with him from his own country, and in part of other bands of men whom Vang Khan had placed under his orders, or who had joined him of their own accord. He was assisted in the command of this body by four subordinate generals or khans, whom he called his four intrepids. They were all very brave and skilful commanders. At the head of this troop Temujin was accustomed to scour the country, hunting out Vang Khan's enemies, or making long expeditions over distant plains or among the mountains, in the prosecution of Vang Khan's warlike projects, whether those of invasion and plunder, or of retaliation and vengeance.

Popular Commanders

Temujin was extremely popular with the soldiers who served under him. Soldiers always love a dashing, fearless and energetic leader, who has the genius to devise brilliant schemes, and the spirit to execute them in a brilliant manner. They care very little how dangerous the situations are into which he may lead them. Those that get killed in performing the exploits which he undertakes cannot speak to complain, and those who survive are only so much the better pleased that the dangers that they have been brought safely through were so desperate, and that the harvest of glory which they have thereby acquired is so great.

Stories of Temujin's Cruelty – Probably Fictions

Temujin, though a great favourite with his own men, was, like almost all half-savage warriors of his class, utterly merciless, when he was angry, in his treatment of his enemies. It is said that after one of his battles, in which he had gained a complete victory over an immense horde of rebels and other foes, and had taken great numbers of them prisoners, he ordered fires to be built and 70 large caldrons of water to be put over them, and then, when the water was boiling hot, he caused the principal leaders of the vanquished army to be thrown in headlong and thus scalded to death. Then he marched at once into the country of the enemy, and there took all the women and children, and sent them off to be sold as slaves, and seized the cattle and other property which he found, and carried it off as plunder. In thus taking possession of the enemy's property and making it his own, and selling the poor captives into slavery, there was nothing remarkable. Such was the custom of the times. But the act of scalding his prisoners to death seems to denote or reveal in his character a vein of peculiar and atrocious cruelty. It is possible, however, that the story may not be true. It may have been invented by Yemuka and Sankum, or by some of his other enemies.

Vang Khan's Uneasiness – Temujin

For Yemuka and Sankum, and others who were combined with them, were continually endeavouring to undermine Temujin's influence with Vang Khan, and thus deprive him of his power. But he was too strong for them. His great success in all his military undertakings kept him up in spite of all that his rivals could do to pull him down. As for Vang Khan himself, he was in part pleased with him and proud of him, and in part he feared him. He was very unwilling to be so dependent upon a subordinate chieftain, and yet he could not do without him. A king never desires that any one of his subjects should become too conspicuous or too great, and Vang Khan would have been very glad to have diminished, in some way, the power and prestige which Temujin had acquired, and which seemed to be increasing every day. He, however, found no means of effecting this in any quiet and peaceful manner. Temujin was at the head of his troops, generally away from Karakorom, where Vang Khan resided, and he was, in a great measure, independent. He raised his own recruits to keep the numbers of his army good, and it was always easy to subsist if there chanced to be any failure in the ordinary and regular supplies.

Vang Khan's Suspicions – A Reconciliation

Besides, occasions were continually occurring in which Vang Khan wished for Temujin's aid, and could not dispense with it. At one time, while engaged in some important campaigns, far away among the mountains, Yemuka contrived to awaken so much distrust of Temujin in Vang Khan's mind, that Vang Khan secretly decamped in the night, and marched away to a distant place to save himself from a plot which Yemuka had told him that Temujin was contriving. Here, however, he was attacked by a large body of his enemies, and was reduced to such straits that he was obliged to send couriers off at once to Temujin to come with his intrepids and save him. Temujin came. He rescued Vang Khan from his danger, and drove his enemies away. Vang Khan was very grateful for this service, so that the two friends became entirely reconciled to each other, and were united more closely than ever, greatly to Yemuka's disappointment and chagrin. They made a new league of amity, and, to seal and confirm it, they agreed upon a double marriage between their two families. A son of Temujin was to be married to a daughter of Vang Khan, and a son of Vang Khan to a daughter of Temujin.

Fresh Suspicions

This new compact did not, however, last long. As soon as Vang Khan found that the danger from which Temujin had rescued him was passed, he began again to listen to the representations of Yemuka and Sankum, who still insisted that Temujin was a very dangerous man, and was by no means to be trusted. They said that he was ambitious and unprincipled, and that he was only waiting for a favourable opportunity to rebel himself against Vang Khan and depose him from his throne. They made a great many statements to the khan in confirmation of their opinion, some of which were true doubtless, but many were exaggerated, and others probably false. They, however, succeeded at last in making such an impression upon the khan's mind that he finally determined to take measures for putting Temujin out of the way.

Plans Laid – Treachery – Menglik

Accordingly, on some pretext or other, he contrived to send Temujin away from Karakorom, his capital, for Temujin was so great a favourite with the royal guards and with all the garrison of the town, that he did not dare to undertake any thing openly against him there. Vang Khan also sent a messenger to Temujin's own country to persuade the chief persons there to join him in his plot. It will be recollected that, at the time that Temujin left his own country, when he was about 14 years old, his mother had married a great chieftain there, named Menglik, and that this Menglik, in conjunction doubtless with Temujin's mother, had been made regent during his absence. Vang Khan now sent to Menglik to propose that he should unite with him to destroy Temujin.

'You have no interest,' said Vang Khan in the message that he sent to Menglik, 'in taking his part. It is true that you have married his mother, but, personally, he is nothing to you. And, if he is once out of the way, you will be acknowledged as the

Grand Khan of the Mongols in your own right, whereas you now hold your place in subordination to him, and he may at any time return and set you aside altogether.'

Vang Khan hoped by these arguments to induce Menglik to come and assist him in his plan of putting Temujin to death, or, at least, if Menglik would not assist him in perpetrating the deed, he thought that, by these arguments, he should induce him to be willing that it should be committed, so that he should himself have nothing to fear afterward from his resentment. But Menglik received the proposal in a very different way from what Vang Khan had expected. He said nothing, but he determined immediately to let Temujin know of the danger that he was in. He accordingly at once set out to go to Temujin's camp to inform him of Vang Khan's designs.

Menglik Gives Temujin Warning – The Double Marriage

In the meantime, Vang Khan, having matured his plans, made an appointment for Temujin to meet him at a certain place designated for the purpose of consummating the double marriage between their children, which had been before agreed upon. Temujin, not suspecting any treachery, received and entertained the messenger in a very honourable manner, and said that he would come. After making the necessary preparations, he set out, in company with the messenger and with a grand retinue of his own attendants, to go to the place appointed. On his way he was met or overtaken by Menglik, who had come to warn him of his danger. As soon as Temujin had heard what his stepfather had to say, he made some excuse for postponing the journey, and, sending a civil answer to Vang Khan by the ambassador, he ordered him to go forward, and went back himself to his own camp.

Temujin's Camp – Karasher

This camp was at some distance from Karakorom. Vang Khan, as has already been stated, had sent Temujin away from the capital on account of his being so great a favourite that he was afraid of some tumult if he were to attempt anything against him there. Temujin was, however, pretty strong in his camp. The troops that usually attended him were there, with the four intrepids as commanders of the four principal divisions of them. His old instructor and guardian, Karasher, was with him too. Karasher, it seems, had continued in Temujin's service up to this time, and was accustomed to accompany him in all his expeditions as his counsellor and friend.

Vang Khan's Plans – His Plans Betrayed by Two Slaves

When Vang Khan learned, by the return of his messenger, that Temujin declined to come to the place of rendezvous which he had appointed, he concluded at once that he suspected treachery, and he immediately decided that he must now strike a decisive blow without any delay, otherwise Temujin would put himself more and more on his guard. He was not mistaken, it seems, however, in thinking how great a favourite Temujin was at Karakorom, for his secret design was betrayed to Temujin by two of his servants, who overheard him speak of it to one of his wives.

Vang Khan's plan was to go out secretly to Temujin's camp at the head of an armed force superior to his, and there come upon him and his whole troop suddenly, by surprise, in the night, by which means, he thought, he should easily overpower the whole encampment, and either kill Temujin and his generals, or else make them prisoners. The two men who betrayed this plan were slaves, who were employed to take care of the horses of some person connected with Vang Khan's household, and to render various other services. Their names were Badu and Kishlik. It seems that these men were one day carrying some milk to Vang Khan's house or tent, and there they overheard a conversation between Vang Khan and his wife, by which they learned the particulars of the plan formed for Temujin's destruction. The expedition was to set out, they heard, on the following morning.

It is not at all surprising that they overheard this conversation, for not only the tents, but even the houses used by these Asiatic nations were built of very frail and thin materials, and the partitions were often made of canvas and felt, and other such substances as could have very little power to intercept sound.

A Council Called

The two slaves determined to proceed at once to Temujin's camp and warn him of his danger. So they stole away from their quarters at nightfall, and, after traveling diligently all night, in the morning they reached the camp and told Temujin what they had learned. Temujin was surprised; but he had been, in some measure, prepared for such intelligence by the communication which his stepfather had made him in respect to Vang Khan's treacherous designs a few days before. He immediately summoned Karasher and some of his other friends, in order to consult in respect to what it was best to do.

Temujin Plans a Stratagem

It was resolved to elude Vang Khan's design by means of a stratagem. He was to come upon them, according to the account of the slaves, that night. The preparations for receiving him were consequently to be made at once. The plan was for Temujin and all his troops to withdraw from the camp and conceal themselves in a place of ambuscade nearby. They were to leave a number of men behind, who, when night came on, were to set the lights and replenish the fires, and put everything in such a condition as to make it appear that the troops were all there. Their expectation was that, when Vang Khan should arrive, he would make his assault according to his original design, and then, while his forces were in the midst of the confusion incident to such an onset, Temujin was to come forth from his ambuscade and fall upon them. In this way he hoped to conquer them and put them to flight, although he had every reason to suppose that the force which Vang Khan would bring out against him would be considerably stronger in numbers than his own.

Chapter VIII
Progress of the Quarrel
1202

The Ambuscade – The Wood and the Brook

TEMUJIN'S STRATAGEM succeeded admirably. As soon as he had decided upon it he began to put it into execution. He caused everything of value to be taken out of his tent and carried away to a place of safety. He sent away the women and children, too, to the same place. He then marshalled all his men, excepting the small guard that he was going to leave behind until evening, and led them off to the ambuscade which he had chosen for them. The place was about two leagues distant from his camp. Temujin concealed himself here in a narrow dell among the mountains, not far from the road where Vang Khan would have to pass along. The dell was narrow, and was protected by precipitous rocks on each side. There was a wood at the entrance to it also, which concealed those that were hidden in it from view, and a brook which flowed by near the entrance, so that, in going in or coming out, it was necessary to ford the brook.

Temujin, on arriving at the spot, went with all his troops into the dell, and concealed himself there.

The Guard Left Behind

In the meantime, the guard that had been left behind in the camp had been instructed to kindle up the campfires as soon as the evening came on, according to the usual custom, and to set lights in the tents, so as to give the camp the appearance, when seen from a little distance in the night, of being occupied, as usual, by the army. They were to wait, and watch the fires and lights until they perceived signs of the approach of the enemy to attack the camp, when they were secretly to retire on the farther side, and so make their escape.

These preparations, and the march of Temujin's troops to the place of ambuscade, occupied almost the whole of the day, and it was near evening before the last of the troops had entered the dell.

Arrival of Vang Khan's Army – False Hopes

They had scarce accomplished this manoeuvre before Vang Khan's army arrived. Vang Khan himself was not with them. He had intrusted the expedition to the command of Sankum and Yemuka. Indeed, it is probable that they were the real originators and contrivers of it, and that Vang Khan had only been induced to give his consent to it – and that perhaps reluctantly – by their persuasions. Sankum and Yemuka advanced cautiously at the head of their columns, and when they saw the illumination of the camp produced by the lights and the campfires, they thought at once that all was right, and that their old enemy and rival was now, at last, within their reach and at their mercy.

Assault Upon the Vacant Camp – Advance of the Assailants

They brought up the men as near to the camp as they could come without being observed, and then, drawing their bows and making their arrows ready, they advanced furiously to the onset, and discharged an immense shower of arrows in among the tents. They expected to see thousands of men come rushing out from the tents, or starting up from the ground at this sudden assault, but, to their utter astonishment, all was as silent and motionless after the falling of the arrows as before. They then discharged more arrows, and, finding that they could not awaken any signs of life, they began to advance cautiously and enter the camp. They found, of course, that it had been entirely evacuated.

They then rode round and round the enclosure, examining the ground with flambeaux and torches to find the tracks which Temujin's army had made in going away. The tracks were soon discovered. Those who first saw them immediately set off in pursuit of the fugitives, as they supposed them, shouting, at the same time, for the rest to follow. Some did follow immediately. Others, who had strayed away to greater or less distances on either side of the camp in search of the tracks, fell in by degrees as they received the order, while others still remained among the tents, where they were to be seen riding to and fro, endeavouring to make discoveries, or gathering together in groups to express to one another their astonishment, or to inquire what was next to be done. They, however, all gradually fell into the ranks of those who were following the track which had been found, and the whole body went on as fast as they could go, and in great confusion. They all supposed that Temujin and his troops were making a precipitate retreat, and were expecting every moment to come up to him in his rear, in which case he would be taken at great disadvantage, and would be easily overwhelmed.

The Ambuscade – Temujin's Victory

Instead of this, Temujin was just coming forward from his hiding place, with his squadrons all in perfect order, and advancing in a firm, steady and compact column, all being ready at the word of command to charge in good order, but with terrible impetuosity, upon the advancing enemy. In this way the two armies came together. The shock of the encounter was terrific. Temujin, as might have been expected, was completely victorious. The confused masses of Vang Khan's army were overborne, thrown into dreadful confusion and trampled underfoot. Great numbers were killed. Those that escaped being killed at once turned and fled. Sankum was wounded in the face by an arrow, but he still was able to keep his seat upon his horse, and so galloped away. Those that succeeded in saving themselves got back as soon as they could into the road by which they came, and so made their way, in detached and open parties, home to Karakorom.

Of course, after this, Vang Khan could no longer dissimulate his hostility to Temujin, and both parties prepared for open war.

Preparations for Open War – Temujin Makes Alliances

The different historians through whom we derive our information in respect to the life and adventures of Genghis Khan have related the transactions which occurred after this open outbreak between Temujin and Vang Khan somewhat differently. Combining their accounts, we learn that both parties, after the battle, opened negotiations with such neighbouring tribes as they supposed likely to take sides in the conflict, each endeavouring to gain as many adherents as possible to his own cause. Temujin obtained the alliance and co-operation of a great number of Tartar princes who ruled over hordes that dwelt in that part of the country, or among the mountains around. Some of these chieftains were his relatives. Others were induced to join him by being convinced that he would, in the end, prove to be stronger than Vang Khan, and being, in some sense, politicians as well as warriors, they wished to be sure of coming out at the close of the contest on the victorious side.

Turkili

There was a certain khan, named Turkili, who was a relative of Temujin, and who commanded a very powerful tribe. On approaching the confines of his territory, Temujin, not being certain of Turkili's disposition toward him, sent forward an ambassador to announce his approach, and to ask if Turkili still retained the friendship which had long subsisted between them. Turkili might, perhaps, have hesitated which side to join, but the presence of Temujin with his whole troop upon his frontier seems to have determined him, so he sent a favourable answer, and at once espoused Temujin's cause.

Solemn League and Covenant – Bitter Water

Many other chieftains joined Temujin in much the same way, and thus the forces under his command were constantly increased. At length, in his progress across the country, he came with his troop of followers to a place where there was a stream of salt or bitter water which was unfit to drink. Temujin encamped on the shores of this stream, and performed a grand ceremony, in which he himself and his allies banded themselves together in the most solemn manner. In the course of the ceremony a horse was sacrificed on the shores of the stream. Temujin also took up some of the water from the brook and drank it, invoking heaven, at the same time, to witness a solemn vow which he made, that, as long as he lived, he would share with his officers and soldiers the bitter as well as the sweet, and imprecating curses upon himself if he should ever violate his oath. All his allies and officers did the same after him.

Recollection of the Ceremony

This ceremony was long remembered in the army, all those who had been present and had taken part in it cherishing the recollection of it with pride and pleasure; and long afterward, when Temujin had attained to the height of his power and glory, his generals considered their having been present at this first solemn league and covenant as conferring upon them a sort of title of nobility, by which they and their descendants were to be distinguished forever above all those whose adhesion to the cause of the conqueror dated from a later time.

Temujin's Strength

By this time Temujin began to feel quite strong. He moved on with his army till he came to the borders of a lake which was not a great way from Vang Khan's dominions. Here he encamped, and, before proceeding any farther, he determined to try the effect upon the mind of Vang Khan of a letter of expostulation and remonstrance; so he wrote to him, substantially, as follows:

His Letter to Vang Khan

'A great many years ago, in the time of my father, when you were driven from your throne by your enemies, my father came to your aid, defeated your enemies, and restored you.

'At a later time, after I had come into your dominions, your brother conspired against you with the Markats and the Naymans. I defeated them, and helped you to recover your power. When you were reduced to great distress, I shared with you my flocks and everything that I had.

'At another time, when you were in circumstances of great danger and distress, you sent to me to ask that my four intrepids might go and rescue you. I sent them according to your request, and they delivered you from a most imminent danger. They helped you to conquer your enemies, and to recover an immense booty from them.

'In many other instances, when the khans have combined against you, I have given you most effectual aid in subduing them.

'How is it, then, after receiving all these benefits from me for a period of so many years, that you form plans to destroy me in so base and treacherous a manner?'

Effect of the Letter – Sankum's Anger

This letter seems to have produced some impression upon Vang Khan's mind; but he was now, it seems, so much under the influence of Sankum and Yemuka that he could decide nothing for himself. He sent the letter to Sankum to ask him what answer should be returned. But Sankum, in addition to his former feelings of envy and jealousy against Temujin, was now irritated and angry in consequence of the wound that he had received, and determined to have his revenge. He would not hear of any accommodation.

Great Accessions to Temujin's Army

In the meantime, the khans of all the Tartar and Mongol tribes that lived in the countries bordering on Vang Khan's dominions, hearing of the rupture between

Vang Khan and Temujin, and aware of the great struggle for the mastery between these two potentates that was about to take place, became more and more interested in the quarrel.

Temujin was very active in opening negotiations with them, and in endeavouring to induce them to take his side. He was a comparatively young and rising man, while Vang Khan was becoming advanced in years, and was now almost wholly under the influence of Sankum and Yemuka. Temujin, moreover, had already acquired great fame and great popularity as a commander, and his reputation was increasing every day, while Vang Khan's glory was evidently on the wane. A great number of the khans were, of course, predisposed to take Temujin's side. Others he compelled to join him by force, and others he persuaded by promising to release them from the exactions and the tyranny which Vang Khan had exercised over them, and declaring that he was a messenger especially sent from heaven to accomplish their deliverance. Those Asiatic tribes were always ready to believe in military messengers sent from heaven to make conquests for their benefit.

Mongolistan

Among other nations who joined Temujin at this time were the people of his own country of Mongolistan Proper. He was received very joyfully by his stepfather, who was in command there, and by all his former subjects, and they all promised to sustain him in the coming war.

Final Attempt at Negotiation

After a time, when Temujin had by these and similar means greatly increased the number of his adherents, and proportionately strengthened his position, he sent an ambassador again to Vang Khan to propose some accommodation. Vang Khan called a council to consider the proposal. But Sankum and Yemuka persisted in refusing to allow any accommodation to be made. They declared that they would not listen to proposals of peace on any other condition than that of the absolute surrender of Temujin, and of all who were confederate with him, to Vang Khan as their lawful sovereign. Sankum himself delivered the message to the ambassador.

'Tell the rebel Mongols,' said he, 'that they are to expect no peace but by submitting absolutely to the khan's will; and as for Temujin, I will never see him again till I come to him sword in hand to kill him.'

Skirmishes

Immediately after this, Sankum and Yemuka sent off some small plundering expeditions into the Mongol country, but they were driven back by Temujin's troops without effecting their purpose. The result of these skirmishes was, however, greatly to exasperate both parties, and to lead them to prepare in earnest for open war.

Chapter IX
The Death of Vang Khan
1202

A Council Called – Mankerule – Debates

A GRAND COUNCIL WAS NOW CALLED of all the confederates who were leagued with Temujin, at a place called Mankerule, to make arrangements for a vigorous prosecution of the war. At this council were convened all the chieftains and khans that had been induced to declare against Vang Khan. Each one came attended by a considerable body of troops as his escort, and a grand deliberation was held. Some were in favour of trying once more to come to some terms of accommodation with Vang Khan, but Temujin convinced them that there was nothing to be hoped for except on condition of absolute submission, and that, in that case, Vang Khan would never be content until he had affected the utter ruin of everyone who had been engaged in the rebellion. So it was, at last, decided that every man should return to his own tribe, and there raise as large a force as he could, with a view to carrying on the war with the utmost vigour.

Temujin Made General-In-Chief

Temujin was formally appointed general-in-chief of the army to be raised. There was a sort of truncheon or ornamented club, called the topaz, which it was customary on such occasions to bestow, with great solemnity, on the general thus chosen, as his badge of command. The topaz was, in this instance, conferred upon Temujin with all the usual ceremonies. He accepted it on the express condition that every man would punctually and implicitly obey all his orders, and that he should have absolute power to punish anyone who should disobey him in the way that he judged best, and that they should submit without question to all his decisions. To these conditions they all solemnly agreed.

He Distributes Rewards – Reward of the Two Slaves

Being thus regularly placed in command, Temujin began by giving places of honour and authority to those who left Vang Khan's service to follow him. He took this occasion to remember and reward the two slaves who had come to him in the night at his camp, some time before, to give him warning of the design of Sankum and Yemuka to come and surprise him there.

He gave the slaves their freedom, and made provision for their maintenance as long as they should live. He also put them on the list of *exempts*. The exempts were a class of persons upon whom, as a reward for great public services, were conferred certain exclusive rights and privileges. They had no taxes to pay. In case of plunder taken from the enemy, they received their full share without any deduction, while all the others were obliged to contribute a portion of their shares for the khan. The exempts, too, were allowed various other privileges. They had the right to go into the presence of the khan at any time, without waiting, as others were obliged to do, till they obtained permission, and, what was more singular still, they were entitled to *nine* pardons for any offenses that they might commit, so that it was only when they had committed 10 misdemeanours or crimes that they were in danger of punishment The privileges which Temujin thus bestowed upon the slaves were to be continued to their descendants to the seventh generation.

His Reasons

Temujin rewarded the slaves in this bountiful manner, partly, no doubt, out of sincere gratitude to them for having been the means, probably, of saving him and his army from destruction, and partly for effect, in order to impress upon his followers a strong conviction that any great services rendered to him or to his cause were certain to be well rewarded.

Organization of the Army – Mode of Attack

Temujin now found himself at the head of a very large body of men, and his first care was to establish a settled system of discipline among them, so that they could act with regularity and order when coming into battle. He divided his army into three separate bodies. The centre was composed of his own guards, and was commanded by himself. The wings were formed of the squadrons of his confederates and allies. His plan in coming into battle was to send forward the two wings, retaining the centre as a reserve, and hold them prepared to rush in with irresistible power whenever the time should arrive at which their coming would produce the greatest effect.

When everything was thus arranged, Temujin set his army in motion, and began to advance toward the country of Vang Khan. The squadrons which composed his immense horde were so numerous that they covered all the plain.

The Two Armies – The Baggage

In the meantime, Vang Khan had not been idle. He, or rather Sankum and Yemuka, acting in his name, had assembled a great army, and he had set out on his march from Karakorom to meet his enemy. His forces, however, though more numerous, were by no means so well disciplined and arranged as those of Temujin. They were greatly encumbered, too, with baggage, the army being followed in its march by endless trains of wagons conveying provisions, arms and military stores of all kinds. Its progress was, therefore, necessarily slow, for the troops of horsemen were obliged to regulate their speed by the movement of the wagons, which, on account of the heavy burdens that they contained, and the want of finished roads, was necessarily slow.

Meeting of the Two Armies – Vang Khan Defeated

The two armies met upon a plain between two rivers, and a most desperate and bloody battle ensued. Karasher, Temujin's former tutor, led one of the divisions of Temujin's army, and was opposed by Yemuka, who headed the wing of Vang Khan's army which confronted his division. The other wings attacked each other, too, in the most furious manner, and for three hours it was doubtful which party would be successful. At length Temujin, who had all this time remained in the background with his reserve, saw that the favourable moment had arrived for him to intervene, and he gave the order for his guards to charge, which they did with such impetuosity as to carry all before them.

One after another of Vang Khan's squadrons was overpowered, thrown into confusion and driven from the field. It was not long before Vang Khan saw that all was lost. He gave up the contest and fled. A small troop of horsemen, consisting of his immediate attendants and guards, went with him. At first the fugitives took the road toward Karakorom. They were, however, so hotly pursued that they were obliged to turn off in another direction, and, finally, Vang Khan resolved to fly from his own country altogether, and appeal for protection to a certain chieftain, named Tayian Khan, who ruled over a great horde called the Naymans, one of the most powerful tribes in the country of Karakatay. This Tayian was the father of Temujin's first wife, the young princess to whom he was married during the lifetime of his father, when he was only about 14 years old.

His Relations with the Naymans

It was thought strange that Vang Khan should thus seek refuge among the Naymans, for he had not, for some time past, been on friendly terms either with Tayian, the khan or with the tribe. There were, in particular, a considerable number of the subordinate chieftains who cherished a deep-seated resentment against him for injuries which he had inflicted upon them and upon their country in former wars. But all these Tartar tribes entertained very high ideas of the obligations of hospitality, and Vang Khan thought that when the Naymans saw him coming among them, a fugitive and in distress, they would lay aside their animosity, and give him a kind reception.

Debates Among the Naymans

Indeed, Tayian himself, on whom, as the head of the tribe, the chief discredit would attach of any evil befalling a visitor and a guest who had come in his distress to seek hospitality, was inclined, at first, to receive his enemy kindly, and to offer him a refuge. He debated the matter with the other chieftains after Vang Khan had entered his dominions and was approaching his camp; but they were extremely unwilling that any mercy should be shown to their fallen enemy. They represented to Tayian how great an enemy he had always been to them. They exaggerated the injuries which he had done them, and represented them in their worst light. They said, moreover, that, by harbouring Vang Khan, they should only involve themselves in a war with Temujin, who would undoubtedly follow his enemy into their country, and would greatly resent any attempt on their part to protect him.

Tayian

These considerations had great effect on the mind of Tayian, but still, he could not bring himself to give his formal consent to any act of hostility against Vang Khan. So the other chieftains held a council among themselves to consider what they should do. They resolved to take upon themselves the responsibility of slaying Vang Khan.

'We cannot induce Tayian openly to authorize it,' they said, 'but he secretly desires it, and he will be glad when it is done.'

Tayian knew very well what course things were taking, though he pretended not to know, and so allowed the other chiefs to go on in their own way.

Vang Khan Beheaded

They accordingly fitted out a troop, and two of the chieftains – the two who felt the most bitter and determined hatred against Vang Khan – placing themselves at the head of it, set off to intercept him. He had lingered on the way, it seems, after entering the Nayman territory, in order to learn, before he advanced too far, what reception he was likely to meet with. The troop of Naymans came suddenly upon him in his encampment, slew all his attendants, and, seizing Vang Khan, they cut off his head. They left the body where it lay, and carried off the head to show it to Tayian.

Tayian's Deceit

Tayian was secretly pleased, and he could not quite conceal the gratification which the death of his old enemy afforded him. He even addressed the head in words of scorn and spite, which revealed the exultation that he felt at the downfall of his rival. Then, however, checking himself, he blamed the chieftains for killing him.

'Considering his venerable age,' said he, 'and his past greatness and renown as a prince and commander, you would have done much better to have acted as his guards than as his executioners.'

Disposal Made of His Head

Tayian ordered the head to be treated with the utmost respect. After properly preparing it, by some process of drying and preserving, he caused it to be enclosed in a case of silver, and set in a place of honour.

While the preparations for this sort of entombment were making, the head was an object of a very solemn and mysterious interest for all the horde. They said that the tongue thrust itself several times out of the mouth, and the soothsayers, who watched the changes with great attention, drew from them important presages in respect to the coming events of the war. These presages were strongly in favour of the increasing prosperity and power of Temujin.

Sankum Slain

Sankum, the son of Vang Khan, was killed in the battle, but Yemuka escaped.

Chapter X
The Death of Yemuka
1202–03

X

The Victory Complete – Exaggeration

IN THE MEANTIME, while these events had been occurring in the country of the Naymans, whither Vang Khan had fled, Temujin was carrying all before him in the country of Vang Khan. His victory in the battle was complete; and it must have been a very great battle, if any reliance is to be placed on the accounts given of the number slain, which it was said amounted to 40,000. These numbers are, however, greatly exaggerated. And then, besides, the number slain in such barbarian conflicts was always much greater, in proportion to the numbers engaged, than it is in the better-regulated warfare of civilized nations in modern times.

The Plunder

At all events, Temujin gained a very grand and decisive victory. He took a great many prisoners and a great deal of plunder. All those trains of wagons fell into his hands, and the contents of many of them were extremely valuable. He took also a great number of horses. Most of these had belonged to the men who were killed or who had been made prisoners. All the best troops that remained of Vang Khan's army after the battle also went over to his side. They considered that Vang Khan's power was now entirely overthrown, and that thenceforth Temujin would be the acknowledged ruler of the whole country. They were accordingly ready at once to transfer their allegiance to him.

Great Accession – The Khans Submit – Sankum and Yemuka

Very soon, Temujin received the news of Vang Khan's death from his father-in-law Tayian, and then proceeded with more vigour than before to take possession of all his dominions. The khans who had formerly served under Vang Khan sent in their adhesion to him one after another. They not only knew that all farther resistance would be useless, but they were, in fact, well pleased to transfer their allegiance to their old friend and favourite. Temujin made a sort of triumphal march through the country, being received everywhere with rejoicings and acclamations of welcome. His old enemies, Sankum and Yemuka, had disappeared. Yemuka, who had been, after all, the leading spirit in the opposition to Temujin, still held a body of armed men together, consisting of all the troops that he had been able to rally after the battle, but it was not known exactly where he had gone.

Hakembu and His Daughter

The other relatives and friends of Vang Khan went over to Temujin's side without any delay. Indeed, they vied with each other to see who should most recommend themselves to his favour. A brother of Vang Khan, who was an influential and powerful chieftain, came among the rest to tender his services, and, by way of a present to conciliate Temujin's goodwill, he brought him his daughter, whom he offered to Temujin as an addition to the number of his wives.

Temujin received the brother very kindly. He accepted the present which he brought him of his daughter, but, as he had already plenty of wives, and as one of his principal officers, the captain of his guards, seemed to take a special fancy to her, he very generously, as was thought, passed over the young lady to him. Of course, the young lady herself had nothing to say in the case. She was obliged to acquiesce submissively in any arrangement which her father and the other khans thought proper to make in respect to the disposal of her.

Hakembu's Fears

The name of the prince her father was Hakembu. He came into Temujin's camp with many misgivings, fearing that, as he was a brother of Vang Khan, Temujin might feel a special resentment against him, and, perhaps, refuse to accept his submission and his proffered presents. When, therefore, he found how kindly he was received, his mind was greatly relieved, and he asked Temujin to appoint him to some command in his army.

Temujin's Gratitude – His Reply

Temujin replied that he would do it with great pleasure, and the more readily because it was the brother of Vang Khan who asked it. 'Indeed,' said he to Hakembu, 'I owe you all the kind treatment in my power for your brother's sake, in return for the succour and protection for which I was indebted to him, in my misfortunes, in former times, when he received me, a fugitive and an exile, at his court, and bestowed upon me so many favours. I have never forgotten, and never shall forget, the great obligations I am under to him; and although in later years he turned against me, still I have never blamed either him or his son Sankum for this, but have constantly attributed it to the false representations and evil influence of Yemuka, who has always been my implacable enemy. I do not, therefore, feel any resentment against Vang Khan for having thus turned against me, nor do I any the less respect his memory on that account; and I am very glad that an opportunity now occurs for me to make, through you, his brother, some small acknowledgment of the debt of gratitude which I owe him.'

So Temujin gave Hakembu an honourable post in his army, and treated him in all respects with great consideration. If he acted usually in this generous manner, it is not at all surprising that he acquired that boundless influence over the minds of his followers which aided him so essentially in attaining his subsequent greatness and renown.

Yemuka Makes His Escape

In the meantime, although Sankum was killed, Yemuka had succeeded in making his escape, and, after meeting with various adventures, he finally reached the country of Tayian. He led with him there all that portion of Vang Khan's army that had saved themselves from being killed or made prisoners, and also a great number of officers. These broken troops Yemuka had reorganized, as well as he could, by collecting the scattered remnants and rearranging the broken squadrons, and in this manner, accompanied by such of the sick and wounded as were able to ride, had arrived in Tayian's dominions. He was known to be a general of great abilities, and he was very favourably received in Tayian's court. Indeed, Tayian, having heard rumours of the rapid manner in which Temujin was extending his conquests and his power, began to be somewhat jealous of him, and to think that it was time for him to take measures to prevent this aggrandizement of his son-in-law from going too far.

Tayian's Conversations with Yemuka

Of course, Tayian held a great many conversations with Yemuka in respect to Temujin's character and schemes. These Yemuka took care to represent in the most unfavourable light, in order to increase as much as possible Tayian's feelings of suspicion and jealousy. He represented Temujin as a very ambitious man, full of schemes for his own aggrandizement, and without any sentiments of gratitude or of honour to restrain him in the execution of them. He threw wholly upon him the responsibility of the war with Vang Khan. It grew, he said, out of plots which Temujin had formed to destroy both Vang Khan and his son, notwithstanding the great obligations he had been under to them for their kindness to him in his misfortunes. Yemuka urged Tayian also to arouse himself, before it was too late, to guard himself from the danger.

Yemuka's Representations of Temujin's Character

'He is your son, it is true,' said he, 'and he professes to be your friend, but he is so treacherous and unprincipled that you can place no reliance upon him whatever, and, notwithstanding all your past kindness to him, and the tie of relationship which ought to bind him to you, he will as readily form plans to compass your destruction as he would that of any other man the moment he imagines that you stand in the way of the accomplishment of his ambitious schemes.'

Plots Formed

These representations, acting upon Tayian's natural apprehensions and fears, produced a very sensible effect, and at length Tayian was induced to take some measures for defending himself from the threatened danger. So he opened negotiations with the khans of various tribes which he thought likely to join him, and soon formed quite a powerful league of the enemies of Temujin, and of all who were willing to join in an attempt to restrict his power.

Alakus

These steps were all taken with great secrecy, for Yemuka and Tayian were very desirous that Temujin should know nothing of the league which they were forming against him until their arrangements were fully matured, and they were ready for action. They did not, however, succeed in keeping the secret as long as they intended. They were generally careful not to propose to any khan or chieftain to join them in their league until they had first fully ascertained that he was favourable to the object of it. But, growing less cautious as they went on, they at last made a mistake. Tayian sent proposals to a certain prince or khan, named Alakus, inviting him to join the league. These proposals were contained in a letter which was sent by a special messenger. The letter specified all the particulars of the league, with a statement of the plans which the allies were intending to pursue, and an enumeration of the principal khans or tribes that were already engaged.

The Plots Revealed to Temujin

Now it happened that this Alakus, who reigned over a nation of numerous and powerful tribes on the confines of China, was, for some reason or other, inclined to take Temujin's side in the quarrel. So he detained the messenger who brought the letter as a prisoner, and sent the letter itself, containing all the particulars of the conspiracy, at once to Temujin. Temujin was greatly surprised at receiving the intelligence, for, up to that moment, he had considered his father-in-law Tayian as one of his best and most trustworthy friends. He immediately called a grand council of war to consider what was to be done.

The Young Prince Jughi

Temujin had a son named Jughi, who had now grown up to be a young man. Jughi's father thought it was now time for his son to begin to take his place and act his part among the other princes and chieftains of his court, and he accordingly gave him a seat at this council, and thus publicly recognized him, for the first time, as one of the chief personages of the state.

Council of War

The council, after hearing a statement of the case in respect to the league which Tayian and the others were forming, were strongly inclined to combine their forces and march at once to attack the enemy before their plans should be more fully matured. But there was a difficulty in respect to horses. The horses of the different hordes that belonged to Temujin's army had become so much exhausted by the long marches and other fatigues that they had undergone in the late campaigns, that they would not be in a fit condition to commence a new expedition until they had had some time to rest and recruit. But a certain khan, named Bulay, an uncle of Temujin's, at once removed this objection by offering to furnish a full supply of fresh horses for the whole army from his own herds. This circumstance shows on what an immense scale the pastoral occupations of the great Asiatic chieftains were conducted in those days.

Yemuka and Tayian

Temujin accepted this offer on the part of his uncle, and preparations were immediately made for the marching of the expedition. As soon as the news of these preparations reached Yemuka, he urged Tayian to assemble the allied troops immediately, and go out to meet Temujin and his army before they should cross the frontier.

'It is better,' said he, addressing Tayian, 'that you should meet and fight him on his own ground, rather than to wait until he has crossed the frontier and commenced his ravages in yours.'

'No,' said Tayian, in reply, 'it is better to wait. The farther he advances on his march, the more his horses and his men will be spent with fatigue, the scantier will be their supplies, and the more difficult will he find it to affect his retreat after we shall have gained a victory over him in battle.'

Temujin Crosses the Frontier

So Tayian, though he began to assemble his forces, did not advance; and when Temujin, at the head of his host, reached the Nayman frontier – for the country over which Tayian reigned was called the country of the Naymans – he was surprised to find no enemy there to defend it. He was the more surprised at this from the circumstance that the frontier, being formed by a river, might have been very easily defended. But when he arrived at the bank of the river the way was clear. He immediately crossed the stream with all his forces, and then marched on into the Nayman territory.

His Advance

Temujin took good care, as he advanced, to guard against the danger into which Tayian had predicted that he would fall – that of exhausting the strength of his men and of his animals, and also his stores of food. He took good care to provide and to take with him abundant supplies, and also to advance so carefully and by such easy stages as to keep both the men and the horses fresh and in full strength all the way. In this order and condition he at last arrived at the spot where Tayian had formed his camp and assembled his armies.

Preparations for Battle – Kushluk and Jughi

Both sides immediately marshalled their troops in order of battle. Yemuka was chief in command on Tayian's side. He was assisted by a young prince, the son of Tayian, whose name was Kushluk. On the other hand, Jughi, the young son of Temujin, who had been brought forward at the council, was appointed to a very prominent position on his father's side. Indeed, these two young princes, who were animated by an intense feeling of rivalry and emulation toward each other, were appointed to lead the van on their respective sides in commencing the battle; Jughi advancing first to the attack, and being met by Kushluk, to whom was committed the charge of repelling him. The two princes fought throughout the battle with the utmost bravery, and both of them acquired great renown.

Great Battle – Temujin Again Victorious

The battle was commenced early in the morning and continued all day. In the end, Temujin was completely victorious. Tayian was mortally wounded early in the day. He was immediately taken off the field, and every possible effort was made to save his life, but he soon ceased to breathe. His son, the Prince Kushluk, fought valiantly during the whole day, but toward night, finding that all was lost, he fled, taking with him as many of the troops as he could succeed in getting together in the confusion, and at the head of this band made the best of his way into the dominions of one of his uncles, his father's brother, where he hoped to find a temporary shelter until he should have time to determine what was to be done.

Yemuka is Beheaded

As for Yemuka, after fighting with desperate fury all day, he was at last, toward night, surrounded and overpowered, and so made prisoner. Temujin ordered his head to be cut off immediately after the battle was over. He considered him, not as an honourable and open foe, but rather as a rebel and traitor, and, consequently, undeserving of any mercy.

Chapter XI
Establishment of the Empire
1203

✖

Plans for the Formation of a Government

THERE WAS NOW a vast extent of country, comprising a very large portion of the interior of the Asiatic Continent, and, indeed, an immense number of wealthy, powerful hordes under Temujin's dominion, and he at once resolved to consolidate his dominion by organizing a regular imperial government over the whole.

There were a few more battles to be fought in order to subdue certain khans who still resisted, and some cities to be taken. But these victories were soon obtained, and, in a very short time after the great battle with Tayian, Temujin found himself the undisputed master of what to him was almost the whole known world. All open opposition to his rule had wholly disappeared, and nothing now remained for him to do but to perfect the organization of his army, to enact his code of laws, to determine upon his capital and to inaugurate generally a system of civil government such as is required for the management of the internal affairs of a great empire.

His Court at Karakorom – Ambassadors

Temujin determined upon making Karakorom his capital. He accordingly proceeded to that city at the head of his troops, and entered it in great state. Here he established a very brilliant court, and during all the following winter, while he was occupied with the preliminary arrangements for the organization and consolidation of his empire, there came to him there a continual succession of ambassadors from the various nations and tribes of Central Asia to congratulate him on his victories, and to offer the allegiance or the alliance of the khans which they respectively represented. These ambassadors all came attended by troops of horsemen splendidly dressed and fully armed, and the gayety and magnificence of the scenes which were witnessed in Karakorom during the winter surpassed all that had ever been seen there before.

Temujin Forms a Constitution

In the meantime, while the attention of the masses of the people was occupied and amused by these parades, Temujin was revolving in his mind the form of constitution which he should establish for his empire, and the system of laws by which his people should be governed. He conferred privately with some of his ablest counsellors on this subject, and caused a system of government and a code of laws to be drawn up by secretaries. The details of these proposed enactments were discussed in the privy council, and, when the whole had been well digested and matured, Temujin, early in the spring, sent out a summons, calling upon all the great princes and khans throughout his dominions to assemble at an appointed day, in order that he might lay his proposed system before them.

Election of Khans

Temujin determined to make his government a sort of elective monarchy. The grand khan was to be chosen by the votes of all the other khans, who were to be assembled in a general convocation for this purpose whenever a new khan was to be installed. Any person who should cause himself to be proclaimed grand khan, or who should in any other way attempt to assume the supreme authority without having been duly elected by the other khans, was to suffer death.

Division of the Country

The country was divided into provinces, over each of which a subordinate khan ruled as governor. These governors were, however, to be strictly responsible to the grand khan. Whenever summoned by the grand khan they were required to repair at once to the capital, there to render an account of their administration and to answer any charges which had been made against them. Whenever any serious case of disobedience or maladministration was proved against them, they were to suffer death.

Organization of the Army – Arms and Ammunition

Temujin remodelled and reorganized the army on the same or similar principles. The men were divided into companies of about 100 men each, and every 10 of these companies was formed into a regiment, which, of course, contained about 1,000 men. The regiments were formed into larger bodies of about 10,000 each. Officers were appointed, of all the various necessary grades, to command these troops, and arrangements were made for having supplies of arms and ammunition provided and stored in magazines under the care of the officers, ready to be distributed to the men whenever they should require.

Temujin also made provision for the building of cities and palaces, the making of roads and the construction of fortifications, by ordaining that all the people should work one day in every week on these public works whenever required.

Hunting

Although the country over which this new government was to be established was now at peace, Temujin was very desirous that the people should not lose the martial spirit which had thus far characterized them. He made laws to encourage and regulate hunting, especially the hunting of wild beasts among the mountains; and subsequently he organized many hunting excursions himself, in connection with the lords of his court and the other great chieftains, in order to awaken an interest in the dangers and excitements of the chase among all the khans. He also often employed bodies of troops in these expeditions, which he considered as a sort of substitute for war.

Slaves

He required that none of the natives of the country should be employed as servants, or allowed to perform any menial duties whatever. For these purposes, the people were required to depend on captives taken in war and enslaved. One reason why he made this rule was to stimulate the people on the frontiers to make hostile excursions among their neighbours, in order to supply themselves and the country generally with slaves.

The right of property in the slaves thus taken was very strictly guarded, and very severe laws were made to enforce it. It was forbidden, on pain of death, to harbour a slave, or give him meat or drink, clothing or shelter, without permission from his master. The penalty was death, too, if a person meeting a fugitive slave neglected to seize and secure him, and deliver him to his master.

Polygamy and Slavery – Concubines

Every man could marry as many wives as he pleased, and his female slaves were all, by law, entirely at his disposal to be made concubines.

Posthumous Marriages

There was one very curious arrangement, which grew out of the great importance which, as we have already seen, was attached to the ties of relationship and family connection among these pastoral nations. Two families could bind themselves together and make themselves legally one, in respect to their connection, by a fictitious marriage arranged between children no longer living. In such a case the contracts were regularly made, just as if the children were still alive, and the ceremonies were all duly performed. After this the two families were held to be legally allied, and they were bound to each other by all the obligations which would have arisen in the case of a real marriage.

This custom is said to be continued among some of the Tartar nations to the present day. The people think, it is said, that such a wedding ceremony, duly solemnized by the parents of children who are dead, takes effect upon the subjects of it in the world of spirits, and that thus their union, though arranged and consecrated on earth, is confirmed and consummated in heaven.

Punishment for Theft

Besides these peculiar and special enactments, there were the ordinary laws against robbery, theft, murder, adultery and false witness. The penalties for these offenses were generally severe. The punishment for stealing cattle was death. For petty thefts the criminal was to be beaten with a stick, the number of the blows being proportioned to the nature and aggravation of the offense. He could, however, if he had the means, buy himself off from this punishment by paying nine times the value of the thing stolen.

Religion – Freedom of Choice

In respect to religion, the constitution which Temujin made declared that there was but one God, the creator of heaven and earth, and it acknowledged him as the supreme ruler and governor of all mankind, the being 'who alone gives life and death, riches and poverty, who grants and denies whatever he pleases, and exercises over all things an absolute power'. This one fundamental article of faith was all that was required. For the rest, Temujin left the various nations and tribes throughout his dominions to adopt such modes of worship and to celebrate such religious rites as they severally preferred, and forbade that anyone should be disturbed or molested in any way on account of his religion, whatever form it might assume.

Assembly of the Khans – Dilon Ildak

At length, the time arrived for the grand assembly of the khans to be convened. The meeting was called, not at Karakorom, the capital, but at a central spot in the interior of the country, called Dilon Ildak. Such a spot was much more convenient than any town or city would have been for the place of meeting, on account of the great troops of horses and the herds of animals by which the khans were always accompanied in all their expeditions, and which made it necessary that, whenever any considerable number of them were to be convened, the place chosen should be suitable for a grand encampment, with extensive and fertile pasture-grounds extending all around.

Their Encampment – Tents and Herds of Cattle

As the several khans came in, each at the head of his own troop of retainers and followers, they severally chose their ground, pitched their tents and turned their herds of horses, sheep and oxen out to pasture on the plains. Thus, in the course of a few days, the whole country in every direction became dotted with villages of tents, among which groups of horsemen were now and then to be seen galloping to and fro, and small herds of cattle, each under the care of herdsmen and slaves, moved slowly, cropping the grass as they advanced along the hillsides and through the valleys.

Temujin's Address

At length, when all had assembled, a spot was selected in the centre of the encampment for the performance of the ceremonies. A raised seat was prepared for Temujin in a situation suitable to enable him to address the assembly from it. Before and around this the various khans and their attendants and followers gathered, and Temujin made them an oration, in which he explained the circumstances under which they had come together, and announced to them his plans and intentions in respect to the future. He stated to them that, in consequence of the victories which he had gained through their co-operation and assistance, the foundation of a great empire had been laid, and that he had now called them together in order that they might join with him in organizing the requisite government for such a dominion, and in electing a prince or sovereign to rule over it. He called upon them first to proceed to the election of this ruler.

Temujin is Elected Grand Khan

The khans accordingly proceeded to the election. This was, in fact, only a form, for Temujin himself was, of course, to be chosen. The election was, however, made, and one of the oldest and most venerable of the khans was commissioned to announce the result. He came forward with great solemnity, and, in the presence of the whole assembly, declared that the choice had fallen upon Temujin. He then made an address to Temujin himself, who was seated during this part of the ceremony upon a carpet of black felt spread upon the ground. In the address the khan reminded Temujin that the exalted authority with which he was now invested came from God, and that to God he was responsible for the right exercise of his power. If he governed his subjects well, God, he said, would render his reign prosperous and happy; but if, on the other hand, he abused his power, he would come to a miserable end.

He is Enthroned and Honoured

After the conclusion of the address, seven of the khans, who had been designated for this purpose, came and lifted Temujin up and bore him away to a throne which had been set up for him in the midst of the assembly, where all the khans, and their various bodies of attendants, came and offered him their homage.

The Old Prophet Kokza

Among others there came a certain old prophet, named Kokza, who was held in great veneration by all the people on account of his supposed inspiration and the austere life which he led. He used to go very thinly clad, and with his feet bare summer and winter, and it was supposed that his power of enduring the exposures to which he was thus subject was something miraculous and divine. He had received accordingly from the people a name which signified *the image of God*, and he was everywhere looked upon as inspired. He said, moreover, that a white horse came to him from time to time and carried him up to heaven, where he conversed face to face with God, and received the revelations which he was commissioned to make to men.

All this the people fully believed. The man may have been an impostor, or he may have been insane. Oftentimes, in such cases, the inspiration which the person supposes he is the subject of arises from a certain spiritual exaltation, which, though it does not wholly unfit him for the ordinary avocations and duties of life, still verges upon insanity, and often finally lapses into it entirely.

His Predictions – The Title Genghis Khan

This old prophet advanced toward Temujin while he was seated on his carpet of felt, and made a solemn address to him in the hearing of all the assembled khans. He was charged, he said, with a message from heaven in respect to the kingdom and dominion of Temujin, which had been, he declared, ordained of God, and had now been established in fulfilment of the Divine will. He was commissioned, moreover, he said, to give to Temujin the style and title of Genghis Khan, and to declare that his kingdom should not only endure while he lived, but should descend to his posterity, from generation to generation, to the remotest times.

Homage of the Khans

The people, on hearing this address, at once adopted the name which the prophet had given to their new ruler, and saluted Temujin with it in long and loud acclamations. It was thus that our hero received the name of Genghis Khan, which soon extended its fame through every part of Asia, and has since become so greatly renowned through all the world.

Temujin, or Genghis Khan, as we must now henceforth call him, having thus been proclaimed by the acclamations of the people under the new title with which the old prophet had invested him, sat upon his throne while his subjects came to render him their homage. First the khans themselves came up, and kneeled nine times before him, in token of their absolute and complete submission to his authority. After they had retired, the people themselves came, and made their obeisance in the same manner. As they rose from their knees after the last prostration, they made the air resound once more with their shouts, crying 'Long live great Genghis Khan!' in repeated and prolonged acclamations.

Inaugural Address

After this, the new emperor made what might be called his inaugural address. The khans and their followers gathered once more before his throne while he delivered an oration to them, in which he thanked them for the honour which they had done him in raising him to the supreme power, and announced to them the principles by which he should be guided in the government of his empire. He promised to be just in his dealings with his subjects, and also to be merciful. He would defend them, he said, against all their enemies. He would do everything in his power to promote their comfort and happiness. He would lead them to honour and glory, and would make their names known throughout the earth. He would deal impartially, too, with all the different tribes and hordes, and would treat the Mongols and the Tartars, the two great classes of his subjects, with equal favour.

Rejoicings – Departure of the Khans

When the speech was concluded Genghis Khan distributed presents to all the subordinate khans, both great and small. He also made magnificent entertainments, which were continued for several days. After thus spending some time in feasting and rejoicings, the khans one after another took their leave of the emperor, the great encampment was broken up, and the different tribes set out on their return to their several homes.

Chapter XII
Dominions of Genghis Khan
1203

Karakorom – Insignificance of Cities and Towns

AFTER THE CEREMONIES of the inauguration were concluded, Genghis Khan returned, with the officers of his court and his immediate followers, to Karakorom. This town, though nominally the capital of the empire, was, after all, quite an insignificant place.

Indeed, but little importance was attached to any villages or towns in those days, and there were very few fixed places of residence that were of any considerable account. The reason is, that towns are the seats of commerce and manufactures, and they derive their chief importance from those pursuits; whereas the Mongols and Tartars led almost exclusively a wandering and pastoral life, and all their ideas of wealth and grandeur were associated with great flocks and herds of cattle, and handsome tents, and long trains of wagons loaded with stores of clothing, arms and other movables, and vast encampments in the neighbourhood of rich and extended pasture-grounds. Those who lived permanently in fixed houses they looked down upon as an inferior class, confined to one spot by their poverty or their toil, while they themselves could roam at liberty with their flocks and herds over the plains, riding fleet horses or dromedaries, and encamping where they pleased in the green valleys or on the banks of the meandering streams.

Account of Karakorom – The Buildings

Karakorom was accordingly by no means a great and splendid city. It was surrounded by what was called a mud wall – that is, a wall made of blocks of clay dried in the sun. The houses of the inhabitants were mere hovels, and even the palace of the king, and all the other public buildings, were of very frail construction; for all the architecture of the Mongols in those days took its character from the tent, which was the type and model, so to speak, of all other buildings.

The new emperor, however, did not spend a great deal of his time at Karakorom. He was occupied for some years in making excursions at the head of his troops to various parts of his dominions, for the purpose of putting down insurrections, overawing discontented and insubordinate khans and settling disputes of various kinds arising between the different hordes. In these expeditions he was accustomed to move by easy marches across the plains at the head of his army, and sometimes would establish himself in a sort of permanent camp, where he would remain, perhaps, as in a fixed residence, for weeks or months at a time.

The Grand Encampments

Not only Genghis Khan himself, but many of the other great chieftains, were accustomed to live in this manner, and one of their encampments, if we could have seen it, would have been regarded by us as a great curiosity. The ground was regularly laid out, like a town, into quarters, squares and streets, and the space which it covered was sometimes so large as to extend nearly a mile in each direction. The tent of the khan himself was in the centre. A space was reserved for it there large enough not only for the grand tent itself, but also for the rows of smaller tents near, for the wives and for other women belonging to the khan's family, and also for the rows of carts or wagons containing the stores of provisions, the supplies of clothing and arms and the other valuables which these wandering chieftains always took with them in all their peregrinations.

Construction of the Tents

The tent of the khan in summer was made of a sort of calico, and in winter of felt, which was much warmer. It was raised very high, so as to be seen above all the rest of the encampment, and it was painted in gay colours, and adorned with other barbaric decorations.

Dwellings of the Women

The dwellings in which the women were lodged, which were around or near the great tent, were sometimes tents, and sometimes little huts made of wood. When they were of wood they were made very light, and were constructed in such a manner that they could be taken to pieces at the shortest notice, and packed on carts or wagons, in order to be transported to the next place of encampment, whenever, for any reason, it became necessary for their lord and master to remove his domicile to a different ground.

Mountains and Wild Beasts – Hunting

A large portion of the country which was included within the limits of Genghis Khan's dominions was fertile ground, which produced abundance of grass for the pasturage of the flocks and herds, and many springs and streams of water. There were, however, several districts of mountainous country, which were the refuge of tigers, leopards, wolves and other ferocious beasts of prey. It was among these mountains that the great hunting parties which Genghis Khan organized from time to time went in search of their game.

There was a great officer of the kingdom, called the grand huntsman, who had the superintendence and charge of everything relating to hunting and to game throughout the empire. The grand huntsman was an officer of the very highest rank. He even took precedence of the first ministers of state. Genghis Khan appointed his son Jughi, who has already been mentioned in connection with the great council of war called by his father, and with the battle, which was subsequently fought, and in which he gained great renown, to the office of grand huntsman, and, at the same time, made two of the older and more experienced khans his ministers of state.

The Danger of Hunting in Those Days

The hunting of wild beasts as ferocious as those that infested the mountains of Asia is a very dangerous amusement even at the present day, notwithstanding the advantage which the huntsman derives from the use of gunpowder, rifled barrels and fulminating bullets. But in those days, when the huntsman had no better weapons than bows and arrows, javelins and spears, the undertaking was dangerous in the extreme. An African lion of full size used to be considered as a match for 40 men in the days when only ordinary weapons were used against him, and it was considered almost hopeless to attack him with less than that number. And even with that number to waylay and assail him he was not usually conquered until he had killed or disabled two or three of his foes.

Thus, the hunting of wild beasts in the mountains was very dangerous work, and it is not surprising that the office of grand huntsman was one of great consideration and honour.

Timid Animals

The hunting was, however, not all of the dangerous character above described. Some animals are timid and inoffensive by nature, and attempt to save themselves only by flight. Such animals as these were to be pursued and overtaken by the superior speed of horses and dogs, or to be circumvented by stratagem. There was a species of deer, in certain parts of the Mongol country, that the huntsmen were accustomed to take in this way, namely:

Stratagems – Mode of Taking Deer

The huntsmen, when they began to draw near to a place where a herd of deer were feeding, would divide themselves into two parties. One party would provide themselves with the antlers of stags, which they arranged in such a manner that they could hold them up over their heads in the thickets, as if real stags were there. The others, armed with bows and arrows, javelins, spears and other such weapons, would place themselves in ambush nearby. Those who had the antlers would then make a sort of cry, imitating that uttered by the hinds. The stags of the herd, hearing the cry, would immediately come toward the spot. The men in the thicket then would raise the antlers and move them about, so as to deceive the stags, and excite their feelings of rivalry and ire, while those who were appointed to that office continued to counterfeit the cry of the hind. The stags immediately would begin to paw the ground and to prepare for a conflict, and then, while their attention was thus wholly taken up by the tossing of the false antlers in the thicket, the men in ambush would creep up as near as they could, take good aim and shoot their poor deluded victims through the heart.

Training of the Horses

Of course, it required a great deal of practice and much skill to perform successfully such feats as these; and there were many other branches of the huntsman's art, as practiced in those days, which could only be acquired by a systematic and special course of training. One of the most difficult things was to train the horses so that they would advance to meet tigers and other wild beasts without fear. Horses have naturally a strong and instinctive terror for such beasts, and this terror it was very difficult to overcome. The Mongol huntsmen, however, contrived means to inspire the horses with so much courage in this respect that they would advance to the encounter of these terrible foes with as much ardour as a trained charger shows in advancing to meet other horses and horsemen on the field of battle.

Great Desert – Cold

Besides the mountainous regions above described, there were several deserts in the country of the Mongols. The greatest of these deserts extends through the very heart of Asia, and is one of the most extensive districts of barren land in the world. Unlike most other great deserts, however, the land is very elevated, and it is to this elevation that its barrenness is, in a great measure, due. A large part of this desert consists of rocks and barren sands, and, in the time of which we are writing, was totally uninhabitable. It was so cold, too, on account of the great elevation of the land, that it was almost impossible to traverse it except in the warmest season of the year.

Pasturage

Other parts of this district, which were not so elevated, and where the land was not quite so barren, produced grass and herbage on which the flocks and herds could feed, and thus, in certain seasons of the year, people resorted to them for pasturage.

No Forests – Burning the Grass on the Plains

Throughout the whole country there were no extensive forests. There were a few tangled thickets among the mountains, where the wild beasts concealed themselves and made their lairs, but this was all. One reason why forests did not spring up was, as is supposed, the custom of the people to burn over the plains every spring, as the Native people were accustomed to do on the American prairies.

In the spring the dead grass of the preceding year lay dry and withered, and sometimes closely matted together, on the ground, thus hindering, as the people thought, the fresh grass from growing up. So the people were accustomed, on some spring morning when there was a good breeze blowing, to set it on fire. The fire would run rapidly over the plains, burning up everything in its way that was above the ground. But the roots of the grass, being below, were safe from it. Very soon afterward the new grass would spring up with great luxuriance. The people thought that the rich verdure which the new grass displayed, and its subsequent rapid growth, were owing simply to the fact that the old dead grass was out of the way. It is now known, however, that the burning of the old grass leaves an ash upon the ground which acts powerfully as a fertilizer, and that the richness of the fresh vegetation is due, in a great measure, to this cause.

The Various Tribes Submit

Such was the country which was inhabited by the wandering pastoral tribes that were now under the sway of Genghis Khan. His dominion had no settled boundaries, for it was a dominion over certain tribes rather than over a certain district of country. Nearly all the tribes composing both the Mongol and the Tartar nations had now submitted to him, though he still had some small wars to wage from time to time with some of the more distant tribes before his authority was fully and finally acknowledged. The history of some of these conflicts will be narrated in the next chapter.

Chapter XIII
Adventures of Prince Kushluk
1203–08

Kushluk's Escape

PRINCE KUSHLUK, as the reader will perhaps recollect, was the son of Tayian, the khan of the Naymans, who organized the grand league of khans against Temujin at the instigation of Yemuka, as related in a preceding chapter. He was the young prince who was opposed to Jughi, the son of Temujin, in the great final battle. The reader will recollect that in that battle Tayian himself was slain, as was also Yemuka, but the young prince succeeded in making his escape.

Tukta Bey – Kashin

He was accompanied in his flight by a certain general or chieftain named Tukta Bey. This Tukta Bey was the khan of a powerful tribe. The name of the town or village which he considered his capital was Kashin. It was situated toward the southwest, not far from the borders of China. Tukta Bey, taking Kushluk with him, retreated to this place, and there began to make preparations to collect a new army to act against Temujin. I say Temujin, for these circumstances took place immediately after the battle, and before Temujin had received his new title of Genghis Khan.

Temujin Pursues Tukta Bey and Kushluk

Temujin, having learned that Tukta Bey and the young prince had gone to Kashin, determined at once to follow them there. As soon as Tukta Bey heard that he was coming, he began to strengthen the fortifications of his town and to increase the garrison. He also laid in supplies of food and military stores of all kinds. While he was making these preparations, he received the news that Temujin was advancing into his country at the head of an immense force. The force was so large that he was convinced that his town could not long stand out against it. He was greatly perplexed to know what to do.

Retreat to Boyrak's Country

Now it happened that there was a brother of Tayian Khan's, named Boyrak, the chief of a powerful horde that occupied a district of country not very far distant from Tukta Bey's dominions. Tukta Bey thought that this Boyrak would be easily induced to aid him in the war, as it was a war waged against the mortal enemy of his brother. He determined to leave his capital to be defended by the garrison which he had placed in it, and to proceed himself to Boyrak's country to obtain re-enforcements. He first sent off the Prince Kushluk, so that he might be as soon as possible in a place of safety. Then, after completing the necessary arrangements and dispositions for the defence of his town, in case it should be attacked during his absence, he took his oldest son, for whose safety he was also greatly concerned, and set out at the head of a small troop of horsemen to go to Boyrak.

Fall and Destruction of Kashin

Accordingly, when Temujin, at the head of his forces, arrived at the town of Kashin, he found that the fugitives whom he was pursuing were no longer there. However, he determined to take the town. He accordingly at once invested it, and commenced the siege. The garrison made a very determined resistance. But the forces under Temujin's command were too strong for them. The town was soon taken. Temujin ordered his soldiers to slay without mercy all who were found in arms against him within the walls, and the walls themselves, and all the other defences of the place, he caused to be levelled with the ground.

He then issued his proclamation, offering peace and pardon to all the rest of the tribe on condition that they would take the oath of allegiance to him. This they readily agreed to do. There were a great many subordinate khans, both of this tribe and of some others that were near, who thus yielded to Temujin, and promised to obey him.

Temujin Returns to Karakorom

All this took place, as has already been said, immediately after the great battle with Tayian, and before Temujin had been enthroned as emperor, or had received his new title of Genghis Khan. Indeed, Temujin, while making this expedition to Kashin in pursuit of Kushluk and Tukta Bey, had been somewhat uneasy at the loss of time which the campaign occasioned him, as he was anxious to go as soon as possible to Karakorom, in order to take the necessary measures there for arranging and consolidating his government. He accordingly now determined not to pursue the fugitives any farther, but to proceed at once to Karakorom, and postpone all farther operations against Kushluk and Tukta until the next season. So he went to Karakorom, and there, during the course of the winter, formed the constitution of his new empire, and made arrangements for convening a grand assembly of the khans the next spring, as related in the last chapter.

Boyrak's Precautions

In the meantime, Tukta Bey and the Prince Kushluk were very kindly received by Boyrak, Tayian's brother. For a time, they all had reason to expect that Temujin, after having taken and destroyed Kashin, would continue his pursuit of the prince, and Boyrak began accordingly to make preparations for defence. But when, at length, they learned that Temujin had given up the pursuit, and had returned to Karakorom, their apprehensions were, for the moment, relieved. They were, however, well aware that the danger was only postponed; and Boyrak, being determined to defend the cause of his nephew, and to avenge, if possible, his brother's death, occupied himself diligently with increasing his army, strengthening his fortifications and providing himself with all possible means of defence against the attack which he expected would be made upon him in the coming season.

Great Battle – Boyrak is Taken and Slain

Boyrak's expectations of an attack were fully realized. Temujin, after having settled the affairs of his government, and having now become Genghis Khan, took the first opportunity in the following season to fit out an expedition against Tukta Bey and Boyrak. He marched into Boyrak's dominions at the head of a strong force. Boyrak came forth to meet him. A great battle was fought. Boyrak was entirely defeated. When he found that the battle was lost he attempted to fly. He was, however, pursued and taken, and was then brought back to the camp of Genghis Khan, where he was put to death. The conqueror undoubtedly justified this act of cruelty toward his helpless prisoner on the plea that, like Yemuka, he was not an open and honourable foe, but a rebel and traitor, and, consequently, that the act of putting him to death was the execution of a criminal, and not the murder of a prisoner.

Flight of Kushluk and Tukta Bey – Ardish

But, although Boyrak himself was thus taken and slain, Kushluk and Tukta Bey succeeded in making their escape. They fled to the northward and westward, scarcely knowing, it would seem, where they were to go. They at last found a place of refuge on the banks of the River Irtish. This river rises not far from the centre of the Asiatic continent, and flows northward into the Northern Ocean. The country through which it flows lay to the north-westward of Genghis Khan's dominions, and beyond the confines of it. Through this country Prince Kushluk and Tukta Bey wandered on, accompanied by the small troop of followers that still adhered to them, until they reached a certain fortress called Ardish, where they determined to make a stand.

Tukta Bey's Adherents

They were among friends here, for Ardish, it seems, was on the confines of territory that belonged to Tukta Bey. The people of the neighbourhood immediately flocked to Tukta's standard, and thus the fugitive khan soon found himself at the head of a considerable force. This force was farther increased by the coming in of broken bands that had made their escape from the battle at which Boyrak had been slain at the same time with Tukta Bey, but had become separated from him in their flight.

Genghis Khan Pursues Them in Winter

It would seem that, at first, Genghis Khan did not know what was become of the fugitives. At any rate, it was not until the next year that he attempted to pursue them. Then, hearing where they were and what they were doing, he prepared an expedition to penetrate into the country of the Irtish and attack them. It was in the dead of winter when he arrived in the country. He had hurried on at that season of the year in order to prevent Tukta Bey from having time to finish his fortifications. Tukta Bey and those who were with him were amazed when they heard that their enemy was coming at that season of the year. The defences which they were preparing for their fortress were not fully completed, but they were at once convinced that they could not hold their ground against the body of troops that Genghis Khan was bringing against them in the open field, and so they all took shelter in and near the fortress, and awaited their enemy there.

Difficulties of the Country

The winters in that latitude are very cold, and the country through which Genghis Khan had to march was full of difficulty. The branches of the river which he had to cross were obstructed with ice, and the roads were in many places rendered almost impassable by snow. The emperor did not even know the way to the fortress where Tukta Bey and his followers were concealed, and it would have been almost impossible for him to find it had it not been for certain tribes, through whose territories he passed on the way, who furnished him with guides. These tribes, perceiving how overwhelming was the force which Genghis Khan commanded, knew that it would be useless for them to resist him. So they yielded submission to him at once, and detached parties of horsemen to go with him down the river to show him the way.

Death of Tukta Bey

Under the conduct of these guides Genghis Khan passed on. In due time he arrived at the fortress of Ardish, and immediately forced Tukta Bey and his allies to come to an engagement. Tukta's army was very soon defeated and put to flight. Tukta himself, and many other khans and chieftains who had joined him, were killed; but the Prince Kushluk was once more fortunate enough to make his escape.

Kushluk Escapes Again – Turkestan

He fled with a small troop of followers, all mounted on fleet horses, and after various wanderings, in the course of which he and they who were with him endured a great deal of privation and suffering, the unhappy fugitive at last reached the dominions of a powerful prince named Gurkhan, who reigned over a country which is situated in the western part of Asia, toward the Caspian Sea, and is named Turkestan. This is the country from which the people called the Turks, who afterward spread themselves so widely over the western part of Asia and the eastern part of Europe, originally sprung.

He Is Received by Gurkhan

Gurkhan received Kushluk and his party in a very friendly manner, and Genghis Khan did not follow them. Whether he thought that the distance was too great, or that the power of Gurkhan was too formidable to make it prudent for him to advance into his dominions without a stronger force, does not appear. At any rate, for the time being he gave up the pursuit, and after fully securing the fruits of the victory which he had gained at Ardish, and receiving the submission of all the tribes and khans that inhabited that region of country, he set out on his return home.

Presentation of the *Shongar*

It is related that one of the khans who gave in his submission to Genghis Khan at this time made him a present of a certain bird called a *shongar*, according to a custom often observed among the people of that region. The shongar was a very large and fierce bird of prey, which, however, could be trained like the falcons which were so much prized in the Middle Ages by the princes and nobles of Europe. It seems it was customary for an inferior khan to present one of these birds to his superior on great occasions, as an emblem and token of his submission to his superior's authority. The bird in such a case was very richly decorated with gold and precious stones, so that the present was sometimes of a very costly and magnificent character.

Urus Inal

Genghis Khan received such a present as this from a chieftain named Urus Inal, who was among those that yielded to his sway in the country of the Irtish, after the battle at which Tukta Bey was defeated and killed. The bird was presented to Genghis Khan by Urus with great ceremony, as an act of submission and homage.

What, in the end, was the fate of Prince Kushluk, will appear in the next chapter.

Chapter XIV
Idikut
1208

Idikut – The Old System of Farming Revenues

THERE WAS ANOTHER great and powerful khan, named Idikut, whose tribe had hitherto been under the dominion of Gurkhan, the Prince of Turkestan, where Kushluk had sought refuge, but who about this time revolted from Gurkhan and went over to Genghis Khan, under circumstances which illustrate, in some degree, the peculiar

nature of the political ties by which these different tribes and nations were bound to each other.

It seems that the tribe over which Idikut ruled was tributary to Turkestan, and that Gurkhan had an officer stationed in Idikut's country whose business it was to collect and remit the tribute. The name of this collector was Shuwakem. He was accustomed, it seems, like almost all tax gatherers in those days, to exact more than was his due.

The system generally adopted by governments in that age of the world for collecting their revenues from tributary or conquered provinces was to *farm them,* as the phrase was. That is, they sold the whole revenue of a particular district in the gross to some rich man, who paid for it a specific sum, considerably less, of course, than the tax itself would really yield, and then he reimbursed himself for his outlay and for his trouble by collecting the tax in detail from the people.

Of course, it was for the interest of the tax gatherer, in such a case, after having paid the round sum to the government, to extort as much as possible from the people, since all that he obtained over and above the sum that he had paid was his profit on the transaction. Then, if the people complained to the government of his exactions, they could seldom obtain any redress, for the government knew that if they rebuked or punished the farmer of the revenue, or interfered with him in any way, they would not be able to make so favourable terms with him for the next year.

Modern System – Independent and Impartial Courts – Waste of the Public Money

The plan of farming the revenues thus led to a great deal of extortion and oppression, which the people were compelled patiently to endure, as there was generally no remedy.

In modern times and among civilized nations, this system has been almost universally abandoned. The taxes are now always collected for the government directly by officers who have to pay over not a fixed sum, but simply what they collect. Thus, the tax gatherers are, in some sense, impartial, since, if they collect more than the law entitles them to demand, the benefit inures almost wholly to the government, they themselves gaining little or no advantage by their extortion. Besides this, there are courts established which are, in a great measure, independent of the government, to which the taxpayer can appeal at once in a case where he thinks he is aggrieved. This, it is true, often puts him to a great deal of trouble and expense, but, in the end, he is pretty sure to have justice done him, while under the old system there was ordinarily no remedy at all. There was nothing to be done but to appeal to the king or chieftain himself, and these complaints seldom received any attention.

For, besides the natural unwillingness of the sovereign to trouble himself about such disputes, he had a direct interest in not requiring the extorted money to be paid back, or, rather, in not having it proved that it was extorted. Thus, the poor taxpayer found that the officer who collected the money, and the umpire who was to decide in case of disputes, were both directly interested against him, and he was continually wronged; whereas, at the present day, by means of a system which provides disinterested officers to determine and collect the tax, and independent judges to decide all cases of dispute, the evils are almost wholly avoided.

The only difficulty now is the extravagance and waste with which the public money is expended, making it necessary to collect a much larger amount than would otherwise be required. Perhaps some future generation will discover some plain and simple remedy for this evil too.

Shuwakem

The name of the officer who had the general charge of the collection of the taxes in Idikut's territory for Gurkhan, King of Turkestan, was, as has already been said, Shuwakem. He oppressed the people, exacting more from them than was really due. Whether he had farmed the revenue, and was thus enriching himself by his extortions, or whether he was acting directly in Gurkhan's name, and made the people pay more than he ought from zeal in his master's service, and a desire to recommend himself to favour by sending home to Turkestan as large a revenue from the provinces as possible, does not appear. At all events, the people complained bitterly. They had, however, no access to Gurkhan, Shuwakem's master, and so they carried their complaints to Idikut, their own khan.

Idikut's Quarrel with Gurkhan's Tax Gatherers

Idikut remonstrated with Shuwakem, but he, instead of taking the remonstrance in good part and relaxing the severity of his proceedings, resented the interference of Idikut, and answered him in a haughty and threatening manner. This made Idikut very angry. Indeed, he was angry before, as it might naturally be supposed that he would have been, at having a person owing allegiance to a foreign prince exercising authority in a proud and domineering manner within his dominions, and the reply which Shuwakem made when he remonstrated with him on account of his extortions exasperated him beyond all bounds. He immediately caused Shuwakem to be assassinated. He also slew all the other officers of Gurkhan within his country – those, probably, who were employed to assist Shuwakem in collecting the taxes.

Rebellion – He Sends to Genghis Khan

The murder of these officers was, of course, an act of open rebellion against Gurkhan, and Idikut, in order to shield himself from the consequences of it, determined to join himself and his tribe at once to the empire of Genghis Khan; so he immediately dispatched two ambassadors to the Mongol emperor with his proposals.

The envoys, accompanied by a suitable troop of guards and attendants, went into the Mongol country and presently came up with Genghis Khan, while he was on a march toward the country of some tribe or horde that had revolted from him. They were very kindly received; for, although Genghis Khan was not prepared at present to make open war upon Gurkhan, or to invade his dominions in pursuit of Prince Kushluk, he was intending to do this at some future day, and, in the meantime, he was very glad to weaken his enemy by drawing off from his empire any tributary tribes that were at all disposed to revolt from him.

His Reception of the Embassy

He accordingly received the ambassadors of Idikut in a very cordial and friendly manner. He readily acceded to the proposals which Idikut made through them, and, in order to give full proof to Idikut of the readiness and sincerity with which he accepted his proposals, he sent back two ambassadors of his own to accompany Idikut's ambassadors on their return, and to join them in assuring that prince of the cordiality with which Genghis Khan accepted his offers of friendship, and to promise his protection.

Idikut's Visit to Genghis Khan

Idikut was very much pleased, when his messengers returned, to learn that his mission had been so successful. He immediately determined to go himself and visit Genghis Khan in his camp, in order to confirm the new alliance by making a personal tender to the emperor of his homage and his services. He accordingly prepared some splendid presents, and, placing himself at the head of his troop of guards, he proceeded to the camp of Genghis Khan. The emperor received him in a very kind and friendly manner. He accepted his presents, and, in the end, was so much pleased with Idikut himself that he gave him one of his daughters in marriage.

Gurkhan in a Rage

As for Gurkhan, when he first heard of the murder of Shuwakem and the other officers, he was in a terrible rage. He declared that he would revenge his servant by laying waste Idikut's territories with fire and sword. But when he heard that Idikut had placed himself under the protection of Genghis Khan, and especially when he learned that he had married the emperor's daughter, he thought it more prudent to postpone his vengeance, not being quite willing to draw upon himself the hostility of so great a power.

Subsequent History of Kushluk – Jena

Prince Kushluk remained for many years in Turkestan and in the countries adjoining it. He married a daughter of Gurkhan, his protector. Partly in consequence of this connection and of the high rank which he had held in his own native land, and partly, perhaps, in consequence of his personal courage and other military qualities, he rapidly acquired great influence among the khans of Western Asia, and at last he organized a sort of rebellion against Gurkhan, made war against him and deprived him of more than half his dominions. He then collected a large army, and prepared to make war upon Genghis Khan.

Genghis Khan sent one of his best generals, at the head of a small but very compact and well-disciplined force, against him. The name of this general was

Jena. Kushluk was not at all intimidated by the danger which now threatened him. His own army was much larger than that of Jena, and he accordingly advanced to meet his enemy without fear. He was, however, beaten in the battle, and, when he saw that the day was lost, he fled, followed by a small party of horsemen, who succeeded in saving themselves with him.

Kushluk's Final Defeat and Flight

Jena set out immediately in pursuit of the fugitive, accompanied by a small body of men mounted on the fleetest horses. The party who were with Kushluk, being exhausted by the fatigue of the battle and bewildered by the excitement and terror of their flight, could not keep together, but were overtaken one by one and slain by their pursuers until only three were left. These three kept close to Kushluk, and with him went on until Jena's party lost the track of them.

At length, coming to a place where two roads met, Jena asked a peasant if he had seen any strange horsemen pass that way. The peasant said that four horsemen had passed a short time before, and he told Jena which road they had taken.

Kushluk's Death

Jena and his party rode on in the direction which the peasant had indicated, and, pushing forward with redoubled speed, they soon overtook the unhappy fugitives. They fell upon Kushluk without mercy, and killed him on the spot. They then cut off his head, and turned back to carry it to Genghis Khan.

Genghis Khan's Triumph

Genghis Khan rewarded Jena in the most magnificent manner for his successful performance of this exploit, and then, putting Kushluk's head upon a pole, he displayed it in all the camps and villages through which he passed, where it served at once as a token and a trophy of his victory against an enemy, and, at the same time, as a warning to all other persons of the terrible danger which they would incur in attempting to resist his power.

Chapter XV
The Story of Hujaku
1211

China – The Chinese Wall

THE ACCOUNTS GIVEN US of the events and transactions of Genghis Khan's reign after he acquired the supreme power over the Mongol and Tartar nations are imperfect, and, in many respects, confused. It appears, however, from them that in the year 1211, that is, about five years after his election as grand khan, he became involved in a war with the Chinese, which led, in the end, to very important consequences.

The kingdom of China lay to the southward of the Mongol territories, and the frontier was defended by the famous Chinese wall, which extended from east to west, over hills and valleys, from the great desert to the sea, for many hundred miles. The wall was defended by towers, built here and there in commanding positions along the whole extent of it, and at certain distances there were fortified towns where powerful garrisons were stationed, and reserves of troops were held ready to be marched to different points along the wall, wherever there might be occasion for their services.

The Frontier

The wall was not strictly the Chinese frontier, for the territory on the outside of it to a considerable distance was held by the Chinese government, and there were many large towns and some very strong fortresses in this outlying region, all of which were held and garrisoned by Chinese troops.

Outside the Wall

The inhabitants, however, of the countries outside the wall were generally of the Tartar or Mongol race. They were of a nation or tribe called *the Kitan*, and were somewhat inclined to rebel against the Chinese rule. In order to assist in keeping them in subjection, one of the Chinese emperors issued a decree which ordained that the governors of those provinces should place in all the large towns, and other strongholds outside the wall, twice as many families of the Chinese as there were of the Kitan. This regulation greatly increased the discontent of the Kitan, and made them more inclined to rebellion than they were before.

Origin of the Quarrel with the Chinese

Besides this, there had been for some time a growing difficulty between the Chinese government and Genghis Khan. It seems that the Mongols had been for a long time accustomed to pay some sort of tribute to the Emperor of China, and many years before, while Genghis Khan, under the name of Temujin, was living at Karakorom, a subject of Vang Khan, the emperor sent a certain royal prince, named Yong-tsi, to receive what was due. While Yong-tsi was in the Mongol territory he and Temujin met, but they did not agree together at all. The Chinese prince put some slight upon Temujin, which Temujin resented. Very likely Temujin, whose character at that time, as well as afterward, was marked with a great deal of pride and spirit, opposed the payment of the tribute. At any rate, Yong-tsi became very much incensed against him, and, on his return, made serious charges against him to the emperor, and urged that he should be seized and put to death. But the emperor declined engaging in so dangerous an undertaking. Yong-tsi's proposal, however, became known to Temujin, and he secretly resolved that he would one day have his revenge.

At length, about three or four years after Temujin was raised to the throne, the emperor of the Chinese died, and Yong-tsi succeeded him. The very next year he sent an officer to Genghis Khan to demand the usual tribute. When the officer came into the presence of Genghis Khan in his camp, and made his demand, Genghis Khan asked him who was the emperor that had sent him with such a message.

The officer replied that Yong-tsi was at that time emperor of the Chinese.

Genghis Khan's Contempt for Him

'Yong-tsi!' repeated Genghis Khan, in a tone of great contempt. 'The Chinese have a proverb,' he added, 'that such a people as they ought to have a god for their emperor; but it seems they do not know how to choose even a decent man.'

It was true that they had such a proverb. They were as remarkable, it seems, in those days as they are now for their national self-importance and vanity.

'Go and tell your emperor,' added Genghis Khan, 'that I am a sovereign ruler, and that I will never acknowledge him as my master.'

Armies Raised – Hujaku

When the messenger returned with this defiant answer, Yong-tsi was very much enraged, and immediately began to prepare for war. Genghis Khan also at once commenced his preparations. He sent envoys to the leading khans who occupied the territories outside the wall inviting them to join him. He raised a great army, and put the several divisions of it under the charge of his ablest generals. Yong-tsi raised a great army too. The historians say that it amounted to 300,000 men. He put this army under the command of a great general named Hujaku, and ordered him to advance with it to the northward, so as to intercept the army of Genghis Khan on its way, and to defend the wall and the fortresses on the outside of it from his attacks.

Many of the Khans Come Over on Genghis's Side

In the campaign which ensued, Genghis Khan was most successful. The Mongols took possession of a great many towns and fortresses beyond the wall, and every victory that they gained made the tribes and nations that inhabited those provinces more and more disposed to join them. Many of them revolted against the Chinese authority, and turned to their side. One of these was a chieftain so powerful that he commanded an army of 100,000 men. In order to bind himself solemnly to the covenant which he was to make with Genghis Khan, he ascended a mountain in company with the envoy and with others who were to witness the proceedings, and there performed the ceremony customary on such occasions. The ceremony consisted of sacrificing a white horse and a black ox, and then breaking an arrow, at the same time pronouncing an oath by which he bound himself under the most solemn sanctions to be faithful to Genghis Khan.

To reward the prince for this act of adhesion to his cause, Genghis Khan made him king over all that portion of the country, and caused him to be everywhere so proclaimed. This encouraged a great many other khans and chieftains to come over to his side; and at length one who had the command of one of the gates of the great wall, and of the fortress which defended it, joined him. By this means, Genghis Khan obtained access to the interior of the Chinese dominions, and Yong-tsi and his great general Hujaku became seriously alarmed.

Victory Over Hujaku

At length, after various marchings and counter-marchings, Genghis Khan learned that Hujaku was encamped with the whole of his army in a very strong position at the foot of a mountain, and he determined to proceed thither and attack him. He did so; and the result of the battle was that Hujaku was beaten and was forced to retreat. He retired to a great fortified town, and Genghis Khan followed him and laid siege to the town. Hujaku, finding himself in imminent danger, fled; and Genghis Khan was on the point of taking the town, when he was suddenly stopped in his career by being one day wounded severely by an arrow which was shot at him from the wall.

Genghis Khan is Wounded

The wound was so severe that, while suffering under it, Genghis Khan found that he could not successfully direct the operations of his army, and so he withdrew his troops and retired into his own country, to wait there until his wound should be healed. In a few months he was entirely recovered, and the next year he fitted out a new expedition, and advanced again into China.

Hujaku Disgraced

In the meantime, Hujaku, who had been repeatedly defeated and driven back the year before by Genghis Khan, had fallen into disgrace. His rivals and enemies among the other generals of the army, and among the officers of the court, conspired against him, and represented to the emperor that he was unfit to command, and that his having failed to defend the towns and the country that had been committed to him was owing to his cowardice and incapacity. In consequence of these representations Hujaku was cashiered, that is, dismissed from his command in disgrace.

Restored Again

This made him very angry, and he determined that he would have his revenge. There was a large party in his favour at court, as well as a party against him; and after a long and bitter contention, the former once more prevailed, and induced the emperor to restore Hujaku to his command again.

Dissensions Among the Chinese

The quarrel, however, was not ended, and so, when Genghis Khan came the next year to renew the invasion, the councils of the Chinese were so distracted, and their operations so paralyzed by this feud, that he gained very easy victories over them. The Chinese generals, instead of acting together in a harmonious manner against the common enemy, were intent only on the quarrel which they were waging against each other.

At length the animosity proceeded to such an extreme that Hujaku resolved to depose the emperor, who seemed inclined rather to take part against him, assassinate all the chiefs of the opposite party, and then finally to put the emperor to death, and cause himself to be proclaimed in his stead.

Advance of the Mongols

In order to prepare the way for the execution of this scheme, he forbore to act vigorously against Genghis Khan and the Mongols, but allowed them to advance farther and farther into the country. This, of course, increased the general discontent and excitement, and prepared the way for the revolt which Hujaku was plotting.

Hujaku's Rebellion – Death of Yong-tsi

At length, the time for action arrived. Hujaku suddenly appeared at the head of a large force at the gates of the capital, and gave the alarm that the Mongols were coming. He pressed forward into the city to the palace, and gave the alarm there. At the same time, files of soldiers, whom he had ordered to this service, went to all parts of the city, arresting and putting to death all the leaders of the party opposed to him, under pretence that he had discovered a plot or conspiracy in which they were engaged to betray the city to the enemy. The excitement and confusion which was produced by this charge, and by the alarm occasioned by the supposed coming of the Mongols, so paralyzed the authorities of the town that nobody resisted Hujaku, or attempted to save the persons whom he arrested. Some of them he caused to be killed on the spot. Others he shut up in prison. Finding himself thus undisputed master of the city, he next took possession of the palace, seized the emperor, deposed him from his office and shut him up in a dungeon. Soon afterward he put him to death.

This was the end of Yong-tsi; but Hujaku did not succeed, after all, in his design of causing himself to be proclaimed emperor in his stead. He found that there would be very great opposition to this, and so he gave up this part of his plan, and finally raised a certain prince of the royal family to the throne, while he retained his office of commander-in-chief of the forces. Having thus, as he thought, effectually destroyed the influence and power of his enemies at the capital, he put himself once more at the head of his troops, and went forth to meet Genghis Khan.

Hujaku Advances

Some accident happened to him about this time by which his foot was hurt, so that he was, in some degree, disabled, but still he went on. At length he met the vanguard of Genghis Khan's army at a place where they were attempting to cross a river by a bridge. Hujaku determined immediately to attack them. The state of his foot was such that he could not walk nor even mount a horse, but he caused himself to be put upon a sort of car, and was by this means carried into the battle.

The Battle – Hujaku's Victory

The Mongols were completely defeated and driven back. Perhaps this was because Genghis Khan was not there to command them. He was at some distance in the rear with the main body of the army.

Hujaku was very desirous of following up his victory by pursuing and attacking the Mongol vanguard the next day. He could not, however, do this personally, for, on account of the excitement and exposure which he had endured in the battle, and the rough movements and joltings which, notwithstanding all his care, he had to bear in being conveyed to and fro about the field, his foot grew much worse. Inflammation set in during the night, and the next day the wound opened afresh; so he was obliged to give up the idea of going out himself against the enemy, and to send one of his generals instead. The general to whom he gave the command was named Kan-ki.

Kan-Ki's Expedition – Hujaku Enraged

Kan-ki went out against the enemy, but, after a time, returned unsuccessful. Hujaku was very angry with him when he came to hear his report. Perhaps the wound in his foot made him impatient and unreasonable. At any rate, he declared that the cause of Kan-ki's failure was his dilatoriness in pursuing the enemy, which was cowardice or treachery, and, in either case, he deserved to suffer death for it. He immediately sent to the emperor a report of the case, asking that the sentence of death which he had pronounced against Kan-ki might be confirmed, and that he might be authorized to put it into execution.

But the emperor, knowing that Kan-ki was a courageous and faithful officer, would not consent.

In the meanwhile, before the emperor's answer came back, the wrath of Hujaku had had time to cool a little. Accordingly, when he received the answer, he said to Kan-ki that he would, after all, try him once more.

'Take the command of the troops again,' said he, 'and go out against the enemy. If you beat them, I will overlook your first offense and spare your life; but if you are beaten yourself a second time, you shall die.'

Kan-ki's Second Trial – The Sandstorm

So Kan-ki placed himself at the head of his detachment, and went out again to attack the Mongols. They were to the northward, and were posted, it seems, upon or near a sandy plain. At any rate, a strong north wind began to blow at the time when the attack commenced, and blew the sand and dust into the eyes of his soldiers so that they could not see, while their enemies the Mongols, having their backs to the wind, were very little incommoded. The result was that Kan-ki was repulsed with considerable loss, and was obliged to make the best of his way back to Hujaku's quarters to save the remainder of his men.

Kan-ki's Desperate Resolution

He was now desperate. Hujaku had declared that if he came back without having gained a victory he should die, and he had no doubt that the man was violent and reckless enough to keep his word. He determined not to submit. He might as well die fighting, he thought, at the head of his troops, as to be ignobly put to death by Hujaku's executioner. So he arranged it with his troops, who probably hated Hujaku as much as he did, that, on returning to the town, they should march in under arms, take possession of the place, surround the palace and seize the general and make him prisoner, or kill him if he should attempt any resistance.

The Attack – Hujaku Is Killed in the Gardens

The troops accordingly, when they arrived at the gates of the town, seized and disarmed the guards, and then marched in, brandishing their weapons, and uttering loud shouts and outcries, which excited first a feeling of astonishment and then of terror among the inhabitants. The alarm soon spread to the palace. Indeed, the troops themselves soon reached and surrounded the palace, and began thundering at the gates to gain admission. They soon forced their way in. Hujaku, in the meantime, terrified and panic-stricken, had fled from the palace into the gardens, in hopes to make his escape by the garden walls. The soldiers pursued him. In his excitement and agitation, he leaped down from a wall too high for such a descent, and, in his fall, broke his leg. He lay writhing helplessly on the ground when the soldiers came up. They were wild and furious with the excitement of pursuit, and they killed him with their spears where he lay.

Kan-ki took the head of his old enemy and carried it to the capital, with the intention of offering it to the emperor, and also of surrendering himself to the officers of justice, in order, as he said, that he might be put to death for the crime of which he had been guilty in heading a military revolt and killing his superior officer. By all the laws of war this was a most heinous and a wholly unpardonable offense.

Kan-ki Is Pardoned and Promoted

But the emperor was heartily glad that the turbulent and unmanageable old general was put out of the way, for a man so unprincipled, so ambitious and so reckless as

Hujaku is always an object of aversion and terror to all who have anything to do with him. The emperor accordingly issued a proclamation, in which he declared that Hujaku had been justly put to death in punishment for many crimes which he had committed, and soon afterward he appointed Kan-ki commander-in-chief of the forces in his stead.

Chapter XVI
Conquests in China
1211–16

War Continued – Grand Invasion

AFTER THE DEATH OF HUJAKU, **the Emperor of China endeavoured to defend his dominions against Genghis Khan by means of his other generals, and the war was continued for several years, during which time Genghis Khan made himself master of all the northern part of China, and ravaged the whole country in the most reckless and cruel manner.**

The country was very populous and very rich. The people, unlike the Mongols and Tartars, lived by tilling the ground, and they practiced, in great perfection, many manufacturing and mechanic arts. The country was very fertile, and, in the place of the boundless pasturages of the Mongol territories, it was covered in all directions with cultivated fields, gardens, orchards and mulberry groves, while thriving villages and busy towns were scattered over the whole face of it. It was to protect this busy hive of wealth and industry that the great wall had been built ages before; for the Chinese had always been stationary, industrious and peaceful, while the territories of Central Asia, lying to the north of them, had been filled from time immemorial with wild, roaming and unscrupulous troops of marauders, like those who were now united under the banner of Genghis Khan.

The wall had afforded for some hundreds of years an adequate protection, for no commander had appeared of sufficient power to organize and combine the various hordes on a scale great enough to enable them to force so strong a barrier. But, now that Genghis Khan had come upon the stage, the barrier was broken through, and the terrible and reckless hordes poured in with all the force and fury of an inundation.

In the year 1214, which was the year following that in which Hujaku was killed, Genghis Khan organized a force so large for the invasion of China, that he divided it into four different battalions, which were to enter by different roads, and ravage different portions of the country. Each of these divisions was by itself a great and powerful army, and the simultaneous invasion of four such masses of reckless and merciless enemies filled the whole land with terror and dismay.

Enthusiasm of the Troops

The Chinese emperor sent the best bodies of troops under his command to guard the passes in the mountains, and the bridges and fording places on the rivers, hoping in this way to do something toward stemming the tide of these torrents of invasion. But it was all in vain. Genghis Khan had raised and equipped his forces by means, in a great measure, of the plunder which he had obtained in China the year before, and he had made great promises and glowing representations to his men in respect to the booty to be obtained in this new campaign. The troops were consequently full of ardour and enthusiasm, and they pressed on with such impetuosity as to carry all before them.

Captives – Immense Plunder

The Emperor of China, in pursuing his measures of defence, had ordered all the men capable of bearing arms in the villages and in the open country to repair to the nearest large city or fortress, there to be enrolled and equipped for service. The consequence was that the Mongols found in many places, as they advanced through the country, nobody but infirm old men, and women and children in the hamlets and villages. A great many of these, especially such as seemed to be of most consequence, the handsomest and best of the women and the oldest children, they seized and took with them in continuing their march, intending to make slaves of them. They also took possession of all the gold and silver, and also of all the silks and other rich and valuable merchandise which they found, and distributed it as plunder. The spoil which they obtained, too, in sheep and cattle, was enormous. From it they made up immense flocks and herds, which were driven off into the Mongol country. The rest were slaughtered, and used to supply the army with food.

Dreadful Ravages

It was the custom of the invaders, after having pillaged a town and its environs, and taken away all which they could convert to any useful purpose for themselves, to burn the town itself, and then to march on, leaving in the place only a smoking heap of ruins, with the miserable remnant of the population which they had spared wandering about the scene of desolation in misery and despair.

Base Use Made of the Captives

They made a most cowardly and atrocious use, too, of the prisoners whom they conveyed away. When they arrived at a fortified town where there was a garrison or any other armed force prepared to resist them, they would bring forward these helpless captives, and put them in the forefront of the battle in such a manner that the men on the walls could not shoot their arrows at their savage assailants without killing their own wives and children. The officers commanded the men to fire notwithstanding. But they were so moved by the piteous cries which the women and children made that they could not bear to do it, and so they refused to obey, and in the excitement and confusion thus produced the Mongols easily obtained possession of the town.

Extent of Mongol Conquests

There are two great rivers in China, both of which flow from west to east, and they are at such a distance from each other and from the frontiers that they divide the territory into three nearly equal parts. The northernmost of these rivers is the Hoang Ho. The Mongols in the course of two years overran and made themselves masters of almost the whole country lying north of this river, that is, of about one third of China proper. There were, however, some strongly fortified towns which they found it very difficult to conquer.

The Siege of Yen-king

Among other places, there was the imperial city of Yen-king, where the emperor himself resided, which was so strongly defended that for some time the Mongols did not venture to attack it. At length, however, Genghis Khan came himself to the place, and concentrated there a very large force. The emperor and his court were very much alarmed, expecting an immediate assault. Still Genghis Khan hesitated. Some of his generals urged him to scale the walls, and so force his way into the city. But he thought it more politic to adopt a different plan.

Proposed Terms of Arrangement

So he sent an officer into the town with proposals of peace to be communicated to the emperor. In these proposals, Genghis Khan said that he himself was inclined to spare the town, but that to appease his soldiers, who were furious to attack and pillage the city, it would be necessary to make them considerable presents, and that, if the emperor would agree to such terms with him as should enable him to satisfy his men in this respect, he would spare the city and would retire.

Difference of Opinion

The emperor and his advisers were much perplexed at the receipt of this proposal. There was great difference of opinion among the counsellors in respect to the reply which was to be made to it. Some were in favour of rejecting it at once. One general, not content with a simple rejection of it, proposed that, to show the indignation and resentment which they felt in receiving it, the garrison should march out of the gates and attack the Mongols in their camp.

Consultation on the Subject

There were other ministers, however, who urged the emperor to submit to the necessity of the case and make peace with the conqueror. They said that the idea of going out to attack the enemy in their camp was too desperate to be entertained for a moment, and if they waited within the walls and attempted to defend themselves there, they exposed themselves to a terrible danger, without any countervailing hope of advantage at all commensurate with it; for if they failed to save the city they were all utterly and irretrievably ruined; and if, on the other hand, they succeeded in repelling the assault, it was only a brief respite that they could hope to gain, for the Mongols would soon return in greater numbers and in a higher state of excitement and fury than ever. Besides, they said, the garrison was discontented and depressed in spirit, and would make but a feeble resistance. It was composed mainly of troops brought in from the country, away from their families and homes, and all that they desired was to be released from duty, in order that they might go and see what had become of their wives and children.

Terms of Peace Agreed Upon

The emperor, in the end, adopted this counsel, and he sent a commissioner to the camp of Genghis Khan to ask on what terms peace could be made. Genghis Khan stated the conditions. They were very hard, but the emperor was compelled to submit to them. One of the stipulations was that Genghis Khan was to receive one of the Chinese princesses, a daughter of the late emperor Yong-tsi, to add to the number of his wives. There were also to be delivered to him for slaves 500 young boys and as many girls, 3,000 horses, a large quantity of silk and an immense sum of money. As soon as these conditions were fulfilled, after dividing the slaves and the booty among the officers and soldiers of his army, Genghis Khan raised the siege and moved off to the northward.

In respect to the captives that his soldiers had taken in the towns and villages – the women and children spoken of above – the army carried off with them all that were old enough to be of any value as slaves. The little children, who would only, they thought, be in the way, they massacred.

The Emperor's Uneasiness

The emperor was by no means easy after the Mongol army had gone. A marauding enemy like that, bought off by the payment of a ransom, is exceedingly apt to find some pretext for returning, and the emperor did not feel that he was safe. Very soon after the Mongols had withdrawn, he proposed to his council the plan of removing his court southward to the other side of the Hoang Ho, to a large city in the province of Henan. Some of his counsellors made great objections to this proposal. They said that if the emperor withdrew in that manner from the northern provinces that portion of his empire would be irretrievably lost. Genghis Khan would soon obtain complete and undisputed possession of the whole of it. The proper course to be adopted, they said, was to remain and make a firm stand in defence of the capital and of the country. They must levy new troops, repair the fortifications, recruit the garrison and lay in supplies of food and of other military stores, and thus prepare themselves for a vigorous and efficient resistance in case the enemy should return.

But the emperor could not be persuaded. He said that the treasury was exhausted, the troops were discouraged, the cities around the capital were destroyed and the whole country was so depopulated by the devastations of the Mongols that no considerable number of fresh levies could be obtained; and that, consequently, the only safe course for the government to pursue was to retire to the southward, beyond the river. He would, however, he added, leave his son, with a strong garrison, to defend the capital.

Abandonment of the Capital

He accordingly took with him a few favourites of his immediate family and a small body of troops, and commenced his journey – a journey which was considered by all the people as a base and ignoble flight. He involved himself in endless troubles by this step. A revolt broke out on the way among the guards who accompanied him. One of the generals who headed the revolt sent a messenger to Genghis Khan informing him of the emperor's abandonment of his capital, and offering to go over, with all the troops under his command, to the service of Genghis Khan if Genghis Khan would receive him.

The Siege of the Capital Renewed

When Genghis Khan heard thus of the retreat of the emperor from his capital, he was, or pretended to be, much incensed. He considered the proceeding as in some sense an act of hostility against himself, and, as such, an infraction of the treaty and a renewal of the war. So he immediately ordered one of his leading generals – a certain chieftain named Mingan – to proceed southward at the head of a large army and lay siege to Yen-king again.

The old emperor, who seems now to have lost all spirit, and to have given himself up entirely to despondency and fear, was greatly alarmed for the safety of his son the prince, whom he had left in command at Yen-king. He immediately sent orders to his son to leave the city and come to him. The departure of the prince, in obedience to these orders, of course threw an additional gloom over the city, and excited still more the general discontent which the emperor's conduct had awakened.

Wan-yen and Mon-yen – Their Perplexity

The prince, on his departure, left two generals in command of the garrison. Their names were Wan-yen and Mon-yen. They were left to defend the city as well as they could from the army of Mongols under Mingan, which was now rapidly drawing near. The generals were greatly embarrassed and perplexed with the difficulties of their situation. The means of defence at their disposal were wholly inadequate, and they knew not what to do.

Suicide Proposed

At length one of them, Wan-yen, proposed to the other that they should kill themselves. This Mon-yen refused to do. Mon-yen was the commander on whom the troops chiefly relied, and he considered suicide a mode of deserting one's post scarcely less dishonourable than any other. He said that his duty was to stand by his troops, and, if he could not defend them where they were, to endeavour to draw them away, while there was an opportunity, to a place of safety.

Wan-yen in Despair

So Wan-yen, finding his proposal rejected, went away in a rage. He retired to his apartment, and wrote a dispatch to the emperor, in which he explained the desperate condition of affairs, and the impossibility of saving the city, and in the end declared himself deserving of death for not being able to accomplish the work which his majesty had assigned to him.

He enveloped and sealed this dispatch, and then, calling his domestics together, he divided among them, in a very calm and composed manner, all his personal effects, and then took leave of them and dismissed them.

His Suicide

A single officer only now remained with him. In the presence of this officer, he wrote a few words, and then sent him away. As soon as the officer had gone, he drank a cup of poison which he had previously ordered to be prepared for him, and in a few minutes was a lifeless corpse.

Mon-yen's Plan – Petition of the Wives

In the meantime, the other general, Mon-yen, had been making preparations to leave the city. His plan was to take with him such troops as might be serviceable to the emperor, but to leave all the inmates of the palace, as well as the inhabitants of the city, to their fate. Among the people of the palace were, it seems, a number of the emperor's wives, whom he had left behind at the time of his own flight, he having taken with him at that time only a few of the more favoured ones. These women who were left, when they heard that Mon-yen was intending to abandon the city with a view of joining the emperor in the south, came to him in a body, and begged him to take them with him.

Sacking of the City by Mingan

In order to relieve himself of their solicitations, he said that he would do so, but he added that he must leave the city himself with the guards to prepare the way, and that he would return immediately for them. They were satisfied with this promise, and returned to the palace to prepare for the journey. Mon-yen at once left the city, and very soon after he had gone, Mingan, the Mongol general, arrived at the gates, and, meeting with no effectual resistance, he easily forced his way in, and a scene of universal terror and confusion ensued. The soldiers spread themselves over the city in search of plunder, and killed all who came in their way. They plundered the palace and then set it on fire. So extensive was the edifice, and so vast were the stores of clothing and other valuables which it contained, even after all the treasures which could be made available to the conquerors had been taken away, that the fire continued to burn among the ruins for a month or more.

Massacres

What became of the unhappy women who were so cruelly deceived by Mon-yen in respect to their hopes of escape does not directly appear. They doubtless perished with the other inhabitants of the city in the general massacre. Soldiers at such a time, while engaged in the sack and plunder of a city, are always excited to a species of insane fury, and take a savage delight in thrusting their pikes into all that come in their way.

Fate of Mon-yen

Mon-yen excused himself, when he arrived at the quarters of the emperor, for having thus abandoned the women to their fate by the alleged impossibility of saving them. He could not have succeeded, he said, in effecting his own retreat and that of the troops who went with him if he had been encumbered in his movements by such a company of women. The emperor accepted this excuse, and seemed to be satisfied with it, though, not long afterward, Mon-yen was accused of conspiracy against the emperor and was put to death.

Treasures

Mingan took possession of the imperial treasury, where he found great stores of silk, and also of gold and silver plate. All these things he sent to Genghis Khan, who remained still at the north at a grand encampment which he had made in Tartary.

Conquests Extended – Governors Appointed

After this, other campaigns were fought by Genghis Khan in China, in the course of which he extended his conquests still farther to the southward, and made himself master of a very great extent of country. After confirming these conquests, he selected from among such Chinese officers as were disposed to enter into his service suitable persons to be appointed governors of the provinces, and in this way annexed them to his dominions; these officers thus transferring their allegiance from the emperor to him, and covenanting to send to him the tribute which they should annually collect from their respective dominions. Everything being thus settled in this quarter, Genghis Khan next turned his attention to the western frontiers of his empire, where the Tartar and Mongol territory bordered on Turkestan and the dominions of the Mohammedans.

Chapter XVII
The Sultan Mohammed
1217

X

THE PORTION OF CHINA which Genghis Khan had added to his dominions by the conquests described in the last chapter was called Katay, and the possession of it, added to the extensive territories which were previously under his sway, made his empire very vast. The country which he now held, either under his direct government, or as tributary provinces and kingdoms, extended north and south through the whole interior of Asia, and from the shores of the Japan and China Seas on the east, nearly to the Caspian Sea on the west, a distance of nearly 3,000 miles.

Sultan Mohammed – Karazm

Beyond his western limits lay Turkestan and other countries governed by the Mohammedans. Among the other Mohammedan princes there was a certain Sultan Mohammed, a great and very powerful sovereign, who reigned over an extensive region in the neighbourhood of the Caspian Sea, though the principal seat of his power was a country called Karazm. He was, in consequence, sometimes styled Mohammed Karazm.

Proposed Embassy

It might perhaps have been expected that Genghis Khan, having subdued all the rivals within his reach in the eastern part of Asia, and being strong and secure in the possession of his power, would have found some pretext for making war upon the sultan, with a view of conquering his territories too, and adding the countries bordering on the Caspian to his dominions. But, for some reason or other, he concluded, in this instance, to adopt a different policy. Whether it was that he was tired of war and wished for repose, or whether the sultan's dominions were too remote, or his power too great to make it prudent to attack him, he determined on sending an embassy instead of an army, with a view of proposing to the sultan a treaty of friendship and alliance.

The time when this embassy was sent was in the year 1217, and the name of the principal ambassador was Makinut.

Makinut and His Suite

Makinut set out on his mission accompanied by a large retinue of attendants and guards. The journey occupied several weeks, but at length he arrived in the sultan's dominions. Soon after his arrival he was admitted to an audience of the sultan, and there, accompanied by his own secretaries, and in the presence of all the chief officers of the sultan's court, he delivered his message.

Speech of the Ambassador

He gave an account in his speech of the recent victories which his sovereign, Genghis Khan, had won, and of the great extension which his empire had in consequence attained. He was now become master, he said, of all the countries of Central Asia, from the eastern extremity of the continent up to the frontiers of the sultan's dominions, and having thus become the sultan's neighbour, he was desirous of entering into a treaty of amity and alliance with him, which would be obviously for the mutual interest of both. He had accordingly been sent an ambassador to the sultan's court to propose such an alliance. In offering it, the emperor, he said, was actuated by a feeling of the sincerest goodwill. He wished the sultan to consider him as a father, and he would look upon the sultan as a son.

The Sultan Not Pleased

According to the patriarchal ideas of government which prevailed in those days, the relation of father to son involved not merely the idea of a tie of affection connecting an older with a younger person, but it implied something of pre-eminence and authority on the one part, and dependence and subjection on the other. Perhaps Genghis Khan did not mean his proposition to be understood in this sense, but made it solely in reference to the disparity between his own and the sultan's years, for he was himself now becoming considerably advanced in life. However this may be, the sultan was at first not at all pleased with the proposition in the form in which the ambassador made it.

Private Interview

He, however, listened quietly to Makinut's words, and said nothing until the public audience was ended. He then took Makinut alone into another apartment in order to have some quiet conversation with him. He first asked him to tell him the exact state of the case in respect to all the pretended victories which Genghis Khan had gained, and, in order to propitiate him and induce him to reveal the honest truth, he made him a present of a rich scarf, splendidly adorned with jewels.

Conversation

'How is it?' said he; 'has the emperor really made all those conquests, and is his empire as extensive and powerful as he pretends? Tell me the honest truth about it.'

'What I have told your majesty is the honest truth about it,' replied Makinut. 'My master the emperor is as powerful as I have represented him, and this your majesty will soon find out in case you come to have any difficulty with him.'

Anger of the Sultan

This bold and defiant language on the part of the ambassador greatly increased the irritation which the sultan felt before. He seemed much incensed, and replied in a very angry manner.

'I know not what your master means,' said he, 'by sending such messages to me, telling me of the provinces that he has conquered, and boasting of his power, or upon what ground he pretends to be greater than I, and expects that I shall honour him as my father, and be content to be treated by him only as his son. Is he so very great a personage as this?'

Makinut Returns a Soft Answer

Makinut now found that perhaps he had spoken a little too plainly, and he began immediately to soften and modify what he had said, and to compliment the sultan himself, who, as he was well aware, was really superior in power and glory to Genghis Khan, notwithstanding the great extension to which the empire of the latter had recently attained. He also begged that the sultan would not be angry with him for delivering the message with which he had been intrusted. He was only a servant, he said, and he was bound to obey the orders of his master. He assured the sultan, moreover, that if any unfavourable construction could by possibility be put upon the language which the emperor had used, no such meaning was designed on his part, but that in sending the embassage, and in everything connected with it, the emperor had acted with the most friendly and honourable intentions.

The Sultan Is Appeased

By means of conciliating language like this the sultan was at length appeased, and he finally was induced to agree to everything which the ambassador proposed. A treaty of peace and commerce was drawn up and signed, and, after everything was concluded, Makinut returned to the Mongol country loaded with presents, some of which were for himself and his attendants, and others were for Genghis Khan.

He was accompanied, too, by a caravan of merchants, who, in consequence of the new treaty, were going into the country of Genghis Khan with their goods, to see what they could do in the new market thus opened to them. This caravan travelled in company with Makinut on his return, in order to avail themselves of the protection which the guard that attended him could afford in passing through the intervening countries. These countries being filled with hordes of Tartars, who were very little under the dominion of law, it would have been unsafe for a caravan of rich merchandise to pass through them without an escort.

Genghis Khan is Pleased

Genghis Khan was greatly pleased with the result of his embassy. He was also much gratified with the presents that the sultan had sent him, which consisted of costly stuffs for garments, beautiful and highly wrought arms, precious stones and other similar articles. He welcomed the merchants too, and opened facilities for them to travel freely throughout his dominions and dispose of their goods.

Opening of the Trade

In order that future caravans might go and come at all times in safety, he established guards along the roads between his country and that of the sultan. These guards occupied fortresses built at convenient places along the way, and especially at the crossing places on the rivers, and in the passes of the mountains; and there orders were given to these guards to scour the country in every direction around their respective posts, in order to keep it clear of robbers. Whenever a band of robbers was formed, the soldiers hunted them from one lurking-place to another until they were exterminated. In this way, after a short time, the country became perfectly safe, and the caravans of merchants could go and come with the richest goods, and even with treasures of gold and silver, without any fear.

The Exorbitant Merchants

At first, it would seem, some of the merchants from the countries of Mohammed asked too much for their goods. At least a story is told of a company who came very soon after the opening of the treaty, and who offered their goods first to Genghis Khan himself, but they asked such high prices for them that he was astonished.

'I suppose,' said he, 'by your asking such prices as these, you imagine that I have never bought any goods before.'

Their Punishment

He then took them to see his treasures, and showed them over 1,000 large chests filled with valuables of every description; gold and silver utensils, rich silks, arms and accoutrements splendidly adorned with precious stones and other such commodities. He told them that he showed them these things in order that they might see that he had had some experience in respect to dealings in merchandise of that sort before, and knew something of its just value. And that, since they had been so exorbitant in their demands, presuming probably upon the ignorance of those whom they came to deal with, he should send them back with all their goods, and not allow them to sell them anywhere in his dominions, at any price.

This threat he put in execution. The merchants were obliged to go back without selling any of their goods at all.

The Next Company – Their Artful Management

The next company of merchants that came, having heard of the adventure of the others, determined to act on a different principle. Accordingly, when they came into the presence of the khan with their goods, and he asked them the prices of some of them, they replied that his majesty might himself fix the price of the articles, as he was a far better judge of the value of such things than they were. Indeed, they added that if his majesty chose to take them without paying anything at all he was welcome to do so.

This answer pleased the emperor very much. He paid them double price for the articles which he selected from their stores, and he granted them peculiar privileges in respect to trading with his subjects while they remained in his dominions.

Genghis Khan Fits Out a Company

The trade which was thus opened between the dominions of the sultan and those of Genghis Khan was not, however, wholly in the hands of merchants coming from the former country. Soon after the coming of the caravan last mentioned, Genghis Khan fitted out a company of merchants from his own country, who were to go into the country of the sultan, taking with them such articles, the products of the country of the Mongols, as they might hope to find a market for there. There were four principal merchants, but they were attended by a great number of assistants, servants, camel drivers, etc., so that the whole company formed quite a large caravan. Genghis Khan sent with them three ambassadors, who were to present to the sultan renewed assurances of the friendly feelings which he entertained for him, and of his desire to encourage and promote as much as possible the commercial intercourse between the two countries which had been so happily begun.

Mohammedans

The three ambassadors whom Genghis Khan selected for this service were themselves Mohammedans. He had several persons of this faith among the officers of his court, although the Mongols had a national religion of their own, which was very different from that of the Mohammedans; still, all forms of worship were tolerated in Genghis Khan's dominions, and the emperor was accustomed to take good officers into his service wherever he could find them, without paying any regard to the nature of their religious belief so far as their general duties were concerned. But now, in sending this deputation to the sultan, he selected the ambassadors from among the Mohammedans at his court, thinking that it would please the sultan better to receive his message through persons of his own religious faith. Besides, the three persons whom he appointed were natives of Turkestan, and they were, of course, well acquainted with the language of the country and with the country itself.

Messengers From the Court

Besides the merchants and the ambassadors, Genghis Khan gave permission to each of his wives, and also to each of the great lords of his court, to send a servant or messenger with the caravan, to select and purchase for their masters and mistresses whatever they might find most curious or useful in the Mohammedan cities which the caravan might visit. The lords and ladies were all very glad to avail themselves of the opportunity thus afforded them.

Large Party

All these persons, the ambassadors and their suite, the merchants and their servants and the special messengers sent by the lords and ladies of the court, formed, as may well be supposed, a very numerous company. It is said that the caravan, when ready to commence its march, contained no less than 450 persons.

Roads Doubly Guarded

Everything being at last made ready, the caravan set out on its long journey. It was accompanied by a suitable escort, and, in order to provide still more effectually for the safety of the rich merchandise and the valuable lives committed to it, Genghis Khan sent on orders beforehand to all the military stations on the way, directing the captains to double the guard on their respective sections of the road while the caravan was passing.

By means of these and other similar precautions the expedition accomplished the journey in safety, and arrived without any misfortune in the Mohammedan country. Very serious misfortunes, however, awaited them there immediately after their arrival, arising out of a train of events which had been for some time in progress, and which I must now go back a little to describe.

The Calif of Bagdad

It seems that some difference had arisen some time before this between the Sultan Mohammed and the Calif of Bagdad, who was the great head of the Mohammedan power. Mohammed applied to the calif to grant him certain privileges and powers which had occasionally been bestowed on other sultans who had rendered great services to the Mohammedan empire. He claimed that he had merited these rewards by the services which he had rendered. He had conquered, he said, more than 100 princes and chieftains, and had cut off their heads and annexed their territories to his dominions, thus greatly enlarging and extending the Mohammedan power.

Mohammed's Demand and the Calif's Reply

Mohammed made this demand of the calif through the medium of an ambassador whom he sent to Bagdad. The calif, after hearing what the ambassador had to say, refused to comply. He said that the services which Mohammed had rendered were not of sufficient importance and value to merit the honours and privileges which Mohammed demanded. But, although he thus declined complying with Mohammed's request, he showed a disposition to treat the sultan himself with all proper deference by sending an ambassador of his own to accompany Mohammed's ambassador on his return, with instructions to communicate the reply which the calif felt bound to make in a respectful and courteous manner.

The Sultan Calls a Council – Mohammed's Plan for Revenge

Mohammed received the calif's ambassador very honourably, and in his presence concealed the anger which the answer of the calif excited in his mind. As soon as the ambassador was gone, however, he convened a grand council of all the great chieftains, generals and ministers of state in his dominions, and announced to them his determination to raise an army and march to Bagdad, with a view of deposing the calif and reigning in his stead. The great personages assembled at the council were very ready to enter into this scheme, for they knew that if it was successful there would be a great many honours and a great deal of booty that would fall to their share in the final distribution of the spoil. So they all engaged with great zeal in aiding the sultan to form and equip his army.

In due time the expedition was ready, and the sultan commenced his march. But, as often happens in such cases, the preparations had been hindered by various causes of delay, and it was too late in the season when the army began to move. The forces moved slowly, too, after they commenced their march, so that the winter came on while they were among the passes of the mountains. The winter was unusually severe, and the troops suffered so much from the frosts and the rains, and from the various hardships to which they were in consequence exposed, that the sultan found it impossible to go on. He was consequently obliged to return, and begin his work over again. And the worst of it was, that the calif was now aware of his designs, and would be able, he knew, before the next season, to take effectual measures to defend himself.

The Calif's Plans

When the calif heard of the misfortunes which had befallen the sultan's army, and his narrow escape from the dangers of a formidable invasion, he was at first overjoyed, and he resolved at once on making war upon the rebellious sultan. In forming his plans for the campaign, the idea occurred to him of endeavouring to incite Genghis Khan to invade the sultan's dominions from the east while he himself attacked him from the west; for Bagdad, the capital of the calif, was to the westward of the sultan' country, as the empire of the Mongols was to the eastward of it.

Objections to Them

But when the calif proposed his plan to his counsellors, some of them objected to it very strenuously. The sultan and the people of his country were, like the calif himself, Mohammedans, while the Mongols were of another religion altogether, or, as the Mohammedans called them, unbelievers or infidels; and the counsellors who objected to the calif's proposal said that it would be very wrong to bring the enemies of God into the country of the faithful to guard against a present and temporary danger, and thereby, perhaps, in the end, occasion the ruin both of their religion and their empire. It would be an impious deed, they thought, thus to bring in a horde of barbarian infidels to wage war with them against their brethren.

Arguments of the Calif

To this the calif replied that the emergency was so critical that they were justified in availing themselves of any means that offered to save themselves from the ruin with which they were threatened. And as to the possibility that Genghis Khan, if admitted to the country as their ally, would in the end turn his arms against them, he said that they must watch, and take measures to guard against such a danger. Besides, he would rather have an open unbeliever like Genghis Khan for a foe, than a Mohammedan traitor and rebel like the sultan. He added, moreover, that he did not believe that the Mongol emperor felt any animosity or ill will against the Mohammedans or against their faith. It was evident, indeed, that he did not, for he had a great many Mohammedans in his dominions, and he allowed them to live there without molestation. He even had Mohammedan officers of very high rank in his court.

So it was finally decided to send a message and invite him to join the calif in making war on the sultan.

Message to Genghis Khan – Artful Device

The difficulty was now to contrive some means by which this message could be conveyed through the sultan's territories, which, of course, lay between the dominions of the calif and those of Genghis Khan. To accomplish this purpose the calif resorted to a very singular device. Instead of writing his communication in a letter, he caused it to be pricked with a needle and some indigo, by a sort of tattooing process, upon the messenger's head, in such a manner that it was concealed by his hair. The messenger was then disguised as a countryman and sent forth. He succeeded in accomplishing the journey in safety, and when he arrived Genghis Khan had only to cause his head to be shaved, when the inscription containing the calif's proposal to him at once became legible.

This method of making the communication was considered very safe, for even if, from any accident, the man had been intercepted on the way, on suspicion of his being a messenger, the sultan's men would have found nothing, in searching him, to confirm their suspicions, for it is not at all probable that they would have thought of looking for a letter among his hair.

The Answer of Genghis Khan

Genghis Khan was well pleased to receive the proposals of the calif, but he sent back word in reply that he could not at present engage in any hostile movement against the sultan on account of the treaty of peace and commerce which he had recently established with him. So long as the sultan observed the stipulations of the treaty, he felt bound in honour, he said, not to break it. He knew, however, he added, that the restless spirit of the sultan would not long allow things to remain in the posture they were then in, and that on the first occasion given he would not fail to declare war against him.

Things were in this state when the grand caravan of merchants and ambassadors which Genghis Khan had sent arrived at the frontiers of the sultan's dominions.

The Caravan Arrives at Otrar – The Governor's Treachery

After passing the frontier, the first important place which they reached was a city called Otrar. They were received very courteously by the governor of this place, and were much pleased with the opportunity afforded them to rest from the fatigues of their long journey. It seems, however, after all, that the governor's friendship for his guests was only pretended, for he immediately wrote to the sultan, informing him that a party of persons had arrived at his city from the Mongol country who pretended to be merchants and ambassadors, but that he believed that they were spies, for they were extremely inquisitive about the strength of the garrisons and the state of the defences of the country generally. He had no doubt, he added, that they were emissaries sent by Genghis Khan to find out the best way of invading his dominions.

One account states that the motive which induced the governor to make these representations to the sultan was some offense which he took at the familiar manner in which he was addressed by one of the ambassadors, who was a native of Otrar, and had known the governor in former times when he was a private person. Another says that his object was to have the expedition broken up, in order that he might seize for himself the rich merchandise and the valuable presents which the merchants and ambassadors had in their possession.

The Party Massacred

At any rate, he wrote to the sultan denouncing the whole party as foreign emissaries and spies, and in a short time he received a reply from the sultan directing him to put them all to death, or otherwise to deal with them as he thought proper. So he invited the whole party to a grand entertainment in his palace, and then, at a given signal, probably after most of them had become in some measure helpless from the influence of the wine, a body of his guards rushed in and massacred them all.

Or, rather, they attempted to massacre them all, but one of the merchants' men contrived in the confusion to make his escape. He succeeded in getting back into the Mongol country, where he reported what had happened to Genghis Khan.

Genghis Khan Hears the Tidings

Genghis Khan was greatly exasperated when he heard these tidings. He immediately called together his sons, and all the great lords and chieftains of his court, and recited to them the story of the massacre of the merchants in such a manner as to fill their hearts with indignation and rage, and to inspire them all with a burning thirst for revenge.

He Declares War

He also immediately sent word to the sultan that, since by so infamous an action he had violated all the engagements which had subsisted between them, he, from that instant, declared himself his mortal enemy, and would take vengeance upon him for his treacherousness and cruelty by ravaging his country with fire and sword.

This message was sent, it was said, by three ambassadors, whose persons ought to have been considered sacred, according to every principle of international law. But the sultan, as soon as they had delivered their message, ordered their heads to be cut off.

Preparations

This new massacre excited the rage and fury of Genghis Khan to a higher pitch than ever. For three days, it is said, he neither ate nor slept, and seemed almost beside himself with mingled vexation, grief and anger. And afterward he busied himself night and day with the arrangements for assembling his army and preparing to march, and he allowed himself no rest until everything was ready.

Chapter XVIII
The War with the Sultan
1217–18

Marshalling of the Army

GENGHIS KHAN MADE HIS PREPARATIONS for a war on an immense scale. He sent messengers in every direction to all the princes, khans, governors and other chieftains throughout his empire, with letters explaining to them the cause of the war, and ordering them to repair to the places of rendezvous which he appointed, with all the troops that they could raise.

Arms and Armor

He gave particular directions in respect to the manner in which the men were to be armed and equipped. The arms required were the sabre, the bow with a quiver full of arrows and the battle axe. Each soldier was also to carry a rope, ropes and cordage being continually in demand among people living on horseback and in tents.

The officers were to wear armour as well as to carry arms. Those who could afford it were to provide themselves with a complete coat of mail. The rest were to wear helmets and breastplates only. The horses were also to be protected as far as possible by breastplates, either of iron or of leather thick and tough enough to prevent an arrow from penetrating.

When the troops thus called for appeared at the place of rendezvous appointed for them, Genghis Khan found, as is said, that he had an army of 700,000 men!

Provision for Contingencies

The army being thus assembled, Genghis Khan caused certain rules and regulations, or articles of war, as they might be called, to be drawn up and promulgated to the troops. One of the rules was that no body of troops were ever to retreat without first fighting, whatever the imminence of the danger might be. He also ordered that where a body of men were engaged, if any subordinate division of them, as one company in a regiment, or one regiment in a battalion, should break ranks and fly before the order for a retreat should have been given by the proper authority, the rest were to leave fighting the enemy, and attack the portion flying, and kill them all upon the spot.

The emperor also made formal provision for the event of his dying in the course of the campaign. In this case a grand assembly of all the khans and chieftains of the empire was to be convened, and then, in the presence of these khans and of his sons, the constitution and laws of the empire, as he had established them, were to be read, and after the reading the assembly were to proceed to the election of a new khan, according to the forms which the constitution had provided.

The Army Commences Its March

After all these affairs had been arranged, Genghis Khan put his army in motion. He was obliged, of course, to separate it into several grand divisions, and to send the several divisions forward by different roads, and through different sections of the country. So large a body can never be kept together on a long march, on account of the immense quantity of food that is required, both for the horses and the men, and which must be supplied in the main by the country itself which they traverse, since neither horses nor men can carry food with them for more than a very few days.

Jughi's Division

Genghis Khan put one of the largest divisions under the command of his son Jughi, the prince who distinguished himself so much in the conflicts by which his father raised himself to the supreme power.

Jughi was ordered to advance with his division through Turkestan, the country where the Prince Kushluk had sought refuge, and which still remained, in some degree, disaffected toward Genghis Khan. Genghis Khan himself, with the main body of the army, took a more southerly route directly toward the dominions of the sultan.

Preparations of the Sultan

In the meantime, the sultan himself had not been idle. He collected together all the forces that he could command. When they were mustered, the number of men was found to be 400,000. This was a large army, though much smaller than that of Genghis Khan.

His Plan

The sultan set out upon his march with his troops to meet the invaders. After advancing for some distance, he learned that the army of Jughi, which had passed through Turkestan, was at the northward of his position, and he found that by turning in that direction he might hope to meet and conquer that part of the Mongol force before it could have time to join the main body. He determined at once to adopt this plan.

The Sultan Meets Jughi

He accordingly turned his course, and marched forward into the part of the country where he supposed Jughi to be. At length he came to a place where his scouts found, near a river, a great many dead bodies lying on the ground. Among the others who had fallen there was one man who was wounded, but was not dead. This wounded man told the scouts that the bodies were those of persons who had been slain by the army of Jughi, which had just passed that way. The sultan accordingly pressed forward and soon overtook them. Jughi was hastening on in order to join his father.

Jughi consulted his generals in respect to what it was best to do. They advised him to avoid a battle.

Opinion of the Generals

'We are not strong enough,' said they, 'to encounter alone the whole of the sultan's army. It is better that we should retreat, which we can do in an orderly manner, and thus join the main body before we give the enemy battle. Or, if the sultan should attempt to pursue us, he cannot keep his army together in doing so. They will necessarily become divided into detachments on the road, and then we can turn and destroy them in detail, which will be a much surer mode of proceeding than for us to attack them in the mass.'

Jughi was not willing to follow this advice.

Jughi's Decision

'What will my father and my brothers think,' said he, 'when they see us coming to them, flying from the enemy, without having fought them, contrary to his express commands? No. We must stand our ground, trusting to our valour, and do our best. If we are to die at all, we had better be slain in battle than in flight. You have done your duty in admonishing me of the danger we are in, and now it remains for me to do mine in trying to bring you out of it with honour.'

So he ordered the army to halt, and to be drawn up in order of battle.

The Battle Commenced

The battle was soon commenced, and it was continued throughout the day. The Mongols, though fewer in numbers, were superior to their enemies in discipline and in courage, and the advantage was obviously on their side, though they did not gain a decisive victory. Toward night, however, the sultan's troops evinced everywhere a disposition to give way, and it was with great difficulty that the officers could induce them to maintain their ground until the darkness came on and put an end to the conflict. When at length the combatants could no longer see to distinguish friend from foe, the two armies withdrew to their respective camps, and built their fires for the night.

Jughi Withdraws

Jughi thought that by fighting during this day he had done all that his father required of him to vindicate the honour of the army, and that now it would be most prudent to retreat, without risking another battle on the morrow. So he caused fresh supplies of fuel to be put upon the campfires in order to deceive the enemy, and then marched out of his camp in the night with all his men. The next morning, by the time that the sultan's troops were again under arms, he had advanced far on his march to join his father, and was beyond their reach.

His Reception by His Father

He soon rejoined his father, and was received by him with great joy. Genghis Khan was extremely pleased with the course which his son had pursued, and bestowed upon him many public honours and rewards.

After this, other great battles were fought between the two armies. At one of them, a great trumpet 15 feet long is mentioned among the other martial instruments that were used to excite the men to ardour in making the charge.

The Mongols Victorious – The Sultan's Plans

In these battles the Mongols were victorious. The sultan, however, still continued to make head as well as he could against the invaders, until at length he found that he had lost 160,000 of his men. This was almost half of his army, and the loss enfeebled him so much that he was convinced that it was useless for him any longer to resist the Mongols in the open field; so he sent off his army in detachments to the different towns and fortresses of his kingdom, ordering the several divisions to shut themselves up and defend themselves as well as they could, in the places assigned to them, until better times should return.

Flying Squadron

The sultan, however, did not seek shelter in this way for himself. He selected from his troops a certain portion of those who were most active and alert and were best mounted, and formed of them a sort of flying squadron with which he could move rapidly from place to place through the country, wherever his aid might be most required.

Genghis Khan

Genghis Khan, of course, now prepared to attack the cities where the several divisions of the sultan's army had entrenched themselves. He wished first to get possession of Otrar, which was the place where the ambassadors and the merchants had been massacred. But the city was not very large, and so, instead of marching toward it himself, he gave the charge of capturing it to two of his younger sons, whom he sent off for the purpose at the head of a suitable detachment.

He himself, with the main body, set off upon a march toward the cities of Samarcand and Bokhara, which were the great central cities of the sultan's dominions.

Chapter XIX
The Fall of Bokhara
1218–19

Description of the Town Bokhara

BOKHARA WAS A GREAT and beautiful city. It was situated in the midst of a very fine and fertile country, in a position very favourable for the trade and commerce of those days. It was also a great seat of learning and of the arts and sciences. It contained many institutions in which were taught such arts and sciences as were then cultivated, and students resorted to it from all the portions of Western Asia.

The city proper was enclosed with a strong wall. Besides this there was an outer wall, 30 miles in circumference, which enclosed the suburbs of the town, and also a beautiful region of parks and gardens, which contained the public places of amusement and the villas of the wealthy inhabitants. It was this peaceful seat of industry and wealth that Genghis Khan, with his hordes of ruthless barbarians, was coming now to sack and plunder.

Zarnuk

The first city which the Mongols reached on their march toward Bokhara was one named Zarnuk. In approaching it a large troop rode up toward the walls, uttering terrific shouts and outcries. The people shut the gates in great terror. Genghis Khan, however, sent an officer to them to say that it was useless for them to attempt to resist him, and to advise them to surrender at once. They must demolish their citadel, he said, and send out all the young and able-bodied men to Genghis Khan. The officer advised them, too, to send out presents to Genghis Khan as an additional means of propitiating him and inducing him to spare the town.

An Immediate Surrender

The inhabitants yielded to this advice. The gates were thrown open. All the young men who were capable of bearing arms were marshalled and marched out to the Mongol camp. They were accompanied by the older men among the inhabitants, who took with them the best that the town contained, for presents. Genghis Khan accepted the presents, ordered the young men to be enrolled in his army, and then, dismissing the older ones in peace, he resumed his march and went on his way.

Nur

He next came to a town named Nur. One of the men from Zarnuk served as a guide to show the detachment which was sent to summon the city a near way to reach it. Nur was a sort of sacred town, having many holy places in it which were resorted to by many pilgrims and other devotees.

Fate of Nur

The people of Nur shut the gates and for some time refused to surrender. But at last, finding that it was useless to attempt to resist, they opened the gates and allowed the Mongols to come in. Genghis Khan, to punish the inhabitants, as he said, for even thinking of resisting him, set aside a supply of cattle and other provisions to keep them from starving, and then gave up all the rest of the property found in the town to be divided among his soldiers as plunder.

The Siege of Bokhara Commenced

At length the army reached the great plain in which Bokhara was situated, and encamped before the town. Bokhara was very large and very populous, as may well be supposed from its outer wall of 30 miles in circuit, and Genghis Khan did not expect to make himself master of it without considerable difficulty and delay. He was, however, very intent on besieging and taking it, not only on account of the general wealth and importance of the place, but also because he supposed that the sultan himself was at this time within the walls. He had heard that the sultan had retreated there with his flying squadron, taking with him all his treasure.

This was, however, a mistake. The sultan was not there. He had gone there, it is true, at first, and had taken with him the most valuable of his treasures, but before Genghis Khan arrived, he had secretly withdrawn to Samarcand, thinking that he might be safer there.

The Sultan's Anxiety – Intercepted Letters

In truth, the sultan was beginning to be very much disheartened and discouraged. Among other things which occurred to disturb his mind, certain letters were found and brought to him, as if they had been intercepted, which letters gave accounts of a conspiracy among his officers to desert him and go over to the side of Genghis Khan. These letters were not signed, and the sultan could not discover who had written them, but the pretended conspiracy which they revealed filled his soul with anxiety and distress.

The Deserter

It was only a pretended conspiracy after all, for the letters were written by a man in Genghis Khan's camp, and with Genghis Khan's permission or connivance. This man was a Mohammedan and had been in the sultan's service; but the sultan had put to death his father and his brothers on account of some alleged offense, and he had become so incensed at the act that he had deserted to Genghis Khan, and now he was determined to do his former sovereign all the mischief in his power. His intimate knowledge of persons and things connected with the sultan's court and army enabled him to write these letters in such a way as to deceive the sultan completely.

The Outer Wall Taken

It was past midsummer when the army of Genghis Khan laid siege to Bokhara, and it was not until the spring of the following year that they succeeded in carrying the outer wall, so strongly was the city fortified and so well was it defended. After having forced the outer wall, the Mongols destroyed the suburbs of the town, devastated the cultivated gardens and grounds and pillaged the villas. They then took up their position around the inner wall, and commenced the siege of the city itself in due form.

Grand Sortie Made by the Garrison

The sultan had left three of his greatest generals in command of the town. These men determined not to wait the operations of Genghis Khan in attacking the walls, but to make a sudden sally from the gates, with the whole force that could be spared, and attack the besiegers in their intrenchments. They made this sally in the night, at a time when the Mongols were least expecting it. They were, however, wholly unsuccessful. They were driven back into the city with great loss. The generals, it seems, had determined to risk all on this desperate attempt, and, in case it failed, at once to abandon the city to its fate. Accordingly, when driven into the city through the gates on one side, they marched directly through it and passed out through the gates on the other side, hoping to save themselves and the garrison by this retreat, with a view of ultimately re-joining the sultan. They, however, went first in a southerly direction from the city toward the River Amoor. The generals took their families and those of the principal officers of the garrison with them.

Pursuit – The Fugitives Overtaken

The night was dark, and they succeeded in leaving the city without being observed. In the morning, however, all was discovered, and Genghis Khan sent off a strong detachment of well-mounted troops in pursuit. These troops, after about a day's chase, overtook the flying garrison near the river. There was no escape for the poor fugitives, and the merciless Mongols destroyed them almost everyone by riding over them, trampling them down with their horses' hoofs and cutting them to pieces with their sabres.

Surrender

In the meantime, while this detachment had been pursuing the garrison, Genghis Khan, knowing that there were no longer any troops within the city to defend it, and that everything there was in utter confusion, determined on a grand final assault; but, while his men were getting the engines ready to batter down the walls, a procession, consisting of all the magistrates and clergy, and a great mass of the principal citizens, came forth from one of the gates, bearing with them the keys of the city. These keys they offered to Genghis Khan in token of surrender, and begged him to spare their lives.

Conditions Made

The emperor received the keys, and said to the citizens that he would spare their lives on condition that, if there were any of the sultan's soldiers concealed in the city, they would give them up, and that they would also seize and deliver to him any of the citizens that were suspected of being in the sultan's interest. This they took a solemn oath that they would do.

The Governor of the Citadel

The soldiers, however – that is, those that remained in the town – were not delivered up. Most of them retired to the castle, which was a sort of citadel, and put themselves under the command of the governor of the castle, who, being a very energetic and resolute man, declared that he never would surrender.

There were a great many of the young men of the town, sons of the leading citizens, who also retired to the castle, determined not to yield to the conqueror.

Genghis Khan Enters the City

Genghis Khan, having thus obtained the keys of the city itself, caused the gates to be opened, and his troops marched in and took possession. He had promised the citizens that his soldiers should spare the lives of the people and should not pillage the houses on condition that the magistrates delivered up peaceably the public magazines of grain and other food to supply his army; also that all the people who had buried or otherwise concealed gold and silver, or other treasures, should bring them forth again and give them up, or else make known where they were concealed. This the people promised that they would do.

After having entered the town, Genghis Khan was riding about the streets on horseback at the head of his troop of guards when he came to a large and very beautiful edifice. The doors were wide, and he drove his horse directly in. His troops, and the other soldiers who were there, followed him in. There were also with him some of the magistrates of the town, who were accompanying him in his progress about the city.

The Emperor in the Mosque

After the whole party had entered the edifice, Genghis Khan looked around, and then asked them, in a jeering manner, if that was the sultan's palace.

'No,' said they, 'it is the house of God.'

The building was a mosque.

Desecration of the Mosque

On hearing this, Genghis Khan alighted from his horse, and, giving the bridle to one of the principal magistrates to hold, he went up, in a very irreverent manner, to a sacred place where the priests were accustomed to sit. He seized the copy of the Koran which he found there, and threw it down under the feet of the horses. After amusing himself for a time in desecrating the temple by these and other similar performances, he caused his soldiers to bring in their provisions, and allowed them to eat and drink in the temple, in a riotous manner, without any regard to the sacredness of the place, or to the feelings of the people of the town which he outraged by this conduct.

Genghis Khan Makes a Speech

A few days after this, Genghis Khan assembled all the magistrates and principal citizens of the town, and made a speech to them from an elevated stand or pulpit which was erected for the purpose. He began his speech by praising God, and claiming to be an object of his special favour, in proof of which he recounted the victories which he had obtained, as he said, through the Divine aid. He then went on to denounce the perfidious conduct of the sultan toward him in making a solemn treaty of peace with him and then treacherously murdering his merchants and ambassadors. He said that the sultan was a detestable tyrant, and that God had commissioned him to rid the earth of all such monsters. He said, in conclusion, that he would protect their lives, and would not allow his soldiers to take away their household goods, provided they surrendered to him fairly and honestly all their money and other treasures; and if any of them refused to do this, or to tell where their treasures were hid, he would put them to the torture, and compel them to tell.

The Inhabitants Give Up Everything – Surrender of the Citadel

The wretched inhabitants of the town, feeling that they were entirely at the mercy of the terrible hordes that were in possession of the city, did not attempt to conceal anything. They brought forward their hidden treasures, and even offered their household goods to the conqueror if he was disposed to take them. They were only anxious to save, if possible, their dwellings and their lives. Genghis Khan appeared at first to be pleased with the submissive spirit which they manifested, but at last, under pretence that he heard of some soldiers being concealed somewhere, and perhaps irritated at the citadel's holding out so long against him, he ordered the town to be set on fire. The buildings were almost all of wood, and the fire raged among them with great fury. Multitudes of the inhabitants perished in the flames, and great numbers died miserably afterward from want and exposure. The citadel immediately afterward surrendered, and it would seem that Genghis Khan began to feel satisfied with the amount of misery which he had caused, for it is said that he spared the lives of the governor and of the soldiers, although we might have expected that he would have massacred them all.

The Town Utterly Destroyed

The citadel was, however, demolished, and thus the town itself, and all that pertained to it, became a mass of smoking ruins. The property pillaged from the inhabitants was divided among the Mongol troops, while the people themselves went away, to roam as vagabonds and beggars over the surrounding country, and to die of want and despair.

What difference is there between such a conqueror as this and the captain of a band of pirates or of robbers, except in the immense magnitude of the scale on which he perpetrates his crimes?

News of the Fall of Otrar

The satisfaction which Genghis Khan felt at the capture of Bokhara was greatly increased by the intelligence which he received soon afterward from the two princes whom he had sent to lay siege to Otrar, informing him that that city had fallen into their hands, and that the governor of it, the officer who had so treacherously put to death the ambassadors and the merchants, had been taken and slain. The name of this governor was Gayer Khan. The sultan, knowing that Genghis Khan would doubtless make this city one of his first objects of attack, left the governor a force of 50,000 men to defend it. He afterward sent him an additional force of 10,000 men, under the command of a general named Kariakas.

Plans for the Defence of Otrar

With these soldiers the governor shut himself up in the city. He knew very well that if he surrendered or was taken he could expect no mercy, and he went to work accordingly strengthening the fortifications, and laying in stores of provisions, determined to fight to the last extremity. The captain of the guard who came to assist him had not the same reason for being so very obstinate in the defence of the town, and this difference in the situation of the two commanders led to difficulty in the end, as we shall presently see.

Sorties – Proposal Made to Genghis Khan

The Mongol princes began the siege of Otrar by filling up the ditches that encircled the outer wall of the town in the places where they wished to plant their battering rams to make breaches in the walls. They were hindered a great deal in their work, as is usual in such cases, by the sallies of the besieged, who rushed upon them in the night in great numbers, and with such desperate fury that they often succeeded in destroying some of the engines, or setting them on fire before they could be driven back into the town. This continued for some time, until at last the Mongol princes began to be discouraged, and they sent word to their father, who was then engaged in the siege of Bokhara, informing him of the desperate defence which was made by the garrison of Otrar, and asking his permission to turn the siege into a blockade – that is, to withdraw from the immediate vicinity of the walls, and to content themselves with investing the city closely on every side, so as to prevent anyone from going out or coming in, until the provisions of the town should be exhausted, and the garrison be starved into a surrender. In this way, they said, the lives of vast numbers of the troops would be saved.

But their father sent back word to them that they must do no such thing, but must go on and *fight their way* into the town, no matter how many of the men were killed.

The Siege Renewed – The Outer Walls Taken

So the princes began again with fresh ardour, and they pushed forward their operations with such desperate energy that in less than a month the outer wall, and the works of the besieged to defend it, were all in ruins. The towers were beaten down, the ramparts were broken and many breaches were made through which the besiegers might be expected at any moment to force their way into the town. The besieged were accordingly obliged to abandon the outer walls and retire within the inner lines.

Desperate Conflicts

The Mongols now had possession of the suburbs, and, after pillaging them of all that they could convert to their own use, and burning and destroying everything else, they advanced to attack the inner works; and here the contest between the besiegers and the garrison was renewed more fiercely than ever. The besieged continued their resistance for five months, defending themselves by every possible means from the walls, and making desperate sallies from time to time in order to destroy the Mongols' engines and kill the men.

Kariakas and the Governor

At length Kariakas, the captain of the guard, who had been sent to assist the governor in the defence of the town, began to think it was time that the carnage should cease and that the town should be surrendered. But the governor, who knew that he would most assuredly be beheaded if in any way he fell into the hands of the enemy, would not listen to any proposal of the kind. He succeeded, also, in exciting among the people of the town, and among the soldiers of the garrison, such a hatred of the Mongols, whom he represented as infidels of the very worst character, the enemies alike of God and man, that they joined him in the determination not to surrender.

Treason

Kariakas now found himself an object of suspicion and distrust in the town and in the garrison on account of his having made the proposal to surrender, and feeling that he was not safe, he determined to make a separate peace for himself and his 10,000 by going out secretly in the night and giving himself up to the princes. He thought that by doing this, and by putting the Mongols in possession of the gate through which his troops were to march out, so as to enable them to gain admission to the city, his life would be spared, and that he might perhaps be admitted into the service of Genghis Khan.

Punishment of Treason

But he was mistaken in this idea. The princes said that a man who would betray his own countrymen would betray *them* if he ever had a good opportunity. So they ordered him and all his officers to be slain, and the men to be divided among the soldiers as slaves.

The Mongols Enter the Town – Citadel Stormed

They nevertheless took possession of the gate by which the deserters had come out, and by this means gained admission to the city. The governor fled to the citadel with all the men whom he could assemble, and shut himself up in it. Here he fought desperately for a month, making continual sallies at the head of his men, and doing everything that the most resolute and reckless bravery could do to harass and beat off the besiegers. But all was in vain. In the end the walls of the citadel were so broken down by the engines brought to bear upon them, that one day the Mongols, by a determined and desperate assault made on all sides simultaneously, forced their way in, through the most dreadful scenes of carnage and destruction, and began killing without mercy every soldier that they could find.

Desperation of the Governor

The soldiers defended themselves to the last. Some took refuge in narrow courts and lanes, and on the roofs of the houses – for the citadel was so large that it formed of itself quite a little town – and fought desperately till they were brought down by the arrows of the Mongols. The governor took his position, in company with two men who were with him, on a terrace of his palace, and refused to surrender, but fought on furiously, determined to kill anyone who attempted to come near him. His wife was near, doing all in her power to encourage and sustain him.

Genghis Khan had given orders to the princes not to kill the governor, but to take him alive. He wished to have the satisfaction of disposing of him himself. For this reason, the soldiers who attempted to take him on the terrace were very careful not to shoot their arrows at him, but only at the men who were with him, and while they did so a great many of them were killed by the arrows which the governor and his two friends discharged at those who attempted to climb up to the place where they were standing.

Courage and Devotion of His Wife

After a while the two men were killed, but the governor remained alive. Yet nobody could come near him. Those that attempted it were shot, and fell back again among their companions below. The governor's wife supplied him with arrows as fast as he could use them. At length all the arrows were spent, and then she brought him stones, which he hurled down upon his assailants when they tried to climb up to him. But at last, so many ascended together that the governor could not beat them all back, and he was at length surrounded and secured, and immediately put in irons.

The Governor's Fate

The princes wrote word at once to their father that the town was taken, and that the governor was in their hands a prisoner. They received orders in return to bring him with them to Bokhara. While on the way, however, another order came requiring them to put the prisoner to death, and this order was immediately executed.

What was the fate of his courageous and devoted wife has never been known.

Chapter XX
Battles and Sieges
1219–20

X

Continuation of the War

AFTER THE FALL OF BOKHARA and Otrar, the war was continued for two years with great vigour by Genghis Khan and the Mongols, and the poor sultan was driven from place to place by his merciless enemies, until at last his cause was wholly lost, and he himself, as will appear in the next chapter, came to a miserable end.

During the two years while Genghis Khan continued the war against him, a great many incidents occurred illustrating the modes of warfare practiced in those days, and the sufferings which were endured by the mass of the people in consequence of these terrible struggles between rival despots contending for the privilege of governing them.

Saganak

At one time, Genghis Khan sent his son Jughi with a large detachment to besiege and take a certain town named Saganak. As soon as Jughi arrived before the place, he sent in a flag of truce to call upon the people of the town to surrender, promising, at the same time, to treat them kindly if they would do so.

Hassan – The Murdered Ambassador

The bearer of the flag was a Mohammedan named Hassan. Jughi probably thought that the message would be better received by the people of the town if brought to them by one of their own countrymen, but he made a great mistake in this. The people, instead of being pleased with the messenger because he was a Mohammedan, were very much exasperated against him. They considered him a renegade and a traitor; and, although the governor had solemnly promised that he should be allowed to go and come in safety, so great a tumult arose that the governor found it impossible to protect him, and the poor man was torn to pieces by the mob.

Jughi's Revenge

Jughi immediately assaulted the town with all his force, and as soon as he got possession of it he slaughtered without mercy all the officers and soldiers of the garrison, and killed also about one half of the inhabitants, in order to avenge the death of his murdered messenger. He also caused a handsome monument to be erected to his memory in the principal square of the town.

Jughi's General Policy

Jughi treated the inhabitants of every town that dared to resist with extreme severity, while those that yielded at once were, in some degree, spared and protected. The consequence of this policy was that the people of many of the towns surrendered without attempting to defend themselves at all. In one case, the magistrates and other principal inhabitants of a town came out to meet him a distance of two days' journey from them, bringing with them the keys of the town, and a great quantity of magnificent presents, all of which they laid at the conqueror's feet, and implored his mercy.

Account of a Stratagem – The Town Taken

There was one town which Jughi's force took by a kind of stratagem. A certain engineer, whom he employed to make a reconnaissance of the fortifications, reported that there was a place on one side of the town where there was a ditch full of water outside of the wall, which made the access to the wall there so difficult that the garrison would not be at all likely to expect an attack on that side. The engineer proposed a plan for building some light bridges, which the soldiers were to throw over the ditch in the night, after having drawn off the attention of the garrison to some other quarter, and then, mounting upon the walls by means of ladders, to get into the town. This plan was adopted.

The bridges and the ladders were prepared, and then, when the appointed night came, a feigned attack was made in the opposite part of the town. The garrison were then all called off to repel this pretended attack, and in this way the wall opposite to the ditch was left undefended. The soldiers then threw the bridges over the ditch, and planted the ladders against the wall, and before the garrison could get intelligence of what they were doing they had made their way into the town, and had opened one of the gates, and by this means the whole army got in.

The engineer himself, who had proposed the plan, went up first on the first ladder that was planted against the wall. To take the lead in such an escalade required great coolness and courage, for it was dark, and no one knew, in going up the ladder, how many enemies he might have to encounter at the top of it.

A Beautiful City

The next place which the army of Jughi approached was a quiet and beautiful town, the seat of several institutions of learning, and the residence of learned men and men of leisure. It was a very pleasant place, full of fountains, gardens and delightful pleasure grounds, with many charming public and private promenades. The name of this place was Toukat, and the beauty and attractiveness of it were proverbial through all the country.

Toukat

Toukat was a place rather of pleasure than of strength, and yet it was surrounded by a wall, and the governor of it determined to make an effort to defend it. The garrison fought bravely, and they kept the besiegers off for three days. At the end of that time the engines of the Mongols had made so many breaches in the walls that the governor was convinced that they would soon get in, and so he sent to Jughi to ask for the terms on which he would allow them to surrender. Jughi replied that he would not now make any terms with him at all. It was too late. He ought to have surrendered at the beginning.

Toukat Taken – Arrangements for Plundering It

So the Mongol army forced its way into the town, and slaughtered the whole garrison without mercy. Jughi then ordered all the inhabitants, men, women and children, to repair to a certain place on the plain outside the walls. In obedience to this command, all the people went to the appointed place. They went with fear and trembling, expecting that they were all to be killed. But they found, in the end, that the object of Jughi in bringing them thus out of the town was not to kill them, but only to call them away from the houses, so that the soldiers could plunder them more conveniently while the owners were away. After being kept out of the town for a time they were allowed to return, and when they went back to their houses they found that they had been pillaged and stripped of everything that the soldiers could carry away.

Kojend – Timur Melek – His Preparations for Defence

There was another large and important town named Kojend. It was situated 200 or 300 miles to the northward of Samarcand, on the River Sir, which flows into Aral Lake. The governor of this city was Timur Melek. He was a very powerful chieftain, and a man of great military renown, having often been in active service under the sultan as one of the principal generals of his army. When Timur heard of the fall of Toukat, he presumed that his city of Kojend would be next attacked, as it seemed to come next in the way of the Mongol army; so he began to make vigorous preparations for defence. He broke up all the roads leading toward the town, and destroyed the bridges. He also laid in great supplies of food to maintain the inhabitants in case of a protracted siege, and he ordered all the corn, fruits and cattle of the surrounding country, which he did not require for this purpose, to be taken away and stowed in secret places at a distance, to prevent their falling into the hands of the enemy.

Engines and Battering Rams

Jughi did not himself attack this town, but sent a large detachment under the orders of a general named Elak Nevian. Elak advanced toward the city and commenced his operations. The first thing that was to be done was to rebuild a bridge over the river, so as to enable him to gain access to the town, which was on the opposite bank. Then he set up immense engines at different points along the line, some of which were employed to batter down the walls, and others, at the same time, to throw stones, darts and arrows over the parapets, in order to drive the garrison back from them. These engines did great execution. Those built to batter down the walls were of great size and power. Some of them, it was said, threw stones over the wall as big as millstones.

The Floating Batteries

Timur Melek was equally active in the defence of the town. He built a number of flat-bottomed boats, which might be called floating batteries, since they were constructed for throwing missiles of all sorts into the camp of the enemy. These batteries, it is said, were covered over on the top to protect the men, and they had portholes in the sides, like a modern man-of-war, out of which, not cannonballs and bombshells indeed, but arrows, darts, javelins and stones were projected. The boats were sent out, some on the upper side of the town and some on the lower, and were placed in stations where they could most effectually reach the Mongol works. They were the means of killing and wounding great multitudes of men, and they greatly disturbed and hindered the besiegers' operations.

The Morass – Obstinate Conflict

Still Elak persevered. He endeavoured to shut up the city on every side as closely as possible; but there was on one side a large morass or jungle which he could not guard, and Timur received a great many reinforcements, to take the place of the men who were killed on the walls, by that way. In the meantime, however, Elak was continually receiving reinforcements too from Prince Jughi, who was not at a great distance, and thus the struggle was continued with great fury.

The Pretended Deserters

At last, Timur contrived an ingenious stratagem, by which he hoped to cause his enemy to fall into a snare. It seems that there was a small island in the river, not far from the walls of the city, on which, before the siege commenced, Timur had built a fortress, to be held as a sort of advanced post, and had garrisoned the fortress with about 1,000 men. Timur now, in order to divert the attention of the Mongols from the city itself, sent a number of men out from the city, who pretended to be deserters, and went immediately to the Mongol camp. Of course, Elak questioned them about the defences of the city, in order to learn where the weak points were for him to attack. The pretended deserters advised him to attack this fortress on the island, saying that it could very easily be taken, and that its situation was such that, when it was taken, the city itself must surrender, for it completely commanded the place.

No More Stones

So Elak caused his principal engines to be removed to the bank of the river, opposite the island, and employed all his energies and spent all his ammunition in shooting at the fortress; but the river was so wide, and the walls of the fortress wore so thick and so high, that he made very little impression. At last, his whole supply of stones – for stones served in those days instead of cannonballs – was exhausted, and as the town was situated in an alluvial district, in which no stones were to be found, he was obliged to send 10 or 12 miles to the upland to procure a fresh supply of ammunition. All this consumed much time, and enabled the garrison to recruit themselves a great deal and to strengthen their defences.

Building of the Jetty – The Horsemen in the Water

The operations of the siege were in a great measure suspended while the men were obtaining a new supply of stones, and the whole disposable force of the army was employed in going back and forth to bring them. At length, an immense quantity were collected; but then the Mongol general changed his plan. Instead of throwing the stones from his engines toward the fortress on the island, which it had been proved was beyond his reach, he determined to build out a jetty into the river toward it, so as to get a standpoint for his engines nearer the walls, where they could have some chance of doing execution.

So he set his men at work to prepare fascines, bundles and rafts of timber, which were to be loaded with the stones and sunk in the river to form the foundation for the proposed bank. The men would bring the stones down to the bank in their hands, and then horsemen, who were ready on the brink, would take them, and, resting them on the saddle, would drive their horses in until they came near the place where the stones were to go, when they would throw them down and then return for others. In this way they could work upon the jetty in many parts at once, some being employed in building at the end where it abutted on the shore, while the horsemen were laying the foundations at the same time out in the middle of the stream. The work of the horsemen was very difficult and dangerous, on account of holes in the sandy bottom of the river, into which they were continually sinking. Besides this, the garrison on the walls were doing their utmost all the time to impede the work by shooting arrows, javelins, stones and fiery darts among the workmen, by which means vast numbers, both of men and horses, were killed.

The Mongols, however, persevered, and, notwithstanding all the opposition which the garrison made, they succeeded in advancing the mole which they were building so far that Timur was convinced that they would soon gain so advantageous a position that it would be impossible for him to hold out against them. So he determined to attempt to make his escape. His plan was to embark on board his boats, with all his men, and go down the river in the night.

Timur's Boats – The Fireproof Awnings

In order to prepare for this undertaking, he employed his men secretly in building more boats, until he had in all more than 70. These boats were kept out of sight, in hidden places in the river, until all were ready. Each of them was covered with a sort of heavy awning or roof, made of wet felt, which was plastered over with a coating of clay and vinegar. This covering was intended both to defend the men from missiles and the boats themselves from being set on fire.

The Fire Boats and the Bridge

There was one obstacle to the escape of the boats which it was necessary to remove beforehand, and that was the bridge which the Mongols had built across the river, just below the town, when they first came to besiege it. To destroy this bridge, Timur one night made a sally from one of the gates, and attacked the men who were stationed to guard the bridge. At the same time, he sent down the current of the river a number of great flat-bottomed boats, filled with combustibles of various kinds, mixed with tar and naphtha. These combustibles were set on fire before they were launched, and, as the current of the river bore them down one after another against the bridge, they set the wooden piers and posts that supported it on fire, while the guard, being engaged with the party which had sallied from the town, could not go to extinguish the flames, and thus the bridge was consumed.

The way being thus opened, Timur Melek very soon afterward embarked his family and the greater part of his army on board the boats in the night; and, while the Mongols had no suspicion of what was going on, the boats were launched, and sent off one after another swiftly down the stream. Before morning came all traces of the party had passed away.

Pursuit – Battle in the River

Very soon, however, the Mongol general heard how his intended prey had escaped him, and he immediately sent off a strong detachment to follow the southern bank of the river and pursue the fugitives. The detachment soon overtook them, and then a furious battle ensued between the Mongol horsemen on the banks and in the margin of the water and the men in the boats, who kept the boats all the time as near as possible to the northern shore.

Sometimes, however, when the stream was narrow, or when a rocky point projected from the northern shore, so as to drive the boats nearer to the Mongol side, the battle became very fierce and bloody. The Mongols drove their horses far into the water, so as to be as near as possible to the boats, and threw arrows, javelins and fiery darts at them, while the Mohammedans defended themselves as well as they could from their windows or portholes.

The Boats Aground

Things went on in this way for some time, until, at length, the boats arrived at a part of the river where the water was so shallow – being obstructed by sandbars and shoals – that the boats fell aground. There was nothing now for Timur to do but to abandon the boats and escape with his men to the land. This he succeeded in doing; and, after reaching the shore, he was able to form his men in array, on an elevated piece of ground, before Elak could bring up a sufficient number of men to attack him.

Timur's Adventures – He Finally Escapes

When the Mongols at length came to attack him, he beat them off in the first instance, but he was obliged soon afterward to leave the field and continue his retreat. Of course, he was hotly pursued by the Mongols. His men became rapidly thinned in number, some being killed, and others getting separated from the main body in the confusion of the flight, until, at last, Timur was left almost alone. At last, he was himself on the very point of being taken. There were three Mongols closely pursuing him. He turned round and shot an arrow at the foremost of the pursuers. The arrow struck the Mongol in the eye. The agony which the wounded man felt was so great that the two others stopped to assist him, and in the meantime Timur got out of the way. In due time, and after meeting with some other hairbreadth escapes, he reached the camp of the sultan, who received him very joyfully, loaded him with praises for the indomitable spirit which he had evinced, and immediately made him governor of another city.

The Governor's Family

In the meantime, some of the boats which had been abandoned by the soldiers were got off by the men who had been left in charge of them – one especially, which contained the family of Timur. This boat went quietly down the river, and conveyed the family to a place of safety.

Kojend Surrendered

The city of Kojend, from which Timur and his men had fled, was, of course, now without any means of defence, and it surrendered the very next day to the Mongols.

Chapter XXI
Death of the Sultan
1220

Pursuit of the Sultan

IN THE MEANTIME, while Jughi and the other generals were ravaging the country with their detachments, and besieging and capturing all the secondary towns and fortresses that came in their way, as related in the last chapter, Genghis Khan himself, with the main body of the army, had advanced to Samarcand in pursuit of the sultan, who had, as he supposed, taken shelter there. Samarcand was the capital of the country, and was then, as it has been since, a great and renowned city.

The Two Ladies – Character of the Queen Mother

Besides the sultan himself, whom Genghis Khan was pursuing, there were the ladies of his family whom he wished also to capture. The two principal ladies were the sultana and the queen mother. The queen mother was a lady of very great distinction. She had been greatly renowned during the lifetime of her husband, the former sultan, for her learning, her piety, the kindness of her heart and the general excellence of her character, so far as her dealings with her subjects and friends were concerned, and her influence throughout the realm had been unbounded.

At some periods of her life, she had exercised a great deal of political power, and at one time she bore the very grand title of *Protectress of the faith of the world*. She exercised the power which she then possessed, in the main, in a very wise and beneficial manner. She administered justice impartially. She protected the weak, and restrained the oppressions of the strong. She listened to all the cases which were brought before her with great attention and patience, and arrived almost always at just conclusions respecting them. With all this, however, she was very strict and severe, and, as has almost always been the case with women raised to the possession of irresponsible power, she was unrelenting and cruel in the extreme whenever, as she judged, any political necessity required her to act with decision. Her name was Khatun.

Her Retirement

Khatun was not now at Samarcand. She was at Karazm, a city which was the chief residence of the court. She had been living there in retirement ever since the death of her husband, the present sultan's father.

Samarcand – Fortifications of the Place

Samarcand itself, as has already been said, was a great and splendid city. Like most of the other cities, it was enclosed in a double wall, though, in this case, the outer wall surrounded the whole city, while the inner one enclosed the mosque, the palace of the sultan, and some other public buildings. These walls were much better built and more strongly fortified than those of Bokhara. There were 12 iron gates, it is said, in the outer wall. These gates were a league apart from each other. At every two leagues along the wall was a fort capable of containing a large body of men. The walls were likewise strengthened with battlements and towers, in which the men could fight under shelter, and they were surrounded by a broad and deep ditch, to prevent an enemy from approaching too near to them, in order to undermine them or batter them down.

Waterworks

The city was abundantly supplied with water by means of hydraulic constructions as perfect and complete as could be made in those days. The water was brought by leaden pipes from a stream which came down from the mountains at some distance from the town. It was conveyed by these pipes to every part of the town, and was distributed freely, so that every great street had a little current of water running through it, and every house a fountain in the court or garden. Besides this, in a public square or park there was a mound where the water was made to spout up in the centre, and then flow down in little rivulets and cascades on every side.

Gates and Towers

The gates and towers which have been described were in the outer wall, and beyond them, in the environs, were a great many fields, gardens, orchards and beautifully cultivated grounds, which produced fruits of all sorts, that were sent by the merchants into all the neighbouring countries. At a little distance the town was almost entirely concealed from view by these gardens and orchards, there being nothing to be seen but minarets, and some of the loftier roofs of the houses, rising above the tops of the trees.

Arrival of the Mongols

There were so many people who flocked into Samarcand from the surrounding country for shelter and protection, when they learned that Genghis Khan was coming, that the place would hardly contain them. In addition to these, the sultan sent over 100,000 troops to defend the town, with 30 generals to command them. There were 20 large elephants, too, that were brought with the army, to be employed in any service which might be required of them during the siege.

This army, however, instead of entering the city at once, encamped about it. They strengthened the position of the camp by a deep ditch which they dug, throwing up the earth from the ditch on the side toward the camp so as to form a redoubt with which to defend the ground from the Mongols. But as soon as Genghis Khan arrived, they were speedily driven from this post, and forced to take shelter within the walls of the city. Here they defended themselves with so much vigour and resolution that

Genghis Khan would probably have found it very difficult to take the town had it not been for dissensions within the walls. It seems that the rich merchants and other wealthy men of the city, being convinced that the place would sooner or later fall into the hands of the Mongols, thought it would be better to surrender it at once, while they were in a condition to make some terms by which they might hope to save their lives, and perhaps their property.

But the generals would not listen to any proposition of this kind. They had been sent by the sultan to defend the town, and they felt bound in honour, in obedience to their orders, to fight in defence of it to the last extremity.

A Deputation

The dissension within the city grew more and more violent every day, until at length the party of the inhabitants grew so strong and decided that they finally took possession of one of the gates, and sent a large deputation, consisting of priests, magistrates and some of the principal citizens, to Genghis Khan, bearing with them the keys of the town, and proposing to deliver them up to him if he would spare the garrison and the inhabitants. But he said he would make no terms except with those who were of their party and were willing to surrender. In respect to the generals and the soldiers of the garrison he would make no promises.

Massacre – Escape of the Governor

The deputation gave up the keys and Genghis Khan entered the city. The inhabitants were spared, but the soldiers were massacred wherever they could be found. A great many perished in the streets. A considerable body of them, however, with the governor at their head, retreated within the inner wall, and there defended themselves desperately for four days. At the end of that time, finding that their case was hopeless, and knowing that they could expect no quarter from the Mongols in any event, they resolved to make a sally and cut their way through the ranks of their enemies at all hazards. The governor, accordingly, put himself at the head of a troop of 1,000 horse, and, coming out suddenly from his retreat, he dashed through the camp at a time when the Mongols were off their guard, and so gained the open country and made his escape. All the soldiers that remained behind in the city were immediately put to the sword.

Forlorn Condition of the Sultan

In the meantime, the sultan himself, finding that his affairs were going to ruin, retreated from province to province, accompanied by as large a force as he could keep together, and vainly seeking to find some place of safety. He had several sons, and among them two whose titles were Jalaloddin and Kothboddin. Jalaloddin was the oldest, and was therefore naturally entitled to be his father's successor; but, for some reason or other, the queen mother, Khatun, had taken a dislike to him, and had persuaded her son, the sultan, to execute a sort of act or deed by which Jalaloddin was displaced, and Kothboddin, who was a great favourite of hers, was made heir to the throne in his place.

The sultan had other sons who were governors of different provinces, and he fled from one to another of these, seeking in vain for some safe retreat. But he could find none. He was hunted from place to place by detachments of the Mongols, and the number of his attendants and followers was continually diminishing, until at last he began to be completely discouraged.

The Sultan Sends Away His Treasures

At length, at one of the cities where he made a short stay, he delivered to an officer named Omar, who was the steward of his household, 10 coffers sealed with the royal signet, with instructions to take them secretly to a certain distant fortress and lock them up carefully there, without allowing any one to know that he did it.

These coffers contained the royal jewels, and they were of inestimable value.

His Flight and His Despondency

After this, one of his sons joined him with quite a large force, but very soon a large body of Mongols came up, and, after a furious battle, the sultan's troops were defeated and scattered in all directions; and he was again obliged to fly, accompanied by a very small body of officers, who still contrived to keep near him. With these he succeeded, at last, in reaching a very retired town near the Caspian Sea, where he hoped to remain concealed. His strength was now spent, and all his courage gone. He sank down into a condition of the greatest despondency and distress, and spent his time in going to the mosque and offering up prayers to God to save him from total ruin. He made confession of his sins, and promised an entire amendment of life if the Almighty would deliver him from his enemies and restore him to his throne.

Narrow Escape

At last, the Mongol detachment that was in pursuit of him in that part of the country were informed by a peasant where he was; and one day, while he was at his prayers in the mosque, word was brought to him that the Mongols were coming. He rushed out of the mosque, and, guided by some friends, ran down to the shore and got into a boat, with a view of escaping by sea, all retreat by land being now cut off.

Rage of His Pursuers

He had scarce got on board the boat when the Mongols appeared on the shore. The men in the boat immediately pushed off. The Mongols, full of disappointment and rage, shot at them with their arrows; but the sultan was not struck by any of them, and was soon out of the reach of his pursuers.

The sultan lay in the boat almost helpless, being perfectly exhausted by the terror and distress which he had endured. He soon began to suffer, too, from an intense pain in the chest and side, which gradually became so severe that he could scarcely breathe. The men with him in the boat, finding that he was seriously sick, made the best of their way to a small island named Abiskun, which is situated near the southeastern corner of the sea. Here they pitched a tent, and made up a bed in it, as well as they could, for the sufferer. They also sent a messenger to the shore to bring off a physician secretly. The physician did all that was in his power, but it was too late. The inflammation and the pain subsided after a time, but it was evident that the patient was sinking, and that he was about to die.

Visit From His Son Jalaloddin

It happened that the sultan's son, Jalaloddin, the one who had been set aside in favour of his brother Kothboddin, was at this time on the mainland not far from the island, and intelligence was communicated to him of his father's situation. He immediately went to the island to see him, taking with him two of his brothers. They were obliged to manage the business very secretly, to prevent the Mongols from finding out what was going on.

On the arrival of Jalaloddin, the sultan expressed great satisfaction in seeing him, and he revoked the decree by which he had been superseded in the succession.

His Dying Words

'You, my son,' said he, 'are, after all, the one among all my children who is best able to revenge me on the Mongols; therefore I revoke the act which I formerly executed at the request of the queen, my mother, in favour of Kothboddin.'

He then solemnly appointed Jalaloddin to be his successor, and enjoined upon the other princes to be obedient and faithful to him as their sovereign. He also formally delivered to him his sword as the emblem and badge of the supreme power which he thus conferred upon him.

Death and Burial

Soon after this the sultan expired. The attendants buried the body secretly on the island for fear of the Mongols. They washed it carefully before the interment, according to custom, and then put on again a portion of the same dress which the sultan had worn when living, having no means of procuring or making any other shroud.

Khatun at Karazm

As for Khatun, the queen mother, when she heard the tidings of her son's death, and was informed, at the same time, that her favourite Kothboddin had been set aside, and Jalaloddin, whom she hated, and who, she presumed, hated her, had been made his successor, she was in a great rage. She was at that time at Karazm, which was the capital, and she attempted to persuade the officers and soldiers near her not to submit to the sultan's decree, but to make Kothboddin their sovereign after all.

Her Cruelty to Her Captives

While she was engaged in forming this conspiracy, the news reached the city that the Mongols were coming. Khatun immediately determined to flee to save her life. She had, it seems, in her custody at Karazm 12 children, the sons of various princes that reigned in different parts of the empire or in the environs of it. These children were either held as hostages, or had been made captive in insurrections and wars, and were retained in prison as a punishment to their fathers. The queen mother found that she could not take these children with her, and so she ordered them all to be slain. She was afraid that the Mongols, when they came, might set them free.

Dissension

As soon as she was gone, the city fell into great confusion on account of the struggles for power between the two parties of Jalaloddin and Kothboddin. But the sultana, who had made the mischief, did not trouble herself to know how it would end. Her only anxiety was to save her own life. After various wanderings and adventures, she at last found her way into a very retired district of country lying on the southern shore of the Caspian, between the mountains and the sea, and here she sought refuge in a castle or fortress named Ilan, where she thought she was secure from all pursuit. She brought with her to the castle her jewels and all her most valuable treasures.

But Genghis Khan had spies in every part of the country, and he was soon informed where Khatun was concealed. So he sent a messenger to a certain Mongol general named Hubbe Nevian, who was commanding a detachment in that part of the country, informing him that Khatun was in the castle of Ilan, and commanding him to go and lay siege to it, and to take it at all hazards, and to bring Khatun to him either dead or alive.

Khatun's Escape – Her Obstinacy

Hubbe immediately set off for the castle. The queen mother, however, had notice of his approach, and the lords who were with her urged her to fly. If she would go with them, they said, they would take her to Jalaloddin, and he would protect her. But she would not listen to any such proposal. She hated Jalaloddin so intensely that she would not, even to save her life, put herself under his power. The very worst possible treatment, she said, that she could receive from the Mongols would be more agreeable to her than the greatest favours from the hand of Jalaloddin.

Cause of Her Hatred of Jalaloddin

The ground of this extreme animosity which she felt toward Jalaloddin was not any personal animosity to *him*; it arose simply from an ancient and long-continued dislike and hatred which she had borne against his mother!

So Khatun refused to retire from the danger, and soon afterward the horde of Mongols arrived, and pitched their camp before the castle walls.

The Siege of the Fortress

For three months, Hubbe and his Mongols continued to ply the walls of the fortress with battering rams and other engines, in order to force their way in, but in vain. The place was too strong for them. At length Genghis Khan, hearing how the case stood, sent word to them to give up the attempt to make a breach, and to invest the place closely on all sides, so as to allow no person to go out or to come in; in that way, he said, the garrison would soon be starved into a surrender.

The Governor's Hopes

When the governor of the castle saw, by the arrangements which Hubbe made in obedience to this order, that this was the course that was to be pursued, he said he was not uneasy, for his magazines were full of provisions, and as to water, the rain which fell very copiously there among the mountains always afforded an abundant supply.

Want of Rain

But the governor was mistaken in his calculations in respect to the rain. It usually fell very frequently in that region, but after the blockade of the fortress commenced, for three weeks there was not the smallest shower. The people of the country around thought this failure of the rain was a special judgment of heaven against the queen for the murder of the children, and for her various other crimes. It was, indeed, remarkable, for in ordinary times the rain was so frequent that the people of all that region depended upon it entirely for their supply of water, and never found it necessary to search for springs or to dig wells.

Great Suffering

The sufferings of the people within the fortress for want of water were very great. Many of them died in great misery, and at length the provisions began to fail too, and Khatun was compelled to allow the governor to surrender.

The Queen Made Captive

The Mongols immediately seized the queen, and took possession of all her treasures. They also took captive all the lords and ladies who had attended her, and the women of her household, and two or three of her great-grandchildren, whom she had brought with her in her flight. All these persons were sent under a strong guard to Genghis Khan.

Cruel Treatment of the Queen Mother

Genghis Khan retained the queen as a captive for some time, and treated her in a very cruel and barbarous manner. He would sometimes order her to be brought into his tent, at the end of his dinner, that he might enjoy his triumph by insulting and deriding her. On these occasions, he would throw her scraps of food from the table as if she had been a dog.

He took away the children from her too, all but one, whom he left with her a while to comfort her, as he said; but one day an officer came and seized this one from her very arms, while she was dressing him and combing his hair. This last blow caused her a severer pang than any that she had before endured, and left her utterly disconsolate and heartbroken.

Some accounts say that soon after this she was put to death, but others state that Genghis Khan retained her several years as a captive, and carried her to and fro in triumph in his train through the countries over which she had formerly reigned with so much power and splendour. She deserved her sufferings, it is true; but Genghis Khan was nonetheless guilty, on that account, for treating her so cruelly.

Chapter XXII
Victorious Campaigns
1220–21

X

Continued Conquests

AFTER THIS, Genghis Khan went on successfully for several years, extending his conquests over all the western part of Central Asia, while the generals whom he had left at home were extending his dominions in the same manner in the eastern portion. He overran nearly all of Persia, went entirely around the Caspian Sea, and even approached the confines of India.

Efforts of Jalaloddin

In this expedition toward India, he was in pursuit of Jalaloddin. Immediately after the death of his father, Jalaloddin had done all in his power to raise an army and carry on the war against Genghis Khan. He met with a great deal of embarrassment and difficulty at first, on account of the plots and conspiracies which his grandmother had organized in favour of his brother Kothboddin, and the dissensions among his people to which they gave rise. At last, in the course of a year, he succeeded, in some measure, in healing this breach and in raising an army; and, though he was not strong enough to fight the Mongols in a general battle, he hung about them in their march and harassed them in various ways, so as to impede their operations very essentially. Genghis Khan from time to time sent off detachments from his army to take him. He was often defeated in the engagements which ensued, but he always succeeded in saving himself and in keeping together a portion of his men, and thus he maintained himself in the field, though he was growing weaker and weaker all the time.

Jalaloddin Becomes Discouraged

At last he became completely discouraged, and, after signal defeat which he met with from a detachment which had been sent against him by Genghis Khan, he went, with the few troops that remained together, to a strong fortress among the mountains, and told the governor that it seemed to him useless to continue the struggle any longer, and that he had come to shut himself up in the fortress, and abandon the contest in despair.

The Governor's Advice

The governor, however, told him that it was not right for a prince, the descendant of ancestors so illustrious as his, and the inheritor of so resplendent a crown, to yield to discouragement and despondency on account of the reverses of fortune. He advised him again to take the field, to raise a new army and continue the contest to the end.

Jalaloddin determined to follow this advice, and, after a brief period of repose at the castle, he again took the field.

Renewed Exertions – Stratagem

He made great exertions, and finally succeeded in getting together about 20,000 men. This was a small force, it is true, compared with the numbers of the enemy; but it was sufficient, if well managed, to enable the prince to undertake operations of considerable importance, and Jalaloddin began to feel somewhat encouraged again. With his 20,000 men he gained one or two victories too, which encouraged him still more. In one of these cases, he defeated rather a singular stratagem which the Mongol general contrived. It seems that the Mongol detachment which was sent out in this instance against Jalaloddin was not strong enough, and the general, in order to make Jalaloddin believe that his force was greater than it really was, ordered all the felt caps and cloaks that there were in the army to be stuffed with straw, and placed on the horses and camels of the baggage, in order to give the appearance of a second line of reserve in the rear of the line of real soldiers. This was to induce Jalaloddin to surrender without fighting.

Quarrel About a Horse

But in some way or other Jalaloddin detected the deceit, and, instead of surrendering, fought the Mongols with great vigour, and defeated them. He gained a very decided victory, and perhaps this might have been the beginning of a change of fortune for him if, unfortunately, his generals had not quarrelled about the division of the spoil. There was a beautiful Arabian horse which two of his leading generals desired to possess, and each claimed it. The dispute became, at last, so violent that one of the generals struck the other in his face with the lash of his whip. Upon this, the feud became a deadly one. Both parties appealed to Jalaloddin. He did not wish to make either general an enemy by deciding in favour of the other, and so he tried to compromise the matter. He did not succeed in doing this; and one of the generals, mortally offended, went off in the night, taking with him all that portion of the troops which was under his command.

Jalaloddin did everything in his power to bring the disaffected general back again; but, before he could accomplish this purpose, Genghis Khan came up with a large force between the two parties, and prevented their effecting a junction.

Jalaloddin's Forces Divided

Jalaloddin had now no alternative but to retreat. Genghis Khan followed him, and it was in this way that, after a time, both the armies reached the banks of the Indus, on the borders of India.

Great Battle in the Defile

Jalaloddin, being closely pursued, took his position in a narrow defile near the bank of the river, and here a great battle was fought among the rocks and precipices. Jalaloddin, it is said, had only 30,000 men at his command, while Genghis Khan was at the head of an army of 300,000. The numbers in both cases are probably greatly exaggerated, but the proportion may perhaps be true.

It was only a small portion of the Mongol army that could get into the defile where the sultan's troops had posted themselves; and so desperately did the latter fight, that it is said they killed 20,000 of the Mongols before they gave in. In fact, they fought like wild beasts, with desperate and unremitting fury, all day long. Toward night it became evident to Jalaloddin that it was all over with him. A large portion of his followers were killed. Some had made their escape across the river, though many of those who sought to do so were drowned in the attempt. The rest of his men were completely exhausted and discouraged, and wholly unable to renew the contest on the following day.

Orders to Take Jalaloddin Alive

Jalaloddin had exposed himself very freely in the fight, in hopes, perhaps, that he should be killed. But Genghis Khan had given positive orders that he should be taken alive. He had even appointed two of his generals to watch carefully, and to see that no person should, under any circumstances, kill him. He wished to take him alive, in order to lead him through the country a prisoner, and exhibit him to his former subjects as a trophy of his victory, just as he had done and was still doing with the old queen Khatun, his grandmother.

He Takes Leave of His Family

But Jalaloddin was determined that his conqueror should not enjoy this pleasure. He resolved to attempt to save himself by swimming the river. He accordingly went first, breathless, and covered with dust and blood from the fight, to take a hurried leave of his mother, his wives and his children, who, as was customary in those countries and times, had accompanied him in his campaign. He found them in his tent, full of anxiety and terror. He took leave of them with much sorrow and many tears, trying to comfort them with the hope that they should meet again in happier times. Then he took off his armour and his arms, in order that he might not be impeded in crossing the river, reserving, however, his sword and bow, and a quiver full of arrows. He then mounted a fresh horse and rode toward the river.

His Escape Across the River

When he reached the bank of the river, the horse found the current so rapid and the agitation of the water so great that he was very unwilling to advance; but Jalaloddin spurred him in. Indeed, there was no time to be lost; for scarcely had he reached the shore when Genghis Khan himself, and a party of Mongols, appeared in view, advancing to seize him. They stopped on the bank when they saw Jalaloddin ride into the water among the rocks and whirlpools. They did not dare to follow him, but they remained at the waterside to see how his perilous adventure would end.

His Defiance of His Pursuers

As soon as Jalaloddin found that he was out of their reach, he stopped at a place where his horse found a foothold, and turned round toward his pursuers with looks of hatred and defiance. He then drew his bow, and began to shoot at them with his arrows, and he continued to shoot until all the arrows in his quiver were exhausted. Some of the more daring of the Mongols proposed to Genghis Khan that they should swim out and try to take him. But Genghis Khan would not allow them to go. He said the attempt would be useless.

'You can do nothing at all with him,' said he. 'A man of such cool and determined bravery as that will defy and defeat all your attempts. Any father might be proud to have such a son, and any son proud to be descended from such a father.'

Struggles of the Horse

When his arrows were all expended, Jalaloddin took to the river again; and his horse, after a series of most desperate struggles among the whirlpools and eddies, and the boiling surges which swept around the rocks, succeeded at length in carrying his master over. The progress of the horse was watched with great interest by Genghis Khan and his party from the shore as long as they could see him.

Night Spent in a Tree

As soon as Jalaloddin landed, and had recovered a little from the fatigue and excitement of the passage, he began to look around him, and to consider what was next to be done. He found himself entirely alone, in a wild and solitary place, which he had reason to fear was infested with tigers and other ferocious beasts of prey, such as haunt the jungles in India. Night was coming on too, and there were no signs of any habitations or of any shelter. So he fastened his horse at the foot of a tree, and climbed up himself among the branches, and in this way passed the night.

Jalaloddin Meets with Friends

The next morning, he came down and began to walk along the bank of the river to see what he could find. He was in a state of great anxiety and distress.

Suddenly, to his great relief and joy, he came upon a small troop of soldiers, accompanied by some officers, who had escaped across the river from the battle as he had done. Three of these officers were his particular friends, and he was overjoyed to see them. They had made their way across the river in a boat which they had found upon the bank at the beginning of the defeat of the army. They had spent the whole night in the boat, being in great danger from the shoals and shelving rocks, and from the impetuosity of the current. Finally, toward morning, they had landed, not far from the place where Jalaloddin found them.

Large Body of Men Escaped

Not long after this he came upon a troop of 300 horsemen, who had escaped by swimming the river at a place where the water was smoother, at some distance below. These men told him that about six miles farther down the stream there was a body of about 4,000 men who had made their escape in a similar manner. On assembling these men, Jalaloddin found himself once more at the head of a considerable force.

Timely Aid from Jamalarrazad

The immediate wants of the men were, however, extremely pressing, for they were all wholly destitute of food and of every other necessary, and Jalaloddin would have been greatly embarrassed to provide for them had it not been for the thoughtfulness and fidelity of one of the officers of his household on the other side of the river. This officer's name was Jamalarrazad. As soon as he found that his master had crossed the river, knowing, too, that a great number of the troops had attempted to cross besides, and that, in all probability, many of them had succeeded in reaching the other bank, who would all be greatly in want of provisions and stores the next morning, he went to work at once, during the night, and loaded a very large boat with provisions, arms, money and stuff to make clothing for the soldiers. He succeeded in getting off in this boat before his plan was discovered by the Mongols, and in the course of the next morning he reached the opposite bank with it, and thus furnished to Jalaloddin an abundant provision for his immediate necessities.

Jalaloddin was so much pleased with the conduct of Jamalarrazad in this affair that he appointed him at once to a very high and responsible office in his service, and gave him a new title of honour.

Fate of the Sultan's Family

In the meantime, Genghis Khan, on the other side of the river, took possession the next morning of Jalaloddin's camp. Of course, the family of the sultan fell into his hands. The emperor ordered all the males to be killed, but he reserved the women for a different fate. Among the persons killed was a boy about eight years old, Jalaloddin's oldest son.

Sunken Treasures

Jalaloddin had ordered his treasure to be sunk in the river, intending, probably, to come back and recover it at some future time. But Genghis Khan found out in some way where it was sunk, and he sent divers down for it, and thus obtained possession of it as a part of his booty.

Jalaloddin's End

After this, Jalaloddin remained five or six years in India, where he joined himself and his army with some of the princes of that country, and fought many campaigns there. At length, when a favourable opportunity occurred, he came back to his own country, and fought some time longer against the Mongols there, but he never succeeded in gaining possession of any substantial power.

Sieges – Logs for Ammunition

Genghis Khan continued after this for two or three years in the Mohammedan countries of the western part of Asia, and extended his conquests there in every direction. It is not necessary to follow his movements in detail. It would only be a repetition of the same tale of rapine, plunder, murder and devastation.

Sometimes a city would surrender at once, when the conqueror approached the gates, by sending out a deputation of the magistrates and other principal inhabitants with the keys of the city, and with magnificent presents, in hopes to appease him. And they usually so far succeeded in this as to put the Mongol soldiery in good humour, so that they would content themselves with ransacking and plundering the place, leaving the inhabitants alive.

At other times the town would attempt to resist. The Mongols would then build engines to batter down the walls, and to hurl great stones over among the besieged. In many instances there was great difficulty in obtaining a sufficient supply of stones, on account of the alluvial character of the ground on which the city stood. In such cases, after the stones found near were exhausted, the besiegers would cut down great trees from the avenues leading to the town, or from the forests near, and, sawing the trunk up into short lengths, would use the immense blocks thus formed as ammunition for the engines. These great logs of heavy wood, when thrown over the walls, were capable of doing almost as much execution as the stones, though, compared with a modern bombshell – a monstrous ball of iron, which, after flying four or five miles from the battery, leaving on its way a fiery train through the air, descends into a town and bursts into a thousand fragments, which fly like iron hail in every direction around – they were very harmless missiles.

Bringing Stones – Occupation of Slaves

In sawing up the trunks of the trees into logs, and in bringing stones for the engines, the Mongols employed the prisoners whom they had taken in war and made slaves of. The amount of work of this kind which was to be done at some of the sieges was very great. It is said that at the siege of Nishabur – a town whose inhabitants greatly offended Genghis Khan by secretly sending arms, provisions and money to Jalaloddin, after they had once surrendered to the Mongols and pretended to be friendly to them – the army of the Mongols employed 1,200 of these engines, all of which were made at a town at some distance from the place besieged, and were then transported, in parts, by the slaves, and put together by them under the walls. While the slaves were employed in works of this kind, they were sometimes protected by wooden shields covered with raw hides, which were carried before them by other slaves, to keep off and extinguish the fiery darts and arrows which were shot at them from the wall.

Protection Against Fire

Sometimes, too, the places where the engines were set up were protected by wooden bulwarks, which, together with the framework itself of the engines, were covered with raw hides, to prevent their being set on fire by the enemy. The number of raw hides required for this purpose was immense, and to obtain them the Mongols slaughtered vast herds of horses and cattle which they plundered from the enemy.

Precautions

In order to embarrass the enemy in respect to ammunition for their engines, the people of a town, when they heard that the Mongols were coming, used to turn out sometimes in mass, several days before, and gather up all the stones they could find, and throw them into the river, or otherwise put them out of the way.

Attempts at Resistance

In some cases, the towns that were threatened, as has already been said, did not attempt to resist, but submitted at once, and cast themselves on the mercy of the conqueror. In such cases the Mongol generals usually spared the lives of the inhabitants, though they plundered their property. It sometimes happened, too, that after attempting to defend themselves for some time, the garrison would become discouraged, and then would attempt to make some terms or conditions with the conqueror before they surrendered. In these cases, however, the terms which the Mongols insisted upon were often so hard that, rather than yield to them, the garrison would go on fighting to the end.

Account of Kubru – His Noble Spirit

In one instance, there lived in a town that was to be assailed a certain sheikh, or prince, named Kubru, who was a man of very exalted character, as well as of high distinction. The Mongol general whom Genghis Khan had commissioned to take the town was his third son, Oktay. Oktay had heard of the fame of the sheikh, and had conceived a very high respect for him. So he sent a herald to the wall with a passport for the sheikh, and for 10 other persons such as he should choose, giving him free permission to leave the town and go wherever he pleased. But the sheikh declined the offer. Then Oktay sent in another passport, with permission to the sheikh to take 1,000 men with him. But he still refused. He could not accept Oktay's bounty, he said, unless it were extended to all the Mohammedans in the town. He was obliged to take his lot with the rest, for he was bound to his people by ties too strong to be easily sundered.

Kubru Slain

So the siege went on, and at the end of it, when the town was carried, the sheikh was slain with the rest in the streets, where he stood his ground to the last, fighting like a lion.

Pusillanimity

All the Mohammedan chieftains, however, did not possess so noble a spirit as this. One chieftain, when he found that the Mongols were coming, caused himself to be let down with ropes from the wall in the night, and so made his escape, leaving the town and the garrison to their fate.

Sorties by the Garrisons

The garrisons of the towns, knowing that they had little mercy to expect from their terrible enemies, fought often very desperately to the last, as they would have done against beasts of prey. They would suddenly open the gates and rush out in large bands, provided with combustibles of all kinds and torches, with which they would set fire to the engines of the besiegers, and then get back again within the walls before the Mongols could recover sufficiently from the alarm and confusion to intercept them. In this manner they destroyed a great many of the engines, and killed vast numbers of men.

Desperation of the People

Still the Mongols would persevere, and, sooner or later, the place was sure to fall. Then, when the inhabitants found that all hope was over, they had become so desperate in their hatred of their foes that they would sometimes set the town on fire with their own hands, and throw themselves and their wives and children into the flames, rather than fall into the hands of their infuriated enemies.

Mode of Disposing of Prisoners

The cruelties which the Mongols perpetrated upon their unhappy victims when, after a long resistance, they finally gained possession of a town, were indeed dreadful. They usually ordered all the people to come out to an open space on the plain, and there, after taking out all the young and able-bodied men, who could be made useful in bringing stones and setting up engines, and other such labours, and also all the young and beautiful women, to be divided among the army or sold as slaves, they would put the rest together in a mass, and kill them all by shooting at them with arrows, just as if they had been beasts surrounded in a chase, excepting that the excitement and pleasure of shooting into such a mass of human victims, and of hearing the shrieks and cries of their terror, was probably infinitely greater to their brutal murderers than if it had been a herd of lions, tigers and wolves that they were destroying.

Prodigious Slaughter

It is said by the historians that in one case the number of people ordered out upon the plain was so great that it took four days for them to pass out and assemble at the appointed place, and that, after those who were to be spared had been separated from the rest, the number that were left to be slain was over 100,000, as recorded by the secretaries who made an enumeration of them.

In another case, the slaughter was so great that it took 12 days to count the number of the dead.

Atrocities

Some of the atrocities which were perpetrated upon the prisoners were almost too horrible to be described. In one case a woman, quite advanced in years, begged the Mongols to spare her life, and promised that, if they would do so, she would give them a pearl of great value.

The Pearl

They asked her where the pearl was, and she said she had swallowed it. The Mongols then immediately cut her down, and ripped her body open with their swords to find the pearl. They found it, and then, encouraged by this success, and thinking it probable that other women might have attempted to hide their jewels in the same way, they proceeded to kill and cut open a great number of women to search for pearls in their bodies, but they found no more.

Genghis Khan's Grandson Killed – His Mother's Revenge

At the siege of a certain city, called Bamiyan, a young grandson of Genghis Khan, wishing to please his grandfather by his daring, approached so near the wall that he was reached by an arrow shot by one of the archers, and killed. Genghis Khan was deeply affected by this event, and he showed by the bitterness of his grief that, though he was so utterly heartless and cruel in inflicting these woes upon others, he could feel for himself very acutely when it came to his turn to suffer. As for the mother of the child, she was rendered perfectly furious by his death. She thought of nothing but revenge, and she only waited for the town to be taken in order that she might enjoy it. When, at last, a practicable breach was made, and the soldiers began to pour into the city, she went in with the rest, and insisted that every man, woman and child should be put to death. Her special rage was directed against the children, whom she seemed to take special pleasure in destroying, in vengeance for the death of her own child. The hatred and rage which she manifested against children extended even to babes unborn, and these feelings she evinced by atrocities too shocking to be described.

The opinions which Genghis Khan entertained on religious subjects appear from a conversation which he held at one time during the course of his campaigns in Western Asia with some learned Mohammedan doctors at Bokhara, which was the great seat at that time of science and philosophy. He asked the doctors what were the principles of their religion. They replied that these principles consisted of five fundamental points:

Principles of the Mohammedan Faith

1. In believing in one God, the creator of all things, and the supreme ruler and governor of the universe.
2. In giving 1/40th part of their yearly income or gains to the poor.
3. In praying to God five times every day.
4. In setting apart one month in each year for fasting.
5. In making a pilgrimage to the temple in Mecca, there to worship God.

Genghis Khan's Opinion

Genghis Khan told them that he believed himself in the first of these articles, and he approved of the three succeeding ones. It was very well, he said, to give 1/40th of one's income to the poor, and to pray to God five times a day, and to set apart a month in the year for a fast. But as to the last article, he could not but dissent from it entirely, for the whole world was God's house, and it was ridiculous, he said, to imagine that one place could really be any more fitting than another as a place for worshiping him.

The Spirit of Religious Bigotry

The learned doctors were much dissatisfied with this answer. They were, in fact, more displeased with the dissent which the emperor expressed from this last article, the only one that was purely and wholly ritual in its character, than they were gratified with the concurrence which he expressed in all the other four. This is not at all surprising, for, from the times of the Pharisees down to the present day, the spirit of sectarianism and bigotry in religion always plants itself most strongly on the platform of externals. It is always contending strenuously for rites, while it places comparatively in the background all that bears directly on the vital and spiritual interests of the soul.

Chapter XXIII
Grand Celebrations
1221-24

The Great Hunting Party

WHEN GENGHIS KHAN FOUND that his conquests in Western Asia were in some good degree established and confirmed, he illustrated his victory and the consequent extension of his empire by two very imposing celebrations. The first was a grand hunt. The second was a solemn convocation of all the estates of his immense realm in a sort of diet or deliberative assembly.

The accounts given by the historians of both these celebrations are doubtless greatly exaggerated. Their description of the hunt is as follows:

Object of the Hunt

It was after the close of the campaign in 1221 that it took place, while the army were in winter quarters. The object of the hunt was to keep the soldiers occupied, so as to avoid the relaxation of discipline, and the vices and disorder which generally creep into a camp where there are no active occupations to engage the minds of the men. The hunt took place in a vast region of uninhabited country, which was infested with wild beasts of every kind. The soldiers were marched out on this expedition in order of war, as if it were a country occupied by armed men that they were going to attack. The different detachments were conducted to the different points in the outskirts of the country, from which they severally extended themselves to the right and left, so as completely to enclose the ground. And the space was so large, it is said, which was thus enclosed, that it took them several weeks to march into the centre.

The General Plan

It is true that in such a case the men would advance very slowly, perhaps only a few miles each day, in order that they might examine the ground thoroughly, and leave no ravine, thicket or other lurking-place, where beasts might conceal themselves, unexplored. Still, the circle was doubtless immensely large.

The Time Arrives

When the appointed morning at length arrived, the men at the several stations were arrayed, and they commenced their advance toward the centre, moving to the sound of trumpets, drums, timbrels and other such instruments of martial music as were in use in those days.

Orders

The men were strictly forbidden to kill any animal. They were only to start them out from their lurking-places and lairs, and drive them in toward the centre of the field.

Great numbers of the men were provided with picks, spades and other similar tools, with which they were to dig out the burrows and holes of such animals as should seek refuge underground.

Progress of the Operations

They went on in this way for some weeks. The animals ran before them, thinking, when they were disturbed by the men, that it was only a momentary danger, which they could easily escape from, as usual, by running forward into the next thicket; but soon the advancing line of the soldiers reached them there, and drove them out again, and if they attempted to turn to the right or the left they soon found themselves intercepted. Thus, as the circle grew narrower, and the space enclosed diminished, the animals began to find themselves mixing with one another in great numbers, and being now irritated and angry, they attacked one another in many instances, the strong falling upon and killing the weak. Thus, a great many were killed, though not by the hands of the soldiers.

Terror of the Animals

At last, the numbers became so great, and the excitement and terror of the animals so intense, that the soldiers had great difficulty in driving them forward. The poor beasts ran this way and that, half distracted, while the soldiers pressed steadily on behind them, and cut them off from every chance of escape by raising terrific shouts and outcries, and by brandishing weapons before them wherever they attempted to turn.

The Inner Circle

At length the animals were all driven into the inner circle, a comparatively small space, which had been previously marked out. Around this space double and triple lines of troops were drawn up, armed with pikes and spears, which they pointed in toward the centre, thus forming a sort of wall by which the beasts were closely shut in. The plan was now for the officers and khans, and all the great personages of the court and the army, to go into the circle, and show their courage and their prowess by attacking the beasts and slaying them.

Condition of the Beasts

But the courage required for such an exploit was not so great as it might seem, for it was always found on these occasions that the beasts, though they had been very wild and ferocious when first aroused from their lairs, and had appeared excessively irritated when they found the circle beginning to narrow around them, ended at last in losing all their spirit, and in becoming discouraged, dejected and tame. This was owing partly, perhaps, to their having become, in some degree, familiar with the sight of men, but more probably to the exhaustion produced by long-continued fatigue and excitement, and to there having been for so many days deprived in a great degree of their accustomed food and rest.

Thus in this, as in a great many other similar instances, the poor soldiers and common people incurred the danger and the toil, and then the great men came in at the end to reap the glory.

The Princes Enter the Ring

Genghis Khan himself was the first to enter the circle for the purpose of attacking the beasts. He was followed by the princes of his family, and by other great chieftains and khans. As they went in, the whole army surrounded the enclosure, and completely filled the air with the sound of drums, timbrels, trumpets and other such instruments, and with the noise of the most terrific shouts and outcries which they could make, in order to terrify and overawe the beasts as much as possible, and to destroy in them all thought and hope of resistance.

Intimidation of the Wild Beasts

And, indeed, so much effect was produced by these means of intimidation, that the beasts, it is said, became completely stupefied. 'They were so affrighted that they lost all their fierceness. The lions and tigers became as tame as lambs, and the bears and wild boars, like the most timorous creatures, became dejected and amazed.'

They Recover Their Ferocity When Attacked

Still, the going in of Genghis Khan and the princes to attack them was not wholly without danger; for, of course, it was a point of honour with them to select the most ferocious and fierce of the animals, and some of these, when they found themselves actually assailed, were aroused again, and, recovering in some degree their native ferocity, seemed impelled to make a last desperate effort to defend themselves. After killing a few of the lions, tigers and bears, Genghis Khan and his immediate suite retired to a place at one side of the enclosure, where a throne had been set up for the emperor on an eminence which afforded a good view of the field. Here Genghis Khan took his seat in order to enjoy the spectacle of the slaughter, and then an immense number of men were allowed to go in and amuse themselves with killing and destroying the poor beasts till they were perfectly satiated with the sight of blood and of suffering.

Petition of the Young Men – End of the Hunt

At last some of the khan's grandsons, attended by several other young princes, approached the throne where the emperor was seated, and petitioned him to order the carnage to cease, and to allow the rest of the animals to go free. This petition the emperor granted. The lines were broken up, the animals that had escaped being massacred made their way back into the wilds again, and the hunt was over.

The several detachments of the army then set out on their march back to the camp again. But so great was the scale on which this grand hunting expedition was conducted, that four months elapsed between the time of their setting out upon it till the time of their return.

The Assembly at Toukat

The grand diet or general assembly of the states of Genghis Khan's empire took place two or three years later, when the conquest of Western Asia was complete, and the sons of the emperor and all the great generals could be called together at the emperor's headquarters without much danger. The place chosen for this assembly was a vast plain in the vicinity of the city of Toukat, which has already been mentioned as one of the great cities conquered by Genghis Khan. Toukat lay in a central and convenient position for the purpose of this assembly. It was, moreover, a rich and beautiful city, and could furnish all that would be necessary for the wants of the assembly. The meeting, however, was not to be held in the city itself, but upon a great plain in the environs of it, where there was space for all the khans, with their numerous retinues, to pitch their tents.

Return of Genghis Khan's Sons

When the khans and chieftains began to assemble, there came first the sons of the king, returning from the various expeditions on which their father had sent them, and bringing with them magnificent presents. These presents, of course, consisted of the treasures and other valuables which they had taken in plunder from the various cities which had fallen into their hands. The presents which Jughi brought exceeded in value those of all the others. Among the rest, there was a herd of horses 100,000 in number. These horses had, of course, been seized in the pastures of the conquered countries, and were now brought to the emperor to be used by him in mounting his troops. They were arrayed in bands according to the colour, white, dappled grey, bay, black and spotted, of each kind an equal number.

The emperor received and welcomed his sons with great joy, and readily accepted their presents. In return, he made presents to them from his own treasuries.

The Khans Arrive – Grand Entertainment

After this, as other princes and khans came in, and encamped with their troops and followers on the plain, the emperor entertained them all with a series of grand banquets and public diversions of all sorts. Among other things a grand hunting party was organized, somewhat similar in the general plan to the one already described, only on a much smaller scale, of course, in respect to the number of persons engaged and the time occupied, while yet it greatly surpassed that one in magnificence and splendour. Several thousand beasts were slain, it is said, and a great number and variety of birds, which were taken by the falcons.

Drinks

At the end of the hunt a great banquet was given, which surpassed all the other feasts in munificence. They had on the tables of this banquet a great variety of drinks – not only rich wines from the southern countries, but beer, metheglin and also sherbet, which the army had learned to make in Persia.

Great Extent of the Encampment

In the meantime, the great space on the plain, which had been set apart for the encampment, had been gradually becoming filled up by the arrival of the khans, until at length, in every direction, as far as the eye could reach, the whole plain was covered with groups of tents and long lines of movable houses, brought on wheels. The ground which the encampment covered was said by the historians to have been seven leagues in extent. If the space occupied was anything at all approaching this magnitude, it could only be that the outer portions of it were occupied by the herdsmen and other servants of the khans, who had to take care of the cattle and horses of the troops, and to provide them with suitable pasture. Indeed, the great number of animals which these wandering tribes always took with them on their journeys rendered it necessary to appropriate a much larger space to their encampments than would have been otherwise required.

Laying Out the Encampment

It is surprising to us, who are accustomed to look upon living in tents as so exclusively an irregular and temporary expedient, to learn how completely this mode of life was reduced to a system in those days, and how perfect and complete all the arrangements relating to it were made. In this case, in the centre of the encampment, a space of two leagues in length was regularly laid out in streets, squares and marketplaces, like a town. Here were the emperor's quarters, with magnificent tents for himself and his immediate household, and multitudes of others of a plainer character for his servants and retainers. The tents of the other grand khans were nearby. They were made of rich materials, and ornamented in a sumptuous manner, and silken streamers of various colours floated in the wind from the summits of them.

The State Tent – The Throne

Besides these there was an immense tent, built for the assembly itself to hold its sessions in. This tent was so large, it is said, that it would contain 2,000 persons. It was covered with white, which made it very conspicuous. There were two entrance gates leading to the interior. One of them was called the imperial gate, and was for the use of Genghis Khan alone. The other was the public gate, and was used in general for the members of the assembly and for spectators.

Within the tent was erected a magnificent throne, intended for the use of the emperor during the sessions of the assembly.

Business Transacted

A great amount of important business was transacted by the assembly while it continued in session, and many important edicts were made by the emperor. The constitution and laws of the empire were promulgated anew, and all necessary arrangements made for the government of the various provinces both near and remote.

Leave-taking – The Assembly Is Dismissed

At length, when these various objects had been accomplished, and the business was concluded, the emperor gave audience individually to all the princes, khans, generals, governors of provinces and other grand dignitaries who were present on the occasion, in order that they might take their leave preparatory to returning to their several countries. When this ceremony was concluded the encampment was broken up, and the various khans set off, each at the head of his own caravan, on the road leading to his own home.

Chapter XXIV
Conclusion
1227

✘

AFTER THE GRAND CONVOCATION described in the last chapter, Genghis Khan lived only three years. During this time, he went on extending his conquests with the same triumphant success that had attended his previous operations. Having at length established his dominion in Western Asia on a permanent basis, he returned to the original seat of his empire in the East, after seven years' absence, where he was received with great honour by the Mongol nation. He began again to extend his conquests in China. He was very successful. Indeed, with the exception of one great calamity which befell him, his career was one of continued and unexampled prosperity.

Death of the Khan's Oldest Son

This calamity was the death of his son Jughi, his oldest, most distinguished and best-beloved son. The news of this event threw the khan into a deep melancholy, so that for a time he lost all his interest in public affairs, and even the news of victories obtained in distant countries by his armies ceased to awaken any joyful emotions in his mind.

Effects of This Calamity

The khan was now, too, becoming quite advanced in life, being about 64 years old, which is an age at which the mind is slow to recover its lost elasticity. He did, however, slowly recover from the effects of his grief, and he then went on with his warlike preparations. He had conquered all the northern portion of China, and was now making arrangements for a grand invasion of the southern part, when at length, in the spring of the year 1227, he fell sick. He struggled against the disease during the summer, but at length, in August, he found himself growing worse, and felt that his end was drawing nigh.

Plan for the Invasion of China

His mind was occupied mainly, during all this interval, by arranging the details of the coming campaign, and making known to the officers around him all the particulars of his plans, in order that they might carry them out successfully after his decease. He was chiefly concerned, as well he might be, lest the generals should quarrel among each other after he should be gone, and he continually exhorted them to be united, and on no account to allow discord or dissensions to creep in and divide them.

The Khan's Sons

His oldest son, next to Jughi, was Jagatay, but he was of a mild and amiable temper, and not so well qualified to govern so widely extended an empire as the next son, whose name was Oktay. The next son to Oktay, whose name was Toley, was with his father at the time when his sickness at last assumed an immediately alarming character.

His Sickness – Change for the Worse

This change for the worse, which convinced the emperor that his death was drawing nigh, took place one day when he was traveling with a portion of his army, being borne on a litter on account of his infirm and feeble condition. A halt was ordered, a camp was formed, and the great conqueror was borne to a tent which was pitched for him on the spot near the borders of the forest. The physicians and the astrologers came around him, and tried to comfort him with encouraging predictions, but he knew by the pains that he felt, and by other inward sensations, that his hour had come.

He accordingly ordered that all of his sons who were in the camp, and all the princes of his family, should be called in to his bedside. When they had all assembled, he caused himself to be raised up in his bed, and then made a short but very solemn address to them.

Farewell Address

'I leave you,' said he, 'the greatest empire in the world, but your preserving it depends upon your remaining always united. If discord steals in among you all will most assuredly be lost.'

He Claims the Right to Name His Successor

Then, turning to the great chieftains and khans who were standing by – the great nobles of his court – he appealed to them, as well as to the princes of his family, whether it was not just and reasonable that he, who had established the empire, and built it up wholly from the very foundations, should have the right to name a successor to inherit it after he was gone.

They all expressed a full assent to this proposition. His sons and the other princes of his family fell on their knees and said, 'You are our father and our emperor, and we are your slaves. It is for us to bow in submission to all the commands with which you honour us, and to render the most implicit obedience to them.'

The khan then proceeded to announce to the assembly that he had made choice of his son Oktay as his successor, and he declared him the Khan of Khans, which was the imperial title, according to the constitution.

The whole assembly then kneeled again, and solemnly declared that they accepted the choice which the emperor had made, and promised allegiance and fidelity to the new sovereign so soon as he should be invested with power.

Other Arrangements

The aged emperor then gave to his second son, Jagatay, a large country for his kingdom, which, however, he was, of course, to hold under the general sovereignty of his brother. He also appointed his son Toley, who was then present, to act as regent until Oktay should return.

Death of the Emperor

The assembly was then dismissed, and very soon afterward the great conqueror died.

Toley, of course, immediately entered upon his office as regent, and under his direction the body of his father was interred, with great magnificence, under a venerable tree, where the khan had rested himself with great satisfaction a few days before he was taken sick.

His Grave and Monument

The spot was a very beautiful one, and in due time a magnificent monument was erected over the grave. Trees were afterward planted around the spot, and other improvements were made in the grounds, by which it became, at length, it was said, one of the finest sepulchres in the world.

Visits of Condolence to the New Emperor

As soon as Oktay, whom the emperor had designated as his successor, returned home, he was at once proclaimed emperor, and established himself at his father's court. The news of the old emperor's death rapidly spread throughout Asia, and a succession of ambassadors were sent from all the provinces, principalities and kingdoms throughout the empire, and also from such contiguous states as desired to maintain friendly relations with the new monarch, to bring addresses and messages of condolence from their respective rulers. And so great was the extent of country from which these ambassadors came that a period of six months was consumed before these melancholy ceremonies were ended.

Fate of the Empire

The fate of the grand empire which Genghis Khan established was the same with that of all others that have arisen in the world, from time to time, by the extension of the power of great military commanders over widely separated and heterogeneous nations. The sons and successors to whom the vast possessions descended soon quarrelled among themselves, and the immense fabric fell to pieces in less time than it had taken to construct it.

The Mongols: A History

ABBOTT'S BOOK IS WHAT IT IS and does not pretend to be otherwise. Today it is still quite useful as an introduction or primer to the study of Chinggis Khan's life, one that defers more robust treatment and fine detail to other more meticulous books. One early such book is Jeremiah Curtin's *The Mongols: A History*, originally published in 1908.

Curtin, a careful and meticulous scholar and translator whose passing President Theodore Roosevelt mourned as having 'robbed America of one of her two or three foremost scholars' (Roosevelt even wrote the Foreword for Curtin's book on Chinggis Khan), wrote not just a biography of Chinggis Khan but a history of the entire Mongol World Empire. His biographical coverage of the career of Chinggis Khan closely follows translations of *The Secret History of the Mongols* (not then fully available in careful English translation directly from the Mongolian-language original), but he occasionally intersperses the biographical narrative with background chapters, such as Chapter V, part of which is on China's Tang dynasty (618–907 CE). His biographical coverage of Chinggis Khan concludes with Chapter VIII; the rest of the book, to its final page 412, covers the course of the Mongol World Empire after the Great Khan's death. Thus, one third of Curtin's book is on Chinggis Khan himself, while the other two thirds are on the later empire. All of the chapters on the Great Khan can be read with profit by scholars and general readers who want to know more about the founder of the most extensive and expansive empire the world has ever known.

Included from Curtin in this reader are his Chapter II on Chinggis Khan's youth until his struggle with Jamuka, and Chapters VI and VII on Chinggis Khan's conquests and depredations in Islamic Central Asia, for which he is the most infamous.

Together the books by Abbott and Curtin will put readers in good stead to digest recent rigorous scholarship on Chinggis Khan based on primary historical records in their original languages. After Abbott and Curtin, curious readers who want to know more will certainly want to consult what remains the nonpareil biography of Chinggis Khan – Paul Ratchnevsky's masterwork *Genghis Khan: His Life and Legacy*. *Chinggis Khan* by Michal Biran, the most prominent historian of the Mongol empire active today, is a close second. Her biography of the Great Khan is part of the 'Makers of the Muslim World' series, and as such it concentrates on the legacy of Chinggis Khan and his empire in the Muslim world, and it draws largely on Islamic sources.

For the other side of the Eurasian landmass, H. Desmond Martin's *Chingis Khan and His Conquest of North China* is an underappreciated and underused biographical resource. Ruth Dunnell's brief but quite serviceable *Chinggis Khan: World Conqueror* is based on a thorough acquaintance with the *Secret History of the Mongols* and with recent scholarship on the Great Khan. Her first chapter, 'Eurasian Nomads: Ecological, Geographical, and Historical Considerations' is especially useful and informative. George Lane's *Genghis Khan and Mongol Rule* is a helpful and readable resource containing the standard historical narrative plus an appendix section containing mini biographies, translated primary documents, a glossary and (perhaps most useful of all) an annotated bibliography.

The bevy of popular books on Chinggis Khan (such as Harold Lamb's *Genghis Khan: The Emperor of All Men*; John Man's *Genghis Khan: Life, Death, and Resurrection*; Frank McLynn's *Genghis Khan: The Man Who Conquered the World*, Cark Fredrik Sverdrup's *The Mongol Conquests: The Military Operations of Genghis Khan and Sübe'etei* and Jack Weatherford's *Genghis Khan and the Making of the Modern World*) make interesting reading but are not as scholarly or thorough. Weatherford, in particular, makes several factual errors and farfetched claims, especially in his Chapter IX.

Chapter II
Temujin Begins His Mighty Career

✗

THIS INTENSE RIVALRY between the descendants of Kabul and Ambagai was the great ruling fact among Mongols at this epoch. Kabul and Ambagai were second cousins, both being third in descent from Kaidu, that little boy saved by his nurse from the Jelairs; the Kaidu whose descendants were the great ruling Mongols of history. Kabul and Ambagai are remarkable themselves, and are notable also as fathers of men who sought power by all means which they could imagine and bring into practice.

Yessugai with his brothers was now triumphant and prosperous. He was terribly hostile to the Buyur Lake Tartars; he was ever watching the Taidjut opposition, which though resting at times never slumbered. Once in the days of his power Yessugai, while hawking along the Onon, saw a Merkit named Yeke Chilaidu taking home with him a wife from the Olkonots. Seeing that the woman was a beauty Yessugai hurried back to his yurta and returned with his eldest and youngest brothers to help him. When Yeke saw the three brothers coming he grew frightened, struck his horse and rushed away to find some good hiding place, but found none and rode back to the cart where his wife was. 'Those men are very hostile,' said the woman. 'Hurry off, or they will kill thee. If thou survive find a wife such as I am, if thou remember me call her by my name.' Then she drew off her shift and gave it to Yeke. He took it, mounted quickly and, seeing Yessugai approaching with his brothers, galloped up the river.

The three men rushed after Yeke, but did not overtake him, so they rode back to the woman, whose name was Hoelun. She was weeping. Her screams when they seized her raised waves on the river, and shook trees in the valley.

'The husband has crossed many ridges already, and many waters,' said Daritai, Yessugai's youngest brother, 'no matter how thou scream he will not come to thee, if thou look for his trail thou wilt not find it. Stop screaming!' Thus, they took Hoelun, and she became a wife then to Yessugai.

Some months after the capture of Hoelun, Yessugai made attacks on the Tartars, and among other captives took Temujin Uge, a chieftain. Hoelun gave birth to a son at that period near the hill Dailiun Baldak. The boy was born grasping a lump of dark blood in his fist very firmly, and since he was born when Temujin Uge was taken they called the child Temujin. After that, Hoelun had three other sons: Kassar, Hochiun and Taimuge, and one daughter, Taimulun.

When this first son had passed his 13th year, Yessugai set out with the lad on a visit to Hoelun's brothers to find among them a wife for him. When between the two mountains Cihurga and Cheksar he met one Desaichan, a man of the Ungirs. 'Whither art thou going 0 Yessugai?' asked Desaichan. 'I am going with my son to his uncles to look out a bride for him among them.' 'Thy son has a clear face and bright eyes,' said Desaichan. 'Last night I dreamed that a white falcon holding the sun and the moon in its talons flew down to my wrist, and perched on it. 'We only know the sun and the moon through our eyesight,' said I to some friends of mine, 'but now a white falcon has brought them both down to me in his talons, this must be an omen of greatness.' At the right time hast thou come hither Yessugai with thy son and shown what my dream means. It presages high fortune undoubtedly. I have a daughter at home, she is small yet but come and look at her.'

Then he conducted the father and son to his yurta. Yessugai rejoiced in his heart very greatly at sight of the girl, who in truth was a beauty. She was 10 years of age, and named Bortai. Next day, Yessugai asked Bortai of Desaichan as a bride for young Temujin. 'Will it show more importance if I give her only after much begging,' asked the father, 'or will it show slight esteem if I give her in answer to few words? We know that a girl is not born to remain in the household forever. I yield her to marry thy son, and do thou leave him here for a time with me.'

The agreement was finished and Yessugai went away without Temujin. On the road home he stopped at Cheksar and met Tartars who arranged there a feast for him. Being hungry and thirsty from traveling he halted. His hosts, who knew well that he had captured and killed very many of their people, Temujin Uge with others, had poison made ready, and gave it in drink to him. Yessugai rode away and reached home in three days, but fell ill on the journey, and his trouble increased as he travelled. 'There is pain in my heart,' said he, 'who is near me?' At that time Munlik, a son of Charaha, happened in at the yurta, and Yessugai called him. 'My children are young,' said he, 'I went to find a bride for my son Temujin, and have found her. On the way home I was poisoned by enemies. My heart is very sore in me, so go thou to my brothers and see them, see their wives also. I give thee this as a duty; tell them all that has happened. But first bring me Temujin very quickly.'

Yessugai died (in 1175) shortly after without seeing Temujin.

Munlik went with all haste to Desaichan. 'Yessugai,' said he, 'wants to see Temujin, he has sent me to bring the boy.' 'If Yessugai is grieving let Temujin go, and return to me afterward.' Munlik took Temujin home as instructed. In the spring following, when Ambagai's widows were preparing the offerings to ancestors before moving to the summer place, they refused to share sacrificed meats with Hoelun, and thus shut her out from their ruling circle and relationship. 'Better leave this woman here with her children, she must not go with us,' said the widows. Targutai Kurultuk, who was then in authority, went from the winter place without turning to Hoelun, or speaking. He with Todoyan Jirisha, his brother, had enticed away Yessugai's people. Munlik's father, Charáha, an old man, strove to persuade Targutai and his brother to take Hoelun, but they would not listen to him or to any. 'The deep water is gone, the bright stone is broken,' said Todoyan, 'we cannot restore them, we have nothing to do with that woman, and her children.' And when Targutai with his brother was starting, a warrior of his thrust a spear into Charáha's back and the old man fell down mortally wounded.

Temujin went to talk with Charáha and take advice from him. 'Targutai and his brother,' said the old man, 'have led away all the people assembled by thy father, and our relatives.' Temujin wept then and turned to his mother for assistance. Hoelun resolved quickly; she mounted, and, directing her attendants to take lances, set out at the head of them. She overtook the deserting people and stopped one half of them, but even that half would not go back with her. So Targutai and Todoyan had defeated Hoelun with her children, and taken one half of Yessugai's people; the second half joined other leaders. But Hoelun, a strong, resolute woman, protected her family and found means to support it. Her children lived in poor, harsh conditions, and grew up in the midst of hostility and hatred. To assist and give help to their mother, they made hooks out of needles and fished in the river Onon which was close to their dwelling. Once Temujin and Kassar went to fish with their half-brothers, Baiktar and Belgutai, Yessugai's children by another wife. Temujin caught a golden-hued trout, and his half-brothers took it from him. He went then with Kassar to Hoelun. 'We caught a golden-hued fish,' said they, 'but Baiktar and Belgutai took it.' 'Why do ye quarrel?' asked the mother, 'we have no friends at present; all have deserted us; nothing sticks to us now but our shadows. We have no power yet to punish the Taidjuts. Why do ye act like the sons of Alan Goa, and quarrel? Why not agree and gain strength against enemies?'

Temujin was dissatisfied; he wished Hoelun to take his side and go against Baiktar. 'The other day,' said he, 'I shot a bird and Baiktar took this bird also. He and his brother today snatched my fish from me. If they act always in this way, how can I live with them?' And he turned from his mother very quickly. Both brothers rushed out, slammed the door flap behind them and vanished.

When they were out, they saw Baiktar on a hill herding horses. Temujin stole up from behind, and Kassar in front; they had taken arrows and were aiming when Baiktar turned and saw them. 'Why treat me like a splinter in the mouth, or a hair on the eyeball?' asked he. 'Though ye kill me spare my brother, do not kill Belgutai.' Then he bent his legs under him, and waited.

Temujin from behind and Kassar in front killed Baiktar with arrows. When they went home Hoelun knew by their faces what had happened. 'Thou wert born,' said she to Temujin, 'grasping blood in thy fingers. Thou and thy brother are like dogs when devouring a village, or serpents which swallow alive what they spring upon, or wolves hunting prey in a snowstorm. The injuries done us by the Taidjuts are terrible, ye might plan to grow strong and then punish the Taidjuts. But what are ye doing?'

Well might she ask, for she did not know then her wonderful son Temujin, for whom it was as natural to remove a half-brother, or even a brother, by killing him as to set aside any other obstacle. He who worked all his life till its end to eliminate opponents was that day beginning his mighty career, and his first real work was the murder of his half-brother Baiktar, whose father was his own father, Yessugai.

No matter who Temujin's enemies were, he removed them as coolly as a teacher in his classroom rubs figures from a blackboard. He struck down the Taidjuts as soon as he felt himself strong enough, but before he could do that his task was to weed out and train his own family. The first work before him was the empire of his household. Neither mother, nor brother, nor anyone must stand between Temujin and his object; in that he showed his great singleness of purpose, his invincible will power, his wisdom in winning the success which his mind saw. The wisdom of Temujin in building up empire was an unerring clear instinct like the instinct of a bee in constructing its honeycomb, or the judgment and skill of a bird in finding the proper material and weaving the round perfect nest for its eggs and its little ones.

Temujin began his career in real practice by killing his half-brother mainly through the hand of his full brother Kassar, who was famed later on as the unerring strong archer, and who in time tried unsuccessfully to rival the invincible Temujin.

Temujin was now master in a very small region, but he was master. His mother and brothers did not dominate, or interfere, they assisted him. The family lived for a time in seclusion and uninjured till at last Targutai roused up his followers to action. 'Temujin and his brothers have grown,' said he, 'they are stronger.' Taking with him some comrades he rode away quickly to find Temujin with his family. From afar Hoelun and her children saw the men coming and were frightened. Temujin seized his horse quickly, and fled before others to the mountain. Belgutai hid his half brothers and sister in a cliff, after that he felled trees to stop the horsemen. Kassar sent arrows to hinder the Taidjuts. 'We want only Temujin, we want no one else,' said they. Temujin had fled to Mount Targunai and hidden there in dense thickets whither they could not follow. They surrounded Targunai and watched closely.

He spent three days in secret places, and then led his horse out to flee from the mountain. When near the edge of the forest the saddle fell. He saw that breast strap and girth were both fixed securely. 'A saddle may fall,' thought he, 'though the girth be well fastened, but how can it fall when the breast strap is holding it? I see now that Heaven is protecting me.'

He turned back and passed three other days hiding; then he tried to go out a second time – a great rock fell in front of him, blocked the road and stopped his passage. 'Heaven wills that I stay here still longer,' said Temujin. He went back and spent three other days on the mountain, nine days in all without eating. 'Must I die here alone and unheard of?' thought he despairingly. 'Better go at all hazards.' He cut a way near the rock and led his horse down the mountain side.

The Taidjuts, who were watching outside very carefully, seized Temujin and took him to Targutai, who commanded that a kang be put on him, and also fetters, and that he live one day and night in each tent. So he passed from one family to another in succession. During these changes he gained the close friendship of one Sorgan Shira, and of an old woman. The old woman was kind and put rags on the kang at the points where his shoulders were galled by it.

Once, the Taidjuts made a feast near the Onon and went home after sunset, appointing a boy to watch over the captive. Temujin had been able to break his own fetters, and seeing that all had gone home felled the boy with the kang in which his own head and both hands were fastened. Then he ran to a forest along the Onon and lay down there, but, fearing lest they might find him, he rose, hurried on to the river and sank in it, leaving only his face above water.

The boy soon recovered and screamed that the captive had fled from him. Some Taidjuts rushed quickly together on hearing him, and searched around everywhere. There was moonlight that evening and Sorgan Shira of the Sulduts, who was searching with others, and had gone quite a distance ahead, found Temujin, but did not call out. 'The Taidjuts hate thee because thou hast wisdom,' said he to the captive, 'thou wilt die if they find thee. Stay where thou art for the present, and be careful, I will not betray thee to anyone.'

The pursuers went some distance while searching. 'This man escaped during daylight,' said Sorgan Shira, when he overtook them. 'It is night now and difficult to find him. Better search nearer places, we can hunt here tomorrow. He has not come thus far, – how could he run such a distance with a kang on his shoulders?'

On the way back, Sorgan Shira went to Temujin a second time. 'We shall come hither tomorrow to search for thee,' said he. 'Hurry off now to thy mother and brothers. Shouldst thou meet any man tell him not that I saw thee.' When Sorgan Shira had gone, Temujin fell to thinking and thought in this manner: While stopping at each tent I passed a day with Sorgan Shira; Chila and Chinbo his sons showed me pity. They took off the kang in the dark from my shoulders and let me lie down then in freedom. He saw me today, I cannot escape till this kang is taken off, he will do that, I will go to him. He will save me.

So Temujin went and when he entered the yurta Sorgan Shira was frightened. 'Why come now to me?' inquired he. 'I told thee to go to thy mother and brothers.' 'When a bird is pursued by a falcon,' said Temujin, 'it hides in thick grass and thus saves itself.'

'We should be of less value than grass were we not to help this poor youth, who thus begs us,' said to himself Sorgan Shira. The boys took the kang from the captive and burned it, then they hid Temujin in a cart which they piled high with wool packs and told Kadan, their sister, to guard the wool carefully, and not speak of Temujin to any living person.

The Taidjuts appeared on the third day. 'Has no one here seen that runaway?' asked they of Sorgan. 'Search where ye will,' was the answer. They searched the whole yurta, then they searched around the house in all places, and threw out the wool till they came to the cart box. They were going to empty this also when Sorgan laughed at them, saying, 'How could any man live in a cart load of wool this hot weather?' They prodded the wool then with lances; one of these entered Temujin's leg, but he was silent and moved not. The Taidjuts were satisfied, and went away without emptying the cart box.

'Thou hast come very near killing me,' said Sorgan to Temujin. 'The smoke of my house would have vanished, and my fire would have died out forever had they found thee. Go now to thy mother and brothers.'

He gave Temujin a white-nosed sorrel mare without a saddle, gave him a boiled lamb which was fat because reared by two mothers, gave him a skin of mare's milk, a bow and two arrows, but no flint lest he strike fire on the way, and betray himself.

Temujin went to the ruins of his first house and then higher up the Onon till he reached the Kimurha. He saw tracks near that river and followed them on to Mount Baitar. In front of that mountain is a smaller one, Horchukin; there he found all his brothers and Hoelun his mother. Temujin moved now with them to Mount Burhan. Near Burhan is the high land Gulyalgu, through this land runs the river Sangur, on the bank of that river is a hill called Kara Jiruge and a green-coloured lake near the foot of it. At this lake Temujin fixed his yurta, trapped marmots and field mice, and thus they lived on for a season. At last, some Taidjut thieves drove off eight horses from Temujin, leaving only the white-nosed sorrel mare which Sorgan had given him, and on which Belgutai had gone to hunt marmots. He came back that evening with a load of them.

'The horses have been stolen,' said Temujin. 'I will go for them,' said Belgutai. 'Thou couldst not find them,' answered Kassar, "I will go.' 'Ye could not find them, and if ye found them ye could not bring them back,' called out Temujin, 'I will go.'

Temujin set his brothers aside as useless at that juncture, their authority and worth were to him as nothing. Temujin's is the only, the genuine authority. He rode off on the white-nosed sorrel mare, and followed the trail of the eight stolen horses. He travelled three days and on the fourth morning early he saw near the road a young man who had led up a mare and was milking her. 'Hast thou seen eight grey horses?' asked Temujin. 'Before sunrise eight horses went past me, I will show thee the trail over which they were driven.' Temujin's weary beast was let out then to pasture; a white horse with a black stripe on its spine was led in to go farther. The youth hid his leather pail and his bag in the grass very carefully. 'Thou art tired,' said he to Temujin, 'and art anxious. My name is Boörchu, I will go with thee for thy horses. Nahu Boyan is my father, I am his one son and he loves me.'

So they set out together and travelled three days in company. On the third day toward evening, they came to a campground and saw the eight horses. 'Stay at this place O my comrade,' said Temujin, 'I will go and drive off those horses.'

'If I have come hither to help thee why should I stay alone and do nothing?' asked Boörchu. So they went on together and drove off the horses. The thieves hurried after them promptly and one, who rode a white stallion, had a lasso and was gaining on the comrades. 'Give me thy quiver and bow,' said Boörchu, 'I will meet him with an arrow.' 'Let me use the bow,' answered Temujin, 'those enemies might wound thee.' The man on the white horse was directing his lasso and ready to hurl it when Temujin's arrow put an end to his action. That night Temujin and Boörchu made a journey which would have taken three days for any other men, and saw the yurta of Nahu Boyan in the distance at daybreak.

'Without thy help,' said Temujin, 'I could not have brought back these horses. Without thee I could have done nothing, so let us divide now these eight beasts between us.' 'I decided to help thee,' answered Boörchu, 'because I saw thee weighed down and weary from sorrow and loneliness, why should I take what is thine from thee? I am my father's one son, his wealth is enough for me, more is not needed. If I should take thine how couldst thou call me thy comrade?'

When they entered the yurta of Nahu Boyan they found the old man grieving bitterly for Boörchu. On seeing them he shed tears and reproached his son sharply. 'I know not,' said Boörchu in answer, 'how I thought of assisting this comrade, but when I saw him worn and anxious I had to go with him. Things are now well again, for I am with thee, my father.' Nahu Boyan became satisfied when he heard the whole story. Boörchu rode off then and brought the leather milk pail, killed a lamb, filled a bag with mare's milk and, tying it to the horse like a pack, gave Temujin all to sustain him. 'Ye are young,' said Nahu Boyan, 'be ye friends, and be faithful.' Temujin took farewell of Boörchu and his father. Three days after that he had reached home with his horses. No words could describe the delight of his mother and brothers when they saw him.

Temujin had passed his 13th year when he parted from Bortai. He went down the Kerulon now with his half-brother, Belgutai, to get her. Several years had passed and he had a wish to marry. Bortai's father rejoiced at seeing Temujin. 'I grieved,' said he, 'greatly and lost hope of seeing thee when I heard of Taidjut hatred.'

Both parents escorted their daughter and her husband. Desaichan, after going some distance, turned homeward, as was usual for fathers, but Bortai's mother, Sotan, went on to Temujin's yurta.

Temujin wished now to have Boörchu, wished him as a comrade forever, and sent Belgutai to bring him. Boörchu said nothing to his father or to anyone; he took simply a humpbacked sorrel horse, saddled him, strapped a coat of black fur to the saddle and rode away quickly to Temujin's yurta; after that he never left him.

Temujin removed from the Sangur to the springs of the Kerulon and fixed his yurta at the foot of the slope known as Burji. Bortai had brought with her a black sable cloak as a present to Hoelun. 'In former days,' said Temujin to his brothers, our father, Yessugai, became a sworn friend, an 'anda,' to Togrul of the Kera ts, hence Togrul is to me in the place of my father, we will go now and show Togrul honour.'

Temujin and two of his brothers took the cloak to Togrul in the Black Forest on the Tula. 'In former days,' said Temujin as he stood before Togrul, 'thou didst become anda to Yessugai, hence thou art to me in the place of my father. I bring thee today, my father, a gift brought by my wife to my mother.' With these words he gave the black sable to Togrul, who was pleased very greatly with the offering.

'I will bring back to thee thy people who are scattered,' said Togrul in answer, 'and join them again to thee, I will keep this in mind very firmly, and not forget it.'

When Temujin returned home, the old man Charchiutai came from Mount Burhan with the bellows of a blacksmith on his shoulders, and brought also Chelmai, his son, with him. 'When thou wert born,' said Charchiutai to Temujin, 'I gave thee a lined sable wrap, I gave thee too my son Chelmai, but as he was very little at that time, I kept the boy with me and trained him, but now when he is grown up and skilful, I bring him. Let him saddle thy horse and open doors to thee.' With that he gave his son Chelmai to Temujin.

Some short time after this, just before daybreak one morning, Hoakchin, an old woman, Hoelun's faithful servant, who slept on the ground, sprang up quickly and called to her mistress: 'O mother, rise, I hear the earth tremble! O mother, the Taidjuts are coming, our terrible destroyers! Hasten, O mother!' 'Rouse up the children,' said Hoelun, 'wake them all quickly!' Hoelun rose to her feet as she was speaking. Temujin and his brothers sprang up and ran to their horses. Hoelun carried her daughter Taimulun. Temujin had only one saddle beast ready. There was no horse for Bortai, so he galloped off with his brothers. Thus showing that self-preservation was his one thought.

Hoakchin, the old woman, hid Bortai, she stowed her away in a small black kibitka (cart), attached a pied cow to it and drove along the river Tungela. As the night darkness cleared and light was approaching, some mounted men overtook the old woman. 'Who art thou?' asked they, riding up to her. 'I go around and shear sheep for rich people, I am on my way home now,' said Hoakchin. 'Is Temujin at his yurta?' asked a horseman. 'Where is it?' His yurta is not far, but I know not where he is at this moment,' answered Hoakchin.

When the men had ridden off the old woman urged on the cow, but just then the axle broke. Hoakchin wished to hurry on foot to the mountain with Bortai, but the horsemen had turned back already and came to her. 'Who is in there?' asked a man as he pointed at the kibitka. 'I have wool there,' replied the old woman. 'Let us look at this wool, brothers,' said one of the mounted men. They dragged Bortai out, and then put her on horseback with Hoakchin. Next they followed on Temujin's tracks to Mount Burhan, but could not come up with him. Wishing to enter the mountain land straightway they tried one and another place, but found no road of any kind open. In one part a sticky morass, in another a dense growth of forest and thicket. They did not find the secret road and could not break in at any point. These horsemen were from three clans of Merkits. The first had been sent by Tukta Bijhi of the Uduts; the second by Dair Usun of the Uasits; the third by Haätai Darmala of the Haäts. They had come to wreak vengeance on Temujin because Yessugai, his father, had snatched away Hoelun from Chilaidu, and this Hoelun was Temujin's mother. They now carried off Bortai, Temujin's wife, who was thus taken in vengeance, as they said, for the stealing of Hoelun.

Temujin, fearing lest they might be in ambush, sent his half-brother, Belgutai, and Boörchu, with Chelmai to examine and discover. In three days when these men were well satisfied that the Merkits had gone from the mountain, Temujin left his hiding place. He stood, struck his breast and cried looking heavenward: 'Thanks to the ears of a skunk, and the eyes of an ermine in the head of old Hoakchin, I escaped capture. Besides that, Mount Burhan has saved me, and from this day I will make offering to the mountain, and leave to my children and their children this duty of sacrifice.' Then he turned toward the sun, put his girdle on his back, took his cap in his hand and, striking his breast, bent his knees nine times in homage; he made next a libation of tarasun, a liquor distilled out of mare's milk.

After that, Temujin with Kassar and Belgutai went to Togrul on the Tula and implored him, 'O father and sovereign,' said Temujin, 'three clans of Merkits fell on us suddenly, and stole my wife, Bortai. Is it not possible to save her?'

'Last year,' said Togrul, 'when the cloak of black sable was brought to me, I promised to lead back thy people who deserted, and those who were scattered. I remember this well, and because of my promise I will root out the Merkits, I will rescue and return to thee Bortai. Inform Jamuka that thy wife has been stolen. Two tumans (a tuman is 10,000) of warriors will go with me, let Jamuka lead out the same number.'

Jamuka, chief of the Juriats at that time, was descended from a brother of Kabul Khan, and was third cousin therefore to Temujin. Temujin sent his brothers to Jamuka with this message: 'The Merkits have stolen my wife, thou and I have the same origin; can we not avenge this great insult?' He sent Togrul's statement also. 'I have heard,' said Jamuka, 'that Temujin's wife has been stolen, I am grieved very greatly at his trouble and will help him.' He told where the three clans were camping, and promised to aid in bringing back Bortai.

'Tell Temujin and Togrul,' said he, 'that my army is ready. With me are some people belonging to Temujin; from them I will gather one tuman of warriors and take the same number of my own folk with them, I will go up to Butohan Borchi on the Onon where Togrul will meet me.' They took back the answer to Temujin, and went to Togrul with the words from Jamuka.

Togrul set out with two tumans of warriors toward the Kerulon and met Temujin at the river Kimurha. One tuman of Togrul's men was led by Jaganbo, his brother. Jamuka waited three days at Butohan Borchi for Togrul and Jaganbo; he was angry and full of reproaches when he met them. 'When conditions are made between allies,' said he, though wind and rain come to hinder, men should meet at the season appointed. The time of our meeting was settled, a given word is the same as an oath, if the word is not to be kept no ally should be invited.'

'I have come three days late,' said Togrul. 'Blame, and punish me, Jamuka, my brother, until thou art satisfied.'

The warriors went on now, crossed the Kilho to Buura where they seized all the people and with them the wife of the Merkit, Tukta Bijhi. Tukta Bijhi, who was sleeping, would have been captured had not his hunters and fishermen hurried on in the night-time and warned him. He and Dair Usun, his brother, rushed away down the river to Bargudjin. When the Merkits were fleeing at night down along the Selinga, Togrul's men hunted on fiercely and were seizing them. In that rushing crowd Temujin shouted: 'Bortai! O Bortai!' She was with the fleeing people; she knew Temujin's voice and sprang from a small covered cart with Hoakchin, the old woman. Running up, she caught Temujin's horse by the bridle. The moon broke through clouds that same moment, and each knew the other.

Temujin sent to Togrul without waiting. 'I have found,' said he, 'those whom I was seeking; let us camp now and go on no farther tonight.' They camped there. When the Merkits with 300 men attacked Temujin to take vengeance for snatching off Chilaidu's wife, Hoelun, Tukta Bijhi, the brother of Chilaidu, with two other leaders rode three times round Mount Burhan, but could not find Temujin, and only took Bortai. They gave her as wife to Chilger, a younger brother of Chilaidu, the first husband of Hoelun, Temujin's mother. (This Chilaidu was perhaps Temujin's father.) Now, when a great army was led in by Togrul and Jamuka, Chilger was cruelly frightened. 'I have been doomed like a crow,' said he, 'to eat wretched scraps of old skin, but I should like greatly the taste of some wild goose. By my offenses against Bortai I have brought evil suffering on the Merkits; the harm which now has befallen them may crush me also. To save my life I must hide in some small and dark corner.' Having said this, he vanished. Haätai Darmala was the only man captured; they put a kang on his neck and went straight toward Mount Burhan.

Those 300 Merkits who rode thrice round Mount Burhan were slain every man of them. Their wives, who were fit to continue as wives, were given to new husbands; those who should only be slaves were delivered to slavery.

'Thou, O my father, and thou my anda,' said Temujin to Togrul and Jamuka, 'Heaven through the aid which ye gave me has strengthened my hands to avenge a great insult. The Merkits who attacked me are extinguished, their wives are taken captive, the work is now ended.' That same year Bortai gave birth to her first son, Juchi, and because of her captivity the real father of Juchi was always a question in the mind of Temujin.

The Uduts had left in their camp a beautiful small boy, Kuichu. He had splendid bright eyes, was dressed in river sable and on his feet were boots made of deer hoofs. When the warriors took the camp, they seized Kuichi and gave him to Hoelun. Temujin, Togrul and Jamuka destroyed all the dwellings of the Merkits and captured the women left in them. Togrul returned then to the Tula. Temujin and Jamuka went to Hórho Nachúbur and fixed a camp there. The two men renewed former times and the origin of their friendship; each promised now to love the other more firmly than before, if possible. Temujin was in his boyhood, 11 years of age, when they made themselves 'andas' the first day; both were guests of Togrul at that period. Now they swore friendship again, – became andas a second time. They discussed friendship with each other: 'Old people,' said Temujin, 'declare that when men become andas both have one life as it were; neither abandons the other, and each guards the life of his anda. Now we strengthen our friendship anew, and refresh it.' At these words Temujin girded Jamuka, with a golden belt, which he had taken from the Merkits, and Jamuka gave him a rich girdle, and a splendid white stallion, which he had captured. They arranged a feast under a broad spreading tree near the cliff known as Huldah, and at night they slept under one blanket together.

Temujin and Jamuka, from love, as it were, of each other, lived 18 months in glad, careless company, but really each of the two men was studying and watching his anda and working against him with all the power possible as was shown very clearly in the sequel. At last, during April, while moving, the two friends spurred on ahead of the kibitkas and were talking as usual: 'If we camp near that mountain in front,' said Jamuka all at once, 'the horse herds will get our yurtas. If we camp near the river the shepherds will have food for their gullets.' Temujin made no answer to words which seemed dark and fateful, so he halted to wait for his wife and his mother; Jamuka rode farther and left him. When Hoelun had come up to him Temujin told her the words of Jamuka, and said, 'I knew not what they could signify, hence I gave him no answer. I have come to ask thy opinion, mother.' Hoelun had not time to reply because Bortai was quicker. 'People say,' declared Bortai, 'that thy friend seeks the new and despises the old; I think that he is tired of us. Is there not some trick in these words which he has given thee? Is there not some danger behind them? We ought not to halt, let us go on all night by a new road, and not stop until daybreak. It is better to part in good health from Jamuka.' 'Bortai talks wisdom,' said Temujin. He went on then by his own road, aside from Jamuka, and passed near one camp of the Taidjuts who were frightened when they saw him; they rose up and hurried away that same night to Jamuka. Those Taidjuts left in their camp a small boy, Kokochu. Temujin's men found the lad and gave him as a present to Hoelun.

After this swift, all-night's journey, when day came Temujin's party was joined by many Jelairs. Horchi of the Barin clan came then to Temujin after daybreak and spoke to him as follows: 'I know through a revelation of the spirit what will happen, and to thee I now tell it: In a vision I saw a pied cow coming up to Jamuka; she stopped, looked at him, dug the earth near his yurta and broke off one horn as she was digging. Then she bellowed very loudly, and cried: 'Give back my horn, O Jamuka. After that a strong hornless bull came drawing the pins of a great ruler's tent behind Temujin's kibitka. This great bull lowed as he travelled, and said: "Heaven appoints Temujin to be lord of dominion, I am taking his power to him." This is what the spirit revealed in my vision. What delight wilt thou give me for this revelation?' 'When I become lord of dominion, I will make thee commander of ten thousand,' said Temujin. 'I have told thee much of high value,' said Horchi. 'If thou make me merely commander of ten thousand, what great delight can I get from the office? Make me that, and let me choose also as wives 30 beautiful maidens wherever I find them, and give me besides what I ask of thee.' Temujin nodded, and Horchi was satisfied.

Next came a number of men from four other clans. These had all left Jamuka for Temujin, and joined him at the river Kimurha. And then was completed a work of great moment: Altan, Huchar and Sachai Baiki took counsel with all their own kinsmen, and when they had finished they stood before Temujin and spoke to him as follows: 'We wish to proclaim thee,' said they. 'When thou art khan we shall be in the front of every battle against all thy enemies. When we capture beautiful women and take splendid stallions and mares, we will bring all to thee surely, and when at the hunt thou art beating in wild beasts we will go in advance of others and give thee the game taken by us. If in battles we transgress thy commands, or in peace we work harm to thee in any way, take from us everything, take wives and property and leave us out then in wild, barren places to perish.' Having sworn thus they proclaimed Temujin, and made him khan over all of them.

Temujin, now khan in the land of the four upper rivers, commanded his comrade Boörchu, whom he called 'youngest brother', together with Ogelayu, Hochiun, Chedai and Tokolku to carry his bows and his quiver. Vanguru and Kadan Daldur to dispense food and drink, to be masters of nourishment. Dagai was made master of shepherds, Guchugur was made master of kibitkas. Dodai became master of servants. After that he commanded Kubilai, Chilgutai and Karkaito Kuraun with Kassar his brother to be swordbearers; his half-brother Belgutai with Karal Daito Kuraun to be masters of horse training. Daichu, Daihut, Morichi and Muthalhu were to be masters of horse herds. Then he commanded Arkai Kassar, Tagai and Sukagai Chaurhan to be like near and distant arrows, that is, messengers to near and distant places. Subotai the Valiant spoke up then and said: 'I will be like an old mouse in snatching, I will be like a jackdaw in speed, I will be like a saddlecloth to hide things, I will ward off every enemy, as felt wards off wind, that is what I shall be for thee.'

Temujin turned then to Boörchu and Chelmai. 'When I was alone, ye two before other men came to me as comrades. I have not forgotten this. Be ye first in all this assembly.' Then he spoke further, and said to other men: 'To you who have gathered in here after leaving Jamuka, and have joined me, I declare that if Heaven keeps and upholds me as hitherto, ye will all be my fortunate helpers and stand in high honour before me;' then he instructed them how to perform their new duties.

Temujin sent Tagai and Sukagai to announce his accession to Togrul of the Keraits. 'It is well,' said Togrul, 'that Temujin is made khan; how could ye live even to this time without a commander? Be not false to the khan whom ye have chosen.'

Temujin sent Arkai Kassar and Belgutai with similar tidings to Jamuka who answered: 'Tell Altan and Huchar, Temujin's uncle and cousin, that they by calumnies have parted me now from my anda, and ask them why they did not proclaim Temujin when he and I were one person in spirit? Be ye all active assist ants to Temujin. Let his heart be at rest through your faithfulness.'

This was the formal official reply, Jamuka's real answer was given soon after.

Taichar, a younger brother of Jamuka, was living not far from Mount Chalma, and a slave of Temujin, named Darmala, was stopping for a season at Sari Keher – a slave was considered in the customs of that age and people as a brother, hence was as a brother in considering a vendetta and dealing with it – Taichar stole a herd of horses from Darmala whose assistants feared to follow and restore them, Darmala rushed alone in pursuit and came up with his herd in the night-time; bending forward to the neck of his horse he sent an arrow into Taichar; the arrow struck his spine and killed the man straightway. Darmala then drove back his horses. Jamuka to take vengeance for his brother put himself at the head of his own and some other clans; with these he allied himself straightway with Temujin's mortal enemies, the Taidjuts. Three tumans of warriors (30,000) were assembled by Targutai and Jamuka. They had planned to attack their opponent unexpectedly and crossed the ridge Alaut Turhau for this purpose. Temujin, in Gulyalgu at that time, was informed of this movement by Mulketokah and by Boldai who were both of them Ikirats. His warriors all told were thirteen thousand in number and with these he marched forth to meet Targutai and Jamuka. He was able to choose his own time and he struck the invaders as suited him. He fought with these enemies at Dalan daljut and gained his first triumph, a bloody victory, and immense in its value as results proved.

Targutai and Jamuka were repulsed with great loss. Their army was broken and scattered, and many were taken prisoners. After this fierce encounter Temujin led his men to a forest not far from the battleground where he ranged all his prisoners, and selected the main ones for punishment. Beyond doubt there were many among them of those who had enticed away people after the poisoning of Yessugai, Temujin's father, men who had left the orphan and acted with Targutai his bitterest enemy. In 70, or, as some state, in 80 large caldrons, he boiled alive those of them who were worthiest of punishment. The boiling continued each day till he had tortured to death the most powerful and vindictive among his opponents.

This execution spread terror on all sides, and since Temujin showed the greatest kindness to his friends not only during those days, but at all times and rewarded them to the utmost, hope and fear brought him many adherents.

The Uruts and Manhuts, the first led by Churchadai, and the second by Kuyuldar, drew away from Jamuka and joined Temujin, the new victor. Munlik of the clan Kuanhotan came also, bringing with him his seven mighty sons who were immensely great fighters, and venomous. This Munlik, a son of that Charaha whom one of Targutai's followers had wounded to death with a spear thrust, was the man who had brought home Temujin from the house of Desaichan his father-in-law when his own father, Yessugai, was dying.

Soon after the boiling to death of those captives in the forest a division of the Juriats, that is Jamuka's own clansmen, came and joined Temujin for the following reason: The Juriat lands touched those of Temujin's people, and on a certain day men of both sides were hunting and the parties met by pure chance in the evening. 'Let us pass the night here with Temujin,' said some of the Juriats. Others would not consent, and one half of the party, made up altogether of 400, went home; the other two hundred remained in the forest. Temujin gave these men all the meat needed, and kettles in which they could boil it, he treated them generously and with friendship.

These Juriats halted still longer and hunted with Temujin's party. They received every evening somewhat more of the game than was due them; at parting they were satisfied with Temujin's kindness and thanked him sincerely. At heart they felt sad, for their position was painful. They wished greatly to join Temujin, but desired not to leave their own people; and on the way home they said to one another as they travelled: 'The Taidjuts are gone, they will not think of us in future. Temujin cares for his people and does everything to defend them.' On reaching home they talked with their elders. 'Let us settle still nearer to Temujin, said they, 'and obey him, give him service.' 'What harm have the Taidjuts done you?' was the answer. 'They are kinsfolk; how could we become one with their enemy, and leave them?' Notwithstanding this answer Ulug Bahadur and Tugai Talu with their kinsmen and dependents went away in a body to Temujin.

'We have come,' said they, 'like a woman bereft of her husband, or a herd without a master, or a flock without a shepherd. In friendship and agreement we would live with thee, we would draw our swords to defend thee, and cut down thy enemies.'

'I was like a sleeping man when ye came to me,' said Temujin, 'ye pulled me by the forelock and roused me. I was sitting here in sadness, and ye cheered me, I will do what I can now to satisfy your wishes.' He made various rules and arrangements which pleased them, and they were satisfied perfectly, at least for a season.

Temujin wished to strengthen his position still further, and desired to win to his alliance Podu who was chief of the Kurulats, whose lands were adjacent to the Argun. This chief was renowned as an archer and a warrior. Temujin offered him his sister in marriage. The offer was accepted with gladness. Podu was ready to give Temujin half his horses, and proffered them.

'Oh,' said Temujin, 'thou and I will not mention either taking or giving; we two are brothers and allies, not traffickers or traders. Men in the old time have said that one heart and one soul cannot be in two bodies, but this is just what in our case I shall show to all people as existing. I desire nothing of thee and thy people, but friendship. I wish to extend my dominion and only ask faithful help from my sister's husband and his tribesmen.' The marriage took place and Podu was his ally.

Soon after this first group of Juriats had joined Temujin, some more of their people discussed at a meeting as follows: 'The Taidjuts torment us unreasonably, they give us nothing whatever, while Temujin takes the coat from his back and presents it. He comes down from the horse which he has mounted and gives that same horse to the needy. He is a genuine leader, he is to all as a father. His is the best governed country.' This fraction also joined Temujin.

Another marriage to be mentioned was that of Temujin's mother to Munlik, son of Charáha, and father of the seven brothers – the great fighters. All these accessions of power, and his victory so strengthened Temujin and rejoiced him that he made for his mother and stepmothers and kinsfolk, with all the new people, a feast near the river Onon, in a forest. At this feast feminine jealousy touching position, and the stealing of a bridle, brought about a dispute and an outbreak. In spite of Temujin's power and authority an encounter took place at the feast which caused one chief, Sidje Bijhi of the Barins, to withdraw with his party. He withdrew not from the feast alone, but from his alliance with Temujin.

The quarrel began in this way: Temujin sent a jar of mare's milk first of all to his mother, to Kassar and to Sachai Baiki. Thereupon Holichin and Hurchin, his two stepmothers grew angry. 'Why not give milk to us before those people, why not give milk to us at the same time with Temujin's mother?' asked they as they struck Shikiur who was master of provisions. This striking brought on a disturbance. Thereupon Temujin commanded his half-brother, Belgutai, to mount his horse and keep order and take Buri Buga on the part of the Churkis to help him. A man of the Hadjin clan and connected with the Churkis stole a bridle and was discovered by Belgutai who stopped him. Buri Buga, feeling bound to defend this man, cut through Belgutai's shoulder piece, wounding him badly.

Belgutai made no complaint when his blood flowed. Temujin, who was under a tree looking on, noted everything. 'Why suffer such treatment?' inquired he of Belgutai. 'I am wounded,' said Belgutai, 'but the wound is not serious; cousins should not quarrel because of me.' Temujin broke a branch from the tree, seized a milk paddle, sprang himself at the Churkis and beat them; then seizing his stepmothers he brought them back to their places, and to reason.

The two Juriat parties which had joined Temujin grew cool in allegiance soon after that feast at the river. They were brought to this state of mind beyond doubt by intrigues of Jamuka; next they fought with each other, and finally deserted.

Jamuka was a man of immense power in plotting, and one who never ceased to pursue his object. Temujin tried to win some show of kindness from Jamuka. In other words, he made every effort to subdue him by deep subtle cunning, but all efforts proved fruitless. These men were bound to win power. Without power life was no life for either one of the two master tricksters. Whatever his action or seeming at any time Jamuka was Temujin's mortal enemy always. He kept undying hatred in his heart, and was ever planning some blow at his rival. When the Juriats were at their best he was plotting, when they were scattered and weak and had in part gone to Temujin, he was nonetheless active and made common cause with the enemies of his opponent wherever he could find them. Temujin cared for no man or woman, and for nothing on earth if opposed to his plans of dominion.

Chapter VI
Destruction of the Kwaresmian Empire

THAT IMMENSE KARA KITAI, or Black Carthay, or Black China was added to the Mongol dominions which conterminous with the Kwaresmian Empire. This empire, begun on Seljuk ruins, was increased soon by other lands, and in 1219 it extended from the Syr Darya or Yaxartes to the Indus, and from Kurdistan to the great roof of the

world, those immense Pamir highlands. The sovereign at the opening of the thirteenth century was Alai ud din Mohammed, great-great-grandson of a Turk slave named Nush Tegin. The master of this slave was a freed man of Melik Shah the Seljuk Sultan, and this freedman transferred Nush Tegin to his sovereign. The slave became cupbearer to Melik Shah, and prefect of Khwaresm at the same time by virtue of his office.

In Mohammedan history, cases of Turkish slaves seizing sovereignty are frequent. Turkish captives in Persia were highly esteemed and appeared there in multitudes. Throughout the vast regions north and east of the Caspian various Turk tribes fought unceasingly; each seized the children of an enemy whenever the chance came, and sold them in the slave marts. These children, reared in the faith of Mohammed, were trained to arms for the greater part, and became trusted bodyguards of princes. They served also as household officials, or managers. Those of them who earned favour gained freedom most frequently, and next the highest places at courts, and in armies. A lucky man might be made governor, and when fortune helped well enough he made himself sovereign.

Turkish slaves grew all-powerful in Moslem lands, till those lands were invaded at last by Turk warriors. Persia, lowered much by Arab conquest, recovered under Bagdad rule in some slight degree, till the eleventh century saw it conquered again by Turk nomads from those immense steppes north and east of the Caspian. Under the descendants of Seljuk these fierce sons of wild herdsmen pushed their way on to the Propontis and to Palestine; camped in Persia, and in lands lying west of it. These self-seeking, merciless adventurers brought torture, oppression and brigandage to all people equally, till at last intestine wars and social chaos put an end to Seljuk rule toward the close of the twelfth century.

Kutb ud din Mohammed, son of the manumitted slave, Nush Tejin, and also his successor, won the title of Kwaresmian Shah, a title used before the Arab conquest. Atsiz, son of Kutb ud din, raised arms repeatedly against Sindjar, the son of Melik Shah, and was forced to render tribute to the Gurkhan. When Sindjar died (1157) Il Arslan, son of Atsiz, seized West Khorassan; his son, Tukush, took Persian Irak from Togrul, who fell in battle. By the death of Togrul and Sindjar, both Persian Seljuk lines became extinct.

Tukush obtained investiture at Bagdad from the kalif, and Persia passed from one line of Turkish tyrants to another. Mohammed, who succeeded his father

Tukush in 1200, seized the provinces of Balkh and Herat and made himself lord of Khorassan. Soon after this, Mazanderan and Kerman passed under his power and direction. Mohammed now planned to shake off the authority of the Gurkhan of Kara Kitai, to whom he, and three of his predecessors, had paid yearly tribute. Besides he was urged to this step by Osman, khan of Samarkand and Transoxiana, who, being also a vassal of the Gurkhan, endured with vexation the insolence of agents who took the tribute in his provinces. Osman promised to recognize Mohammed as his suzerain (a feudal overlord), and pay the same tribute that he had paid to the Gurkhan. The shah accepted this offer with gladness; he merely waited for a pretext, which appeared very quickly: An official came to receive the yearly tribute, and seated himself at the shah's side, the usual place in such cases, though it seemed now that he did so somewhat boldly. Mohammed's pride, increased much by recent victory over Kipchaks living north of the Caspian, would endure this no longer, so in rage he commanded to cut down the agent and hack him to pieces.

After this act Mohammed invaded the lands of the Gurkhan immediately (1208), but was defeated in the ensuing battle, and captured with one of his officers. The officer had the wit to declare that the shah, whose person was unknown in those regions, was a slave of his. In a short time, the amount of ransom for the officer was settled; he offered to send his slave to get the sum needed. This offer was taken and an escort sent with the slave to protect him. Thus did Mohammed return in servile guise to his dominions, where reports of his death had preceded him. In Taberistan his brother, Ali Shir, had proclaimed his own rule, and his uncle, the governor of Herat, was taking sovereign power in that region.

The following year, Mohammed and Osman, the Samarkand ruler, made a second attack on the Gurkhan. Crossing the Syr Darya at Tenakit, they met their opponents, commanded by Tanigu, and won a victory.

They conquered a part of the country as far as Uzkend, and instated a governor. The news of this sudden success caused immense joy in the Kwaresmian Empire. Embassies were sent by neighbouring princes to congratulate the victor. After his name on the shield was added 'Shadow of God upon earth'. People wished to add also 'Second Alexander', but he preferred the name Sindjar, since the Seljuk prince Sindjar had reigned 41 years successfully. After his return, the shah gave his daughter in marriage to Osman, and the Gurkhan's lieutenant in Samarkand was replaced by a Kwaresmian agent. Soon, however, Osman was so dissatisfied with this agent that he gave back his allegiance to the Gurkhan, and killed the Kwaresmians in his capital.

Mohammed, enraged at this slaughter, marched to Samarkand, stormed the city, and for three days and nights his troops did naught else but slay people and plunder; then he laid siege to the fortress and captured it. Osman came out dressed in grave shroud; a naked sword hung from his neck down in front of him. He fell before Mohammed and begged for life abjectly. The shah would have spared him, but Osman's wife, the shah's daughter, rushed in and demanded the death of her husband. He had preferred an earlier wife, the daughter of the Gurkhan, and had forced her, the shah's daughter, to serve at a feast that detested and inferior woman. Osman had to die, and with him died his whole family, including the daughter of the Gurkhan.

Mohammed joined all Osman's lands to the empire, and made Samarkand a new capital. He further increased his empire a by a part of the kingdom of Gur, which extended from Herat to the sacred river of India, the Ganges.

After the death, in 1205, of Shihab ud din, fourth sovereign of the Gur line, his provinces passed under officers placed there as prefects. When Mohammed took Balkh and Herat, Mahmud, nephew of Shihab, kept merely Gur the special domain of the family, and even for this he was forced to give homage to the Kwaresmian monarch. Mahmud had reigned seven years in that reduced state when he was killed in his own palace. Public opinion in this case held the shah to be a murderer, and beyond doubt with full justice.

Ali Shir, the shah's brother, who had proclaimed himself sovereign so hurriedly when Mohammed was returning, disguised as a slave, from his war against the Gurkhan, was now at the Gur capital; he declared himself Mahmud's successor and begged the shah to confirm him as vassal. Mohammed sent an officer, as it seemed, for this ceremony, but when Ali Shir was about to put on the robe of honour sent him the officer swept off his head with a sword stroke, and produced thereupon the command of his master to do so. After this revolting deed, the Gur principality was joined to Mohammed's dominion (1213).

Three years later, 1216, Mohammed won Ghazni from a Turk general once a subject of Shihab ud din. This Turk had seized the province at the dissolution of Gur dominion. In the archives of Ghazni the shah came on letters from the Kalif Nassir at Bagdad to the Gur Khans, in which he gave warning against the

Kwaresmian Shahs, and incited to attack them, advising a junction with the Kara Kitans for that purpose.

These letters roused the shah's wrath to the utmost. The kalif, Nassir, who ascended the throne in 1180, had laboured without success, though unceasingly, to stop Kwaresmian growth and aggression. He could not employ his own forces to this end, since he had none. The temporal power of the Prophet's successors had shrunk to the narrow limits of Kuzistan and Arabian Irak. The other parts of their once vast dominions had passed to various dynasties whose sovereigns were supposed to receive lands in fief from the kalif. If these sovereigns asked for investiture, it was simply for religious, or perhaps more correctly, for political reasons.

Outside the bounds of their own little state, the Abbasid kalifs had only two emblems of sovereignty: their names were mentioned in public prayer throughout Islam, and were stamped on the coins of all Moslem commonwealths. They were not masters, even in their own capital always.

When the Seljuk Empire, composed at that time of Persian Irak alone, was destroyed by disorder under Togrul its last Sultan, the kalif, a man of quick mind and adventurous instincts, did much to bring on the dissolution of the tottering state, through his intrigues, and by calling in Tukush, the Kwaresmian monarch. He had hoped to win Persian Irak, but when Tukush had won that great province he would cede not a foot of it to any man. The kalif saw himself forced to invest a new line with the sanction of sacredness, a line which threatened Bagdad far more than that which he had helped so industriously to ruin.

When Mohammed succeeded Tukush, Nassir roused Ghiath ud din of Gur to oppose him. This prince, lord already of Balkh and Herat, desired all Khorassan, and began war to win it. His death followed soon after. Shihab ud din, the next ruler, continued the struggle but lost his whole army, which was slaughtered and crushed in the very first battle. When at Ghazni, Mohammed found proof of the kalif's intrigues, he despatched to Nassir an envoy; through this envoy he demanded the title of sultan for himself; a representative in Bagdad as governor; and also that his name be mentioned in public prayers throughout Islam. Nassir refused these demands and expressed great surprise that Mohammed, not content with his own immense empire, was coveting also the capital of the kalif.

On receiving this answer, Mohammed resolved to strip the Abbasids of the succession, or kalifat. To do this he must obtain first a sanctioning fetva from

Mohammedan theologians (the Ulema). So he proposed to that body the following questions: 'May a monarch whose entire glory consists in exalting God's word and destroying the foes of true faith, depose a recalcitrant kalif, and replace him by one who is deserving, if the kalifat belongs by right to descendants of Ali, and if the Abbasids have usurped it, and if besides they have always omitted one among the first duties, the duty of protecting the boundaries of Islam, and waging sacred wars to bring unbelievers to the true faith, or, if they will not accept the true faith, to pay tribute?'

The Ulema declared that in such cases deposition was justified. Armed with this decision, the shah recognized Ali ul Muluk of Termed, a descendant of Ali, as kalif, and ordered that in public prayers the name of Nassir be omitted. The shah assembled an army to carry out the sentence against Nassir.

Ogulmush, a Turk general who had subdued Persian Irak and then rendered fealty to Mohammed, was murdered at direction of the kalif, under whose control a number of assassins had been placed by their chieftain at Alamut. In Persian Irak the name of the shah was dropped from public prayers, after the slaying of Ogul mush. The princes of Fars and Azerbaidjan hastened promptly to seize upon Irak, at the instance of Nassir. Sád, prince of Fars, was taken captive, but secured freedom by ceding two strongholds, and promising the third of his annual income as tribute. Euzbek of Azerbaidjan fled after defeat, and the shah would not pursue, as the capture of two rulers in the space of one year was unlucky. Euzbek, on reaching home, sent envoys with presents, and proclaimed himself a vassal. Mohammed annexed Irak to the empire, and moved his troops on toward Bagdad.

Nassir sent words of peace to his enemy, but those words had no influence, and the march continued. Nassir strove to strengthen Bagdad and defend it, while Mohammed was writing diplomas, which turned Arabian Irak, that whole land of which Bagdad was the capital, into military fiefs and taxpaying districts.

The shah's vanguard, 15,000 strong, advanced toward Heulvan by the way of the mountains, and was followed soon by a second division of the same strength. Though the time was early autumn, snow fell for 20 days in succession, the largest tents were buried under it; men and horses died in great numbers, both when they were marching through those mountains and when they halted. A retreat was commanded at last when advance was impossible. Turks and Kurds then attacked the retreating forces so savagely that the ruin of the army was well-nigh total. This was attributed by Sunnite belief to divine anger for that impious attack on the person of the kalif.

The reports of Mongol movements alarmed the shah greatly and he hastened homeward, first to Nishapur, and later on to Bukhara, where he received the first envoys from Jinghis Khan, his new neighbour.

It is well to go back to the time when the shah chose a new kalif from among the descendants of Ali, the cousin and son-in-law of Mohammed. In the Moslem world there are 73 or more sects, varying in size and degree of importance, but the two great divisions of Islam are the Sunnite and Shite, which differ mainly on the succession. Among Sunnites the succession was from Abbas, the uncle of Mohammed the Prophet of Islam; that is the succession which took place in history. Among Shiites the succession which, as they think, should have taken place, but which did not, was that through Ali, the husband of Fatima, the daughter of Mohammed.

The Shiites of Persia thought that the day of justice had come after six centuries of abasement and waiting, and that the headship of Islam would be theirs through the accession of Ali ul Muluk of Termid to the Kalifat. In their eyes the Kwaresmian shah had become an agent of Allah, a sacred person. His act created an immense effect throughout Persia, and certainly no less in the capital of Islam at Bagdad, where the Kalif Nassir called a council at once to find means of defence against so dreadful an enemy as Shah Mohammed. After long discussion, one sage among those assembled declared that Jinghis Khan, whose fame was sounding then throughout Western Asia, was the man to bring the raging shah to his senses.

The kalif, greatly pleased with this statement, resolved to send an envoy, but the journey was perilous, since every road to the Mongols lay through Shah Mohammed's dominions. Should the envoy be taken and his message read, the shah, roused by resentment and anger, would spare no man involved in the plot, least of all Kalif Nassir and his servants. To avoid this chance, they shaved the envoy's head and wrote out, or branded, his commission upon it. His skull was then covered with paint, or a mixture of some kind. The entire message to Jinghis was fixed well in the mind of the envoy, and he set out on his journey.

After four months of hard traveling he reached Mongol headquarters, delivered his message in words, and was admitted soon after to the khan of the Mongols in secret. The envoy's head was shorn a second time and the credentials traced with fire on his crown became visible. There was branded in also an invitation to invade the Kwaresmian Empire, and destroy the reigning dynasty.

Jinghis meditated over this invitation. The thought of conquering a new empire did not leave him, but as he had spoken not long before with its ruler in friendship, he waited till a reason to justify attack should present itself.

In 1216–17 in Bukhara, as mentioned already, Shah Mohammed received three envoys from Jinghis; these men brought ingots of silver, musk, jade and costly white robes of camels' hair, all creations and products of Central Asia, sent as presents to the Kwaresmian sovereign. 'The great khan has charged us,' said the envoys, 'to give this message: "I salute thee! I know thy power and the great extent of thy empire. Thy reign is over a large part of the earth's surface. I have the greatest wish to live in peace with thee; I look on thee as my most cherished son. Thou art aware that I have subdued China, and brought all Turk nations north of it to obedience. Thou knowest that my country is swarming with warriors; that it is a mine of wealth, and that I have no need to covet lands of other sovereigns. I and thou have an equal interest in favouring commerce between our subjects."'

This message was in fact a demand on Mohammed to declare himself a vassal, since various degrees of relationship were used among rulers in Asia to denote corresponding degrees of submission.

The shah summoned one of the envoys in the night-time. 'Has Jinghis Khan really conquered China?' asked he. 'There is no doubt of that,' said the envoy. 'Who is this who calls me his son? How many troops has he?' The envoy, seeing Mohammed's excitement, replied that Mongol forces were not to be compared with his in any case. The shah was calmed, and when the time came he dismissed the envoys with apparent good feeling and friendliness. When they reached the boundary of the shah's land they were safe, for wherever Jinghis Khan became sovereign there was safety for travellers immediately, even in places where robbery had been the rule for many ages.

Since Kara Kitai had fallen, Mohammed's possessions reached the heart of Central Asia, and touched the land of the Uigurs, now tributary to Jinghis, hence commercial relations were direct and of very great value. Soon after the khan's envoys had made their visit, a party of between 400 and 500 merchants from Mongolian places arrived at Otrar on the Syr Daryá. Inald juk, the governor of the city, tempted by the rich stuffs and wares which those strangers had brought with them, imprisoned the whole party, and declared to the shah that the men were spies of the Mongol sovereign. The shah gave command to slay them in that case immediately, and Inaldjuk obeyed without waiting. When news of this terrible slaughter was borne to Jinghis he wept with indignation as he heard it, and went straightway to a mountain top where he bared his head, put his girdle about his neck and fell prostrate. He lay there imploring Heaven for vengeance, and spent three days and nights, it is stated, imploring and prostrate. He rose and went down then to hurl Mongol strength at the Kwaresmian Empire.

The request of the Kalif of Islam ran parallel now with the wish of the Mongols. But before striking the empire, Jinghis had resolved to extinguish Gutchluk, his old enemy, the son of Baibuga, late Taiyang of the Naimans. Meanwhile, he sent three envoys to the shah with this message: 'Thou didst give me assurance that thou wouldst not maltreat any merchant from my land. Thou hast broken thy word! Word breaking in a sovereign is hideous. If I am to believe that the merchants were not slain at Otrar by thy order, send me thy governor for punishment; if thou wilt not send him, make ready for conflict.'

Shah Mohammed, far from giving Jinghis Khan satisfaction, or offering it, slew Bajra, the first envoy, and singed off the beards of the other two. If Mohammed had wished to punish or yield up Inaldjuk he could not have done so, for the governor was a kinsman of Turkan Khatun, the Shah's mother, and also of many great chiefs in the Kwaresmian army.

And now it is important to explain the position of Turkan Khatun, the unbending, savage mother of Mohammed. This woman was a daughter of Jinkeshi, Khan of the Baijut tribe of Kankali Turks; she married Tukush, the Kwaresmian Shah, and became then the mother of Shah Mohammed. A large number of Kankali chiefs who were related to Turkan followed her with their tribesmen to serve in the Kwaresmian Empire.

The influence of this relentless, strong-willed woman, and the valour of Turkish warriors raised those chiefs to the highest rank among military leaders; their power was enormous, since commanders of troops governed with very wide latitude. Amid this aristocracy of fighters, the power of the sovereign was uncertain; he was forced to satisfy the ambition of men who saw in all things their own profit only. The troops controlled by those governors were the scourge of peaceful people; they ruined every region which they lived in or visited.

Turkan Khatun, the head of this military faction, not only equalled her son in authority, but often surpassed him. When two orders of different origin appeared in any part of the empire, the date decided which had authority; that order was always carried out on which the date was most recent, and the order of recent date was the order of that watchful woman. When Mohammed won a new province, he always assigned a large part to the appanage of his mother. She employed seven secretaries at all times, men distinguished for ability. The inscription on her decrees was 'Protectress of the world and the faith, Turkan, queen of women.' Her device was: 'God alone is my refuge.' 'Lord of the world' was her title.

The following example shows clearly the character of the Shah's mother: She had obtained from Mohammed the elevation of Nassir ud din, a former slave of hers, to the position of vizir, or prime minister of the empire; soon the shah came to hate the man, for personal and also other reasons. His ability was small, and his greed without limit. At Nishapur, the shah appointed a new judge, one Sadr ud din, and forbade him to give the vizir any presents. Friends, however, warned the judge not to neglect this prime dignitary, so he sent Nassir ud din a sealed purse containing 4,000 gold pieces. The shah, who was watching both judge and vizir, caused the latter to send the purse to him. It was sent straightway, and the seal was intact on it. The judge was summoned, and when he appeared the shah asked before witnesses what gift he had made the vizir; he denied having made any, persisted in denial, and swore by the head of his sovereign that he had not given one coin to the minister. The shah had the purse brought; the judge was deprived of his dignity. The vizir was sent home without office to his patroness.

Nassir ud din went back to the shah's mother. On the way he decided every case that men brought him. On the vizir's approach Turkan Khatun ordered people of all ranks and classes to go forth and meet him. The vizir grew more insolent now than he had been. The shah sent an officer to bring the recalcitrant minister's head to him. When the officer came to her capital, Turkan Khatun sent him to the vizir, who was then in the divan and presiding. She had given the officer this order: 'Salute the vizir in the shah's name, and say to him: "I have no vizir except thee, continue in thy functions. No man in my empire may destroy thee, or fail in respect to thee."'

The officer carried out the command of the woman. Nassir ud din exercised his authority in defiance of Mohammed; he could do so since Turkan Khatun upheld him, and she had behind her a legion of her murderous kinsmen. The sovereign, who had destroyed so many rulers unsparingly, had not the power or the means to manage one insolent upstart who defied him.

The murder of the merchants in Otrar was followed soon by such a tempest of ruin as had never been witnessed in Asia or elsewhere. Shah Mohammed had mustered at Samarkand a large army to move against Gutchluk, whom he wished to bring down to subjection or destroy altogether, but hearing that a body of Merkits was advancing through Kankali regions lying north of Lake Aral, he marched to Jend straightway against them, and learned upon reaching that city, that those Merkits, being allies of Gutchluk, were hunted by Jinghis, and that Gutchluk himself had been slain by the Mongols.

He returned swiftly to Samarkand for additional forces, and following the tracks of both armies, found a field strewn with corpses, among which he saw a Merkit badly wounded; from this man the shah learned that the Jinghis had gained a great victory, and gone forward.

One day later, Mohammed came up with them and formed his force straightway to attack them. The Mongol leader (perhaps Juchi) declared that the two states were at peace, and that he had commands to treat the shah's troops with friendliness; he even offered a part of his booty and prisoners to Mohammed. The latter refused these and answered: 'If Jinghis has ordered thee not to meet me in battle, God commands me to fall on thy forces. I wish to inflict sure destruction on infidels and thus earn Divine favour.'

The Mongols, forced to give battle, came very near victory. They had put Mohammed's left wing to flight, pierced the centre where the shah was, and would have dispersed it, but for timely aid brought by Jelal ud din, the shah;s son, who rushed from the right and restored the battle, which lasted till evening and was left undecided.

The Mongols lighted vast numbers of campfires and retired in the dark with such swiftness that at daybreak they had made two days' journey.

After this encounter, the Shah knew Mongol strength very clearly. He told intimates that he had never seen men fight as they had.

Jinghis, having ended Gutchluk and his kingdom (1218), summoned his own family and officers to a council where they discussed war with Mohammed, and settled everything touching this enterprise and its management. That same autumn the Mongol conqueror began his march westward, leaving the care of home regions to his youngest brother. He spent all the following summer near the Upper Irtish, arranging his immense herds of horses and cattle. The march was resumed in the autumn, when he was joined by the prince of Almalik, the Idikut of the Uigurs, and by Arslan, khan of the Karluks.

Shah Mohammed was alarmed by the oncoming of this immense host of warriors, more correctly this great group of armies, though his own force was large, since it numbered 400,000. His troops were in some ways superior to the Mongols, but they lacked iron discipline and blind confidence in leaders; they lacked also that experience of hardship, fatigue and privation, that skill in desperate fighting, which made the Mongols not merely a terror, but, at that time, invincible. The Kwaresmian armies were defending a population to which they were indifferent, and which they were protecting, hence victory gave scant rewards in the best case, while the Mongols, in attacking rich, flourishing countries, were excited by all that can rouse human greed, or tempt wild cupidity. The disparity in leaders was still more apparent. On the Mongol side was a chief of incomparable genius in all that he was doing; on the other side a vacillating sovereign with warring and wavering counsels. The shah had been crushing and assassinating rulers all his reign, and now he feared to meet a man whom he had provoked by his outrages. Instead of concentrating forces and meeting the enemy, he scattered his men among all the cities of Transoxiana, and then withdrew and kept far from the fields of real struggle. Some ascribed this to the advice of his generals, others to his faith in astrologers, who declared that the stars were unfavourable, and that no battle should be risked till they changed their positions. It is also reported that Jinghis duped the Shah, and made him suspect his own leaders. The following is one of the stories:

A certain Bedr ud din of Otrar, whose father, uncle and other kinsmen had been slain by Mohammed, declared to Jinghis that he wished to take vengeance on the shah, even should he lose his own soul in so doing, and advised the Grand Khan to make use of the quarrels kept up by Mohammed with his mother. In view of this Bedr ud din wrote a letter, as it were, from Mohammed's generals to Jinghis, and composed it in this style: 'We came from Turkistan to Mohammed because of his mother. We have given him victory over many other rulers whose states have increased the Kwaresmian Empire. Now he pays his dear mother with ingratitude. This princess desires us to avenge her. When thou art here, we shall be at thy orders.'

Jinghis so arranged that this letter was intercepted. The tale is, that the shah was deceived by it and distrusted his generals, hence separated them each from the others, and disposed them in various strong cities. It is more likely by far, that he and they, after testing Mongol strength, thought it better to fight behind walls than in the open. They thought also, no doubt, that the Mongols, after pillaging the country and seizing many captives, would retire with their booty.

The shah was light-minded and ignorant. He knew not with whom he was dealing. He had not studied the Mongols, and could not have done so; he had no idea whatever of Jinghis Khan and could not acquire it; he knew not the immense power of his system, and the far reaching nature of his wishes.

Jinghis arrived at the Syr Daryá with his army, and arranged all his troops in four great divisions. The first he fixed near Otrar and placed two of his sons, Ogotai and Jagatai, in command of it; the second, commanded by his eldest son, Juchi, was to act against the other cities, from Jend to Lake Aral; the third division he directed against Benakit on the river, south of Jend. While the three divisions were taking these cities on the Syr Darya, Jinghis himself moved toward Bokhara to bar Shah Mohammed from the Transoxiana, and prevent him from reinforcing any garrison between the two rivers.

Otrar was invested late in November 1218. The walls had been strengthened, and the city, with its fortress, provisioned very carefully. The strong garrison had been increased by 10,000 horsemen. After a siege of five months, the troops and the citizens were discouraged, and the commander thought it best to surrender, but Inaldjuk, the governor, could not hope for his life, since he was the man who had slain the Mongol merchants; hence, he would not hear of surrender. He would fight, as he said, to the death, for his sovereign. The chief of the horsemen felt differently, and led out his best troops in the night to escape, but was captured. He and they offered then to serve the besiegers. The Mongols inquired about conditions in the city, and, when the chief had told what he knew, they informed him that he and his men, being unfaithful to their master, could not be true to another. They thereupon slew him, and all who were with him.

The city was taken that day, April 1219, and its inhabitants driven to the country outside, so that the captors might pillage the place in absolute freedom. Inaldjuk, the governor, withdrew with 20,000 men to the fortress, and fought for two months in that stronghold. When the Mongols burst in, he had only two men left; with these he retired to a terrace. The two men at his side fell soon after. When his arrows were gone, he hurled brickbats. The besiegers had orders to seize the man living. He struggled like a maniac, but they caught and bound him at last, and bore him to the camp before Samarkand. Jinghis had molten silver poured into his ears and eyes to avenge the slaughtered merchants. The surviving inhabitants of Otrar were spared but the fortress was levelled.

Juchi, before marching on Jend, went to Signak and asked that the gates be thrown open. Scarcely had the message been given when the furious inhabitants tore Hassan Hadji, Juchi's envoy, to pieces and called on God's name as they did so.

Juchi gave the order at once to attack, and forbade his men to cease fighting till the city was captured. Fresh troops relieved those who were wearied. After seven days of storming, the Mongols burst in and slew every soul in that city.

Juchi made a son of Hassan Hadji commandant of the ruins; then he moved up the river and sacked every place that he visited.

As the Mongols drew near to Jend, Katluk Khan, the commandant, fled in the night-time, crossed the Syr Darya and took the desert road for Urgendj beyond the southern shore of the Oxus. Juchi demanded surrender through Chin Timur his envoy. Deserted by their chief, the people were in doubt what to do, and when Chin Timur came they wished to kill him, but he told them of Signak, and promised to turn aside Mongol vengeance in case they were prudent. The people then freed him, but very soon saw the enemy under the walls, which they thought proof against every besieger. The Mongols scaled those walls quickly, and rushed in from all sides. No hand was raised then against them. The inhabitants were driven to the open country and left nine days and nights there, while the pillage continued. Excepting those who had abused Chin Timur, the people were spared, since they had made no resistance.

Meanwhile a detachment of the army had seized Yengikend, the last town on the river, and Juchi's work was done on the right bank with thoroughness.

The third division of the army moved from Otrar to the left up the river, and attacked Benakit which was garrisoned by Kankalis. At the end of three days, the officers wished to capitulate. Their lives were promised them, and they surrendered. The inhabitants were driven from the city. The Turks were taken out to one side, and cut down to the last man, with swords and other weapons. Being warriors whom the Mongols could not trust, they were slaughtered. The artisans were spared and divided among the Mongol army. Unskilled, young and strong men were taken to assist in besieging; all other people were slain immediately.

The march was continued to Khodjend, and soon the invaders were in front of that city and storming it. In Khodjend, Timur Melik, a man of great valour, commanded. He took 1,000 chosen warriors to a fort on an island far enough from either bank to be safe from stones and arrows. The besiegers were reinforced by

20,000 Mongols for conflict, and 50,000 natives of the country to carry on siege work. These natives were employed first of all at bearing stones from a mountain three leagues distant, and building a road from the shore to the fortress in the river. Timur Melik meanwhile built 12 covered barges, protected from fire with glazed earth, which was first soaked in vinegar. Every day, six of these boats went to each shore and sent arrows, through openings, at the Mongols. Night attacks were made suddenly and wrought much harm on the invaders.

But despite every effort, Timur saw that failure would come if he stayed there. He was met by preponderant and crushing numbers at last. So he put men and baggage in seventy strong boats and his chosen warriors in the 12 covered barges; and they sped down the swift river at night by the light of many torches fixed on the boats of his flotilla. The boats snapped a chain stretched across from one bank to the other by Mongols near Benakit, and passed along, hunted by the enemy on both sides.

Timur learned now that Juchi had posted a large corps of men on the two banks, close to Jend, captured recently; he learned also that balistas were ready and that a bridge of boats had been made near the same place. He debarked higher up, therefore, and took to horse to avoid capture. Pursued by the enemy, he gave battle till his baggage was brought near him. He repeated this day after day till forced at last to abandon the baggage. Finally, having lost all his men, he was alone and pursued by three Mongols. He had only three arrows left, one of these had no metal point on it; he shot that and put out an eye of the nearest pursuer. Then he cried to the other men: 'There are two arrows still in my quiver, ye would better go back with your eyesight.' They did so. Timur Melik made his way to Urgendj, and joined Jelal ud din, whom he followed till the death of that sovereign.

Meanwhile, Jinghis moved against Bokhara with his main forces and arrived at that city during June of 1219. On the way he seized Nur and Charnuk, which he pillaged; then he took from those places all stalwart men useful in siege work. Bokhara, the great city with a garrison of 20,000, was invested on all sides, and attacked by relays of fresh warriors, who gave neither respite nor rest to it.

After some days, the defenders lost hope of success and resolved to burst through in the night-time, trusting in that way to save themselves. They fell on the Mongols unexpectedly, and scattered them, but instead of pursuing this advantage and fighting, those escaping defenders hastened forward. The Mongol troops rallied, and hunted the fugitives to the river, where they cut down nearly all of them.

Next morning early, the Ulema and notables came out to give homage to the great Mongol Khan, and open the gates to him. Jinghis rode in, and going to the main mosque of the city entered it on horseback. Dismounting near the minbar, or pulpit, he ascended some steps of it and said to the people who assembled there quickly before him: 'The fields now are stripped; feed our horses in this place!'

The boxes which had been used to hold copies of the Koran were taken to the courtyard to hold grain for Mongol horses; the sacred volumes were thrown under the hoofs of those animals and trampled. Skins of wine were brought into the mosque with provisions; jesters and singers of the city were summoned, and while wild warriors were revelling in excesses of all sorts, and shouting songs of their own land and people, the highest chiefs of religion and doctors of law served them as slaves, held their horses and fed them. While thus employed one great man whispered to his neighbour: 'Why not implore the Almighty to save us?' 'Be silent,' said the other, 'God's wrath is moving near us; this is no time for beseeching. I fear to pray to the Almighty lest it become worse with us thereby. If life is dear to thee hold their beasts now for the Mongols, and serve them.'

From the mosque, Jinghis went to the place of public prayer beyond the city, and summoned all people to meet there. He stood in the pulpit and inquired: 'Who are the richest men in this multitude?' Two hundred and eighty persons were presented; 90 of these had come from other cities. The khan commanded all those wealthy persons to draw near, and then he spoke to them. He described the shah's cruelties and injustice, which had brought on the ruin of their city: 'Know,' continued he, 'that ye have committed dreadful deeds, and the great people of this country are the worst of its criminals. Should ye ask why I speak thus, I answer: I am Heaven's scourge, sent to punish. Had ye not been desperate offenders I should not be standing here now against you.' Then he said that he required no one to deliver wealth which was above ground, his men could discover that very easily, but he asked for hidden treasures. The wealthy men were then forced to name their agents, and those agents had to yield up the treasures, or be tortured. All strong men were set to filling the moats encircling the city; even copies of the Koran and furniture of mosques were hurled in to fill ditches. The fortress was stormed and not a man of its defenders found mercy.

When the fortress was taken, all its inhabitants were driven from the city with nothing but the clothes which they had on their bodies. Then began the great pillage. The victors slew all whom they found in any place of hiding. At last Mongol troops were sent out to surround the inhabitants on the plain, and divide them into parties. Deeds were done there which baffle description. Every possible outrage was enacted before those to whom it was most dreadful to be present, and have eyesight. Some had strength to choose death instead of looking at those horrors; among spectators of this kind were the chief judge of the city, and the first Imam, who seeing the dishonour of their women rushed to save them, and perished.

Finally the city was fired; everything wooden was consumed, nothing was left save the main mosque, and a few brick palaces.

Jinghis Khan left the smoking ruins of Bokhara the Noble, to march on Samarkand, which was only five days distant. He passed along the pleasant valley of Sogd, covered at that time with beautiful fields, orchards and gardens and with houses here and there in good number. All inhabitants of Bokhara taken to toil in the coming siege were driven on behind the army. Whoso grew weak on the way or too weary for marching was cut down at once without pity.

Samarkand was one of the great commercial cities of the world. It had a garrison which numbered 40,000. Both the city and the citadel had been fortified with care, and all men considered that a siege of that place would continue for months, nay, for years perhaps.

The three other army corps appeared now, for every place on the lower river had been taken, and Northern Transoxiana was subjected. These divisions brought with them all captives who were young, firm and stalwart, men who might be of service in siege work; there was an immense host of those people arranged in groups of 10, and each 10 had a banner. Jinghis, to impose on the doomed city, paraded his legions before it; cavalry, infantry, and at last those unfortunate captives who had the seeming of regular warriors.

Two days were spent in examining the city defences and out works; on the third morning early, the Mongol conqueror sounded the onset. A host of brave citizens made a great sally, and at first swept all before them but not being sustained by their own troops, who feared the besiegers, they met a dreadful disaster. The Mongols retired before the onrushing people, who pressed forward with vigour till they fell into ambush; being on foot they were surrounded very quickly and slaughtered before the eyes of the many thousands looking from the walls, and the housetops. This great defeat crushed the hopes of the citizens.

The Kankali troops being Turks believed that the Mongols would treat them most surely as kinsmen. In fact, Jinghis had promised, as they thought, to take them to his service. Hence this great multitude, the real strength of the city, issued forth that same day with their leaders, their families and their baggage, in one word, with all that belonged to them. On the fourth day, just as the storm was to be sounded, the chief men of the city went to the Mongol camp, where they received satisfactory answers concerning themselves with their families and dependents; hence they opened the gates of Samarkand to the conqueror; but they were driven from the city save 50,000 who had put themselves under the protection of the cadi and the mufti. These 50,000 were safeguarded, the others were all slaughtered.

The night following the surrender, Alb Khan, a Turk general, made a sortie from the citadel and had the fortune to break through the Mongols, thus saving himself and those under him. At daybreak the citadel was attacked simultaneously on all sides. That struggle lasted till the evening, when one storming party burst in, and the stronghold was taken. One thousand defenders took refuge in a mosque and fought with desperation. The mosque was fired then, and all were burned to death in it. The Kankalis who had yielded on the third day, that is the first day of fighting, were conducted to a place beyond the city and kept apart from others. Their horses, arms and outfits were taken from them, and their hair was shaved in front, Mongol fashion, as if they were to form a part of the army. This was a trick to deceive them till the executioners were ready. In one night, the Kankalis were murdered to the very last man.

When vast numbers of the citizens had been slaughtered, a census was made of the remnant: 30,000 persons of various arts, occupations and crafts were given by Jinghis to his sons, his wives and his officers; 30,000 more were reserved for siege labour; 50,000, after they had paid 200,000 gold pieces, were permitted to return to the city, which received Mongol commandants. Requisitions of men were made at later periods repeatedly, and, since few of those persons returned to their homes, Samarkand stood ruined and unoccupied for a long time.

Jinghis Khan so disposed his forces from the first, that Shah Mohammed could not relieve any city between the two rivers; now all those cities were taken, and the forces defending them were slaughtered. The next great work was to seize Shah Mohammed himself, and then slay him, and with him his family.

Thirty thousand chosen men were employed now in chasing the Kwaresmian ruler. Never had a sovereign been hunted like this victim of the Mongols. He fled like a fox, or a hare; he was hunted as if he had been a dreadful wild beast, which had killed some high or holy person, or as if he were some outcast, who had committed a deed which might make a whole nation shudder. But here we must say a few words concerning the hunted man, and explain his position.

Chapter VII
Flight and Death of Mohammed

WHILE THE MONGOLS WERE RUINING Northern Transoxiana Mohammed held aloof from every action, and was discouraged so deeply that his weakness affected all people of the empire. While fortifying Samarkand he passed by the moat one day, and made this remark: 'The Mongols are so many that they could fill this moat with their horsewhips.' When Jinghis had captured the northern line beyond the Oxus, Mohammed moved southward by way of Naksheb, telling all people to care for themselves, since his troops could not protect them. The diversity of opinions among his commanders and ministers increased his hesitation. The best warriors declared that Transoxiana was lost, but that Khorassan and Irak must be guarded; that troops must be concentrated, a general levy enforced and the Amu Darya be defended at all costs. Others advised to fall back upon Ghazni, and there meet the Mongols; if beaten, the shah might retire beyond the Indus. This being the most timid course Mohammed favoured and chose it; but, joined at Balkh by Amad ul mulk, the vizir, he altered that plan at the instance of Amad, who was prime minister of Rokn ud din, the shah's son who held Persian Irak as an appanage, and had sent Amad to his father hoping thus to be rid of him.

The position of Amad was of this sort: He wished to be near Shah Mohammed, his protector, and he was drawn toward his birthplace, the home of his family; so he persuaded the shah to change plans and go to Persian Irak, where he would find men and means to force back the Mongols. Jelal ud din, the best son of Mohammed, in fact the only brave man in the family, was opposed to both projects; he would not talk of retreat, he would stop the invasion at the Oxus. 'If thou retire to Irak,' said he, 'give me thy forces. I will drive back the Mongols, and liberate the empire.' Every discussion, however, was fruitless; the shah treated all his son's reasons as folly. 'Success,' said Mohammed, 'is fixed from eternity, defeat is averted by a change in the stars, and not otherwise.'

Before he left his position at Balkh, Mohammed sent men to Pendjde, a point north of Termed, to collect information of the enemy's movements. Tidings came quickly that Bokhara had been captured, that Samarkand had surrendered. Delaying his journey no longer, the shah started off in hot haste through Khorassan. Most of the troops who went with him were Turks whose chiefs were his mother's adherents and kinsmen; these formed a plot very quickly to kill him. Forewarned of their treachery, Mohammed left his tent during night hours; next morning it was seen to be riddled with arrows. His fears increased greatly, and he hastened on till he reached Nishap, where he halted, thinking that the Mongols would not cross the river Oxus in any case.

From Samarkand, Jinghis despatched Chepé with 10,000, Subotai with a second 10,000 and Tuguchar with a third corps of similar numbers. The order given these was to ride with all speed to the camp of the Shah. If they found him at the head of large forces to wait till reinforcements came up to them; if he had few, to attack and secure him; if fleeing, to pursue, and with Heaven's help take and keep him; to spare cities which yielded; to ruin utterly those which resisted.

The pursuing Mongols swept through Khorassan untiringly. This splendid province had four famous cities: Balkh, Herat, Merv and Nishapur. Besides these there were others of considerable, though minor, importance. When the Mongols were near Balkh that city sent forth a deputation with presents and submission. A Mongol governor was placed in it. Zaveh closed its gates and refused all supplies; unwilling to lose time there at siege work the Mongols pressed forward, but since people mounted the walls then, and stood beating drums and abusing them, they turned and attacked that foolish city which reviled them. They stormed the place, put to the sword every man in it, and burned what they had not the power to take with them.

On and on rode the Mongols. People met on the way to Nishapur were seized and put to torture till they told what they knew of the fleeing Mohammed. Cities were summoned to surrender; those that surrendered were spared and received new commandants. If cities which resisted were weak, they were stormed; if strong, they were left till a later occasion, since the work then on hand was to capture Mohammed.

When the shah learned that the enemy had entered Khorassan, he left Nishapur with a small escort under pretext of hunting. Consternation filled that place when the truth grew apparent. After the shah deserted the city, the vizir with the mufti and the cadi ruled, pending the arrival of a governor, who was on the way from Urgendj, the Kwaresmian capital. This man died when three days from the end of his journey; his household officials kept his death secret lest the escort might seize all his movable property. One of the regents went forth as if to meet him, and brought in his treasure. The escort, 1,000 in number, would not stay in the city, but went in search of Mohammed. Next day those men, when nine miles from Nishapur, were met by a new host of Mongols who attacked very quickly and cut them to pieces.

The city was summoned to open its gates and the three regents gave answer as follows: 'When Shah Mohammed is captured, Nishapur will surrender.' The first Mongol party that demanded provisions received them and vanished. Day after day new bodies rushed up to the city, received what they asked for and rode away swiftly. At last, Chepé came and commanded the vizir, the mufti and cadi to appear at headquarters. Three supposititious men were sent out to meet him with gifts and provisions. The general gave these men the khan's proclamation in Uigur characters, and this was its import: 'O commandants, officials and people! Know ye that Heaven has given me the empire of the earth, both the east and the west of it. Those who submit will be spared; woe to those who resist, they will be slaughtered with their children, and wives and dependents. Give provisions to all troops that come, and think not to meet water with fire, or to trust in your walls, or the numbers of those who defend them. If ye try to escape utter ruin will seize you.'

The three bodies of Mongols, 10,000 each which were speeding on now in pursuit of Mohammed were rushing toward Irak. Subotai passed through Damegan and Simnan, and crossed the Kumus River. Chepé Noyon, who had gone by Mazanderan, rejoined Subotai at Rayi. This place they took by surprise, and then sacked it.

From Nishapur, Mohammed hastened on to Kazvin, where his son Rokn un din had an army; there he took counsel with the leaders of that army which was 30,000 in number, and sent for Hezerasp, prince of Lur, who advised a retreat across the mountain chain lying between Fars and Lur. The shah wished to stay in Irak and increase his defence there; he had just stated that wish when news came that Rayi had been taken and plundered. Chiefs and princes fled straightway on hearing this. Each went his own road, and the whole army vanished immediately, so great was the terror inspired by the onrushing Mongols.

The shah fled for safety to his sons in Karun. On the way Mongol forces were in sight and almost caught him, unwittingly. They sent arrows at the fleeing man though not knowing who he was and wounded the horse which he was riding, but the beast held out and bore him safely to the fortress. Next morning, he fled farther along the road lying westward toward Bagdad. Barely had he ridden away when the Mongols, who knew now whose horse they had wounded, rushed in, thinking to seize the hunted man surely. They attacked the fort furiously at first, but learning soon that the shah had escaped they hurried after him. On the way they met men who professed to be guides dismissed by Mohammed; from these men they heard that he was fleeing to Bagdad. They took the guides then and rushed forward, but the shah was on a new road at that time. The Mongols soon saw that they had lost his trail, and were tricked, so they cut down the guides and returned to Karun.

Mohammed had fled to Serdjihan, a strong place northeast of Kazvin on a mountain. Seven days he remained there; he then fled to Gilan, and next to Mazanderan, where he appeared stripped of property and almost unattended. The Mongols had preceded him, having sacked two towns already, Amol the capital, and Astrabad a place of much commerce. 'Where am I to find safety from Mongols? Is there no spot on earth where I can be free of them?' Such was the cry of Mohammed. 'Go to some little island in the Caspian, that will be the safest place!' said some of his friends. This advice pleased Shah Mohammed, so he stopped in a village on the seashore, intending to follow it. He prayed five times each day in the mosque, had the Koran read to him and promised God tearfully that justice would reign in his empire as never on earth up to that day, should power ever come to him a second time.

While Mohammed was thus engaged in that village, Mongols appeared on a sudden. They were guided by Rokn ud din, a small prince of that region. This man's uncle and cousin had been killed by Shah Mohammed, who seized their lands in the days of his insolence and his greedy ambition. Rokn ud din's hatred had sent him as a guide to the Mongols, and thus he recovered his family inheritance. The shah had barely time to spring into a boat and push out from shore when his enemies were upon him. Enraged at the loss of their victim, many horsemen sprang after the boat, but they failed to reach it and were drowned in the Caspian.

Mohammed, who was suffering gravely from pleurisy and weakness, declared as he sailed from the shore, that after reigning over many kingdoms and lands he lacked even a few ells of earth for a resting place. The fallen man reached a small island and was childishly joyous at finding a safe place of refuge. His house was a tent with little in it, but the people of the coast brought him food, and whatever else might be pleasing to the monarch, as they thought. In return Mohammed gave them brevets of office, or titles to land which they wrote themselves frequently, since he had sent most of his small suite to bring his sons to him. Later on, when Jelal ud din had regained some part of his possessions he honoured all gages of this kind.

The shah's illness increased, and he lost hope of recovery. His sons came and then he withdrew from Oslag the inheritance. 'Save Jelal ud din there is none of you who can recover the empire,' declared Mohammed. The failing monarch took his own sabre which he girded on Jelal ud din, and commanded the younger brothers to show him obedience. Mohammed breathed his last some days later, January 10, 1221, and was buried on that island. There was no cloth for a shroud, so he was buried in another man's shirt. His funeral was small and the ceremony scant at his burial. Such was the end which Jinghis gave a great sovereign who, till his attack on the Kalif of Islam, ruled over a vast country and found success everywhere save in the struggles with his mother.

Before crossing the Oxus, Mohammed directed Turkan Khatun, who governed Urgendj, the modern Khiva, to retire to Mazanderan and live there in the mountains, taking with her his harem. Jinghis, informed clearly of the quarrels between the shah and his mother, sent Danishmend, his chancellor, to that relentless, harsh woman, and this was his message: 'Thy son is ungrateful, I know that. If thou agree with me, I will not touch Kwaresm, which thou art ruling. I will give thee, moreover, Khorassan when I win it. Send a trusty man, he will hear this assurance from my own lips directly.'

Turkan Khatun gave no answer, but left Kwaresm as soon as she heard that her son had Aed westward. Before going, however, she put to death all the princes whom the Shah had despoiled and imprisoned; among these were both sons of Togrul, the last Seljuk sultan of Irak; the Balkh prince and his son, the sovereign of

Termed; the prince of Bamian; the Vakhsh prince, the two sons of the lord of Signak, and the two sons of Mahmud, last prince of Gur. She had all these men thrown into the Oxus and drowned, sparing only Omar, Khan of Yazer, who could be of use on her journey, since he knew all the roads which led to his own land and birthplace. In fact, he served the woman well, till they were near Yazer, when his head was cut off at her order, as she had no further use for him.

When Mohammed had fled to Mazanderan he directed his mother, as we have seen, to live in Ilak, the best stronghold in all that great region of mountain. Later on, Subotai, who was hunting Mohammed, left a body of men to invest that strong fortress. As Ilak was in a rainy, damp climate no reservoirs had been made for dry periods; while the place was invested that happened which came to pass rarely, a dry season. After a blockade of some months, drought forced a surrender. But just after the Mongols had taken possession, the sky was covered densely with clouds which brought a great rainfall.

Turkan Khatun and the harem were taken to the camp of Jinghis, who was before Talekan at that time and besieging it. She was held captive there strictly. All the sons of Mohammed found in the harem were put to death promptly. Two of his daughters were given to Jagatai, who made one of them his concubine, and gave the other as a present to his manager; a third was given as wife to the chancellor, Danishmend. The widow of Osman, Khan of Samarkand, she who had insisted on the execution of her husband, and was the daughter of the Gurkhan, was given in marriage to a dyer, but by another account she was given to Juchi, who had by her afterward several children. Turkan Khatun, the strong, brutal woman, was taken to Kara Kurum, the Mongol capital, where she died eight years later. Just before she was captured a eunuch had urged her to find refuge with Jelal ud din, her own grandson, who was nearby, he declared, with a numerous army. Turkan replied that captivity of any kind was sweeter to her than salvation at his hand. Such was the hate which she felt toward her grandson. Nassir ud din, the vizir who had defied Shah Mohammed, was put to death at Talekan with a number of others.

Mohammed's three elder sons made their way to Mangishlak by the Caspian and thence to Urgendj, the Kwaresmian capital. Since the flight of their grandmother, the capital had been without rule; in her haste she had left no governor there. Seventy thousand men gathered round the three princes immediately. The commanders, being Kankali Turks, were dissatisfied that Jelal ud din had succeeded his father; they feared his strong will and plotted to kill him. The new shah saw very clearly that his one chance of safety was flight, and he seized that chance quickly. With 300 warriors under Timur Melik, that Khodjend commandant who had escaped through the Mongol investment, he fled across the desert to Nessa.

After the capture of Samarkand, Jinghis stationed his troops between that place and Naksheb where they spent the spring of 1221 and also the summer. Toward autumn his forces were reorganized thoroughly. Having rested, they were strong and now ready for action. The return of Mohammed's sons at Urgendj and the gathering of forces there roused the khan's vigilance, so he despatched thither an army at once under his sons, Juchi, Jagatai and Ogotai. To cut off retreat toward the Indus he formed a cordon on the southern rim of the desert; a part of this cordon was already near Nessa when Jelal ud din and his party arrived there. He attacked this line of men valiantly, forced it to flight and pushed on without stopping. This was the first victory won over Mongols in the Kwaresmian Empire. The two younger brothers, hearing of the advance on Urgendj, set out three days later, but failed of such fortune as their brother, and perished near Nessa. Their heads fixed on lances were borne through Khorassan.

When the Mongol troops arrived before Urgendj, Juchi, who was in command, sent to the capital a summons to surrender, informing the people that his father had given him the city and that he did not wish to injure it in any way. As no attention was paid to this summons the siege was begun at once. The Mongols endeavoured to divert the waters of the Oxus above the town, but with no success, for the workmen were killed by the garrison. Quarrels between Juchi and Jagatai impeded siege work very greatly. Jinghis, angered by this delay, placed Ogotai in command. Juchi was enraged at being thus superseded by a younger brother, but he could not withdraw. The siege lasted seven months and gained great renown through the desperate defence made by citizens. After the general assault which decided the fate of the city the people continued resistance with fury; driven from one street they fought in the next. Women and even children took part in these struggles, which continued seven days and nights without ceasing. At last, the inhabitants asked to capitulate. 'We have felt thy wrath,' declared they to the Mongol commander, 'thy time has come now to show favour.' 'How!' exclaimed Ogotai. They mention our wrath, they who have slain so many of our army? We have felt their wrath very heavily and now we will show them what ours is!'

He ordered all the inhabitants to go forth from the city and wait on the plain; the artisans were to group themselves separately. These artisans were spared, but were sent to Mongolia. Some of them fearing such an exile, joined with the people and waited. Except artisans no one was spared unless youthful women, and also children; all were cut down by Ogotai, without mercy.

After this slaughter, the Mongols plundered Urgendj of everything which had value. Then they opened the sluices of the Oxus and flooded the city; those who were hidden there perished. In other places, some persons saved themselves always, but here, those who escaped Mongol fury and hid themselves were drowned by the water let in on them.

Jinghis camped that summer on the rich Naksheb steppes, where his vast herds of horses found rest and good pasture. In the autumn, a new and great campaign was begun by the siege laid to Termed. This city, on the north or right bank of the Oxus, refused to surrender and was taken by storm on the 10th day of action. All the inhabitants were driven beyond the suburbs and massacred; a certain old woman stopped the sword above her head and promised a rare pearl if they spared her. When they asked for the treasure, she answered, 'I have swallowed it.' They ripped her body open and found the costly pearl in her stomach. Thinking that others might have swallowed jewels in like fashion, Jinghis commanded to rip bodies open thenceforward.

The Mongol Khan passed the next winter between Balkh and the Badakshan boundary, subduing, ravaging, destroying all cities of note, and every place of distinction or value. Before the winter had ended that whole region north of the Oxus was ruined, and was a horror to look upon. In spring he crossed the river at a ford and was met by a Balkh deputation with gifts and submission. Humility brought that rich famous place no salvation. Jinghis, who knew that Jelal ud din, the new sovereign, was at Ghazni with an army, would not leave a strong fortress behind him. Under pretext of making a census he directed the people in Balkh to assemble outside near the suburbs. They went forth and were slaughtered most brutally; the city was pillaged, then burned, and all its defences demolished.

The time of terror came next to Nusrat i kuh in the Talekan district. This place, strong by position, by its works, and its garrison, defended itself for six months with immense strength, and successfully. Prisoners in large numbers were forced to fight in the front lines of investment. Those who turned back were cut down without mercy by the Mongols behind them. A huge earth mound was reared and catapults placed on it; with these the besiegers battered the interior of the fortress. At last, the brave garrison made a great sally on foot and on horseback; the horsemen escaped to the mountains, but the foot forces were like wild beasts at bay; they fought till the enemy had slain every man of them. The Mongols then burst into the city; they spared no living soul in it and left not one stone on another.

While the khan's army was destroying Nusrat i kuh, Tului returned to his father after wasting Khorassan, the richest and most beautiful part of the empire. When Tului had set out for this work of destruction Khorassan had been already ravaged by Subotai and by Chepé, who did the work only in part as they rushed along hunting Mohammed. These two chiefs left a commandant in each place which yielded. After they had passed, and when news came of victories won, as men said, by Mohammed, people hitherto terrified recovered their courage. For instance, the chief of militia in Tus killed the Mongol commandant and sent his head to Nishapur, the next city, as a trophy; but this chief suffered soon after for his levity and rashness. A strange captain came with a detachment to Tus, put nearly all native troops to the sword, and forced the Tus citizens to destroy their defences.

When Tului received the command in 1220 to march on Khorassan, he sent forward 10,000 men, under Togachar, as a vanguard. This body went on toward Nessa and when approaching that city a part of it met with resistance. Belgush, its commander, fell in the action which followed. Togachar, to avenge the death of Belgush, besieged Nessa. Shah Mohammed, when fleeing, had sent an official to advise Nessa people: 'The Mongols,' said he, 'will abandon the empire when they have plundered it, so flee to the desert, or to mountainous regions, unless ye wish to rebuild the old fortress, which was razed by my father.' They rebuilt the old fortress.

Togachar attacked Nessa, using 20 catapults handled by captives, who, whenever they fell back, were massacred by Mongols behind them. On the 16th day at dawn, a breach in the wall was affected; the Mongols burst through and drove out the inhabitants. On the plain near Nessa some were forced to bind others; when the hands of each man were bound behind his back the Mongols slaughtered all who were there, 70,000 in number.

The ancient city of Meru, or Merv, renowned in Persian story, and still more in Sanscrit poems, was the first place attacked by Tului with the main army. It was one of the four ruling cities, and the one which Melik Shah and Sindjar, the Seljuk Sultans, had favoured. It stood on a broad, fertile plain through which flowed the Murghab, or Bird, River. When Mohammed fled from Jinghis he directed Merv troops and officials to retire on Meraga, a neighbouring fortress. 'All people who remain must receive Mongol troops with submission,' this was his order. Mohammed's fear, not his counsel, remained in that city. His governor, Behai ul Mulk, did not think Meraga strong and found elsewhere a refuge; some chiefs returned to Merv, others fled to distant places. The new governor, a man of no value, declared for submission, and so did the mufti, but the judge and descendants of the Prophet demanded resistance. The governor lost his place soon and was followed in office by a former incumbent named Mojir ul Mulk, who managed Mery matters till Tului appeared with a force 70,000 in number, made up in some part of captives. Next day, he surrounded the outworks and within a week's time his whole army had enclosed that doomed city, February 1221.

The besieged made two sorties from different sides but were hurled back each time with great violence. The assailants then passed the whole night near the ramparts, so that no living soul might escape them. Mojir ul Mulk sent a venerable imam next morning to visit headquarters. This holy man brought back such mild words and fair speeches that the governor himself went to visit the camp, bearing with him rich presents. Tului promised him the office of governor, and the lives of all citizens. He gave him a rich robe of honour and spoke of the governor's friends and adherents: 'I desire to attach them to my person,' said he, 'and confer on them fiefs and high office.' The governor sent for his friends and adherents. When Tului had all these men in his power he bound them. He bound Mojir ul Mulk also and forced him to name the richest Mery citizens. A list was drawn up of 200 great merchants and men of much property, who were sent to the Mongols with 400 artisans. After this, the troops entered the city and drove out the people. The command had been given that each man must go forth with his family and all he had of most value. The multitude spent four whole days marching out of the city.

Tului mounted a gilded throne on a plain near the suburbs and had the war chiefs brought first to his presence. That done, he commanded to hew off their heads in presence of the immense wailing multitude of people, for whom no better lot was in waiting.

Men, women and children were torn from one another never to meet in this life after that day. The whole place was filled with groans, shrieks and wild terror; the people were given in groups to divisions of the army whose office it was to cut them down to the last without pity or exception. Only 400 artisans were set aside, and some boys and girls intended for servitude. Wealthy persons were tortured unsparingly till they told where their treasures were hidden; when the treasures were found these men were slaughtered as well as the others. The city was plundered to the utmost;

the tomb of the sultan, Sindjar, was pillaged; the walls of the ancient city and the fortress were made level with the country about them.

Before he left that city of carnage and terror, Tului appointed a governor, one of the inhabitants whom he had spared for some reason, and then he joined a Mongol commandant to that man. When the army had marched away to destroy Nishapur, about 500 persons crept forth from underground places of hiding, but short was the breathing space given them. Mongol troops following Tului wished also a share in the bloodshed. Halting outside the dark ruins, they asked that these ill-fated people bring wheat to their campground. The unfortunates were sent and were slaughtered.

This corps cut down every man whom it met in the wake of Tului.

Nishapur stood 12 days' journey distant from Merv and in attacking it Tului was preparing to avenge Togachar, his sister's husband, killed at Nessa. The Nishapur people had done what they could to the harm of the Mongols, and had prepared to defend themselves with all the strength of their souls and their bodies. They had mounted 3,000 ballistas on the walls and 500 catapults.

The siege was begun by laying waste the whole province, of which Nishapur was the capital. Three thousand ballistas, 300 catapults, 700 machines to throw pots of burning naphtha, and 4,000 ladders were among the siege implements. At sight of these, and of the vast multitude of savage warriors surrounding their city, the leaders felt courage go from them.

A deputation of notables, with the chief judge of Khorassan, went to offer Tului submission, and an annual tribute.

Tului refused every offer and held the judge captive. Next morning, he rode round the walls and roused his troops to the greatest endeavour. They attacked all sides at once, fighting that day and the night following. In the morning, the moats were full; in the walls were 70 breaches; 10,000 Mongols had entered. New assailants rushed in from every side, and there were desperate encounters at many points. Before that day had ended, the city was occupied. The assailants took terrible vengeance. Togachar's widow, one of Jinghis Khan's daughters, rushed in herself with 10,000 warriors who cut down all before them. The slaughter continued four days without ceasing. The Mongols destroyed every living thing; even the cats and dogs in the city were killed by them (April 1221).

Tului had heard that in the destruction of Merv many persons had saved their lives by lying down among corpses, so now he ordained that all heads be cut from the bodies; of these, three pyramids were constructed, one of men's heads, a second from heads of women, and a third of children's heads. Fifteen days did destruction of the city continue; the place disappeared altogether, and the Mongols sowed barley on the site of it. Of the inhabitants only a few hundred men were left living; these were skilled artisans. Lest some should find refuge in underground places, troops were left near the ruins to slay all who might creep out later on into daylight.

The Mongol army marched now against Herat, the last city left in Khorassan. The governor, who had slain the envoy sent by Tului to summon the place to surrender, exhorted all men to fight desperately, to fight to the death. The struggle continued eight days, and Herat fought with immense resolution and fury; on that day the governor fell, and a small party sprang up which declared for submission. Tului knowing this state of mind in the city, promised to spare the people, if they would submit to him straightway. The offer was accepted. He spared all the citizens, excepting 12,000 devoted to Jelal ud din, the new sovereign, and appointed a Mohammedan governor, with a Mongol commandant to help him.

Eight days later, Tului received from Talekan a command to go to his father.

While Tului was ruining Khorassan, a small group of Turkmans, Khankalis, who were living near Merv, fearing the Mongols, moved westward, and after some wandering in Asia Minor, settled at last near Angora under Ertogrul their tribe chieftain. They numbered in those days 440 families. These Turkmans formed the nucleus of the Ottoman Empire, so famous in history until our day.

After he had destroyed Talekan, Jinghis held his summer camp for a time in the neighbouring mountains. His sons, Jagatai and Ogotai, returned from Urgendj and other ruined places on the Oxus. Juchi went north of Lake Aral and in deep and unquenchable anger began to establish the monarchy of Kipchak, known later as the Golden Horde, and never again saw his father. Jinghis learning, toward the autumn of 1221, that Jelal ud din had large forces in Ghazni, directed his march toward that city to crush him.

The great khan was detained a whole month at Kerduan, a firm fortress, but he destroyed it at last, with all its defenders. He crossed the Hindu Kush after that and besieged Bamian, where he lost one grandson stricken dead by an arrow; this was Moatagan, son of Jagatai. To avenge this death Bamian was stormed promptly, and taken. Jinghis would not have it in another way. The command was given to leave nothing alive, and take no booty of any kind. Every living creature had to die, and everything of value was broken or burned. Bamian was renamed Mobalig (the city of woe), and the region about it was turned to a desert. A hundred years later it contained no inhabitants.

Just after this destruction came the news of Jelal ud din's victory over a Mongol division, commanded by Kutuku, who had been protecting the khan's operations and those of Tului on the south side. This victory was gained at Peruan, not far from the Bamian boundary. It brought more harm to the victor, however, than profit, for it caused a sudden rupture between his commanders, some of whom deserted and led away many warriors. With reduced ranks, he was forced to fall back upon Ghazni, and thence farther south when he heard that Jinghis was advancing rapidly to avenge the defeat of Kutuku, his general.

The Mongol army reached Ghazni 15 days after its opponent had retreated. Jinghis left a governor in the city, and flew toward the Indus with all the speed possible to horses when men are sitting on them and urging them to the utmost. But this time the great Mongol had to do with a man of more mettle than he had met in his warfaring thus far. Jelal ud din had gathered in forces from all sides; he sent urgent messages to the chiefs who had left him, but, though willing to return, they had no chance to do so at that day. Jinghis was between them and their leader.

The Mongols urged forward their horses with the energy of madmen. The great task was to stop the young shah from crossing the Indus with his army and his harem – his wives and children were all with him. Time was in this case preeminent in value. The Mongols pressed Jelal ud din savagely, but he was, as ever, unterrified. Just before reaching the Indus, he fell at night on the rear of his enemy's vanguard, and cut it down to a man very nearly.

On reaching the river there was no time to cross, so the shah ranged his army for battle. The left wing was covered by a mountain, which ended sheer in the river. The mountain could not be turned, and could not be crossed, as the shah thought; it protected the left from flank attack also; the Indus protected the right from flank movements, and Jelal ud din could be met straight in front only. His army was 30,000, while that of his enemy was many times larger.

And now began the unequal and desperate encounter. The shah's right wing, to which he sent reinforcements repeatedly, repulsed the left wing of the Mongols, and he himself broke Jinghis Khan's centre. For a time, the Mongol conqueror was in personal peril, since a horse was killed under him in the struggle. Jelal ud din would have held his own, and perhaps won a victory, had not Bela Noyon been sent with 10,000 picked men to pass the mountain at all costs. Over cliffs and on the edge of abysses the Mongols crept carefully, pushing forward till at last they were in the rear of the weakened left wing and the centre which, at tacked from rear and front, were pierced through and forced out of contact with each other.

Rallying 7,000 men around him Jelal ud din made a desperate charge on the line of his enemy, which gave way for some distance, then he turned quickly, sprang on a fresh horse, threw off his armour and spurring to the Indus leaped from a bank given variously as from 20 to 60 feet higher than the plain of the water. His shield was at his shoulder, and his standard in his hand. Jinghis, who spurred to the riverbank swiftly and gazed at his fleeing opponent, cried: 'How could Shah Mohammed be the father of this man!'

The eldest son of Jelal ud din was a lad of eight years. He with his brothers were tossed into the Indus and drowned like superfluous puppies. Jinghis disposed of the harem and treasures as pleased him.

Jelal ud din vanished then for a time from the conflict to appear later on in various struggles till weakness, treachery and death put an end to him. Mongol generals crossed the river and pursued, but returned after fruitless endeavours.

Jinghis marched up the right bank of the Indus in the spring of 1222, and sent his son Ogotai to take Ghazni and destroy it. Here, as in most other places, the inhabitants were sent from the city, as it were to be counted, but were slaughtered most brutally; none were spared except artisans. An army corps was sent also to ruin Herat, the one city left in Khorassan. Herat had risen in revolt on hearing of the Peruan triumph over Mongols; the people had had such action in view since the time of surrender, and had stored away arms and supplies under pretext that they were for Mongol use should the need come.

Not far from Herat was the Kaliun fortress, known later on as Nerretu. To reach this strong place men had to pass single file on the high, narrow ridge of a mountain which resembled the back of a colossal hog of the razorback species. The place was beyond reach of arrows, or of stones sent by catapults. Though they had attacked Kaliun twice, the Mongols had failed in their efforts to take it. The Kaliun men, fearing lest they might come a third time, and impress Herat people, had planned to involve that strong and wealthy city, which would then have one cause with them. They sent letters to the Mongol governors ruling in Herat stating: 'We are ready to surrender, but fear Mongol rigor; we beg for a written safe-conduct.'

The governors answered that they would give such a letter, and advised the petitioners to visit the city and come to them. This was all that the other men needed; so 70 strong warriors went down from Kaliun, disguised as simple husters; they had arms covered up in the packs which they carried. They entered the city, each man by himself, combined later on and slew both the governors. Herat rose immediately, and killed every partisan of the Mongols.

In addition to his own men, the Mongol commander led now 50,000 impressed from conquered places. A siege followed soon and a desperate resistance. Six months and 17 days did it last till the fall of the city. The sword was turned then on all save the choice youth of both sexes. For one week the Mongols slew, pillaged, burned, ruined. It was said that one million six hundred thousand people perished in the conflict and subsequent slaughter. Jinghis received the richest of the plunder, and with it went several thousands of youthful captives.

When Herat was destroyed, the commander went back to the main army; somewhat later troops were sent to capture all who might have escaped and appeared in the ruins; they found about 2,000. These they slew, and then returned to those who had sent them.

Sixteen persons took refuge on a steep mountain peak, and when they saw no Mongols coming back, they went down to Herat. A few others came also and joined them. There was then a new population, 40 persons in number. Their only refuge was the chief mosque of the city.

After its terrible ruin, Merv had been repeopled to some extent, but later 5,000 Mongols were sent to that city and they slaughtered all whom they found in it. When these 5,000 had done their work thoroughly a commandant, Ak Melik, was left with the order to kill all who might reappear in the ruins. This man did his best to find people and slay them. He sent muezzins to summon to prayer from the minarets. Whenever a Moslem crept out of his hiding place and entered the mosque he was seized and his life taken. Forty-one days did Ak Melik lurk there and wait for more people. The survivors were few when he left the ruins. Merv remained a sad desert till the days of Shah Ruk, son of Tamerlane.

Jinghis cut down on the banks of the Indus all who had been faithful to Jelal ud din, the new shah, and now he destroyed all who had deserted that sovereign and been foolishly treacherous. On deserting Jelal ud din, Agrak had gone with Azam to Bekerhar. After a visit there he set out for Peshawur, and from the first halting place sent back this message: 'Let not my mortal enemy remain in thy country.' This enemy was Nuh Jaudar, the chief of 5,000 or 6,000 Kolluj families. Azam sent back this answer: 'Never has there been among Moslems such need as there now is not to quarrel.' And taking an escort of 50, Azam followed to make peace between Agrak and Jaudar. He could not move Agrak or persuade him; they ate together and also drank wine; Agrak's brain grew excited, he mounted, took 100 men and rode to the camp of the Kollujes. Jaudar thinking that Agrak wished peace rode forth with his son to greet him. On seeing his enemy Agrak drew his sabre as if to strike, and was cut down by Jaudar's men the next moment. When Agrak's adherents heard that their leader had been slain they thought that Jaudar and Azam had plotted his ruin, and right away they slew Azam. Then they attacked Jaudar's camp, where they massacred him and his children. Soon after this, they encountered the Gur men and killed a great number. As a close to this tragic insanity of action a corps of mounted Mongols fell upon all and slew them indiscriminately; a small remnant fled in various directions.